Doreen Hopwood

A Dynasty of Dragons

Copyright © Doreen Hopwood 2024

All rights reserved.

No part of this book may be reproduced, or stored in a retrieval system, or transmitted in any form or by any means, electronic, mechanical, photocopying, recording, or otherwise, without express written permission of the publisher.

ISBN: 9798323278169

Editor: Kathryn Hall — www.cjhall.co.uk
Cover art: Joseba Altuna, Seklev Designs
Formatting: Catherine Arthur — www.catherinearthur.com

Dedication

For my beloved husband Billy, my Mum, Doreen, and my sons, Ross & Kyle.

My late father, Alex, would have been tickled pink to have an author in the family.

Contents

LIST OF CHARACTERS		vi
MAP OF SIDHTHEAN		x
PROLOGUE		xi
ONE	Strange Wildlife	3
TWO	Harry's Return	22
THREE	The Fairy Queen	33
FOUR	Blood Will Out	54
FIVE	The Great Citadel	65
SIX	The Goblin King	74
SEVEN	A Royal Princess	81
EIGHT	A Traitor Amongst Us	92
NINE	A Council of War	106
TEN	Portals and Dragons	111
ELEVEN	The Reckoning	125
TWELVE	The Cauldron Speaks	139
THIRTEEN	The Goblin Queen	154
FOURTEEN	The Thinning of the Veil	164
FIFTEEN	Forests and Fireflies	180
SIXTEEN	Maps and Ley Lines	195
SEVENTEEN	Samhain (Summer's End)	206
EIGHTEEN	The Cailleach	221
NINETEEN	A Dangerous Cargo	237
TWENTY	To The Western Gate	249
TWENTY-ONE	A Surreal Experience	264
TWENTY-TWO	The Troll King	274
TWENTY-THREE	Siren Song	283
TWENTY-FOUR	Retribution	296

TWENTY-FIVE	Melusine	311
TWENTY-SIX	The Queen is Magnanimous	324
TWENTY-SEVEN	A Declaration of Love	335
TWENTY-EIGHT	Tigh Falloch	342
TWENTY-NINE	A Winter Betrothal	359
THIRTY	The Isle of Clouds	367
THIRTY-ONE	The Tongue That Cannot Lie	384
THIRTY-TWO	An Unexpected Arrival	394
THIRTY-THREE	The Anunnaki Lands	413
THIRTY-FOUR	Benign Deceit	438
THIRTY-FIVE	The Wormhole	447
THIRTY-SIX	Castles in the Air	453
THIRTY-SEVEN	The Waters of Forgetfulness	469
THIRTY-EIGHT	Let Battle Commence	490
THIRTY-NINE	The Day of the Dead	500
FORTY	The Mine	505
FORTY-ONE	Metamorphosis	513
FORTY-TWO	The Dragon Queen	528
ACKNOWLEDGEMENTS		548

A Dynasty of Dragons

List of characters

(in order of appearance)

Molly Colman ~ Museum & Arts Curator (retired)
Dolores Reid ~ Molly's nosy neighbour and long-time friend of Fred's
Laura Tweedie ~ Molly's lifelong best friend
Fred Colman ~ Molly's late husband, Retired Investment Banker
Jimmy Thomson ~ an Australian aborigine
James Gordon ~ Molly's father ~ Oil Company Geologist
Harry Bamford ~ Molly's first love.
Morven Gordon ~ Molly's mother & retired art teacher
Gwynnie Williams ~ Morven's sister and Molly's aunt
Nan Williams ~ Morven & Gwynnie's mother
Tad Williams ~ Morven & Gwynnie's father.
Morfan ~ Ceriddwen's younger son
Ceriddwen ~ Fairy Queen of the Tuatha de Danaan
Gwion ~ Ceriddwen's elder son and Harry's father
Xander Bamford ~ Molly's long-lost son
Chrissie Bamford ~ Harry's mother
Elsa & Maddie ~ Harry's sisters
Eleanor ~ Laura's friend and a priestess at Glastonbury Goddess Temple
Lord Lleu ~ Ceriddwen's husband
Anywn ~ Gatekeeper of the Citadel Portal
The Arianrhod ~ Head of the Great Crystal, the fairies' seat of learning and power
Brighid ~ Molly's fairy maid
Lord Gwyn ap Nudd ~ Goblin king
Meyrick ~ Ceriddwen's major-domo

Melusine ~ a water fairy
Mistress Holda ~ Supervisor of the Royal Dressmakers & Wardrobe
Tabitha The Epona ~ Keeper of the Royal Stables, Horses & Unicorns
Jarol, Paris & Rollo ~ royal stable grooms
Lord Cernunnos ~ Tribal Chief of the Forest Fairies
Oonagh ~ Manager of the hospital stud farm
Morello ~ head groom at the hospital stud farm
Lord Taliesin ~ Queen's Warrior & Justiciar of the Four Gates
The Morrigan ~ Commander of the Queen's Armed Forces
Andraste ~ the Elfin Queen
Tanith ~ Cauldron Bearer ~ one of the Ladies of Astarte ~ nine fairies who tend
Ceriddwen's cauldron
Jasper ~ Lord Nudd's eldest son ~ goblin prince
Lord Llyr ~ Tribal Chief of the Water Fairies
Lady Thetis ~ Lord Llyr's wife
Grainne ~ Lord Nudd's wife & Goblin Queen
Birca ~ a forest fairy
Lord Dubh ~ King of the Gnomes
Lady Froya ~ Queen of the Gnomes
Lady Flidais ~ Lord Cernunnos' wife
The Cailleach ~ Troll princess ~ given name Velecia
Lord Varik ~ Lord Taliesin's Deputy
Taranis ~ Festival events manager
Tuke ~ farmer & truffle hunting champion
Iken Faria ~ truffle hunt competitor
Master Lenus ~ senior doctor in the palace hospital
Master Heka ~ junior doctor
King Jontar ~ the Cailleach's father and King of the Trolls
Dala ~ one of the Cailleach's attendants
Lady Sulis ~ Admiral of the Fleet
Lord Ruka ~ Council official

Lord Ravenna ~ Captain of the Queen's Frigates
Luca ~ a village innkeeper
Muirin ~ his wife
Scatha ~ Warrior teacher on the Isle of Clouds
Morgaine ~ Taliesins's former betrothed
Nuada ~ Taliesin's rival for Morgaine
Master Jax ~ young midshipman
Sue ~ woman who helps in Harry's shop
Lady Keres ~ The Morrigan's second-in-command
King Ossian ~ King of the Fianna ~ the Mountain Fairies
Queen Tiya ~ King Jontar's wife
Lorien ~ royal bard/druid
Luss ~ Melusine's baby boy
Master Jorax ~ Melusine's prosecuting counsel
Master Loran ~ Melusine's defence counsel
Lady Rowan ~ cauldron bearer and Lady of Astarte
Idris ~ Lord Nudd's younger son ~ goblin prince
Arden ~ Taliesin's estate manager
Mistress Tansy ~ Nurse to Baby Luss
Lord Brude ~ Taliesin's father
Lady Adwena ~ Taliesin's mother
Lady Kiya ~ Keeper of the Royal Kennels
Lord Pan ~ Cernunnos's eldest son
Enya ~ Taliesin's former nurse ~ now Housekeeper at Tigh Falloch
Finlas ~ Tigh Falloch butler
Kip ~ palace pageboy
Lady Erena ~ bard
Captain Midir ~ a captain of the Fleet
Lord Erien ~ Governor of the palace prison
Lady Nimue ~ temporary Arianrhod
Lord Adarn & Lady Etain ~ Morgaine's parents
Lord Igor & Lady Loti ~ Nuada's parents

Mistress Mesket ~ The Taweret ~ chief midwife
Alaria ~ Molly & Taliesin's daughter
Ares ~ Molly & Taliesin's son
Nuala ~ Alaria and Ares' nanny
Lady Arnemetia ~ a Selkie
Lord Rodon ~ a Selkie
Lady Ceto ~ a Selkie
Lord Varun ~ a Selkie
Lord Harek ~ elfin commander
Hwyel ~ another of Lord Nudd's sons ~ goblin prince
Fili ~ military bard/druid
Tepi ~ a Selkie guide
Lord Conal ~ Sidhe warrior
Rudi & Draco ~ two of Taliesin's warriors
Dru ~ Tigh Falloch groom
Mr. Morrison ~ Molly's next door neighbour
Vix ~ Troll commander

Animals

Joey ~ a baby kangaroo found in Molly's garden
Buster ~ Mr Morrison's dog
Fafnir ~ a captured dragon
Flambeaux ~ Molly's unicorn
Soffo ~ prize winning truffle hunting pig
Chasach Luath ~ Taliesin's prized stallion
Storm ~ Taliesin's unicorn
Flambeaux ~ Molly's unicorn
Jassie & Sassy ~ pet amarok hounds
Toffy ~ one of Tuke's prize pigs
Abraxas ~ another of Molly's unicorns
Roja ~ Lleu's stallion

Map of Sidhthean

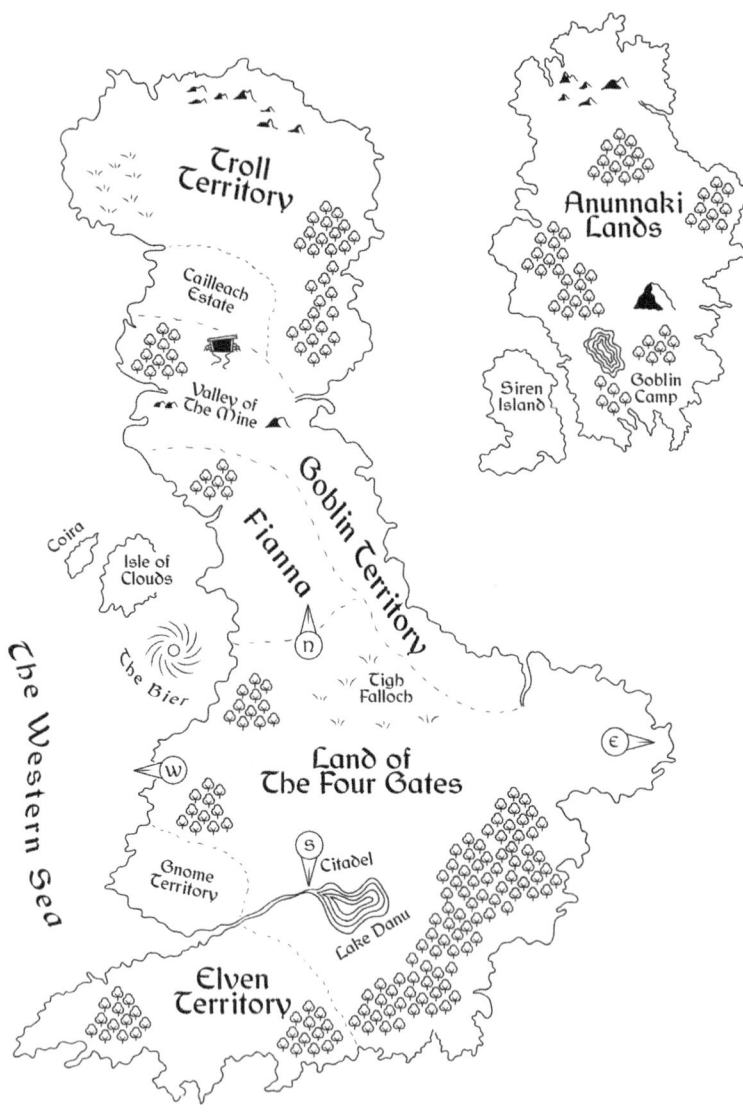

Prologue

On a warm spring day, the huge citadel bell rang out mournfully from its high bell tower, echoing across the vast palace estate and through the surrounding countryside and townships. All flags were flying at half-mast, fluttering feebly in a gentle, dancing breeze that belied the all-consuming grief enveloping the entirety of Sidhthean. Windows and shutters were closed, and drapes drawn in a beautiful suite of rooms overlooking the palace gardens. Finally, the doors were locked, and sacred knots, bearing Queen Ceriddwen's seal, tied across the handles. These doors were never to be opened again. After searching the entire kingdom and surrounding territories and lands for seven long years, and in the absence of a body or a ransom demand, the grief-stricken Queen finally accepted her son, Crown Prince Gwion, must be dead, never to return.

The last time Queen Ceriddwen's subjects heard the citadel bell ring and watched the flags being lowered to half-mast, was when word had arrived, too late, to tell them Gwynn ap Nudd, King of the Goblins, had invaded the Anunnaki lands far from Queen Ceriddwen's kingdom, and, to everyone's horror, slaughtered the entire population, including the Anunnaki dragon fairies and the Flowered Ones, flower fairies who shapeshifted and interacted with flowers, plants and trees, watching over, and protecting all plant life in their magical world. Some people believed their tribal leader, Blodeuwwed, shapeshifted into an owl and managed to escape, perhaps into another world, but no one knew for certain, and certainly no one in Ceriddwen's kingdom could speak to plants nor read the Anunnaki language.

If anyone wondered why the Queen hadn't summoned an army to drive the goblins from the Anunnaki lands to avenge the dragon fairies and the flower fairies, they kept it to themselves. No one would ever risk the capricious and mercurial Queen's fury by questioning her motives.

So, life went on without Prince Gwion, gradually returning to a semblance of normality and so far, the goblin king had made no attempt to wage war on Ceriddwen, and the genocide of the Anunnaki and the Flowered Ones became little more than an unpleasant memory. But unbeknown to Sidhthean, Gwynn ap Nudd had other plans...

one

Strange Wildlife

Molly gazed into the garden as fat raindrops gleefully battered the kitchen window as her yellow rudbeckia daisies drooped beneath the downpour. She filled a plate with cat food for her hedgehogs and piled another plate with chicken legs for the resident fox family, trying not to think about the strange dogs she'd seen lurking around the garden. According to the internet they were Australian dingoes. This revelation tied in with the rest of the mysterious animal appearances the garden was experiencing. Filling the bird feeders, she added another for the equally mysterious parakeets she'd noticed feeding with her regular garden birds the previous day. She peeked into the deep pocket of the makeshift apron she'd run up on her sewing machine. The baby kangaroo was still fast asleep, although Molly knew he'd soon wake up for a feed. Sighing, she began to prepare his bottle. When she first began to care for him — she'd named him Joey, of course — he didn't thrive at all, which Molly initially put down to stress and missing his mother, and as he began to grow weaker, she realised she would have to take him to the local vet. Naturally, the vet practising in the chilly north of England, wondered how and why Molly had acquired such a creature, but accepted, with some scepticism, her story that he was a misplaced exotic pet. Fortunately, the vet had trained in tropical veterinary medicine at Edinburgh University, and quickly explained that kangaroos are lactose intolerant and need special marsupial milk.

'I'll order some in,' the vet had offered, 'but in the meantime, you'll need to buy lactose-free baby milk.' Then added, 'And put disposable nappies on your shopping list, too,' as Molly was just about to leave the surgery.

The sudden shrill of the telephone jolted Molly out of her reverie. She sighed, hoping it wasn't that officious woman from the council — she'd called a few days earlier with her briefcase and impertinent questions about Molly's gardening skills. Someone had made a complaint that apparently, her garden was an eyesore and lowered the tone of the neighbourhood.

Resisting the urge to slam the door in the woman's face, she forced herself to smile politely as the woman proceeded to harangue her on the antisocial evils of unkempt gardens, particularly in a conservation village. When she finished, she handed Molly a leaflet outlining the council's policies on antisocial behaviour. Molly took the leaflet, muttering through gritted teeth, 'Thank you for letting me know. Goodbye,' then closed the door firmly before she tore it to shreds and made an extremely rude and very satisfying gesture in the direction of the woman's retreating back.

She had no doubt that the culprit was the ghastly creature from number 11, Dolores, a woman whose name she couldn't bear to use. She couldn't care less what some council official had to say, no one was going to tell her how she should look after her own garden!

Joey was now wide awake and looking for his bottle. Molly hoped and prayed his mother would come back for him soon. To say she'd been astonished to see a fully-grown kangaroo race through her garden, tossing her baby onto the compost heap as she fled, was putting it mildly. She could only assume the mother had been frightened by next-door's barking dog, but where had she come from? Naturally, she immediately phoned the local animal home, the police, and the nearest zoo, but no one was missing a kangaroo, and the zoo and animal home made it clear they wanted no part of rearing a baby kangaroo either, saying they didn't have the facilities or the staff to cope. She could tell she was dealing with the same young people she spoke to when she phoned about the platypus — they simply thought she was delusional. Disgusted, Molly decided to look after Joey herself. By the time she reached the phone, it had stopped ringing. *Good*, she thought, glaring at it sitting innocently on the hall table.

Molly's garden had a secret, well, it was only a secret because her late husband, Fred, didn't want anyone else to know about it. He made the discovery as he was building a rockery in the back garden near the pond. While he was digging, the ground collapsed, revealing a deep, dark, cave-like hole and he subsequently called in a ranger from the national park who duly pronounced it a sinkhole.

'Unusual down here in the village,' he opined. 'More often found on the moors, but it's definitely a sinkhole.' He looked over the garden wall at the local river. 'The river must have flowed along here at some point in the past creating it, then changed course.'

After scrambling back down, the ranger expressed some enthusiasm for exploring it with a local caving and pot-holing group. But Fred refused outright and swore the surprised ranger to absolute secrecy. No way were legions of spelunkers trampling all over his precious lawns and flower beds, sinkhole or no sinkhole. Fred had loved order—his idea of a beautiful garden involved regimented rows of colour coordinated hardy annuals complimenting his immaculate bowling-green lawns. Anything else was a weed. In Fred's opinion, all wildflowers were weeds to be exterminated.

After his funeral, Molly had sat out in the rain with a large gin & tonic and promised the garden free rein to do whatever it wanted. She then sealed the promise by scattering wildflower seeds all over the lawns and flower beds, and now left it pretty much to its own devices, the pond becoming a quiet little sanctuary for local wildlife. However, an odd incident at the pond a few months later alerted her suspicions that there were strange things going on. She was scattering food on the bird table one morning when she thought she saw an otter glide beneath the surface of the sun-dappled water. Thrilled, she stood stock still and waited for it to surface; what did emerge was so ridiculous and out of place that she thought she was hallucinating. Pulling itself onto one of the rocks was a fully-grown, dark brown, duckbilled platypus. It surveyed her for a few moments before slipping behind the rock and into the sinkhole. Molly rubbed her eyes in disbelief then crept stealthily around the pond to the sinkhole entrance. All was dark and still. Confined spaces unnerved her. She had no idea how deep the sinkhole was, or if it was big enough to provide some sort of den, and she wasn't about to go inside and find out.

The platypus must have come from somewhere, someone must be missing it, Molly reasoned, and she resolved to find out who. She telephoned the local animal home, who were unhelpful to say the least. She knew they'd assume she was just a batty old woman and they told her to ring the zoo instead. The staff at the zoo were dismissive also saying that, no, they hadn't lost a platypus because they didn't have any platypuses, and was she sure she hadn't seen an otter or a beaver. Didn't she know beavers had been re-introduced to the wild? Molly sighed and hung up. Perhaps it was just a lost exotic pet, and if she left it alone it would find its way back home.

She ignored the pond for a few days, resisting the urge to peer into its pellucid depths, or peek into the sinkhole, busying herself instead with pottering around the front garden, cutting back the delphiniums, deadheading roses and splitting a couple of variegated hostas for replanting as she muttered expletives to herself about interfering council jobsworths. She roared at a couple of spotty youths who sniggered at her as they passed the garden gate, probably because they thought she looked ridiculous in Fred's old gardening overalls that were much too big for her. But the steel toecaps she also wore made her feel protected, as did the spade she menacingly pointed in their direction. The youths hurled some teenage cheek about tigers lurking in the undergrowth before sprinting down the avenue, their raucous laughter ringing in her ears. Molly sighed. So, this was her life now. They wouldn't have dared shout like that if Fred was still alive, that's for sure — Fred commanded respect.

'Oh, for goodness' sake, woman, give yourself a shake!' she muttered to herself. 'You always told Fred you weren't helpless. Stop proving him right, getting upset over a couple of mouthy kids!'

She rammed the spade into the centre of a hosta plant with such force that the split sections jumped apart and lay at each end of what used to be a pristine flower bed, bristling with indignation.

'Stop pretending you can feel pain!' she scolded them as she dumped each half into separate plant tubs. 'I'm the one who's been insulted, not you!' The hostas appeared to turn their leaves up and ignored her.

Later that week, she was dazzled by a flock of beautiful blue, yellow and green birds fluttering and chirping around the bird feeders hanging on the branches of the rowan tree. The platypus, meanwhile, was sunning itself by the pond. Molly realised the birds were parakeets, she knew there were lots of them in southern England, flocks which had grown from a few escapees or birds deliberately released. Nevertheless, she was puzzled by the idea that they had spread this far north and why had she never noticed them around here before?

A few days later, on her way to tea with her friend Laura, Molly was accosted by Dolores at number 11 as she unavoidably passed her garden gate on the way to the bus stop. Bristling with self-righteous indignation, the unfavourable woman fixed Molly with a steely glare.

'You do realise your garden's become a magnet for vermin?' she started. 'It really won't do, you know. Fred would have been horrified. I'm sorry but I've had no alternative but to notify the authorities.'

Refusing to rise to the bait, Molly just rolled her eyes, shrugged, and stuck her nose in the air as she gamely marched on towards the distant bus stop. *Interfering busybody*, she thought furiously. *I knew it was her!* Dolores had been thick as thieves with Fred. They enjoyed the same kind of boring gardening, often accompanying each other to the local garden centre and the village gardening club. Molly was sure Number 11 would have made Fred a much better wife than she — they certainly had a lot more in common.

Unfortunately, she missed her usual bus and took the next, which crawled around a different route, up through the sprawling housing estate on the edge of town. It then made its way along the country road, through a tunnel of splendid trees resplendent in their glorious autumnal colours of red, yellow and gold, with the sunlight spiking through their branches and dappling everything in little splashes of sunshine.

At last, the bus pulled up at Molly's stop in the High Street. She leapt off and dashed to their favourite tearoom overlooking the river, where Laura was waiting patiently, looking effortlessly bohemian as usual. Today, she was wearing a long, purple skirt splashed with fuchsia flowers, a pretty silk blouse, and a pink crochet waistcoat topped with a white straw hat. On anyone else, it would have looked ridiculous. But Laura just looked fabulous. Acutely aware of her shapeless skirt and baggy, washed-out sweater, Molly sighed as she approached the table. *To think I used to be an avant-garde designer*, she thought morosely, and then wondered why on earth she should think about her long-lost student days as she threw herself into a chair.

'The bus was late and then it took the long way round!'

'You mean you got on the 1A instead of the 1.' Laura was not to be fooled.

Since Fred's death, Molly had *let herself go*, according to Laura, though Molly ignored her. It was such a huge relief not to have Fred telling her what to wear all the time, fussy twinsets with pearls and tweedy suits, cocktail dresses (who wore those nowadays?), and ghastly evening gowns. He insisted she blend in with his friends. Long gone fashion companies like Country Casuals, Laura Ashley, and Jaeger were amongst his favourite shops, not forgetting the ever popular Marks and Spencer for basics, of course.

'Such sensible quality clothes for our sort of people,' he used to say.

Laura hadn't quite grasped the fact that it was Molly's idea of heaven to roam around braless wearing whatever took her fancy. Laura simply thought Molly needed "sorting out" because she was in the throes of some sort of irrational grief process.

'So, what else is up?' demanded Laura. 'You're looking more frazzled than usual!'

'I'm fine.' Molly forced a bright smile. 'Although I've just had a run-in with the old battleaxe at Number 11. She says my garden's a magnet for vermin.'

'She's still furious poor old Freddie didn't leave you for her,' Laura declared unsympathetically, beckoning to the waitress. 'You should have left him and his boring garden years ago. I've been telling you that forever!'

Mercifully, the waitress arrived to take their order and Molly, feeling the need for a huge sugar rush, ordered a large slice of chocolate cake and a Belgian bun.

'You'll get fat,' Laura warned darkly. She was stick thin and always looked slim and trim no matter how much she ate. Molly would love to be like her, a free spirit who cared little for other people's opinions. In fact, Laura was the only person Molly felt she could discuss the garden with. When their order arrived, she took a large slurp of tea and plunged in.

'Actually, I do have a bit of a problem with the garden,' she ventured.

'You really do have vermin?' Laura asked with a chuckle.

'Well, I wouldn't say vermin, more like unwanted foreign wildlife.'

Laura raised an eyebrow but listened patiently as Molly ploughed on.

'And you're quite sure no one is missing the birds or the platypus?' she asked through a mouthful of meringue.

'I've tried everywhere. No one's interested — they all think I'm mad!'

Laura's face wore an interested, thoughtful look.

'I'll pop round and check it out but only after we've done some meditating and chakra balancing — you look as though you could do with a spot of reiki, too. I'll come for lunch, but it will have to be next week sometime; I'm busy 'til then.'

Molly groaned inwardly. Since retiring from her teaching

post, Laura had embraced alternative therapies and spirituality with a vengeance and found Molly a reluctant but useful guinea pig for her various therapies and treatments. She had also taken to attending monthly meetings called "Moon Rituals" and had recently been trying to encourage Molly to go "Forest Bathing" with her. It all made Molly feel very nervous.

'Ok, that's fine, just let me know what day you're coming.'

Molly was relieved to have a week to psyche herself up for Laura's visit. She loved her friend dearly, but since Fred's demise, Laura viewed her as some sort of project, and it was intensely irritating. However, by submitting herself to Laura's ministrations, she at least had someone to discuss the problem with. No one else was interested.

~

'I think your sinkhole is some sort of portal!' pronounced Laura after meditating for a while amongst the daisies beside the pond. Molly thought she must be extremely uncomfortable sitting cross-legged for all that time, but Laura looked serene as always, although the daisies beneath Laura's weight appeared somewhat forlorn.

'What do you mean by a portal?' Molly asked, mystified.

'Well, you needn't look at me as if I've just lost my marbles!' Laura snapped, serenity forgotten. 'You must have realised there's something supernatural going on by now?'

When Laura came for lunch on that first occasion, she was puzzled, yet intrigued. She loved getting her teeth into a good mystery and attacked the project with gusto. She even ventured into the sinkhole, crawling down so far that Molly began to panic. When she finally clambered out, it was to tell Molly that the cave gradually narrowed down to a very small opening. It certainly didn't look big enough for kangaroos or dingoes to come through and, apart from that, there was no sign of any animal activity, despite the fact they had both seen the platypus slipping in and out on several occasions. By this time, Joey was installed in Molly's apron, the dingoes had made their furtive appearance, and bower birds and honeyeaters had joined the parakeets.

It was Laura who noticed the mysterious antipodean animals never ventured outside the garden, as though the area was inside a protective bubble. The indigenous creatures came and went as normal, and paid no attention to the interlopers, even to assert territorial rights. It was all very perplexing, and Laura was determined to get to the bottom of it. Her research on the internet about the needs of these animals hadn't been able to explain how or why they'd suddenly appeared in Molly's garden.

She had become excited, however, when she read an article on *Aboriginal Dreaming* and after a spell of intense meditation, decided a magical ritual was needed to invoke the spirits she was sure were responsible for the crack, which she believed was opening a portal between dimensions. Molly's heart sank. Laura's rituals involved a lot of chanting and cavorting around naked, or "sky clad", as she called it. Although the garden was large and not overlooked, which was why she assumed most of the goings-on hadn't been noticed by neighbours, you never knew who might drop in.

'Where's your sense of adventure? Stop being such a prude,' Laura said, brushing Molly's misgivings away.

The following afternoon, Laura installed herself by the pond, her naked, pale, slim body gleaming in the sunlight, and began by calling in the four directions. After spending what seemed like ages talking to thin air, she turned to face south and began the chant again. Molly, meanwhile, went inside and began to boil the kettle, rolling her eyes in despair at her friend's seemingly odd antics. She returned ten minutes later carrying a tray filled with cups and a plate of biscuits only to find the garden was empty, apart from a solitary bee humming lazily around the sunflowers and Japanese anemones festooning the edges of the drying green. Laura was nowhere to be seen. Molly called her name a couple of times, but her friend seemed to have vanished into thin air, her clothes still neatly folded on the garden bench. She was perplexed, sensing a smugness in the atmosphere. 'You know where she is,' she berated the climbing roses as they scrambled over the wall. The pansies ignored her, and the daisies closed their little yellow faces before she had a chance to start on those, too. 'You don't fool me!' she muttered, making her way around the pond. The water lilies scuttled to the faraway bank as she approached, appearing to be deep in conversation with an iridescent blue dragonfly. Taking a deep breath, she crept into the sinkhole and peered around, catching a whiff of Laura's very distinctive floral perfume. 'Laura,' she called, 'are you there?' The interior of the cave remained true to its dark and secretive self, betraying nothing, and she quickly ducked back out.

'Ungrateful wretches!' she growled at the traitorous plants as she stomped across the grass. 'I've a good mind to come back with the lawnmower and shears!' She could have sworn she heard little trills of laughter as she slammed the kitchen door.

She then busied herself feeding Joey and preparing the evening meal, hoping she'd find Laura meditating on the grass when she went outside again, but the garden was still and quiet, the clothes on the bench becoming damp in the evening air. She gathered them up and took them inside. 'She'll just have to come to the door starkers when she gets back,' she grumbled to Joey, who was gently snoring.

~

Molly woke with a start. The room was in darkness apart from a sliver of moonlight silvering the blinds. She heard the noise again, a deep rumbling musical drone. Furious with herself for falling asleep, she gently lifted the still-sleeping Joey and crept into the garden to learn the droning was coming from the pond area. Peering through the roses and trying not to scratch herself on their thorns, she made out the vague shadow of a man blowing through a long tube of some sort. *I know what that is*, she thought, *it's a didgeridoo!* She remembered borrowing one for an exhibition at the museum a few years back. Slapping off the roses, Molly crossed the grass, relieved to see that Laura was there, too.

'Where have you been and who's that?' she hissed.

The man was too intent on blowing the instrument to notice her, his brow furrowed and cheeks puffed as he forced the sounds out.

'This is Jimmy Thomson,' said an unperturbed Laura, still naked apart from a shell necklace and white body paint.

Molly stared open-mouthed. 'Jimmy Thomson?' He was obviously a native Australian, an aborigine with dark, wavy hair and a well-muscled torso also covered in body paint.

'I met him in Australia.'

'You went through the portal!' Molly exclaimed in amazement.

'Yes,' said Laura, cool as a cucumber. 'There's a tear in the fabric between dimensions, just as I thought. The animals have been blundering through by accident, poor things. Jimmy's a Ngangkari, a traditional healer, he's going to try and sing the tear closed with the didgeridoo. The healing music will bring the torn parts together, but it may take some time.'

'How long?' Molly asked, staring nervously at the strange man, afraid the whole street would awaken and complain to the police about the noise.

'Oh, I don't know, maybe a couple of weeks, ten days at the earliest.'

Molly was aghast. 'Why so long? He can't blow that thing for two weeks; he's disturbing the peace!'

'I don't think anyone outside the garden can hear a thing,' Laura said, shrugging. 'The ripple between dimensions means that we're not actually here. At this moment, we exist in another dimension of time and space — we could be light years away from here in reality.'

Molly stared at her incredulously.

'But we *are* here, it *is* real, *Joey's* real!' She stroked his soft furry ears for reassurance. 'His mother threw him out of her pouch and ran away when Buster barked at her!'

'Buster was probably barking at next door's cat; I doubt if he saw a kangaroo. You know the local wildlife act as though there's nothing amiss, even if they can see the other animals, I don't think they can sense or smell them. I think it's a bit like looking at a film.'

'I don't believe a word of it,' Molly scoffed. 'The birds can see each other!'

'They probably can't; you only think they do,' said Laura dismissively.

Molly's voice rose, and she was beginning to feel an inexplicable creeping sense of panic.

She turned to Jimmy Thomson, still diligently producing long mournful tones from his didgeridoo.

'Thank you very much, Mr Thomson, you can go home now and please take your musical instrument with you. I'm going to bed. Goodnight!'

Turning on her heel, she was pulled up short by a long stem of goosegrass wrapping itself around her ankle. 'Let me go, you nasty little weed,' she yelped, as the goosegrass wrapped itself tighter and she tried in vain to free herself.

'Molly, calm down,' snapped Laura, 'you're being ridiculous! Do you know what I think? I think you don't want any of this to go away at all; I think you're using the sinkhole as some sort of crutch!'

'A crutch?' spluttered Molly. 'What on earth are you talking about?'

Jimmy droned on, joined by two dingoes, howling in unison.

'It's a distraction taking your mind off the fact that you've wasted the last forty years of your life,' Laura continued.

Molly was outraged. 'Not this again. How often do I have to tell you this is a really boring conversation?'

Undeterred, Laura ploughed on. 'I told you not to marry that selfish loser. He refused to let you have children — they didn't fit in with his plans, plans that obviously saw you as his surrogate mummy; cooking, cleaning, washing and ironing! He even wanted you to give up your job too, if you remember.'

Molly rolled her eyes. 'Well, I didn't as you very well know!' she snapped. 'I had a very successful career.'

'But you could have had a glittering career instead of a *make do* one,' Laura riposted.

Molly could feel her eyes filling with treacherous tears. 'Why do you keep saying these things? I didn't want children, either. You're supposed to be my friend. I did love Fred, Laura, you know I did. I still do!' She gulped convulsively, dabbing ineffectually at the tears now streaming down her face.

'Yes, you thought you did,' replied Laura, adopting a more conciliatory tone. 'Then you just made the best of it. All that time making the best of a life you should have walked away from years ago.'

'Dad spent so much money on the wedding, and he was so proud I'd bagged a man like Fred — it would have killed him if I'd divorced Fred. Not that I ever wanted to,' she added quickly.

'You bagged him?' Laura was incredulous. 'More like he couldn't believe his luck in bagging you!'

'Dad knew he'd provide for me, and I'd have a very happy and comfortable life—I was very lucky to marry Fred.'

'As opposed to marrying a hippie with a health shop and a lovely cottage on the moor. You loved Harry to bits, and you gave him up to please your father—another outrageously selfish man!' Laura was on a roll now. 'It could all have been so different. What a waste!'

'Don't you dare call my father selfish,' Molly cried. 'He was my rock! He knew what was best for me. He always meant well and…and he knew I was too young, anyway,' she added defiantly.

Laura was unimpressed. 'He turned you against the only man you ever truly loved, and you've spent your entire life in denial. Harry's still on his own, by the way, after all these years. You broke his heart and he never got over it.'

'You're just making that up. Sometimes, I think you don't really know me at all, Laura. How do you know what Harry's doing? You haven't seen him since the 1970s. I never think about him, and I certainly haven't been in love with him for years, either. Why do we keep having this pointless conversation?'

Molly was perilously close to breaking point. She swallowed hard and tried to compose herself.

'All right, then,' she began, 'so what happens if the didgeridoo music works? Will all the animals go back to Australia? How will they know the tear has been healed? Won't they be stuck here if they don't know they have to go back through the portal?'

She paused for breath, feeling wretched. Laura was like a dog with a bone. She knew discussing Harry was verboten, it was an unspoken agreement through all the intervening years, an agreement Laura chose to ignore on a regular basis. Everyone knows you never forget your first love, but Harry was ancient history. Her decision had been made and she had stood by it for forty years. She couldn't fathom Laura's unremitting hostility towards Fred. It was as if she didn't want to believe she'd moved on years ago. But Laura was her best friend and thought that gave her special insights into Molly's life. And Laura was up to something. Why else would she bring Harry up right now?

'Jimmy says he'll know when it's time,' Laura said, interrupting Molly's train of thought. 'That's when we'll have to guide the animals back through.'

'What if they don't want to go? I think they like it here.'

'Only because you feed them,' Laura replied in a cynical tone.

'Why are you being so nasty and awkward? I thought you loved the whole idea?'

'I did at first,' Laura said. 'I really did. It's proof that what we consider magic, or science fiction, is real. You really can travel between dimensions.' She fingered the shell necklace at her throat. 'I was even thinking about going up to the university to invite a couple of the science bods along. And then I changed my mind.'

Molly stared at her, wondering if this was perhaps a dream. She'd wake up soon and everything would be back to normal. Normal? What was that? Normal life ceased when Fred died. And yet... She tried to concentrate as her mind scrabbled about for something just beyond the reach of conscious thought... but about what...Fred or Harry? Or something else? Her heart lurched treacherously at the memory of Harry's laughing face and crinkly blue eyes. His hair had been long and wild, one of the features that most infuriated her father, who was mortified to learn that Harry had dropped out of Durham School of Medicine, taking over a health shop in town to train as a herbalist. Harry had also made the mistake of mentioning to James Gordon that he was very interested in Druidry. That was the final straw. Harry instantly became persona non grata.

'He's just a hippie drop-out!' her father had scoffed. 'Who's going to take all that mumbo-jumbo seriously?'

She cringed at the memory, remembering how rude he had been to Harry, and how she hadn't stood up for him or herself when Dad had ordered him out of the house, shouting after him that he would never be good enough for his daughter. She should have told him the truth and things might have been completely different...or would they? She hadn't been in love with Harry for years, and yet she couldn't throw off that unnerving feeling of total discombobulation.

'Molly! Are you listening?' Her musings were rudely interrupted. 'This is a momentous discovery, and we can't let it become a media circus. Can you imagine the hysteria? The whole village would be overrun by government scientists and the military, and the media would be everywhere — we'd have a permanent audience of gawpers and UFO hunters. Our lives would be ruined!'

Molly was aghast. 'The military? What's it got to do with the military?'

'For goodness' sake, Molly, wake up and smell the coffee!' Laura snapped in exasperation. 'They'd be expecting little green men and all sorts of aliens to come through the portal — the whole village would become like Area 51 in America!'

Laura paced back and forth, her naked breasts bouncing around as though they had a life of their own.

'Could you at least get dressed?' Molly suggested. 'You must be cold — it's chilly out here now.'

'Molly, please focus on what's important for once, will you?' Laura said, her eyes glittering in the moonlight. She swung around suddenly as the drone of the didgeridoo abruptly stopped. 'What is it, Jimmy?' she asked. 'What's wrong?'

Jimmy stood up and laid the instrument down on the grass, his face and upper body shiny with sweat from the exertion of blowing. 'I can't do it on my own, Laura. My magic isn't strong enough.'

'How do you know?' she demanded.

'I can feel it. I can feel the vibrations from the portal. They're too strong for me to close on my own. We need someone else.'

'Couldn't you bring someone else through from your side? Another Ngangkari?'

Jimmy bent to lift the didgeridoo. 'Maybe,' he grunted, hefting the instrument onto his shoulder, 'but the tear is powerful magic, and the moon makes it stronger, the nearer we get to the *full* moon.'

'What's the moon got to do with it?' Molly asked, becoming increasingly confused.

'Because the moon's gravitational pull affects everything on the planet,' explained Jimmy patiently. 'The tides, the migrations of birds, the growth of plants, and even women's menstrual cycles. The pull can be stronger when the moon is full, so we don't want to take any chances. We have less than two weeks.' He headed towards the sinkhole. 'I must go back and prepare. Find me a healer on this side.'

'Less than two weeks before what?' Molly called to his retreating back. 'What's going to happen?' But Jimmy was gone, swallowed by the deep, silent darkness of the cave.

The following days passed in a blur, and Jimmy appeared like clockwork every day and spent hours producing strange mysterious sounds from his didgeridoo. Laura had said she wouldn't be around for a couple of days, adding enigmatically that she had *something to do*. Molly, meanwhile, carried on with her usual routine of housework, shopping, looking after Joey, and feeding the animals. She even tried to catch up on a couple of her favourite television programmes but found she couldn't concentrate. She did notice, though, that some of the Australian birds were missing and began to wonder if Jimmy's sterling efforts were working after all. He never spoke to her, just nodded when she brought him a drink; he wouldn't eat anything, and only ever drank water. He made her feel quite nervous and she decided not to ask him about the birds, preferring to wait until Laura reappeared.

TWO

Harry's Return

Molly seldom acted on impulse, surprising herself the next day on the way back from town by staying on the bus instead of alighting at her normal stop. She enjoyed travelling by bus, a welcome relief after all the years of work-related driving, visiting art galleries, auctions, and dealers all over the country. Her flashy Saab, a present from Fred, was firmly parked in the garage.

She carried on for another three stops before hopping off at the edge of the moor. As the bus disappeared over the hill, she gazed up the old Heathervale track, travelling back to October 1970 in her thoughts. It had been a glorious autumn day and she was going to meet Harry. It looked very different in the years before the area became a National Park. The path, little more than a farm track back then, was now a proper road with fingerpost signs pointing in all directions to well-known local sites. She knew every one of these places like the back of her hand: *The Hill of The Standing Stones*, *Heathervale Neolithic Burial Chamber*, and the *Witches Stone Circle*. Few people visited them in the 1970s, apart from the occasional archaeologist, hill walkers & ramblers.

Now people flocked like bees around a honey pot thanks to clever marketing by the National Park Authority. But Molly couldn't get her head around this at all. Some of the visitors defaced the burial chamber with graffiti, lit fires in the middle of the stone circle and clambered all over the standing stones. The litter was appalling, and the park authority was forever asking for teams of volunteers to help clear up the mess. She just couldn't make the connection between conservation and this level of degradation to the moors and monuments. The new roads and paths encouraged boy-racers and bikers to speed over the once peaceful moorland, disturbing wildlife and livestock, infuriating farmers and residents alike.

Sighing, she looked up the road, and mustering her courage, began to walk up the hill. She didn't remember it being this steep, and then reminded herself she was no longer fit and agile with her whole life ahead of her. As she crested the hill she stopped, momentarily confused, unable to see the cottage. Had it been demolished? Heart pounding and panting slightly from the climb, she made her way further along the road, and then, to her relief, saw the cottage nestling behind a screen of trees and bushes. Of course! She had completely forgotten about the rowan trees and hawthorn bushes she helped Harry plant. They were fully-grown now and hid the house from view. A magnificent red fuchsia bush hung over the dry-stone wall at the front of the cottage. Harry's friend, Gus, had built the wall around the garden, and repaired the crumbling wall surrounding the little paddock behind the cottage. He was always in demand from farmers needing running repairs, and after the inauguration of the National Park, he was working flat out. She wondered if Harry knew his friend had recently died.

The cottage looked much the same. Built from local red sandstone, it glowed in the late afternoon sunshine, blending organically into the landscape. That was the beauty of using local stone for building, it made the houses look as if they'd always been there. Harry always maintained he would never live in a "modern pebbledash shoebox", as he called most new-build houses whether they had pebbledash or not. Molly smiled to herself. Despite the hyperbole, you always knew what Harry meant, and he was usually correct. Whoever owned the cottage maintained it well; a smart green door with matching paintwork around the window frames, facia and guttering. The garden was still blooming, and as she walked up the side to the paddock, she could see a well-stocked vegetable patch, a pretty greenhouse and sturdy outbuildings. Harry would be pleased to see his beloved cottage so well-cared for.

She then skirted the paddock and headed towards the stone circle. She used to enjoy sitting in the centre of the stones; it was inexplicably peaceful and relaxing. The bracken fronds bent themselves back to clear a path as she strode through. 'I should think so, too!' she admonished them. 'Don't want any nasty ticks jumping on me, do we?'

Molly had always taken her mysterious ability to communicate with plants for granted. It astounded Harry who maintained she was a *Very Special Person*. He loved to sing Handel's *Where'er You Walk* in his dodgy baritone voice, 'Because the trees do crowd into a shade for you, Molly!' he would insist. 'They keep you dry when it rains, and shady when it's hot. They really do bend their branches over you.' Molly almost laughed out loud, remembering how earnestly he believed she had inherent magical powers. Where were they now? And had she and Harry ever been that young? After spending a while examining the circle and tutting to herself at the blackened earth where some thoughtless picnicker had lit yet another fire, she made her way back to the bus stop.

Getting off the bus and turning the corner into Heathervale Avenue, her heart sank as she saw the council jobsworth talking to Dolores just outside her gate. They turned as she approached, and Molly couldn't help noticing the smug little smirk on the woman's face. Molly began to panic. What if they had gone into the garden and encountered Jimmy Thomson blowing his didgeridoo? Thankfully, she couldn't hear anything, and mustering her courage once again, prepared to confront the enemy.

'Ah, Mrs Colman, I thought I'd missed you,' Jobsworth announced officiously. 'I was just asking your neighbour if she knew where you were.'

Molly glared at them. 'I don't think it's any of your business where I was!'

'I just popped round to see if you'd made any improvements on the gardening front, but I see you haven't. This really won't do, Mrs Colman!'

Molly took a couple of deep calming breaths the way Laura had taught her and faced them down.

'Unless I have piles of rotting rubbish and a huge infestation of rats in my garden, my *privately owned garden*,' she emphasised, 'how I tend it is nobody's business but mine.' She looked pointedly at her neighbour.

'Your garden's a disgrace,' Dolores spluttered, thrusting her large breasts at Molly in indignation. 'It's like a jungle! The weeds are spreading everywhere!'

'You mean the wildflowers,' Molly snapped, turning her attention back to Jobsworth.

'You of all people should be aware of the protected bat roost in my garden.' Molly hurriedly crossed her fingers behind her back. The roost, strictly speaking, wasn't in her garden at all. It was under the stone bridge behind her back garden wall. 'My garden's a haven for wildlife of all descriptions, including our crashing bee population. Isn't that why the council aren't spraying their verges and mowing green spaces until all the flowers and plants have seeded? Helping the bee and insect populations? And, of course, the bats who feed on the insects!'

She took another couple of deep breaths to stop herself from shouting. *As soon as you lose your temper, you've lost the argument,* her father always said. 'You do liaise with the National Park Authority, don't you?'

She smiled as sweetly as she could at Jobsworth, who was now furiously leafing through her clipboard, keeping her head down to hide the perturbed look on her face. Molly remembered Fred once commenting that Dolores was very friendly with a council employee who attended her yoga class, and he used this as an excuse for his extreme gardening policy. This woman was "shit hot" apparently, on antisocial behaviour including untidy gardens as well as noisy neighbours and barking dogs. He had been quite indignant when Molly remarked that she just sounded like a nosy parker who had found the perfect job.

'Dolores says she's been promoted twice in the last year because she's so good!' Fred had asserted pompously.

Good at making other people's lives a misery, Molly thought darkly.

Checking out the woman's increasingly shifty behaviour, she began to wonder if this was a bit of a put-up job—Jobsworth doing an unofficial favour for her friend.

Sensing unauthorised dodgy dealings, Molly announced, 'I'm just going to phone the park rangers who look after the bat roosts and ask them what they can tell me about the problem you seem to have with my garden.'

As she began to open the garden gate, Jobsworth, now adopting a more conciliatory tone and wearing what she obviously hoped was a pleasant expression, quickly said, 'Oh, hang on a minute, I'm so sorry. It seems I should be visiting Heatherdale Road up on the council estate, not Heathervale

Avenue here in the village. I do apologise. It seems the admin team back at the office have mixed things up.' She paused for breath. 'Can't get the staff these days!' she added, with an insincere little laugh.

'You expect me to believe that?' Molly shot them a withering look as she slammed the gate shut and flounced down the path. The discomfited look on Dolores' face was a joy to behold. She couldn't wait to tell Laura.

Joey was beside himself when she let herself into the house, trying to jump into her lap, and she realised he would soon be too big to be carried around in the apron pocket. 'I know, I know,' she crooned to him. 'I was away too long and you're hungry and cross with me for leaving you on your own. I'm sorry, poppet.' She then quickly made up his bottle before popping out to see how Jimmy was doing.

'Hi, Jimmy, how's things?' He raised his eyebrows in acknowledgement as he puffed stoically away on the didgeridoo. 'Any sign of Laura yet?' To her surprise, he nodded but kept on blowing. As usual, Jimmy wasn't going to stop and have a conversation.

Giving up on expecting him to stop the music for just a moment, she dashed back inside and rang Laura.

'Thanks for telling me you're home! What's happening and where have you been?' Molly snapped into the receiver.

Laura quickly cut her off. 'I'm just back. I popped in to see you, but you were out. I'll be over later. Calm down, for goodness' sake!' Then the phone went dead and Molly stood staring at the receiver, sighing in exasperation.

Laura arrived about an hour later. 'Can't talk now, have to let Jimmy know what's happening!'

'I think it's time you told me what's going on,' Molly shouted after her, furious at herself for allowing Laura to barge past her in her own home.

Laura and Jimmy turned around, looked at her, then at each other again. Jimmy nodded rather grimly, and Laura took Molly's arm, guiding her towards the garden bench.

'I think you'd better sit down.' Molly did as she was told, nervously knotting her shirt with her fingers. 'I've been to see Harry.'

'Harry?'

'Yes. You know — Harry, erstwhile love of your life? I googled him ages ago. According to all the rave reviews on the internet, he's a very well-respected shamanic healer, and he's agreed to help us close the portal, but you must be part of this, too. You don't have a choice, Molly, because this may have more to do with you than you think — it may even be your fault!' Laura pursed her lips and Molly's heart began to hammer furiously, moving up into her throat to push out the scream she was trying to swallow.

Making an almighty effort to control herself, she managed to say indignantly, 'My fault? Harry said this is my fault?' Her voice was choking on the words. 'And you say he's coming here?' She couldn't believe what she was hearing. 'How dare you do this behind my back!'

'Yes,' replied Laura, completely ignoring Molly's outrage. 'He's driving up tomorrow. He'll be here around lunchtime.'

'No, no, he can't, it's not possible, I'm not having it! He can't come, we'll do it without him, we must be able to do it without him! And you still haven't told me why Harry thinks it's my fault.' Once again, Molly felt inexplicably panic-stricken.

'Because of your powers.' Laura let out an exasperated sigh. 'The powers you pretend you don't have and don't know anything about. You really are one of the most repressed people I've ever met! And he's coming tomorrow whether you like it or not — we need him!'

'I don't have powers,' retorted Molly furiously. 'I've got green fingers, that's all. You and Harry always did have an overactive imagination where that's concerned, and I see nothing's changed. How dare he suggest this is my fault. What a cheek!' Laura mentally crossed her fingers behind her back. Harry had said no such thing, in fact, he said he thought the whole scenario sounded preposterous, but he did say, albeit reluctantly, that he would come and have a look. Jimmy thought it had more to do with Molly than Harry did and he rolled his eyes. He'd been quick to notice how the plants and flowers in Molly's garden reacted to her. In all his years as a Ngangkari, he'd never seen anything like it. Plants consciously interacting with humans? This was big magic indeed. He'd discussed it at length with Laura and they both reached the conclusion this wasn't happening in Molly's garden by accident, although they couldn't explain why.

~

After a sleepless night, Molly finally dragged herself out of bed and staggered downstairs. Today was the day. She felt sick as her stomach continually clenched and unclenched, tying itself in knots. The thought of seeing Harry after all this time filled her with dread. She knew she was being ridiculous — it was all ancient history now. Nevertheless, mouth dry, she wandered into the kitchen and immediately wondered why there was no Joey bounding over, looking for breakfast. Come to think of it, she had been in such a state last night, she couldn't remember if he'd been in the house or not when she locked up. She opened the back door to call him, noticing with a start how the air was thrumming with energy. As all the plants and flowers turned to bid her good morning, she noticed each of them was surrounded by a different coloured aura, shimmering and shooting little spikes of colour into the air. The effect was dazzling and very beautiful and Molly was entranced, though soon jolted out of her reverie by the sudden appearance of Jimmy Thomson looming at her side.

'Oh, Jimmy, you startled me! Look at the plants. Aren't they gorgeous? And look how they've all turned to let me see them.'

The plants were also the first thing Jimmy noticed when he arrived. He felt a bit unnerved by it all — this was well out of his range of expertise, but he had his own theory.

'I think they're trying to draw on your energy and magic to save them. The energy from the portal will rip them to pieces if we can't close it. That's all I can think of. I've never seen anything like this before — plants projecting colour and energy around themselves. I don't think it's because they're happy to see you,' he added apologetically. 'Perhaps if your friend is the powerful Ngangkari Miss Laura says he is, he will know more than me.'

Molly frowned irritably at Jimmy's comments. 'I don't know — I haven't seen Harry for forty years. I don't know what he's capable of.'

'Well, we'll find out soon enough. Would you be kind enough to bring me some water to drink before I begin today's music?'

'Yes, of course. Oh, and by the way, have you seen Joey? He's not in the house.'

'He went back through the portal last night. He heard his mother calling for him. He's happy and safe and today we concentrate on making everything else safe, too.'

At that, he turned and made his way over to his didgeridoo before she could answer.

Molly never knew how she made it through the next few hours. She fed the animals as usual, noting all the Australian birds were gone, no sign of the platypus, and, of course, no Joey. She tried not to be sad about that — it was right and proper that he was reunited with his mother, but the thought of never gazing into those liquid brown eyes or stroking his soft fur almost made her break down and cry. He would have been such a comfort in the hours ahead.

The intense atmosphere in the garden, together with the stress of Harry's imminent arrival, had induced a terrible headache. The paracetamols she swallowed earlier just took the edge off and she couldn't rid herself of a nagging feeling of impending dread as the morning wore inexorably on.

Laura asked her to provide lunch, as Harry was sure to be hungry after his long drive. This threw Molly into a fit of indecisiveness about whether Harry was a vegetarian or a vegan. For the life of her, she couldn't remember, and finally decided on a vegetarian lunch with tuna mayonnaise and ham for everyone else. She made potato salad and a mixed bean salad with sweet peppers, humus, crusty bread, and a nice selection of cheese and fruit, then she stood nervously at the living room window until a car finally pulled up at the gate — an old, battered Volvo — just as she had imagined. Laura was already waiting for Harry and got out of her car to greet him. Molly's stomach churned in apprehension as she watched Laura make her way up the path. She knew Laura would be irritated because she wasn't standing at the door, arms wide and wearing a brilliant welcoming smile.

Steeling herself, she opened the door and Laura immediately pushed past her, rushing into the kitchen without saying a word. Molly looked down the garden path and stared at the figure coming through the gate. Was this ascetic-looking man, with the austere face and close-cropped grey hair, her Harry? He made his way up the path and nodded curtly.

'Hello, Harry,' she said, almost stumbling over the words. 'How are you?'

'As well as can be expected under the circumstances,' he replied, with no smile or acknowledgement of what they once meant to each other. To him, this was business, nothing else. 'If you would take my bag, please. I have to help my son unload our equipment.'

His son? Molly's mind began to race, and she was about to point out that Laura had never told her he'd got married, then quickly pulling herself together, she managed a bright smile and replied, 'Yes, of course,' and relieved him of the proffered bag.

Leaving the front door open, she retreated swiftly to the kitchen. 'You didn't tell me he had a son,' she hissed at Laura, dumping the bag on the floor. 'He obviously got over me long enough to father a child and he isn't being friendly at all!'

Avoiding both Molly's eyes and the outburst, Laura went to the back door and called Jimmy, the sonorous drone of the didgeridoo tailing off as he made his way across the garden.

'Your big Ngangkari here, then?' he asked. Laura nodded, handing him a plate, indicating he should fill it with food.

'Yes, a few minutes ago. Ah...here they are now!' she replied, as Harry and another man appeared at the kitchen door.

Molly's heart skipped a beat, and her temples began to pound as Harry and his son came through the doorway. She felt the blood draining from her face as something began to tug at her heart. The younger man's feline, topaz-coloured eyes and dark hair reminded her of someone...but who? A terrible truth crept into her consciousness, and she began to understand the dark forebodings she had about Harry's visit. It was all so long ago. She knew she had been ill, staying in Hereford with Aunt Gwynnie for a while, but the rest was just a foggy blank — if only she could remember what had happened...

THREE

The Fairy Queen

Molly was nineteen, and the worst thing that could happen to a well brought-up young woman in 1971, according to some people, had just happened to her, and at the worst possible time. The swinging sixties and permissiveness really didn't exist much outside of London. She was pregnant and unmarried with no plans for a reconciliation with her child's father. Morven, her lovely, practical mother, immediately swung into action. Dad was told Molly had enrolled at Hereford College of Art & Design to study textiles for a year as part of her degree course, the distraction hopefully making her forget about Harry, and she would stay with her mother's younger sister, Aunt Gwynnie. Her father thought this a wonderful idea, the further away from that chap the better, doing the right thing and getting on with her life. Molly had, in fact, taken a sabbatical from her Fine Arts degree. Doing a textiles course was entirely optional as far as her degree was concerned, but provided the perfect cover for her pregnancy, and Dad didn't suspect a thing.

Aunt Gwynnie lived in a little village just outside Hay-on-Wye, roughly 22 miles from Hereford. The cottage was well over two hundred years old and, as far as anyone knew, had always been in the family. She never married and looked after Nan and Tad, Molly's grandparents. Aunt Gwynnie was notoriously fey and called herself a hedge witch, and she got on famously with Harry, who thought she was wonderful. Harry and Molly often visited Nan & Tad where Harry and Aunt Gwynnie spent many happy hours swapping recipes for herbal remedies and potions. She was the perfect person to turn to.

Nan and Tad eventually decided Aunt Gwynnie should get on with her own life, moving to a comfortable retirement home in Hay, much to the family's initial dismay but, eventually, they had reluctantly given way to their parents' wishes and Nan and Tad were now happily settled in their new home. 'It's just wonderful here, Gwynnie,' they enthused when she visited. 'We love the pretty gardens and the scones and jam every afternoon.' The family was greatly reassured, and Aunt Gwynnie settled into life on her own in the lovely old cottage.

Molly was roughly ten weeks pregnant when she arrived in the pretty little Border Marches village deep in the Wye Valley. The textiles course was three days a week and ran from September to March and all being well, she would be able to finish the course before the baby was born and have a textiles certificate to present to Dad. The fashions of the day in 1971 were particularly fortuitous for pregnant women — floaty smock-style dresses were all the rage and Molly had several very pretty garments in various fabrics. She was very slim, and the voluminous frocks were the perfect disguise for her expanding girth.

The textiles course introduced her to the joy of knitting, something she always thought of as passé and boring — it never occurred to her to think of it as an art form. She revelled in the stylish creations of Sonia Rykel, Marion Foale, and Sally Tuffin, and the wonderful Bill Gibb who influenced the artist Kaffe Fassett, destined to become a world-famous designer. She knitted obsessively, her creativity running wild, fuelled by pregnancy hormones, producing wonderful designs, scooping up many accolades and plaudits before being finally invited to have an end-of-term exhibition. The photos from the exhibition were still buried in a box in the cottage's attic. She had never looked at them again. Mum and Aunt Gwynnie had been so proud. Fortunately, Dad was in South America on one of his geology trips for the oil company he worked for, blissfully ignorant of everything.

Molly wore two of her creations for the exhibition; an intricate calf-length lace dress in a fine laceweight yarn, encrusted with free-form crochet motifs, and lined with silk. It was a generous one-size design, disguising her pregnancy reasonably well, and worked beautifully in dove-grey. She wore it with a stunning floor-length drape-front coat in subtle shades of pink and lilac. Buyers for Lee Bender from Bus Stop and Barbara Hulanicki from Biba vied with each other for the chance to buy the designs. It was a triumph — all her designs were sold and on the way home, her waters broke in the back seat of Aunt Gwynnie's beloved Morris Traveller.

Molly was never going to keep the baby. That was a non-negotiable given. She had made her decision. Through the long hours of labour, her mother and Aunt Gwynnie had taken turns to sit with her, encouraging her when the midwife told her to push or pant, and always sweeping the medical staff away on some pretext whenever they started making effusive noises about new mothers and their darling little babies. She nursed the baby and looked after him for the first week because back in the 1970s, new mothers and babies stayed in the hospital maternity unit for a week, a lovely idea for mother and baby to get to know each other, but torture for someone like Molly who was giving her baby away. She told her mother she didn't want to know the details and would they please make all the arrangements on her behalf. She was slightly surprised she had no forms to fill in, sure she would have to sign away her rights as the baby's mother, but no such forms appeared. To be honest, she didn't really care. She just wanted the ordeal to be over.

What Molly didn't know was that her mother had contacted Harry to tell him about the pregnancy, thinking that as the father, he should know, and her instincts were correct. Harry was furious with them all, lit up by the incandescent rage only a betrayed and broken heart could muster. He listened incredulously, but politely, as Morven told him about her daughter's condition and how Molly wished to have the baby adopted. Harry was horrified and insisted there was no way any child of his was going to be adopted by strangers. If Molly didn't want their child, he would raise the baby himself.

At first, Morven scoffed at the idea. How could a single man on his own look after a newborn baby? She wouldn't even consider it and told him so in no uncertain terms. But Harry was determined and persistent. A force to be reckoned with, as was his mother, Chrissie, who swept in and announced, to Morven's amazement, that she would raise the child with the help of Harry and his two married sisters, Elsa and Maddie. Elsa was pregnant also, and Maddie already had a two-year-old daughter. The baby would be raised in a large extended family surrounded by love and security, with his or her real family. They pointed out that as the father, Harry did have certain rights, although ultimately, the decision was Molly's. Every time Molly's name was mentioned, her mother could feel the waves of anger and hostility. Love, loyalty, and the need to protect her daughter prevented her from telling them she was just as broken-hearted and upset by the situation as they were. Morven was a strong woman, but weak as a kitten when it came to her husband. She adored him, as did Molly, but his word was law. She had tried to discuss Molly and Harry's relationship with him, to no avail. He was adamant. Harry was just not good enough.

When Molly left hospital, a nurse carried the baby to the hospital door and handed him to her as soon as she was seated in the taxi. The taxi left the car park and stopped in a layby behind Aunt Gwynnie's little dark blue car. Morven took the baby out of Molly's arms, kissed her goodbye, and watched as she climbed in beside Gwynnie. That was the last time Molly saw her baby.

After the birth, Molly sank into a deep post-natal depression. She seldom went out, ate like a bird, and took little or no interest in anything or anyone. Aunt Gwynnie's gentle attempts to cajole her out into the world were met with the same reactions. Outright, rude refusal, retreating to her room, or outbursts of hysterics with floods of tears. She refused all medical help and offers of counselling, spending long hours lying in bed, not bathing or dressing for days on end. Morven came regularly to try and persuade her to seek professional help, but Molly would just sit and howl in anguish, rocking back and forth in her grief. She wouldn't talk about the baby, or Harry, and after several months, Aunt Gwynnie asked Morven to come for a family conference with Nan at the retirement home and, as the matter of the family's fairy blood was reluctantly raised, so the witchery began.

To say that Nan was an unwilling vessel for the fairy blood was an understatement. Her mother had been a great believer, however, insisting Nan learn as much as she could teach her about fairy lore, and ensuring she could speak and write the fairy language. Nan always hated being "different" and vowed never to inflict the same burden upon her own children. She initially told her daughters nothing about their unusual heritage. Morven appeared to be unaffected, but Aunt Gwynnie was fey from the moment of her birth, and Nan's mother eventually stepped in telling Nan, whether she liked it or not, blood would triumph, and Gwynnie would have to be taught how to use and control it wisely. She was a formidable little woman with a will of iron, and Nan knew that argument was useless, stepping back and contenting herself with the fact that her other daughter seemed totally oblivious to it all.

'No!' Nan was implacable. 'I want nothing to do with it. Just leave me in peace!'

'We're desperate,' pleaded Gwynnie, 'we need you to form the Triad, you know that!'

'I'm surprised at you, Morven — why don't you just take her to a doctor instead?'

'You know why, Mum. You're being deliberately awkward.'

'Don't take that tone with me! I might be old, but I'm still your mother.'

'It's because you're old we need you. We've tried everything else — I've told you dozens of times — this is a sickness only Ceriddwen can cure. You, of all people know that. Please, Mum,' pleaded Gwynnie.

Tad, who appeared to be dozing on the sofa, interjected: 'Fairies indeed — a load of superstitious old nonsense if you ask me!'

All three women turned to look at him.

'Nobody asked you,' Nan said, at her most imperious, 'because it has nothing to do with you. You don't have the blood, so you can just go back to sleep and let us get on with our business!'

Gwynnie and Morven exchanged glances. They knew the signs; their father had deliberately intervened. Nan would help them just because she thought it would annoy Tad who gave his daughters a sly wink as he settled back to continue his snooze.

Fairy queens are flighty, haughty, and difficult creatures to say the least, so the story goes. Asking a favour is a very tricky, if not downright dangerous business. There's no such thing as a free lunch in Sidhthean. Everything has its price; every favour, every boon or piece of wise advice must be paid for. No questions asked. Then there's the protocol. Fairy society is extremely hierarchical, and you must be deferential at all costs. Fairy folk think they are superior to humans because they believe they are the indigenous and rightful heirs to the land. *We are the usurpers, the Johnny-Come-Latelies who stole their birth right and forced them to live in the Hollow Hills*, as Nan pointed out, *they call the dimension of time and space they now occupy.* What humans don't know, they make up anyway, according to Nan, who wasn't happy about it at all. In fact, she was terrified, terrified of the fairy Queen, her reaction and the payment she would exact, but still sprang resolutely into action, and thus began one of the most unforgettable and terrifying experiences of the women's lives.

They had to decide how and when to approach the Queen and this knowledge had been handed down through generations of the blood from mother to daughter. For once, Nan grimly thanked her determined mother who insisted she absorb it all. 'You never know when you'll need it,' she'd said. And she was right. Now the knowledge was needed. They had to write a letter in the fairy tongue and leave it, with a gift in a special place, a large outcropping of rock beside a stream deep in the forest several miles from the village. The rock was partially screened by bushes and trees and covered in moss and ferns. The letter had to be inserted into a cleft just above the waterline of the stream. If the stream was in spate because of heavy rain, the cleft was hidden underwater, so timing was crucial. Nan wrote the letter in a strange script, folded it and placed it along with a pair of beautiful lace gloves, another of Molly's many creations, into a little leather drawstring bag, and on a cool cloudy day, they made their way into the forest. It was the best kind of weather in Nan's opinion. 'We're less likely to meet tourists or ramblers in this part of the forest on a dull day, it's too damp,' she announced.

Aunt Gwynnie clambered across the mossy stones, clinging to overhanging willow branches, before finally reaching down to push the leather bag deep into the cleft. The women then stood and waited. After a few minutes, a young man materialised from behind a large oak tree beside the rock. He was tall and athletic-looking, with large feline eyes and long, glossy black hair. Ignoring Aunt Gwynnie and Morven, he spoke directly to Nan in a strange sing-song language. Nan replied in the same tongue, then bowed to him, signalling her daughters to do the same, before turning on her heel and walking away.

'Don't look back at him!' she hissed. 'Just keep walking.'

'What happens if I look back at him?' whispered Morven curiously. 'He looks rather nice.'

'He's not nice,' retorted Nan, 'not nice at all. He'll beguile you with those cat's eyes and persuade you to go with him, and that's the last anyone will ever see of you. They like to enslave humans — you read about missing persons all the time. It's a fair bet a lot of these people have been snatched by fairy folk.'

Morven suppressed a sceptical retort and instead responded by asking, 'What are our chances with this fairy Queen, then? How do we know she won't just grab us instead of helping us?'

'Because they are bound by honour, it's their code of life; everything they do hinges on protocol and honour. A fairy is bound by his oath, just the way ancient people made blood oaths and swore fealty to their feudal lords and kings. If they agree to make a bargain with you, they will stick to it unless you break it, and then they are free to do whatever they like. They kidnap unwary humans by tricking them with their charm. I warn you, don't be fooled. When they venture into our dimension, they use their glamour, not the glamour you're thinking of — no, they use their glamour to shapeshift into beings that are acceptable and even beautiful to our eyes. Their own forms are not human at all.'

Nan had no idea what fairies really looked like in their natural form, she knew she was just repeating age-old myths, but felt that as fairies were supposed to be dangerous, that was reason enough to repeat the stories.

'So, what do they really look like?' persisted Morven.

'Hungry,' replied Nan darkly. 'You haven't even asked us what he said, have you? This is about your daughter's life, and you seem very complacent. Give this matter the respect it deserves!'

'Sorry,' replied a chastened Morven, 'it just seems so...so far-fetched and ridiculous! Well, tell me, then, what did he say?'

By this time, they were climbing into Aunt Gwynnie's trusty little car. Nan settled herself into the front seat.

'He has agreed on the Queen's behalf to our request for a boon on the understanding that we will be giving the gifts promised, plus perhaps, another gift or two of the Queen's own choosing. The granting of the boon depends on us agreeing totally to the Queen's additional demands should she choose to make any. And that's what I'm afraid of.' Nan sighed deeply. 'This is when it can become very dangerous. She might take a fancy to one of us, or demand Molly's baby in return for Molly's sanity, or just make some ridiculous request she knows we can't keep.'

'When do we meet her?' Morven's voice was beginning to rise. 'Can't we just back out and I'll take Molly to a psychiatrist after all? Do we have to do this?'

'We've committed ourselves, and we need to keep calm and focused, not descend into hysterics,' snapped Nan, turning her frowning face to Morven. 'Pull yourself together, for goodness' sake!'

Aunt Gwynnie drove stoically on, bumping along the rough forest track before turning onto the main road. The forest seemed to loom threatening and ominous behind them.

'I always loved this forest,' Morven muttered from the back seat. 'I don't think I'll ever feel the same about it now.'

'Don't be so ridiculous!' Nan said crisply. 'You're of the blood. I'm not saying that makes us safe from any fairy who might take a malign interest in us, but it makes us more able to protect ourselves. We can speak the fairy tongue, so we can talk ourselves out of trouble if we're lucky, and some of them have a grudging respect for humans with the blood.'

'I can't speak the language,' Morven cried. 'How can I protect myself?'

'Well, once this business is over, you'll be off home.' Nan shrugged. 'I doubt they'll be chasing you all over the country, especially if this goes well and the Queen accepts our terms.'

Morven looked doubtful.

'She knows I'm the baby's grandmother.'

'Well, you've always been a sensible and practical girl. Let's just hope she's not interested in the baby, but if she is, I'm sure the blood will out, and you'll cope.' Nan popped a mint into her mouth to signal that the matter was closed for now.

Eye of toad and toe of newt might have worked wonders for Shakespeare's witches, but Nan and her daughters were so uptight they could hardly brew a cup of tea, never mind a cauldron of spells. Nan bustled about tight-lipped, hoping constant activity would hide her abject terror at their imminent meeting with the dread Ceriddwen. She had no way of knowing what the Queen would demand, and the thought terrified her. The Queen's son had decreed they would meet at the next full moon beside the rock in the forest. They should present themselves and wait.

In the meantime, Morven and Gwynnie sought out Molly's recently cleaned beautiful lace dress and coat, then carefully wrapped each garment in tissue paper, ready for their journey into the unknown.

The day of the full moon dawned dull and grey with leaden clouds and a cool easterly breeze. Not the most propitious start, but nevertheless, the women gathered their courage and set off. It had proved surprisingly easy to persuade Molly to accompany them. They initially thought she would resist, preferring as usual, to sit and mope in her room. She allowed herself to be gently bundled into the car. Almost catatonic, she showed absolutely no interest in the journey. When they arrived, she obediently climbed out of the car, sat on a fallen log, and stared into space. The others waited in a state of heightened tension, nerves taut as bowstrings. Morven chewed her nails while Nan and Aunt Gwynnie paced around the small clearing keeping a watchful eye on the rock and surrounding trees.

After about ten minutes, the young man with the cat's eyes appeared from behind the same oak tree. The three women bowed immediately before he could speak.

'Greetings, ladies.' He smiled, bowing gracefully in return. 'Allow me to introduce myself this time. My name is Morfan and my Lady Mother, the Queen, will be here presently. You will bow before her and not rise until given permission.' He stared directly at them. 'Any non-compliance will be viewed with great displeasure.' His expression became sterner, more business-like. 'Who speaks for you?'

Nan stepped forward. 'I am the matriarch. I will speak.'

Morfan nodded his approval. 'Very well, make ready for the Queen.'

He turned to face the rock just as a brilliant coruscating light began to pour from its base, gradually moving upwards until it formed a doorway of shimmering brilliance. The women stood rooted to the spot as figures began to stream through the light door and form themselves into a circle around the clearing. A loud fanfare sounded, and taking their cue from the people surrounding them, the women bowed except for Molly, who appeared oblivious to it all.

Morfan whispered his command, 'You may rise,' and the women stood up and looked around. The light from the rock was dazzling, but they could see they were standing in the circle surrounded by a group of very beautiful people, much like the Queen's son. A large cauldron was placed in the centre and standing beside it was a tall woman with wild dark hair piled on top of her head, bound up with a glittering silver chain. A statement slash of white curls tumbled down one side of her beautiful face. Her eyes were feline, like her son's, lustrous and glittering.

'Where is the child you wish me to cure?' She spoke without preamble. Her voice was deep and musical, with an underlying threat of great authority. This was someone used to being obeyed instantly.

Nan stepped forward with a bravado she didn't feel, indicating towards Molly, still seated on the log. 'This is my granddaughter, Molly.'

'Leave her!' the Queen snapped imperiously. 'I can see she is ill. She does not even realise we are here. What kind of parents are you to allow your child to fall into this state?' She looked at them distastefully as she moved nearer the cauldron and began to stir it with her staff. 'This may prove more difficult than first we thought.'

Nan looked fearfully at her daughters, and then back to the Queen. This was not boding well. The Queen carried on stirring the cauldron and they noticed how strong and lithe she was beneath her sheath-like gown. Her courtiers, whom they assumed all these people to be, stood silent and watchful.

The Queen withdrew her staff from the cauldron and walked over to where Molly sat with a vacant expression. She began to shake the staff over Molly and droplets of the cauldron's contents flew onto her face and hair. She blinked a few times but didn't move. The Queen bent forward and began sniffing at Molly like a dog sniffing an unfamiliar object. She sniffed hard several times and then stiffened. The gathering of fairy folk also stiffened imperceptibly. Nan noticed this and began to feel even more uneasy. Something was wrong, very wrong.

'What's this?' demanded the Queen, whirling around to face her courtiers. 'I smell Gwion on this human. Now why should that be?' She stood, white-faced with shock, wheeling her staff around the circle, pointing it at each fairy in turn. 'I repeat, why does this human smell of Gwion?' She then began to pace menacingly around the gathering, screaming at the unfortunate fairies and prodding them with the sharp crystal-tipped point of her staff. 'Who knew that Gwion had fathered a child with a human? If you value your lives and do not wish to die young in the world of humans, speak now!'

She stopped and turned, glaring at Nan and her daughters, taking a step towards them. All three instinctively stepped backwards.

'And who,' she hissed, 'is the father of your granddaughter's child?'

'His name is Harry. Harry is my baby's father.'

Every eye in the circle turned to look at Molly. Hands around her knees, she was rocking gently back and forth, staring dreamily into space.

'And who is Harry, child?' purred the Queen, advancing on Molly. 'I should very much like to meet him.'

'I can't remember.' Molly blinked at the Queen, appearing to surface briefly, then, abruptly, her face became closed and shuttered as she withdrew once more.

Whirling around again, Ceriddwen once more addressed her entourage. 'I am waiting. Tell me who knew. Make yourselves known if you do not wish to remain here and perish!' She banged her staff so hard on the ground that Nan, Gwynnie and Morven felt the ground tremble beneath them. Her fury was terrifying.

A murmur arose amongst the fairies as they whispered to each other, passing messages around the circle, wide-eyed with fear, the air thick with nervous trepidation. Finally, a couple stepped forward, spoke briefly to Morfan, then prostrated themselves in front of Ceriddwen, the others in the circle following suit. Only the Queen's son remained standing behind her, along with the three women and Molly.

The fairy on the ground in front of the Queen began to speak, his voice trembling with fear. 'Many of us knew, my Queen. Gwion begged us not to betray him, and because we all loved him, we remained silent.'

An ominous silence ensued as the Queen digested this information, but it was short-lived. All hell broke loose as she erupted into a paroxysm of fury, screaming and shrieking torrents of abuse as her subjects quailed before her, some of them covering their heads as she swung her staff viciously at anyone who moved. It seemed that Nan and her daughters had been forgotten as she lapsed into the fairy tongue, howling and berating the fairies with an intense and terrifying ferocity.

Amid the furore, no one noticed Molly rise from her log and make her way towards the shining brightness of the rock. Too late; Morven glanced over just in time to see her fey, will o' the-wisp daughter disappearing into the glamorous, coruscating light. She let out a piercing scream. The Queen, in the middle of her tirade, turned furiously, ready to swing her staff at whoever had the temerity to interrupt her in full flow. Morven was clutching Nan's arm, babbling and pointing at the rock.

'Molly went into the rock...the light...it swallowed her...oh Mum, do something!' Then turning to the Queen, she screamed, 'Give me back my daughter, you bitch, stealing her wasn't part of the deal.'

The assembled fairies, some of them now scrambling to their feet, gasped in horrified unison at this insult to their Queen. Ceriddwen lowered her staff and gazed at Morven in cool appraisal.

'You think I planned to steal your daughter? I had no such thought, but it would appear your daughter thinks otherwise. Why else would she volunteer to cross the threshold into my domain?'

Morven was having none of it. 'She's ill, she doesn't know what she's doing!'

'Well enough to tell me the name of her child's father,' Ceriddwen replied, a little too reasonable for Nan's liking.

'You covered her in that foul-smelling liquid from your pot. What did that do to her, you evil hag?'

Another sharp intake of breath from the fairies. The Queen seemed unperturbed.

That's because she knows she's holding all the cards, thought Nan.

'The liquid from my cauldron brings wisdom to those who partake of it — it also releases genetic information when it encounters a living being. My people are far advanced in science and medicine — I would not expect small people like you to understand. We have possessed this knowledge for thousands of years, and we continue to expand and learn. We have also spent thousands of years trying to civilize homo sapiens since the Great Catastrophes, but you are a stubborn, ignorant, and slow-to-learn race. I have honoured your daughter, and you abuse me!' She glared contemptuously at the three women.

'Just give me back my daughter!' shouted Morven. 'I don't know what you're talking about!'

'Of course, you don't,' sneered Ceriddwen.

Morven opened her mouth to answer, but Nan laid a warning hand on her arm. She sensed great danger and knew she would have to do some fast talking and even faster thinking.

'I apologise for my daughter's insolence.'

'I'm not sorry...' Morven protested, but a sharp dig from Nan's elbow silenced her.

'She is overwrought. We are all overwrought. My granddaughter's illness is a matter of great concern to us. We have heard of your powerful healing skills, and we would be honoured if you would consider using them to help her.'

Ceriddwen regarded them through narrowed eyes.

'The matter of her child's parentage changes any agreement that went before. I was unaware of the betrayal this meeting would expose.'

'As were we,' replied Nan stoutly. 'We know of no Gwion in relationship to Harry!'

'Ah, the mysterious Harry,' mused the Queen, casting a baleful glance in the direction of the cringing crowd of fairies. 'We shall have to investigate him further.' Raising her arm and snapping her fingers, she regarded Nan with open dislike as her son stepped forward. 'Show me your gifts.'

Nan turned to Aunt Gwynnie who had been clutching the tissue-wrapped dress and coat throughout the entire drama. Aunt Gwynnie placed them into Morfan's arms as two fairy women approached, unwrapped them, and presented them to Ceriddwen, holding the garments up as she examined each in turn, caressing the delicate lace stitches and turning the fabric over to peer at the underside.

'Very fine work,' she grudgingly conceded. 'And which of you created these garments?'

'Why, Molly, of course,' Morven replied, realising her mistake when Nan stamped on her foot, causing her to cry out in pain.

Ceriddwen turned a crafty eye on them. 'The child? So, beneath the mask, she has hidden depths and talents. Only a human with our blood could make such beautiful things. She must make more.'

The last sentence was spoken as a statement, not a suggestion, and Nan's heart sank to her boots. She knew what was coming.

'I shall engage her in creating more beautiful gowns and coats. I shall heal her mind and her spirit — she shall be like a butterfly emerging from her chrysalis!'

'And where will this healing take place?' asked Nan cautiously, knowing the answer before it was given. Ceriddwen regarded her incredulously.

'Why, in my home, of course. Where else? I shall brook no disagreement. Our meeting is over, humans. My son shall explain the details.'

With that, she turned on her heel, and with the fairy band scurrying behind her, made her way back to the rock.

'There will be much trouble, I fear.' Morfan looked miserable. A far cry from the arrogant and confident fairy who had earlier instructed them on protocol.

'So, what will happen now?' demanded a distraught Morven. 'What's going to happen to Molly? How long will the Queen keep her?' Morfan held up his hand to stem Morven's verbal assault.

'Until my mother sees fit. She will almost certainly keep her until she finds out the whole truth about Gwion. If she calms down, she may be reasonable, but she is not one to be disobeyed. Gwion committed a mortal offence by leaving our world without permission, therefore those of us who knew may also face severe punishment.'

The brilliant light disappeared after swallowing the last fairy, returning the moss-covered rocky outcrop to its normal brooding presence. Morven's wail of anguish startled a blackbird, and it screamed in alarm, swooping low in front of them, causing rooks high in the canopy above to caw loudly in sympathetic disapproval. Once again, their beloved forest seemed a dark and sinister place.

Morven and Gwynnie roamed this forest freely as children, setting off on sunny days with a bottle of water and jam sandwiches to sustain them as they galloped about climbing trees, watching forest creatures, and playing games. On other days their grandmother accompanied them, teaching them how to forage, recognise plants and herbs, which mushrooms to pick and which ones to avoid. Morven, always keen on drawing and painting, would bring a sketchbook to draw the plants and flowers Granny pointed out. Gwynnie was more interested in their properties and how they could be used and thus, Morven went to art school and became a teacher. Gwynnie followed in Granny's footsteps, much to Nan's annoyance, becoming a hedge witch and, over time, the village postmistress.

Morven had never taken the fairy blood part of their ancestry seriously. She humoured Nan who insisted they leave small gifts for the fairy folk whenever they went to the forest — little sweets, or a loaf of newly baked bread, and at Hallowe'en or Samhain as Nan called it, sprinkling salt all around the perimeter of the house and garden, *To keep the fairies away when the veil thins.*

Faced with the reality that fairy folk did exist and were possibly every bit the malign, otherworldly beings Nan said they were, Morven, normally practical and down-to-earth, fell apart. Morfan, who appeared to have regained his composure, was the first to speak.

'My mother will not harm your Molly. I give you my solemn promise. She will heal her and return her soon.'

'And what do you mean by soon?' Nan suddenly felt every one of her seventy-five years. *I'm too old for this,* she thought. 'I believe time moves differently in your world. Fairies do not age as we do, so how will this affect my granddaughter?'

'Ah yes, I see how you may be concerned by this, but it actually works to your advantage.'

'Our advantage?' Nan was sceptical. 'How so?'

'Molly will believe she has been in our world for a very long time, because, as you say, time behaves differently there, but when she returns, only a few hours of your time will have passed.'

Morven gave a shriek of hysterical laughter. 'I've never heard such nonsense! Bring my daughter back, now. I don't know what game you're all playing, lighting the place up and disappearing into rocks — what is it you've got over there? A hidden cave? A secret door?'

She stumbled across the clearing and began frantically pushing at the rock surface, pulling off handfuls of moss, breaking her nails in the process.

Gwynnie rushed over and pulled her back. 'Morven, Morven, calm down, please!' Morven collapsed, weeping, into her sister's arms.

Ignoring Morven's sobs, Nan continued her conversation with Morfan. 'If I was your mother, I might think twice about returning Molly to the world of humans,' she said, looking him directly in the eye. 'I imagine Molly is of great value to Ceriddwen, being the mother of a royal prince.'

'Ah,' Morfan nodded, 'you understand our ways more than I thought.'

'I'm not stupid,' Nan replied irritably. 'If your mother's a queen, her sons are princes, and her grandchildren are also royal. She will not allow Molly to just leave. She will want something in return, and it will no doubt be something impossible for us to give.'

Morfan had the grace to look uncomfortable and began to shift about uneasily.

'I see I have touched a nerve,' observed Nan dryly. 'I may only have a human's scant knowledge of fairy folk and their ways, but I do know you set great store by honour and protocol and keep your word once given. Will you give me your word again that Molly will not be harmed and returned to us healed and restored? And,' she added emphatically, 'that your mother will not interfere in Molly's son's life, MY great-grandson's life, until he is old enough to understand who he really is?' Adding as an afterthought, 'If he has to know at all.'

Morfan looked at the three women; Morven's crumpled, tear-stained face, Gwynnie, white and shocked, and Nan's wrinkled frown and fierce eyes boring into him, daring him to refuse. He liked this feisty, elderly human, protecting her family like a bear guarding her cubs, and he felt sorry for Molly's mother — he remembered Ceriddwen's grief when Gwion left. On the other hand, he risked his mother's wrath if he made promises she was not minded to honour, and she was already furious with him. He regarded them thoughtfully for a while.

'Very well,' he said at last, 'I give you my word. Molly shall be returned healed and restored. She will remember nothing of her time in our world until her son is of age. Molly shall have forty human years' grace — her son will be a man and know his own mind — and, *if* it pleases my mother, she will come for him then. That is my final word.'

Morven went to argue, but Nan held up her hand to silence her. She knew further negotiations were pointless. She also knew Morfan had already overstepped his authority. No doubt he would be facing more of his mother's wrath when he returned to his own world. They had no choice but to accept his terms.

'Very well,' agreed Nan. 'But when may we expect Molly's return?'

'Go home now,' urged Morfan, 'return at sunset — Molly will be waiting. And do not worry, she will remember nothing. Take her home and when she awakens in the morning, she will be restored to her old self, content that her adopted child is well and happy and that she has made the correct choice. She will always be aware, in some part of her mind, that she has a child, but will not fret for him while she is under my mother's enchantment. As I said, she will remember nothing for forty years and she will never seek out her son. She will consider that chapter of her life closed. You must never reveal your part in this to her until the forty years have passed, or all your efforts to help her will crumble to nothing. She must never know. After tomorrow, her journey through her human life is hers and hers alone.'

He gave them a wan smile. 'Please go, now. I must return and advise my mother of our deliberations.' With a polite bow, he turned on his heel and strode across the clearing to disappear in a flash of brilliant white light.

FOUR

Blood Will Out

Laura watched Molly's expression change to one of horror as the shock of realisation at who Harry's son really was, began to dawn on her. She thought she knew Molly, they were lifelong best friends, but the woman standing beside her was a stranger. Someone, she realised, she didn't know at all.

Through her new-found interest in spirituality, Laura had discovered an old university friend who now lived in Glastonbury and was a priestess at the town's pretty Goddess Temple, just off the High Street. She was delighted to learn that Eleanor also knew Harry quite well as he regularly frequented the temple to help with various events. Laura had immediately enlisted her help in obtaining Harry's address and set off to find him.

Harry's shop was tucked away in Benedict Street near the ruins of Glastonbury Abbey. Laura remembered her first visit into the shop's shadowed interior, feeling overwhelmed by the all-pervading aromas of herbs and aromatic oils, and she'd suddenly began to feel quite faint, grabbing at a shelving unit for support. Immediately concerned, the man behind the counter rushed to her side.

'Can I help you, are you feeling unwell?'

'It's just the smell of the herbs and oils...it's overpowering.'

'It is, but I suppose I'm used to it,' he replied, sympathetically.

Feeling slightly foolish, Laura smiled weakly and pulling herself together, rearranged her features into what she hoped was a normal expression, and asked for Mr Harry Bamford. As he replied, she noticed he had striking topaz-coloured eyes.

'I'm afraid my father isn't here just now, but please, let me bring you a glass of water.'

She froze in shock. His father? Did Molly and Harry have a son she knew nothing about? Molly hadn't confided in her nor had she said much about Harry for forty years, always refusing to talk about him. Eleanor said Harry had never married, and to her knowledge, had never been in a recognised relationship with anyone. He was a very private man who lived a simple life, completely dedicated to his work.

Laura studied Harry's son from beneath her lashes as he handed her a glass of water. He was difficult to age precisely, but he could, she considered, be a very youthful forty-year-old, which would be correct if he was indeed Molly and Harry's son. The time frame appeared to be indisputable. Although he didn't look anything like Harry, she did think there was a look of Molly, but couldn't identify the cat-like topaz eyes nor the mane of black hair. He was very handsome, no doubt about it.

Now Laura understood, or at least thought she did. Molly had been so obdurate about Harry because she wanted to keep their son a secret — but why? In truth, Laura knew nothing.

When Harry and Molly broke up, Laura was reading English Literature at Glasgow University and having a torrid affair with a hunky maths student called Alastair. When she wasn't cramming for exams, or rushing to lectures, she was sailing on Loch Lomond, hill climbing or walking the West Highland Way, and spending riotous weekends partying with Alastair and their friends. She barely gave Molly a thought, and when her mother told her she heard Molly had taken a year out to study textiles in Hereford, Laura assumed she was going away to avoid seeing Harry for a while. In the days before mobile phones, people were often out of contact with friends for long periods, unless they were letter writers, or had good access to a telephone. Laura had no idea what Molly's new address was, and just assumed they'd catch up eventually.

~

'Jimmy, please allow me to introduce you to Harry and his son — Harry, Xander, this is Jimmy.'

Jimmy was the first to stretch out his hand in greeting, and as they shook hands, Harry said abruptly, 'Pleased to meet you, I'm sure. Are we ready to get started?'

'Don't you think you should eat something? You must be hungry after your journey,' Laura queried. Jimmy had cleared his plate and was already heading towards the door. Harry ignored her and followed him into the garden.

The brilliant multi-coloured light display from the plants was more dazzling than ever as they continued their struggle against the incessant pull of the portal. Harry and Xander automatically shielded their eyes as they entered, Jimmy already having grown used to it and now questioning the other men about the plan of action.

'Before I discuss anything,' Harry rudely interrupted, 'I need to see this portal, if a portal is what it really is.'

Jimmy wasn't in the least offended. 'Of course,' he said, grinning, 'I should have known you'd want to see the portal first. Follow me.'

Harry watched as Jimmy ducked into the small cave-like opening, then got down on his hands and knees for a better look. He was much taller than Jimmy and there was no question of him ducking down far enough to follow him. He crawled to the entrance and stuck his head and shoulders inside and waited as his eyes adjusted to the gloom. No sign of Jimmy — the little cave was only a few feet long and seemed to come to a dead end — it looked as though Jimmy had simply vanished into thin air. He scanned the walls to check for any hidden corners Jimmy might be hiding behind but dismissed the idea that he would be stupid enough to do that and think he could get away with it. He backed out and sat on his hunkers, looking thoughtfully at the sinkhole. There had to be a rational explanation for this; Harry didn't believe in magic; this was simply a natural phenomenon no one yet understood. Laura said she had been through the portal too, and although he had doubted her when she first told him about it, why would she lie? As a trained druid and shamanic healer, he respected the ancient Ngangkari tradition, and if Jimmy thought singing the tear in the dimensional fabric might work, he was certainly willing to give it a try. A few moments later, Jimmy reappeared.

'You satisfied it's a portal, then, Mr Harry?'

'It's certainly something I don't understand, but let's do our best to fix the problem.' He turned to Xander. 'Ready to get started?'

'I might be if I could see what I was doing — it's too bright!' complained Xander. 'Where did you put my harp?'

'Put your sunglasses on!' retorted Harry. 'Your harp's on the bench under the window.'

'You think harp music will be powerful enough?' Jimmy asked. 'Isn't harp music a bit too genteel?'

Harry and Xander exchanged glances.

'Absolutely no idea,' said Harry quietly, watching as Xander twiddled with the pegs on his harp, tightening the strings with practised fingers. 'We've just been asked to help up the ante.'

By now Xander had begun to play, and Harry accompanied with a gentle hypnotic rhythm on his shamanic drum. Molly was entranced by the beautiful music. It was unearthly and magical, and something began to uncurl itself deep within her brain. This music was familiar, but she couldn't work out why. The haunting ethereal chords wove themselves around the garden, soothing the flowers, calming the trees and bushes, caressing the grass, and moving softly across the pond, wrapping the water lilies in an invisible cloak of love and protection. She knew this feeling; she had experienced it before. Where and when had she last heard the music and that sense of peace and intense love? If only she could remember…

As the beautiful sound continued to weave itself around the garden, Molly began to feel more and more uneasy. A small memory seedling was pushing itself through the deeply compacted compost in the depths of her brain. What was it about this music? If only the fogginess would clear. There was a secret, a secret about what?

It's about Harry and my baby…Xander's my baby! Molly's knees almost buckled in shock. She'd known the minute she saw him in the kitchen, but it hadn't really sunk in until now. *Why did I never wonder about my baby? How could I just give him away and never think of him?*

She sank onto the garden seat beneath the kitchen window, hoping no one would notice how much she was shaking. And it was becoming obvious he had been raised by Harry. How had that happened? Taking deep breaths to calm herself, she tried to focus on the events of forty years ago, knowing those events were connected to what was happening now. But how did she know that? What happened all those years ago? Mum and Aunt Gwynnie were in their eighties now; when Dad died, Mum went to live with Aunt Gwynnie. Molly had a sudden urge to phone her mother and ask what she knew but was distracted by the sound of Xander and Harry arguing.

'What do you mean Jimmy will have to go back?' Harry sounded really exasperated.

'I think it's just a fluke that the portal opened in Australia, I don't think that's part of the plan at all,' Xander retorted hotly.

'Plan? What plan?' Harry exploded. 'What are you talking about? We've only just got here and suddenly you know this is a plan. How can you possibly know that?'

Molly was listening intently.

'I just know — I can't explain it. When I saw the plants and their reaction to the music, I realised this has nothing to do with Jimmy, I can feel it in my blood.' He paused, running his hands through his hair. 'I have this feeling, gut instinct. I can't describe it any other way. My blood is singing, it started as soon as I came through Molly's gate. There's real danger here, I don't understand what it is yet, but I'm sure it will reveal itself to us if we don't close the portal soon or deal with whatever is causing the breach. Jimmy must go back. Please.'

Harry turned to Jimmy. 'What do you think?'

Placing his didgeridoo on the grass, Jimmy replied, 'My magic has been growing weaker, I can feel the power of the portal and this power is something I have not experienced in my homeland. We work with the ancestors and the Dreamtime, this is something different, not of my people and I fear your son is correct. Ngangkari magic is no use here. I will return to my home now'

'I thought you said this was just gravitational pull?' Molly forced herself off the bench and crossed the grass to join them. 'Controlled by the moon like the tides and animal migration.' She paused, trying to steady her voice.

'I got it wrong, Molly, I'm sorry.' Jimmy spread his hands apologetically.

Ignoring him, she tried to stop her voice from shaking. 'And now it's nothing to do with that, it's become something else?' She was now breathing hard as she emphasised the words, and turning to Xander thought, *You're my baby.* Trying to push her treacherous feelings aside as she continued: 'Something else, just because you feel it in your blood?'

As soon as she uttered the words, the little memory seedling uncurled itself a bit further. 'I've got the blood!' she exclaimed, before she turned swiftly and ran into the house, slamming the door and leaning against it, her heart thudding against her chest. *I have the blood, I know I have the blood! What does it mean? Did I give Xander the blood? God, I wish I could remember!*

Meanwhile, back in the garden, Laura stood open-mouthed, trying to grasp all that was happening. Her well-intentioned plans of reuniting Harry and Molly, and for all three of them to bask forever in the knowledge that there was indeed such a thing as inter-dimensional time travel, were crumbling to dust in front of her eyes. Of course, she hadn't factored Xander into her plans, how could she? And how could Molly have kept this from her all these years? This man, well, these three men, were turning what had seemed like a magical adventure into a nightmare. And Jimmy was leaving? Abruptly, Laura shook herself and refocused on what Harry and Xander were saying.

'Why should Jimmy leave just because you say so?' she demanded. Three pairs of eyes turned to look at her.

'No, Miss Laura,' Jimmy's voice was sad, but he spoke kindly. 'Your druid friends are correct, this is not about me or my people. I stumbled through by accident — I am not meant to be here.'

Xander interjected indignantly, 'I'm not a druid!'

Ignoring him, Laura demanded, 'Then why did you come? You didn't stumble through. You came through with me, quite happily, as I recall!' and immediately felt ashamed of the sarcastic emphasis she had used.

'Because magic isn't perfect.' Harry's voice was calm and measured. 'Whoever or whatever caused the portal to open in the first place may have stumbled over a word or made a small navigational error. As I said, it isn't a perfect science — and that's all magic is — science we don't yet understand. And that miscalculation caused the portal to open somewhere else at the same time, and not where it was supposed to open.' Everyone stared at him as he continued: 'And I think that's why whoever opened the portal hasn't appeared yet — they haven't managed to open it correctly at their end, so to speak.' He turned to Jimmy and asked, 'Do you know what ley lines are?' Jimmy nodded. 'It may well be that your home is on the same ley line as Molly's, and the parties responsible have simply made a mathematical error, causing the portal to open in the wrong place.'

Laura was becoming totally confused and irritated — she liked to feel she was in charge, and not understanding what was going on meant she was completely losing control of events.

'Let me be clear. Are you saying they have ley lines in Australia?' Harry and Xander stared at her, Xander raising a questioning eyebrow which further infuriated her. *He thinks I'm stupid. Why did I say that?* she thought.

'We call them turingas,' explained Jimmy, 'and I must traverse back along these turingas to my homeland. Goodbye, Miss Laura.' He gave a courteous little bow, picked up his didgeridoo, and headed towards the portal.

'Wait!' cried Laura. 'What year is it in Australia?'

Jimmy laughed and called over his shoulder, 'Same year as it is here. Come and visit us again in the Blue Mountains!' And with that, he was gone.

Molly's breath was coming in great gasps as she desperately tried to calm down, her chest tight with a fear she didn't quite understand. The stress of seeing Harry after all this time, then realising that Xander was their son, was so shocking she could hardly bear it. Frantically trying to gather her thoughts, she became aware of the shrill insistent ring of the telephone. She tried to ignore it, assuming it was just another cold call, but to her exasperation, the ringing went on and on until finally she made her way into the hall and grabbed the receiver.

'Hello?' she bellowed into the handset.

'Is that you, Molly?' an all-too familiar voice boomed down the line. 'It's me, Dolores, from number 11.'

Molly could hardly believe her ears; Dolores never called, at least not since Fred had died. Panic began to mount: She's onto us...*She'll phone the authorities...Laura was right — it'll be a circus!*

'What do you want?'

'Erm...I'm phoning on behalf of the Garden Club about this year's Fred's Shed award.'

'What are you talking about? Get to the point, please. I'm actually very busy right now!'

Well, as you know, the Garden Club...'

'I don't know anything about the Garden Club! Look, I have to go...' Before she had a chance to put the phone down, Dolores jumped straight back in.

'The award's in Fred's honour — we all loved him so much at the club.'

And you more than anyone else, you shameless tart, thought Molly.

'His meticulous shed keeping was an inspiration to us all,' Dolores cooed, 'such an inspiration, in fact, that we decided to hold a special competition every year in his memory. Mr Carstairs from The Glen won it last year, his seed boxes and potting shelves are to die for.'

Molly suppressed a surge of hysterical laughter. 'If you don't get to the point, I'm hanging up, in fact, I'm hanging up right now...'

A Dynasty of Dragons

'No, please, Molly, don't do that. I know we've had our differences, but for the sake of Fred's memory, let me finish.'

'Oh, for goodness' sake! Will you just get on with it, then!'

'Thank you, Molly, I'll be as brief as I can,' and with that, she launched into a garrulous preamble as Molly prepared to lose the will to live. It occurred to Molly that she was feeling much calmer; her antipathy towards Dolores had temporarily banished Harry and Xander from her mind.

'And so, we've decided we would like you to present this year's award to Tom Montgomery for his fabulous Fairy Castle shed, it's got little turrets and everything...'

As Dolores gushed on, something snapped into place inside Molly's head. *Fairies! That's it! It's not aliens or Australians, it's all about the fairies!* Heart thudding, Molly dropped the phone and rushed into the garden, leaving Dolores talking to herself.

'I remember!' she blurted to three astonished faces. 'The portal is about me! Someone is coming for me. At least I think it's me they're coming for...'

As she paused for breath, Harry put down his drum and guided her to the garden bench. 'Take a deep breath.' He spoke in very soothing tones as he sat down beside her. 'That's it, and another deep breath in...and out...it's alright, everything's going to be fine.' He was now holding her hand and stroking it gently. 'Now, start at the beginning, and tell me, who is coming?'

Molly frowned with concentration. 'Ceriddwen is coming. She said I would be safe here for forty years, and then she would come and take me home.' She turned to Harry then looked across the garden to the portal before blurting out, 'But...but not here, this isn't right! I've to go back to the rock in the forest. Something's wrong, very wrong!'

Xander looked at Harry in bewilderment.

'What is she talking about? A Celtic Goddess is coming after forty years? I'm afraid you've lost me now.' He shook his head in bemusement. 'Don't you think we've got more important things to get on with right now than talk about ancient Celtic deities?' His voice was heavy with sarcasm as Molly's face took on an increasingly worried and confused appearance.

Harry was the only person who noticed the plants and flowers as they turned and shone their tired, depleted auras in her direction. 'To comfort her,' he marvelled. 'They're exhausted by this, yet they would die for her.' He remembered how she had laughed good-naturedly at him for pointing this out years ago and immediately felt ashamed of his earlier coldness towards her. 'My, how you've changed your tune!' he snapped at Xander. 'A few moments ago your blood was singing, and you were convinced we're all in mortal danger!' Xander opened his mouth to protest, but Harry cut in again. 'There's a lot you don't know, Xander, very important things I should have told you long ago, but I let my stupid pride get in the way.' He gripped Molly's hand tighter. 'I'm sorry I was rude to you before, Molly — please tell us what you remember.' He glared at Xander. 'We have some time to spare, so a little patience, if you don't mind. And let's not forget you're the one who sensed danger!'

Xander gave a sceptical shrug and sat down beside Laura on the wall of the raised flower bed in front of the bench. And so, bathed in the warm glow of her beloved garden, with Harry holding her hand, Molly began her tale…

FIVE

The Great Citadel

When Molly slipped through the portal, she found herself in a long stone passageway, its high vaulted ceiling lit by glowing crystal lights placed along the walls. On her dreamlike journey through this mysterious corridor, feet padding softly on the smooth flagstones, she recalled a feeling of being enveloped in warmth and well-being so intense she found herself smiling for the first time in months. At the end of the corridor, she was confronted by two enormous iron gates, standing open, waiting for the Queen's return. The gates were flanked by high granite walls, with a semi-circular flight of broad steps leading up to a walkway and another wall. The steps were worn down and smoothed by age — the whole structure looked extremely old to Molly; even on trips to ruined castles and ancient historical sites as a child she couldn't remember seeing anything as remotely old-looking like these walls and stairs. Crossing the walkway, she was just tall enough to look over the wall, and the vista took her breath away.

Glancing to her left and right, she took in crenelated walls and tall turrets topped with fluttering flags and pennants overlooking a gloriously beautiful, wooded valley of lush meadows, fields of crops, and farm animals surrounded by rolling green hills. A gleaming river wound its way from a sparkling lake in the distance and far below the walls, she could see ships and a busy harbour. Little clusters of houses and buildings were dotted at intervals along a broad white road. The air was pure, clean, and warm, and Molly breathed deeply as she watched the tiny, ant-like figures below bustling about their business. She realised she was standing on the battlements of an enormous castle-like structure, and its sheer forbidding size belied the peaceful scene below.

The sound of footsteps and voices echoed up from the corridor and she turned to see the Queen striding through the iron gates with her fairy entourage scuttling apprehensively behind.

'Gatekeeper, the gates!' Ceriddwen bellowed. Molly had seen no one since coming through the portal. She hadn't noticed at the time, being so enthralled by her surroundings, but now it struck her as strange she hadn't been challenged.

Spying Molly at the top of the stairs, the Queen frowned ferociously, and again loudly summoned the absent gatekeeper. All eyes turned at the sound of a door opening. A tall figure began a stately descent from a flight of steps further along the battlements. He had a long-plaited beard and his dark hair fell in a similar braid down his back. He seemed to shimmer in the light and Molly thought he was wearing a garment of little metal plates until she realised, as he drew closer, his long coat was made from small squares of mother of pearl. He was followed by a huge bear of a man wearing a leather breastplate; a huge bunch of keys hung from his broad leather belt. This man was white with fear.

'Ceri, Ceri, my dear! What is amiss? Anwyn has abandoned his post in terror. Can anything be that serious? Your bellowing has terrified the entire citadel. What ails you?'

His voice was rich and mellifluous, but with an air of quiet authority. Ceriddwen looked slightly mollified, but quickly grabbed hold of Molly's arm and thrust her towards him.

'Examine this human and you will soon learn the reason for my fury!'

He turned to Molly with a benevolent look on his face. 'Ah, welcome, my dear. For some reason you have incurred the wrath of our beloved Queen. My name is Lleu,' he paused and gave a wicked smile, 'and I have the misfortune to be her husband!'

'Stop flirting and smell her!' snarled Ceriddwen.

'I do wish you would refrain from being so indelicate, my dear,' he replied calmly as he tucked Molly's arm into his. 'Let's go for a little stroll.' As the huge man with the keys made to follow them, Lleu said curtly, 'Anwyn, resume your duties before the goblins realise you aren't there.'

Anwyn nodded and scurried past the outraged Queen, who took a swipe at him with her staff as he passed.

'How dare you leave your post! I'll deal with you later!' she howled to his rapidly retreating bulk.

'You mustn't mind the Queen,' Lleu said, smiling down at Molly, 'or be afraid of me, for that matter. Much of the Queen's furious outbursts and eye-popping rages are for show. I should know, after all, I am her husband.'

'But I don't know who any of you are, or where I am, or what I'm doing here!' All of this came out in a tumbling rush of words, more words than Molly had spoken in many months. 'There was a lot of shouting and arguing, and when I opened my eyes I saw a great doorway of light — I just got up and walked through and here I am!'

'You are only here because the Queen wishes you to be here, if she didn't wish it, the doorway of light would have closed against you. Now, let us find out why you are here, but first, a little walk and then some refreshments. Does that sound good to you?'

She nodded happily. This man, Lleu, made her feel somehow safe and she knew instinctively she could trust him.

They made their way along the battlements, Lleu pointing to houses and telling her who lived there, what their occupations were, as well as other points of interest along the way. As they turned yet another corner, Molly gasped at the sight of a huge glassy tower glittering in the distance. It was shaped like a spiral and enormously high, the sunlight coruscating in great dazzling bursts from the building's myriad facets.

'What's that building?' she asked. 'It looks as though it's just made of glass — I don't see any metal or bricks.'

'It's not glass,' replied Lleu, 'it's a single quartz crystal, and it's our seat of learning. All our teachers, bards, elders, healers, and musicians learn their craft there.'

'Crystal?' Molly exclaimed incredulously. 'But it's enormous!'

'It's been hollowed out and transformed over many thousands of years. We have used crystal technology for thousands of years, too. Each piece of crystal taken from the master crystal has been carefully preserved and used, along with other crystals, to power our civilisation.'

Molly gazed at the magnificent edifice. 'I would love to visit it.'

'I'm sure that can be arranged,' Lleu affirmed. 'I will introduce you to the Arianrhod.'

'Arianrhod? As in the Welsh goddess?'

Lleu let out a bellow of laughter. 'You humans have such a quaint way of memorising and describing events and people lost to you through the ages and mists of time!' He smiled at her. 'The Arianrhod is Keeper of the Crystal Tower. The title is handed down to every keeper who always happens to be a bard or a very wise and powerful teacher.'

'I knew someone who wanted to be a bard,' Molly confided. 'He was going to medical school and decided to drop out to study druidry and herbal medicine instead.' Her voice quavered, and she could feel tears starting to prick behind her eyelids. 'My father said he wasn't good enough for me.'

'A bard not good enough? Now that is a strange concept.' Lleu looked bemused. 'Bards are very powerful, respected people here, and I do know it was also the case with humans long ago in your history. You humans are a strange lot, if you don't mind me saying so.'

By now, they were strolling down another broad flight of stairs and through great double doors into a large airy room lit by south-facing, floor-length windows. The windows were flung open and sheer gauzy curtains billowed in a gentle breeze. Molly noticed the windows opened onto a balcony and she could see comfortable chairs around a low, beautifully inlaid rosewood table. She gazed in awed pleasure at the sumptuous furnishings, wall hangings, and ornamental sculptures gracing the beautiful room as Lleu led her over thick, luxurious carpets towards the balcony. Handing his lustrous coat to a hovering attendant, he invited his guest to sit, and she made herself comfortable amongst the soft cushions and velvet upholstery of her chosen chair. Charming people flitted about offering food and drink and arranging plates of delicious-looking snacks on the rosewood table.

Molly remembered with great clarity that afternoon with Lleu. She marvelled at how he put her at ease, helping to maintain her feelings of calm and wellbeing, even everyone's courtesy in speaking English, albeit in a somewhat archaic manner in a strange and beautiful accent. Their conversation was constantly interrupted by officials bringing Lleu papers to sign and asking long involved questions. He was obviously an extremely busy person yet never appeared irritated or bored, smiling and chatting to them all equally. No one seemed curious or surprised by Molly's presence until, eventually, the surreality of the situation got the better of her and she summoned the courage to ask, 'Where exactly am I and why am I here?'

She knew very well that Harry, Laura and Xander were probably thinking this entire memory was a figment of her imagination triggered by her post-partum psychosis, and it was a known fact that in the early 1970s, psychotic patients were sometimes prescribed LSD, despite the hallucinatory effects of the drug. Indeed, at the time, Molly began to wonder if she was in the middle of a wonderful dream.

Lleu smiled patiently. ' When you passed through the portal, you left your world, Earth, and entered our world, Sidhthean. You are a guest in the Land of The Four Gates, our kingdom, because the Queen wishes it.

'Who is Gwion? And why do I smell like him? Do you think I smell like this person?'

Again, her words came out in a great rush, and she hoped she wasn't breaching some unknown code of etiquette. Lleu was, after all, a king. Or was he? Was he just the Queen's consort? Her head was beginning to ache with sensory overload.

'Yes, you smell of Gwion. A very pleasing scent indeed. It comforts me a great deal…you comfort me because of that.' He paused for a moment, his brow creasing slightly. 'There is another scent about you I can't identify, but no matter, it can wait.'

Molly persisted. 'So, who exactly is this Gwion? And why has he, or perhaps it's me, made the Queen so angry?'

Lleu let out a great sigh. 'Gwion was our firstborn son.'

'Was?'

'Yes, unfortunately he is dead. We suspected he defied our laws by falling in love with a human and leaving our world to be with her, and you have just confirmed that suspicion. As soon as he did that, he became subject to the physical laws of your world. In other words, his life was cut preternaturally short. We will never cease to grieve for him.'

'But I don't understand what this has to do with me.'

'You have recently given birth and your child's father is Gwion's son. This is what we can sense. You carry the scent of your child. Our people have the sensory ability to detect the essence of our kin on others.'

'My grandmother says we have your blood, too,' Molly ventured as she digested this new information.

'Perhaps.' Lleu nodded thoughtfully. 'I do not yet know enough about you, but what I do know is that your child and his father have royal blood, and that is important. What I do not understand is why you are here without your child. Where is he?'

Soothed by Lleu's warmth and kindliness, Molly told him everything.

He listened intently and said nothing, now waving away the stream of officials intent on gaining his attention.

Molly's nervousness of the Queen and the inhabitants of Sidhthean proved to be unfounded. As that first afternoon wore on, she was eventually shown to her quarters, trotting after a bustling little fairy woman, through long corridors, pretty halls, and seemingly endless flights of stairs, eventually climbing up a twisting spiral staircase into a suite of comfortably furnished turret rooms. The fairy woman asked if she would like to bathe and busied herself running water and pouring scented oils into a huge bath set in the middle of a lovely bathroom. The fairy told her there were fresh clothes in the bedroom and after her bath she should sleep for a while, stating she would return later in the evening to guide her to the Great Hall for dinner.

Molly lay in the warm fragrant water and tried to gather her thoughts. She knew she was ill but marvelled at how well she now felt. She searched her mind for the black, despairing fog that had almost suffocated her for so long, and to her immense relief, found it gone. Her initial feelings of wellbeing and comfort were reinforced by the soothing warmth of the water and the sheer beauty of her surroundings. The bath stood in front of an open window, inviting the eyes to linger on the lush rolling hills and distant mountains. She could hear a thrush singing outside, and to her surprise, her eyes filled with tears of happiness. *I've just arrived, and I feel at home, as though I've always lived here.* She relaxed a while in the warm, perfumed water before stepping out to dry herself on one of the soft fluffy towels beside the bath.

~

Molly paused for breath, gripping Harry's hand with such ferocity he winced.

'I forgot all about this for forty years, yet now it seems like yesterday. I was so happy there. Was that wrong of me? I barely gave my parents, nor Nan or Aunt Gwynnie, or any of you, a second thought and I was there for such a long time.'

The others exchanged puzzled glances.

'I don't remember you being away anywhere apart from the few months you spent with Aunt Gwynnie when you…erm… had the baby.' Laura cast Harry and Xander an apologetic glance. 'Not that I knew anything about that — I just thought you were busy enjoying yourself designing more stuff for all the big names who snapped up your clothes at the exhibition and…well…too busy being successful to be bothered with me anymore.' Laura looked shamefaced. 'I was so jealous when my mum told me all about it,' she admitted.

'And I thought you'd put your father and your future career before me,' Harry added softly. 'I was incredibly hurt. I was even more dumbfounded when your mother told me you left because you were pregnant. I just couldn't get my head round that one. I hated you for that.'

Fat tears began to trickle down Molly's stricken face.

'But I'm beginning to understand now,' he admitted. 'Of course my mother knew who my father was, and I also understand she must have been sworn to secrecy. It explains why she was so quick to insist that we look after Xander—she didn't tell me my father was a fairy prince until she was dying, and I didn't believe a word of it!'

'A royal prince of the Tuatha de Danaan.' Molly turned to Xander. 'And you've been denied that knowledge your entire life. Ceriddwen was horrified to learn you would lead a normal mortal human life and never fulfil your potential, as she saw it. She wanted to send me back immediately to fetch you, but Morfan had given his word to Mum and Nan that the fairies wouldn't interfere in your life until you were old enough to understand the implications of your birthright. Ceriddwen was livid, and it took Lleu ages to calm her down.' A puzzled frown made its way across Xander's face.

Six

The Goblin King

Dressed in a simple, perfectly fitted, cream-coloured empire-line silk dress magically produced by the motherly fairy, Molly nervously followed her through the labyrinthine corridors and stairs of the great citadel palace which, the fairy informed her, guarded the Southern Gate. She was unprepared for the maelstrom about to unfold as she entered a great hall with high arched ceilings, huge crystal chandeliers hanging down and lighting the hall in a soft, yet very clear light. Upon the walls were vibrantly-coloured shields that Molly assumed to be coats of arms and family crests.

It's like being at a real-life medieval banquet, she thought, somewhat hysterically, half expecting to see King Arthur and Queen Guinevere at the top table!

Her musings quickly evaporated when she realised that the assembled fairy diners were staring at the top table in horrified silence, listening to Ceriddwen shrieking at Morfan, spittle flying from her lips as she heaped abuse and insults upon his bowed head.

'How dare you deal behind my back and make promises to humans without my permission! Forty human years? Are you mad?' She drew back her hand as if to strike him, then threw herself into her chair, declaring, 'I am minded to condemn you to the same fate as your brother for your insolence!'

The assembled crowd drew a collective shocked breath at the mention of Prince Gwion, and the previous silence was broken by concerned whispers up and down the table.

'Silence, ingrates,' Ceriddwen screamed, 'or you too shall suffer the fate of Prince Gwion!'

Before Molly could hurry to the seat her fairy helper had pointed towards, raised voices drowned out the rest of Ceriddwen's tirade, then shocked silence as a loud voice boomed out.

'Why don't I just allow them to join me at my court? I could do with some pretty hostages.'

All eyes, including Molly's, turned in the direction of the voice. A tall man with a mane of thick red hair and the broadest shoulders she had ever seen stood inside the door of the Great Hall. He was escorted by the Queen's guard, and he stood within a circle of crossed pikestaffs, as a flustered-looking man who, Molly later learned, was Meyrick, Ceriddwen's major domo, flew the length of the table towards the royal party. He was followed at a slower pace by a man, who was obviously a military officer, with a long braid like Lleu's hanging down his back.

'Had I known I would receive such an inhospitable welcome, I would have brought Fafnir and sat him on your roof with the promise of easy pickings,' the red-haired man shouted scornfully above the hubbub of guards yelling and the shocked chatter of the diners.

The entire company shrank into their seats, stealing fearful glances at the high beamed ceiling as if waiting for some fearful monster to burst through the roof. Ceriddwen stood white-faced in shock and anger as the guard held their ground.

'That's right,' sneered the stranger, 'consider yourself lucky Fafnir isn't resting on your roof.' He paused and looked lazily down the table. 'A nice fat fairy would suit him very well!'

Meyrick wrung his hands in distress as the officer spoke quietly to the royal party. Lleu got to his feet and addressed the obviously unwelcome visitor.

'You trespass, Lord Nudd. Why are you here?'

Molly wondered at the bravado of this Lord Nudd, whoever he was, as she cast a nervous glance at the ferocious fairy guards watching the intruder intently.

'I never conduct business with minions,' Gywn ap Nudd replied mildly. 'What's the phrase our human friends use? Ah yes, I recall. I never talk to the monkey, only the organ grinder!' He turned to Ceriddwen and swept a mocking bow. 'And that, dear lady, would be you.'

'State your business and leave,' replied Ceriddwen stiffly, trying to regain some semblance of control over the situation.

'Leave? Why, that is most ungracious and inhospitable of you.' He pretended to look affronted. 'Is the king of another state going to be denied hospitality at your table? Where is your famed fairy code of honour now?'

Lleu gestured to hovering attendants and they quickly laid another place beside Ceriddwen, as Molly digested the news that this man seemed to be a king — but king of whom and what? She didn't have to wait long to find out.

Ceriddwen, obviously composing herself with great difficulty, reluctantly announced as imperiously as she could muster, 'Very well. Welcome to our hall, Lord Gwynn ap Nudd, King of the Goblins. We invite you to dine at our table.'

He doesn't look like a goblin, but how would I know what a real goblin looks like? thought a bemused Molly, as the military officer made his way back down the hall to escort Gwynn ap Nudd to the royal dais. With an infuriating smirk at the guard as they reluctantly let him pass, the goblin king swaggered the length of the table, climbed onto the dais, and settled himself beside an outraged Ceriddwen, ignoring her venomous glare.

At Lleu's signal, the musicians in the minstrel's gallery began to play and immediately the soothing sound of music filled the room. Attendants moved seamlessly back and forth, placing tureens of soup along the length of the table, serving platters of food to the top table first and then the rest of the company. Protocol deemed the Queen ate first. Everyone waited nervously for Ceriddwen to begin. Finally, she picked up her spoon and began taking delicate sips of soup, the others following suit. Molly reflected that she had never tasted anything so delicious, although she hadn't the faintest idea what she was eating. The meal consisted of several courses, each better than the last, and Lord Nudd loudly proclaimed his enjoyment, slurping his wine, and smacking his lips before finally emitting a very loud belch. Ceriddwen threw him a poisonous look, but he just laughed.

'You fairy folk and your ridiculous manners!'

Ceriddwen ignored the jibe and continued: 'Our meal is over, Lord Nudd, perhaps now you will explain your business?'

'Have I not explained?' He affected a mocking regretful tone. 'How remiss of me and after such a superlative repast.' He cast a long look around the hall, and said slyly, 'I have it on good authority that Crown Prince Gwion is…ahem…no longer with us.'

The room fell into shocked silence, the atmosphere in the beautifully lit hall becoming oppressive and threatening. The musicians stopped playing and it seemed as though everyone was collectively holding their breath.

'And what business is that of yours?' Ceriddwen's voice took on a low and menacing tone. 'Why come all the way to my kingdom and say such a thing?'

Lord Nudd was unperturbed and, pretending to examine his fingernails, remarked rather mildly, 'I have come to your kingdom to challenge you to mortal combat, dear Queen. Lord Dubh told me your eldest son is dead and he leaves no children. Under the laws of these lands, I am free to challenge you for your throne. I am here to set a date. What say you?'

Ceriddwen was speechless with fury as Lleu leapt to his feet and lunged at Nudd. The goblin king ducked out of his way, leaning back in his chair as Lleu was prevented from reaching him by Morfan and one of the attendants, who grabbed his arms and forced him back into his chair. The hall was in an uproar, people screaming at Nudd and calling for the guard to arrest him.

Nudd was on his feet now, shouting at the top of his voice, 'You fools, you are honestly trying to deny your own protocols? You are denying you have no crown prince?'

Ceriddwen raised her staff and banged it hard on the table. The crowd settled into an outraged murmuring, as Lord Nudd once again took control.

'As I was saying, your crown prince is dead and he has no offspring, so by the laws of these lands, I am entitled to challenge your Queen for the throne.'

'I'll see you dead first!' snarled Lleu.

Before Nudd could reply Morfan leapt to his feet, his handsome face drawn and pale, glossy black hair tousled and unkempt after the scuffle. Looking the goblin king fiercefully in the eyes, he said, 'You are very much mistaken, Lord Nudd. My brother's line is alive and well!'

The goblin king slowly looked him up and down. 'And how can this be, Prince Morfan?' he sneered contemptuously. '*You* are not crown prince material, so surely you cannot be putting yourself forward?'

Before anyone could reply, and before she knew what she was doing, Molly found herself on her feet. 'Prince Gwion's son is the father of my son,' she started in a shaky voice. 'I may be human, but I have fairy blood, and my blood combined with Gwion's royal blood, makes my son the crown prince.' Looking directly at Lleu, she added, 'Is that correct, my Lord?'

~

Back in the garden, Molly closed her eyes, concentrating hard on getting the details correct. The snapdragons in the flower beds beside the garden seat had pulled themselves up to their full height and set their fierce little faces towards Xander, glaring balefully at him as he heaved a great sigh of exasperation at this latest twist in Molly's tale. The roses on the wall behind her crowded protectively around, their sharp thorns primed and aimed at Harry should he, too, decide to display any inappropriate behaviour.

'So,' said Xander acidly, 'you are saying that I am Crown Prince of *Fairyland*.' He made no attempt to hide the contempt in his voice. 'And the Queen of the Fairies is going to burst through the portal, kidnap me to fight the goblin king, and, excuse me, I nearly forgot, close the portal and save the world?'

'Xander,' howled Harry, 'show some respect!'

Laura, who had been lost in a reverie of trekking in the Outback with Jimmy, jumped to her feet, jabbing an accusing finger at Xander. 'Don't you dare speak to my friend…your mother…like that! She's the sweetest, loveliest…'

'Please stop fighting,' pleaded Molly, 'we don't have time for this. Please let me finish and then you'll understand. I know it's hard for you to take in, Xander, but have you any idea how hard this is for me? I've had amnesia for forty years and now I find myself in the middle of a nightmare!'

'Seriously?' exclaimed Xander, totally unrepentant. 'Perhaps we should be taking you to the nearest psychiatric unit for an urgent assessment. You sound totally unhinged! I know there's something strange about this, I'm not stupid — I've already said I can feel it, but I mean in a scientific, quantum physics sort of way, not fairy dust and magic wands!'

'Molly, I'm sorry.' Harry glowered ferociously at Xander. 'He's not normally such a rude, inconsiderate person.'

'It's ok, Harry.' Molly smiled ruefully at Xander. 'You're in shock, that's all. Part of you knows it's all true, and the rational part of you can't handle it.'

'Absolute nonsense!' Xander snorted. 'That's it, I'm off. See you back home, Dad, unless you get dragged off to *Fairyland* by little green men!'

Harry watched Xander's retreating back with an amused look on his face.

'Let him have his little moment — he'll be back, I promise you.'

'How do you know?' Laura asked, absent-mindedly unwinding some bindweed that had coiled itself around her arms in case she too should make any threatening gestures towards Molly.

'I've got the car keys,' replied Harry, with a conspiratorial wink at her.

'I think we could all do with a nice cup of tea,' announced Laura, and Molly and Harry nodded in agreement. As Laura bustled off, Harry turned to Molly.

'You were telling Lord Nudd that you are the mother of the fairy crown prince?' he encouraged gently.

SEVEN

A Royal Princess

The goblin king stared incredulously at Molly. 'You? A human? The mother of the crown prince? By Fafnir's teeth, I have never heard such nonsense!' Turning to Ceriddwen and Lleu, he added, 'You must be very afraid of losing if you think I'm going to believe that!'

Ceriddwen drew herself to her full height, magnificent in a shimmering cream-coloured, velvet sheath dress with a huge amber choker glowing at her throat, giving her strong, beautiful face a radiant bloom. She was back in full control.

'She speaks the truth. Why else would a human be seated at our table? Why else would a human be housed in royal apartments, and why else,' she thundered, 'would a human be subject to our royal protection?' She looked haughtily at Lord Nudd, and Molly noticed for the first time that Ceriddwen was the same height as him and could look him directly in the eye. The goblin king was the first to look away.

'This is unheard of,' he blustered. 'I am entitled by the laws of these lands to challenge you. This is but a ruse to throw me off the scent. I am not fooled!'

'But you are a fool!' exclaimed Ceriddwen, looking down the table to Molly. 'Come, my dear!' she said, indicating that Molly should approach the top table. Molly tentatively made her way towards Ceriddwen and nervously mounting the dais, took her outstretched hand, watched curiously by the rest of the diners.

Still holding Molly's hand, the Queen stamped her staff hard on the floor, calling for silence. The uproar hushed as everyone looked expectantly at the top table.

'Lord Nudd and all who are present, I present to you my granddaughter, Princess Molly.'

Molly stood, frozen like a rabbit caught in headlights, watching as Ceriddwen's glittering, feline eyes scanned the hall, daring anyone to contradict her. The goblin king's defiant demeanor began to crumble as the hall erupted into thunderous cheers and applause. Lleu took Molly's other hand, and she was turned left and right so that the entire company could view their princess. Nudd's face twisted into an ugly snarl as he realised he was defeated.

'You may have won this battle, Queen,' he hissed, 'but you have yet to win the war. You haven't heard the last of this!'

Swiftly turning on his heel, he shouldered his way through the crush of cheering fairy folk as he was ushered out. Ceriddwen smiled grimly as he made his blustering exit, and then sat down, signalling the company to do likewise. Turning a solemn expression to Molly she said gravely, 'This is not what I expected when I received your family's request for my help.' Her face softening somewhat, she added, 'but I am beginning to understand your place in our future.'

'My place?'

But the Queen had already turned away to speak to Lleu. Molly strained to hear what was being said but was distracted by a gentle touch on her arm. She turned to find a fairy woman who looked much the same age as herself. The fairy had cool blue eyes and gleaming ash-blonde hair held back from her face by a silver circlet studded with sparkling blue crystals. Shimmering fin-like wings graced her back and as she smiled at Molly, she displayed small, white, and alarmingly sharp-looking teeth. Molly looked down at the hand on her arm and noticed that the fingers were webbed with fingernails whose greenish tones reminded her of abalone shells.

'Greetings, Princess,' she smiled, bobbing a little curtsey. 'I am Melusine, Keeper of the Fish. I hope you enjoyed your meal. It was prepared especially in honour of your arrival.'

Melusine's voice resembled a silvery stream babbling over sand and pebbles.

'To honour my arrival?' Molly exclaimed in amazement. 'Before Lord Nudd's arrival I was under the impression the Queen was very displeased by my presence, although Lleu and everyone else have been very kind to me.'

Melusine gurgled merrily, looking left and right, before leaning towards Molly. 'Her rages are legendary, and only rarely does she mean what she says, but no one ever takes the chance. That's how she maintains power,' she whispered.

Molly was quite shocked by this remark, although she admired the fairy-woman's lack of concern regarding her indiscretion. Just as she was about to reply, Morfan appeared from the other side of the dais. Melusine bobbed a little curtsey and gave him an innocent, demure look from beneath her eyelashes. Molly watched in fascination as Melusine excused herself and undulated her way through the milling throng like flowing water, exiting the hall now that the excitement seemed to be over.

'Watch out for that one,' murmured Morfan, 'she's a water fairy and her loyalties flow like water whichever way they wish — it's in her nature — she would have switched allegiance to Gwynn ap Nudd in a heartbeat!'

Molly was surprised by this statement, and couldn't help herself asking, 'Why do you employ her, then? I can't imagine the Queen tolerating such a fickle subject.'

Morfan smiled ruefully. 'It's a matter of pragmatics. Water fairies are the fish keepers — without their influence and knowledge of fish and their ways, we would not have fish to eat.' Noting Molly's quizzical look he added, 'Our world is different from yours in many ways — we live in harmony with nature and everything in it as much as possible to preserve the precious symbiotic balance. We do not eat other creatures lightly; we honour their sacrifice and take only what we need. Water fairies speak the language of fish and understand them. You may find this strange, but not as strange as we find your world. Much misery infects your world, and we do all we can to protect ourselves from it.'

'Speaking of pragmatics,' said Molly, 'why does the Queen say I am her granddaughter? Surely, I am no relation to her whatsoever!'

'It is custom,' replied Morfan. 'As the mother of her grandson's child, you automatically become my mother's granddaughter and a royal princess. It also makes you my niece.'

'I'll never get my head around this. It's all a bit much to take in, and the squabble with the goblin king wasn't very harmonious, was it?'

Morfan laughed. 'Touché! But I did say "as much as possible". Not everyone in this world wants to live in peace, which I suppose, is very much like your world.'

'At least you're honest — I don't believe anywhere is a perfect paradise, although I'm finding your world absolutely fascinating.' Molly stifled a yawn. 'Would it be very rude of me to leave now and go back to my room? I'm feeling very tired, and to be honest, a bit overwhelmed.'

'Of course,' Morfan said, nodding sympathetically. 'I'm not surprised. It's been quite a day for you — quite a day for all of us,' he added as an afterthought. He snapped his fingers and the fairy housekeeper who brought Molly to the hall seemed to appear from nowhere, dipped a curtsey, and spirited Molly back to her rooms.

~

Molly's life settled into a calm and peaceful routine as weeks spread into months. Each morning she breakfasted with Ceriddwen, Lleu and Morfan, listening attentively to the planned business of the day. Ceriddwen was anxious that she be fully educated in all aspects of fairy life, their customs and ways, their history, and the histories of the other inhabitants of their world. Most days, after breakfast, she was despatched to the Crystal Tower for lessons with, amongst others, the incumbent Arianrhod, a wise and venerable woman who, to Molly's youthful eyes, appeared to be impossibly old. She also made lots of friends who helped her settle into her new life.

Molly learned the most amazing things. She was taught that Planet Earth suffered two enormous extinction events many thousands of years ago, that a comet and a comet fragment collided with Earth at different times, partially melting the ice caps and causing devastating floods throughout the planet. The fairies, or to give them their correct name, the Tuatha de Danaan, were the dominant civilization, slowly and painstakingly bringing civilization to the other species of hominids scattered throughout Earth. Just before the comet collisions, they accidentally discovered a portal into another dimension as they mined for precious gems and minerals. This discovery enabled them to save the lives of many species before the floods swept everything away. Unfortunately, millions of lives were still lost and the great Earth-based civilisation of the Tuatha de Danann was destroyed.

Eventually, more portals were discovered, and after many years, the fairies built great ships Earth-side and sent volunteers across the oceans to assess the damage and search for surviving pockets of mankind. They found survivors in various parts of the world, mainly homo sapiens, as they had proven to be the more resourceful, but reduced to a savage and primitive existence. This was when strange and remarkable human behaviours began to manifest themselves; behaviours and beliefs still held in Molly's mid-twentieth century world. The fairy people disembarking from their ships to help and educate the scraps of humanity struggling to survive, found themselves becoming the focus of blossoming religious beliefs. The native peoples began to see the fairies as supernatural beings believing they were great spirits with magical powers — from Africa, the Middle East, Egypt, Asia, and the Americas — in fact, everywhere they shared their knowledge of agriculture, reading, writing and other rudiments of civilisation, they were deified as gods and goddesses based on human experience of the fairies' knowledge and expertise. She learned that many humans who had accidentally stumbled into the fairy realm were reviled and often executed as heretics when they returned and tried to describe their experiences.

'I have never been religious,' Molly admitted to the Arianrhod, 'but even I feel a bit nervous about saying God was a member of a lost civilisation.'

'There is no need to be nervous about the truth. There is a grain of truth in every myth. A myth is simply a fact that has been greatly distorted by time and loss of memory. You will learn more truths day by day.'

'Including the fact that there really was a Noah's Ark?'

'There were many "arks", as you call them. Our ships circumnavigated the globe. We had our military ships and a huge merchant fleet. We used every single ship to transport as many people and animals as possible to the portal, but the floods very quickly overwhelmed everything and despite all our efforts, most didn't make it.' The Arianrhod smiled sadly. 'We did our best.'

'What you did was incredible—not only did you save thousands of people and animals, but you also re-built a new life for everyone in a new world. That is just so amazing!'

She felt as though her head might explode with all the information she was expected to absorb, but determined to fit in, she gritted her teeth and persevered.

Ceriddwen kept her word regarding Molly's needlecraft skills, introducing her to the dressmakers, tailors, weavers, knitters, and skilled craft workers who produced the beautifully crafted goods she was becoming accustomed to seeing everywhere she went. Ceriddwen had placed the beautiful dress and coat Molly had designed on display in the Crystal Tower, and Molly was astonished to discover they were her designs and that Ceriddwen wished her to design similar garments, something she never actually got round to doing. Her new life was far more interesting as far as she was concerned. She toured the vast weaving sheds and looms, marvelling at the fact people still spun wool using spinning wheels and spindles, watching in fascination as three fairy women worked a warp-weighted loom, passing the shuttle back and forth between them, producing a glorious, patterned fabric in the process. It was an activity repeated on all the looms and Molly reckoned there must be hundreds of fairies diligently producing great reams of cloth.

'It all looks so laborious and time-consuming,' she commented when the fairy showing her around told her it could take a month to produce enough cloth for a particular garment. 'In my world we stopped using this type of loom hundreds of years ago.' She ploughed on, ignoring the frosty look on her guide's face. 'Have you not considered mechanisation? You know humans have the technology, so why don't you use it, too? You would only need to employ a fraction of the workers you have now.'

Molly's guide gave her a withering look from under her shock of strawberry-blonde hair. Holda was a stern-looking fairy in sole charge of the weaving sheds and all the fairies who were employed there.

'And what, may I ask,' she chided, 'would these good fairy folk do without gainful employment to provide for themselves and their families?'

Back in Molly's early 1970s world, computer technology was still in its infancy, and unwary people were being beguiled by claims that computers would eventually make life easier and free people from the labours of the workplace. Talk of shorter working weeks and lots more leisure time, with no loss of earnings, was a much-promoted, disingenuous concept.

'Well, surely they would have more time to relax and enjoy themselves; have more time with their families?'

'We are not slave-drivers,' Holda said with disdain. 'We have plenty of leisure time. The difference between the Tuatha de Danann and humans, Princess Molly, is that we are not *greedy*.' She placed such emphasis on the word *greedy* that Molly could almost see it spelled out in huge capital letters. Holda warmed to her theme as Molly gaped at her. 'In your world, you use technology and mechanisation not to free people, but to further enslave them. The greedy people who possess the technology want to employ as few people as possible and pay them even less. You humans are obsessed with your money — we do not employ such a concept. People are valued for their skills and are properly recompensed by availing themselves of other people's skills. I believe you would call this bartering — so be it. But no one in this land starves or goes without medical care, clothing, housing, or warmth in winter. We provide for each other — you will discover this as you learn more about us and our ways and, I can assure you, mechanisation is not our way!'

Molly felt quite chastened as Holda ushered her through a doorway into a busy cobbled street teeming with people hurrying about their business. It was lined with workshops and stores, and behind the quaint little wrought iron-fronted windows, Molly could see artisans hard at work, making the beautiful hand-crafted goods Holda pointed out to her.

'We are rather like bees in a hive,' Holda continued, 'we serve our Queen and look after one another. We each have our talents, and we work according to what we can do best.'

'Sounds like communism, or is it socialism?' Molly replied doubtfully. 'I can never remember the difference — Modern Studies was never my best subject, although I don't think either works very well in my world, not that I can actually remember very much about anything.'

Holda laughed. 'Well, I don't mean to sound patronising, Princess, but you are still very young and naïve. As I said earlier, humans are *greedy*, that's why the world of human economics is of no interest to us. You must never, ever confuse the psyche of the Tuatha de Danann with that of humans. We are very different.'

Molly was just about to reply when she almost collided with someone coming out of a workshop doorway.

'Oh, I do beg your pardon...' she began when she realised that standing in front of her was Melusine, the water fairy she had first met the night Lord Nudd had challenged Ceriddwen.

'We meet again, Princess,' said Melusine in her babbling brook voice as she bobbed a quick curtsey under the disapproving eye of Holda.

'Fancy meeting you here,' Molly said, a chuckle in her voice. 'I thought you spent your time catching fish for the table!'

'An oversimplification of my duties, Princess.' Melusine's voice seemed a little sharper, as though the babbling brook had been whipped up by a stiff breeze. 'Amongst other things, I also collect and deliver the royal pearls, if you would care to look.' She pulled open a little velvet pouch and poured several large lustrous pearls into her palm.

Molly was just reaching for one of the gleaming treasures when Holda said crisply, 'That's enough now, mind your manners, water fairy, and be about your business!' and with a final glare at Melusine, she shepherded Molly around her and into a little store crammed with beautifully crafted boots and shoes.

'You didn't have to be so rude,' grumbled Molly when they were safely inside.

Holda was unrepentant. 'You will learn not to trust water fairies — they are fickle, just like their element, their loyalties flow wherever they like. They will gush over you if they want something, and then drain you dry until you have given them every drop. You have been warned!'

'Actually, Morfan warned me to be careful of her, too,' admitted Molly, not daring to say she quite liked Melusine.

'Good advice — be sure to take heed. Come!'

Holda steered Molly through the little shop and up a flight of wooden stairs, which led onto a beautiful little mezzanine where several women were working on intricate pieces of embroidery; some were working on gowns and jackets, and one was stitching beads onto delicate fabric slippers. Molly was entranced when two women approached her, after a nod from Holda, and shyly held up a saffron-coloured dress lavishly embroidered in gold thread and beautifully-placed peridot gemstones. The effect was stunning. 'Would the princess care for a fitting?' one of them asked hesitantly, glancing at Holda for approval. There was no doubt that Holda was mistress of all she surveyed, but even she had to acknowledge Molly's status.

'The princess will choose whichever items she wishes; we are here to serve.' She then turned to Molly and said, 'Your Highness?'

Molly was embarrassed at the idea of just walking in and commandeering their beautiful work. But apparently, she could, and she was also expected to.

'I...I couldn't possibly impose on your good nature...all your hard work...I have nothing to pay you with.'

The fairy women looked mortified and Holda was aghast. She took Molly aside. 'Your Highness,' she whispered, 'you are not expected to give us anything, the fact that you have come here to inspect their work is recompense enough. You are the Queen's granddaughter, and my needlewomen will think you are unhappy with their efforts.' She took a deep breath and continued, 'I do not mean to offend, Princess, but surely you are becoming familiar with at least some of our customs by now?'

Molly chewed her bottom lip in exasperation. She could almost hear the Arianrhod scolding her. 'Molly, never forget who you are and what that means to the Queen's subjects. They look up to you and expect you to lead the way even when you don't know where you are going. Always maintain the appearance of confidence.' It was a mantra Molly would hear repeatedly and would be grateful for very soon.

Forcing a bright smile, she turned back to the women who were hovering nervously.

'Thank you, I would love a fitting.'

The women visibly relaxed and ushered her into a fitting room with four large mirrors positioned to ensure garments could be seen from all angles. Holda asked her if she required help with undressing and trying on the gown, and when she shook her head in response, Holda curtsied and withdrew, telling Molly to ring the bell on the table when she was ready.

EIGHT

A Traitor Amongst Us

'Molly, have you ever ridden a horse?' asked Ceriddwen over breakfast one morning, her hair and jewels gleaming in the bright morning sunshine.

Molly thought for a moment. 'Apart from fat little beach ponies and donkeys, I can't say I've ever ridden properly.' She smiled as she recalled hot summer days on holidays to Bournemouth and the Isle of Wight, blue skies and sandy beaches. 'Why do you ask?'

Ceriddwen finished spreading honey on a slice of toast, laid down her knife and smiled.

'You will no doubt have noticed that we do not charge around in the noisy mechanical contraptions so beloved of your world?' she said.

'I did actually wonder about that,' admitted Molly. 'I mean, you are obviously very advanced in so many other ways.'

'You think the absence of these awful machines makes us somehow less advanced than your world?' A little warning frown slipped across Ceriddwen's face.

'No, no, I didn't mean that at all,' Molly replied hastily, remembering Holda's irritation. 'I like the fact that it's so quiet and peaceful here. I don't remember very much about my own world, but I do know I much prefer riding in a carriage to mechanised transport. Do you wish me to ride a horse for a particular reason?' She fervently hoped not.

'I most certainly do!' Ceriddwen beamed at Molly. 'You won't be studying at the Crystal Tower today. Morfan will take you to the stables and introduce you to Tabitha the Epona.' Molly's heart sank. She didn't want Ceriddwen to know she was quite nervous of horses. Fat little Thelwell ponies were one thing, huge powerful horses quite another. Before she could protest, Ceriddwen continued, this time in a grimmer tone.

'You must learn to ride for we will be journeying far and wide to rally support. We have much work to do before the goblin king thinks I have forgotten his outrageous visit and gathers his troops to begin more mischief making!'

Molly gamely swallowed a mouthful of fruit and smiling as brightly as she could, murmured, 'Lovely,' as she glanced over at Morfan, who grinned and gave her a cheeky wink.

'Good! That's settled, but you will have to wear something more suitable. You can't ride in that dress.' She was wearing a fine wool button-front dress in soft tones of green and ochre that swirled around her calf-length boots.

Ceriddwen banged her staff on the floor and screeched, 'Brighid!' A few seconds later, the little fairy, who was now in charge of looking after Molly's daily needs, bustled into view, dipping a neat curtsey to Ceriddwen. 'Princess Molly is meeting the Epona shortly, see that she is suitably attired.'

'Of course, Your Majesty,' replied Brighid. Turning to Molly she curtsied again and said, 'As soon as you have finished breakfasting, Your *Royal Highness.*'

Half an hour later, Molly and Brighid emerged into the huge kitchen area after what seemed like an endless trek through numerous corridors and passageways. Molly was kitted out in sturdy green breeches, a close-fitting grey jacket, and black riding boots. She felt quite self-conscious as they made their way through the busy, bustling kitchen, amid the clatter of pots and pans and shouts of the head cook ordering the kitchen staff about as they prepared the palace meals.

The kitchen courtyard was just as noisy with goods being unloaded from carts, barking dogs, and horses stamping and snorting. Several of the fairy workers stopped to stare at Molly as Brighid pushed her way through, telling everyone to make way for Princess Molly. She may have lived there for many months by now, but the citadel was so huge that many of its inhabitants had never seen her before.

She was relieved when they emerged into another courtyard, this one large and welcoming compared to the rather dark and claustrophobic atmosphere of the kitchen yard. A large stable block and a long, low building, which Molly assumed were offices, storerooms, and tack rooms, faced a lovely tree fronted building with quaint stairs at each end leading up to a covered veranda overflowing with pots of glorious flowers. Several languorous cats lay around basking in the sun, blinking down at them as they passed by. This appeared to be staff living accommodation.

She followed Brighid, trotting down a narrow lane at the side of the stable block that led to another large stable at the bottom of a small paddock. Molly was enchanted. The paddock was surrounded by shady trees and ducks swam on a small pond fed by the stream running alongside the lane. The air was filled with birdsong and once again, she was enveloped in that same sense of warmth and wellbeing she experienced when she came through the portal.

Brighid opened a gate into the paddock shooing Molly through as she closed it behind them. They made their way across the cropped turf to the stable building, opening and closing another five-bar gate, as Brighid called out to announce their arrival. 'Epona, I've brought Princess Molly!'

A jolly smiling face topped with a tousled mop of unruly auburn hair popped over a loosebox door.

'Good morning, Your Royal Highness. I am so very pleased to meet you!'

Brighid turned to Molly and in a rather formal and somewhat grand voice said, 'Your Royal Highness, allow me to present the Epona, Keeper of the Royal Stables and Steward of all horses and unicorns of this Realm.'

Molly suppressed a grin as the smiling face gave a conspiratorial wink behind Brighid's very straight back. 'But do please call me Tabitha,' the Epona said as she emerged from the box leading, to Molly's utter amazement, a large, solid-looking black unicorn with shaggy fetlocks, a luxuriantly flowing mane and tail, and a most impressive gleaming white horn spiralling from the middle of its forehead. The unicorn whickered softly, regarding Molly with kindly eyes. Molly stared in amazement, taking in its bridle and huge comfortable-looking saddle.

'This is Flambeaux, your humble steed, Your Highness,' said Tabitha, fondling Flambeaux's soft muzzle.

'Please call me Molly and am I expected to ride him now?' Panicking slightly, she stammered, 'I can't ride properly! Dad thought it was too dangerous, so I never did learn.' Then she wondered briefly who "Dad" was. Someone she once knew? Yet another unbidden memory. Never mind, more important things at hand right now.

Tabitha gave her an encouraging smile. 'Nothing to worry about. You are fairy — you will adapt quickly, as ducklings adapt to water; it's in your blood.'

Leading Flambeaux over to a mounting block, Tabitha helped Molly into the high-backed saddle. It felt like she was sitting in a big armchair. Tabitha adjusted the stirrup leathers, and once she was sure Molly was comfortable, left her to go and collect her own mount.

Brighid bustled over to pat Flambeaux on the nose, advising that she was returning to the palace to get on with her daily business, adding that Tabitha would ensure she was safely returned in time for lunch.

'Enjoy your lessons,' she called over her shoulder as she left the yard, closing the paddock gate behind her.

'Thank you!' Molly called to her retreating back as Tabitha emerged from the stables, this time leading a beautiful palomino unicorn and speaking to a young man Molly assumed to be one of the grooms.

'We'll be taking the Larkspur Trail and heading towards The Watermeadows. Make sure Rollo and Paris follow at a discreet distance.'

'Yes, Epona,' the young man replied as he gave her a leg-up into the saddle.

Adjusting her stirrups, she called over to Molly, 'Pick up your reins, Jarol will show you how to hold them.'

Molly obediently allowed the groom to fold her fingers over the reins, pulling them gently to the correct tension, at the same time telling her to push her heels down and maintain a relaxed, yet straight back position.

'Shouldn't I be on a leading rein or something?' she asked nervously.

'No need,' said Tabitha. 'Flambeaux knows exactly what to do.'

Jarol showed Molly how to use the reins, guiding him left or right and backwards, and how to squeeze with her legs to move him forward.

'Epona will teach you better when you are out on the trail, Highness,' he whispered. 'No need to worry!'

'Ready?' asked Tabitha.

'Yes, Epona,' replied Jarol, with a little bow to Molly.

'Then let us be off,' she instructed, laughing as she urged her mount forward. 'Walk on, Merrily. Walk on, Flambeaux,' she cried.

The unicorns walked obediently across the yard, turning down the little lane beside the stable block. Flambeaux had a slow, steady gait and Molly began to relax and enjoy the ride. Tabitha rode in front along the lane, cutting through the stable yard and into another lane behind the flower-filled living quarters. This area led to a broad tree-lined avenue bordering lush fields and meadows. Tabitha reined Merrily in, allowing Flambeaux to come alongside, and she began to teach Molly the rudiments of horsemanship. Molly tried to concentrate but her eyes were everywhere, as usual taking in her surroundings. She never tired of the sheer beauty of the landscape, so green and peaceful — beautiful flowers crowding the meadows and farm animals grazing contentedly in the warm sunshine. She was entranced by the birdsong — the air seemingly alive with music. When Tabitha's voice broke into her reverie, it startled her.

'Just give him a squeeze with your legs, and a little dig with your heels. Tell him firmly to trot on!'

Molly didn't have to say anything as Flambeaux's ears pricked forward at Tabitha's command, and both steeds quickened their pace to a trot. At first, Molly bumped up and down uncomfortably, but she soon settled into the rhythm of Flambeaux's gait. After a while, she noticed Tabitha was no longer instructing her and she realised that she really did feel as though she belonged in a saddle. Her fairy blood was working its magic as promised.

As they made their way along the road, Tabitha explained they were going to the unicorn mare and foal hospital stud situated in a little valley called The Watermeadows.

'Hospital?' queried Molly. 'Are they all sick?'

'Yes, and deeply traumatised.' Tabitha's face took on a dark, grim look as she continued: 'Most of them have been rescued from goblin studs. Unicorns are horses with manipulated genes and DNA. It sounds very clever, but goblins are cruel and crude creatures. When the foals are born, they already have perfectly formed sharp little horns, and the mares often die giving birth or are horribly injured, hence the trauma. I won't go into detail — I'm sure you get the idea.'

'That's barbaric,' agreed Molly, horrified.

She was just about to say something else when Flambeaux started to plunge and toss his head, rolling his eyes in terror.

'What's happening?' she cried as Merrily suddenly reared up, almost unseating Tabitha, who was struggling to remain in the saddle and calm both unicorns at the same time.

'Easy now, there, there,' she said, soothingly.

Molly's heart was hammering as she struggled to settle Flambeaux, who was now trembling and sweating profusely.

'Don't worry, Your Highness,' gasped Tabitha, 'both are too well trained to bolt.' Molly blanched at the thought of being astride a runaway. 'But something has seriously upset them!'

Tabitha was using all her experience to control both animals, reaching over to grasp Flambeaux's reins, telling Molly to cling to the pommel of the saddle, when Rollo and Paris came galloping towards them.

'Epona! Epona! Fire! Fire at the hospital! Goblins are trying to steal the foals! Look, the smoke is blowing this way!'

They turned to see thick, black plumes of smoke blowing towards them. This was obviously the cause of the unicorns' distress.

'Who told you this?' Tabitha demanded.

'Lord Cernunnos' messengers, Epona — he has sent word to the Queen, asking for Lord Lleu to bring troops — they passed us on the Larkspur Fork. They took the river trail to summon the water fairies to deal with the fire and now they're heading for the palace!'

Turning to Molly, Tabitha asked her if she would be able to sit Flambeaux at a gallop. Molly nodded fiercely. 'Yes, let's go!' she confirmed, and Tabitha nodded her approval.

'Quickly then,' she cried. 'We must fly!' She then urged Merrily into a headlong gallop along the road with Flambeaux thundering behind, and Molly was relieved to see Rollo and Paris flanking her on each side, keeping pace with Flambeaux. No doubt they were under strict orders to ensure her safety.

Fortunately, the wind had changed direction, and an easterly breeze was now blowing the smoke across the fields and away from them as they pulled up on the brow of the hill, their mounts lathered and blowing, to survey the pretty Watermeadows stud farm below. A scene of utter chaos met their eyes. Two large barns were blazing fiercely, billowing clouds of smoke high into the air and over the valley. Terrified unicorns were milling around the yards and Molly shuddered to hear the screams of animals still trapped in the barns. They could see lines of people scurrying backwards and forwards, darting into the barns and chivvying terror-stricken unicorns to safety.

Rollo suddenly spoke in a low urgent voice. 'Look, Epona. Goblins with foals heading our way!'

Sure enough, just below them, partially screened by leafy bushes, three men were rushing a herd of yearling foals up the hill straight into their path.

'We can take them by surprise,' whispered Tabitha. 'Rollo, hide behind those trees,' she added, pointing to a stand of silver birches, 'and Paris, take the other side of the road. Princess, you must stay out of sight.'

Molly started to protest but Tabitha was adamant.

'If anything happens to you, the Queen will have my head! She may have it yet for leading you into this danger!' she added grimly.

Molly reluctantly turned Flambeaux's head and urged him off the road and down into the shelter of a little copse of trees, noticing the trees quickly bending themselves into a screen, hiding her from view.

Tabitha moved Merrily beside Rollo and waited until the little herd of yearlings rushed by, then Tabitha, Rollo and Paris launched themselves out of the trees to confront the startled goblins. Molly noticed all three fairies were wielding what looked like long pieces of crystal, aiming them directly at the goblins. All three collapsed, clutching their heads, and one appeared to be unconscious.

The little yearlings milled about whinnying in distress until Tabitha yelled to Molly, 'Bring up Flambeaux, bring him up now!' Molly urged Flambeaux up the bank and onto the road. Although she was holding down a moaning goblin with her foot planted firmly on his back, Tabitha called out, 'Flambeaux! Tatu! Tatu!'

At Tabitha's command, the big gentle unicorn began whickering softly to the foals, nuzzling and calming them until they gathered and stood quietly around him.

'Good boy!' crooned Tabitha as she watched Rollo and Paris swiftly bind and secure the three goblins before leaving them hidden in the trees.

'We will deal with them later, but now we must take the foals back to the hospital and do what we can to help.'

With Tabitha galloping ahead, and Molly tightly hemmed in by Rollo, Paris and the foals, they sped down the hill, across the valley and into the burning hospital where a frantic smoke-blackened groom greeted them.

'Epona! Epona! They took us by surprise!' His eyes darted beyond Rollo, Paris and Molly. 'Is Lord Lleu not with you? We sent for help immediately.'

'He will be here shortly,' soothed Tabitha, her heart sinking as she dismounted. The hospital appeared to be devastated.

'Attend to these foals — we took them from three goblins on the trail above the hill. Make sure Oonagh examines them before they are fed and bedded down.'

'At once, Epona,' replied the groom, bobbing a quick bow before scurrying off. By this time, several fairy people had gathered around Tabitha, all babbling and clamouring for her attention at the same time.

'One at a time, please,' she thundered and Molly wondered if she was related to Ceriddwen; she had the same authoritative voice. 'Where is Lord Cernunnos? Lord Taliesin? I must be fully appraised of the situation before Lord Lleu arrives.'

'They're with the water fairies at the main barn. They sent the river through the courtyard well and the fairies are directing the waterspout.'

'Good, good.' Tabitha nodded. 'How many unicorns have we lost?'

Molly noticed that some of the staff were sobbing uncontrollably.

'Cadenza and Poppy were suffocated by the smoke before we could get them out, Epona,' wailed a little dark-haired, elf-like woman, raising her tear-stained, sooty face to Tabitha. 'We tried our best to reach them…Oh, I can't bear it,' she choked, then turned and ran into one of the stables.

'Our best surrogate mothers,' sighed Tabitha. 'It will be hard to replace them, and Cadenza was a particular favourite of the Queen. She will be most displeased with Lord Nudd, I can tell you. Morello!' she called to an exhausted-looking man, 'walk with me and tell me all.' She then began to walk away but stopped suddenly. 'Forgive me, Your Highness, I have not introduced you to the hospital staff.'

Molly wanted to say there were more important things to worry about and then remembered all that the Arianrhod had taught her about fairy protocol.

'Attention everyone!' Tabitha called to the assembled fairies. 'Before you return to your duties, it is my honour to introduce you to Her Royal Highness, The Princess Molly.'

Molly flushed in embarrassment, smiling nervously as each fairy gave her a polite bow before taking their leave.

'I hate all this Royal Highness stuff when everyone has this horror to deal with!' she hissed at Tabitha.

'It is our way,' replied Tabitha. 'They would think it odd and unseemly if I hadn't introduced you. Please walk with us as I assess the damage.'

Molly fell into step beside them and listened intently as Morello outlined the details of the attack and the ensuing damage. As they made their way to the still smouldering barns, Morello explained they had just finished feeding the animals and mucking out the stables when a raiding party of around twenty goblins charged into the main yard, making their way straight to the barn holding the yearling foals, opened the doors and herded the foals out.

'How did they get through the shields?' Tabitha asked with a frown.

'Lord Cernunnos fears there is a traitor amongst us who turned them off,' Morello replied glumly.

'A traitor?' Molly was astounded at the thought of such treachery.

'It would appear so, Your Highness,' replied Morello. 'There's no other explanation.'

He went on to outline how Lord Cernunnos and Lord Taliesin, along with several of the grooms, had immediately launched a counterattack after sending word to Lleu and the water fairies. They succeeded in chasing them off but not before the goblins had set fire to the other barns and one of the stable blocks, and the three now-captive goblins had made off with the yearlings.

'I wouldn't like to be in their shoes when they face the Queen,' said a grim-faced Tabitha. Molly couldn't decide whether Morello was trembling with shock or at the prospect of Ceriddwen's fury.

The air was still acrid and smoky and great spouts of water were gushing from the well in the centre of the courtyard between the blackened, ruined barns. Molly watched in fascination as fairies with the same webbed fingers as Melusine used their hands to guide the great spumes of water wherever they were most needed. As they approached, Tabitha called to a tall figure helping two grooms lift a fallen beam. After putting the beam down, he rushed to Tabitha with open arms.

'Tabby, my dear!' he cried as he enfolded her in an enormous bear hug. Molly tried not to stare at him, but curiosity got the better of her. He had greenish skin with an almost bark-like appearance, his hair and beard looked like twigs, but they were plaited in the same fashion as Lleu's; he was also wearing breeches that looked as though they were sewn from leathery leaves, as did his knee-length boots.

'We have three of them,' Tabitha stated without preamble. 'We ambushed them on the hill. The foals are safe!' and turning towards Molly, she said, 'Lord Cernunnos, may I present Her Royal Highness, The Princes Molly.'

Cernunnos released Tabitha and bowed deeply. 'It is a great honour to finally meet Your Royal Highness. I only wish it were in happier circumstances.'

'I am pleased to meet you, Lord Cernunnos,' answered Molly, 'and I can see you have much work to do. Please do not let me detain you further.' She could hardly believe how formal she sounded. *I must be getting the hang of this*, she thought.

Cernunnos took Tabitha's elbow and propelled her towards the barns. 'Come, Tabby,' he said, then nodding towards Molly, added, 'Your Royal Highness. Let me show you the extent of the damage.'

They were just about to enter the shell of the main barn when they heard shouting and the clatter of many hooves thundering into the yard. They turned as Lleu's sweat-lathered horse slithered to a halt in front of them, closely followed by Morfan and a large troop of fierce-looking fairy warriors. Lleu leapt from the saddle, tossing his reins to the nearest groom, and clasped Cernunnos' arm in greeting.

'Hail, brother, Lady Epona,' he said, and spying Molly, exclaimed, 'Molly! Thank goodness you're safe, my dear. The Queen is beside herself with worry!'

He gave Molly a warm smile, despite his obvious distress, then turned back to Cernunnos and Tabitha as they proceeded into the barn. Morfan appeared at Molly's side and accompanied her a little way behind the others.

'Oh, Morfan, this is so awful! What will happen now? What will Ceriddwen do?'

Morfan hesitated for a moment, then said carefully, 'I think, Molly, that Lord Nudd has just declared war on my mother. She cannot treat this as just another of his petulant tantrums. She will call a Council of War and go ahead with rallying our allies as planned.'

Molly looked bleakly around the smoking, water-sodden hospital, the smoke-darkened sky and at the faces of the desperately tired and bewildered staff. The joy and peace of mind she had felt earlier that morning seemed far away now, but she noticed with mounting surprise, that she, too, felt deeply hurt and violated. It gradually dawned on her that these were her people, this was her world, her home, she WAS fairy, and she would do everything in her power to stop Lord Nudd and his wicked plans for ruling the Fairy Realm and beyond.

nine

A Council of War

When Lleu and Tabitha had been fully briefed on the extent of the raid and damage to the hospital, Lleu, Lord Taliesin, and Cernunnos retreated into one of the undamaged stable blocks to await delivery of the three goblin prisoners. They arrived, still securely bound, across the backs of three ponies and were unceremoniously thrown onto the ground before being hauled in front of Lleu and the others. Much to Molly's disappointment she was not going to witness the interrogation as the Queen had decreed that she return to the palace immediately. Assisted by Morfan, Molly leapt astride Flambeaux and urged him into a startled canter through the hospital gates, quickly pursued by Morfan, Paris, Rollo, and several of the mounted warriors. Melusine, standing with some of the other water fairies, waved to Molly as she cantered by.

It was a sombre journey back to the palace. Morfan frowned as he tried to think who would betray them by turning off the shields. Molly asked how the shields worked and he reminded

A Dynasty of Dragons

her of how they had harnessed the powerful energy inherent in crystals thousands of years ago, learning to use that technology to their advantage. It was a well-kept secret and only a few people were entrusted with the knowledge.

'You use this energy as a weapon too, don't you?' queried Molly, remembering how Tabitha and the others used their crystal weapons against the goblins.

'Yes,' Morfan replied with a nod. 'We are all trained how to use our crystal wands, but only if there is no other way to defend ourselves or prevent harm. If we are engaged in actual warfare, though, I'm afraid we mostly use swords and battle-axes — too many crystal weapons would be needed in such situations, raising the likelihood of them falling into the wrong hands. They kill very effectively, and the goblins would love to know how to use them, which is why the fact we seem to have a traitor among us is so disturbing.'

'When do you think the Queen will call a Council of War?'

'Very soon, I think,' replied Morfan, pointing into the distance. Then, 'look at the flags, Molly — we have visitors!'

They crested a small hill before descending towards the royal stables, and beyond the stables, fluttering in the breeze, were two new flags flying from the palace battlements: A large crimson flag, sporting a huge black bird in flight, adorned the centre of one, with a slightly smaller yellow flag emblazoned with a leaping hare flying next to it.

'Whose flags are those?' asked Molly.

'The red flag is the Morrigan's — she is Commander in Chief of my mother's armies, and the yellow flag is Andraste's. Both flags fly when they are here on official business.'

'Andraste?'

'The Elfin Queen,' Morfan called over his shoulder, as he turned into the little lane leading to the royal stable yard, cantering over to greet Jarol who was waiting with a worried-looking Brighid at his side. She fluttered over like a frightened bird as Molly trotted towards them.

'Oh, Your Highness, I've been so worried! Are you alright? Have you been injured?' She babbled on, fussing over Molly as she dismounted, handing Flambeaux's reins to Jarol.

'Yes, Brighid, I'm fine,' Molly reassured her. 'I just need a bath and something to eat—I'm famished!'

'Your bath is already drawn, Your Highness; we will go to your chambers directly before it cools, and I will fetch a plate of food while you bathe.'

Before Molly could reply, Brighid tucked her arm through Molly's and steered her firmly through the paddock gate and back towards the kitchen courtyard.

Refreshed after her bath, some food and a short nap, Molly was deciding what to wear when Brighid popped her head round the door after a quick tap.

'Sorry to intrude, Your Highness,' she said apologetically, 'but you have been summoned to the Council of War.'

'But...but...' stammered Molly. 'I don't know anything about war...why do I have to go?' Brighid came into the room, closing the door behind her.

'Forgive me, Your Highness,' she held up her hand to ward off Molly's entreaties for informality, 'but I have been commanded to bring you at once. Please let me help you dress, and we will be on our way.'

Brighid led Molly through the usual maze of corridors and stairs, deep into a part of the palace she had never visited. Huge double doors lined one wall of a wide tapestry-hung corridor opening into a large room with dancing, coloured light streaming through tall stained-glass windows. Some of the doors in the corridor were flung wide, and Molly saw a great walled courtyard alive with people rushing to and fro, horses whinnying and stamping, and raised voices issuing all manner of orders and instructions.

'The war machine trundles into action,' Brighid observed sadly. 'We have been waiting for this to happen since Lord Gwion left us. Hopefully, it will come to nothing.' When they reached the room at the end of the corridor, two guards barred their entrance with crossed pikes but stood aside after a tongue lashing from Brighid.

'I should think so!' She sniffed primly as she swept Molly across the vast room, skirting a huge circular table, heading towards a tall fairy woman with silvery blonde hair.

'Lady Tanith, may I present Her Royal Highness, The Princess Molly. The Queen requires her presence, but she is presently engaged. Please take the princess to her as soon as she is free.' The fairy woman looked slightly fazed at being ordered about by Brighid, giving her a slight nod before turning a long cool gaze on Molly.

The old Molly would have been intimidated by this woman's obvious hostility, but after the horror of today's attack, she wasn't in the least perturbed. She acknowledged the fairy's presence in the formal manner she had been taught.

'I am pleased to make your acquaintance, Lady Tanith. What is your House?' As a member of the royal family, she was entitled to query another fairy's status. This protocol had been firmly instilled by the Arianrhod:

You must always exert your royal position and authority. To do otherwise implies weakness to be exploited. Even if you are quaking in your boots, mask it and always appear confident.

Tanith appeared taken aback by Molly's assertiveness and hesitated before answering. After a few seconds, she admitted to being elevated to the House of Astarte, the Queen's cauldron bearers.

'The Queen has brought her cauldron here?'

At Molly's query, Tanith nodded and pointed to the cauldron standing on a tripod in the centre of the room. Molly hadn't noticed it when she'd first arrived, and now counted eight fairies standing around it. Tanith smiled thinly. 'I am the ninth bearer. Once I have taken you to the Queen, I must resume my position.'

'Why is the cauldron here?' Molly was intrigued.

'Apparently, there is a traitor amongst us.' Tanith flicked a strand of hair away from her face; she had the most beautiful high cheekbones and creamy skin. Molly felt plain and insignificant beside her.

'The cauldron knows all — if the traitor IS one of us, they shall soon be unmasked! The Queen has summoned everyone from the hospital stud for testing. She will systematically work her way through everyone who knows anything about the shields.' She paused, looking across the huge, polished table. 'Ah, the Queen is free, hurry and we shall catch her before someone else gets there first!'

TEN

Portals and Dragons

'What I can't understand,' announced Laura as she handed mugs of tea around, 'is why you didn't seem frightened by this "experience", if that's the correct word. I would have been terrified!'

Molly gazed thoughtfully over the rim of her mug. 'I suppose it was like being in a dream. We do strange things in dreams, visit weird places, and get involved in all sorts of things, yet because you're in the dream world, you don't question it, it's just the way it is—it feels perfectly normal.'

'But didn't you remember anything about our world?' persisted Laura. 'Your mum must have been out of her mind with worry.'

'I wasn't away long enough in our time for Mum to be worried, although none of this was ever mentioned to me. Ceriddwen must have made them promise never to tell me.' Molly put her mug of tea down. 'I was aware I was the mother of the new crown prince, but I never questioned why he wasn't with me. I simply accepted that I was living another life and embraced it totally. I'm beginning to understand that I was, for want of a better expression, under an enchantment, an enchantment, I think, arranged by Mum, Aunt Gwynnie, and Nan to heal me. I was very ill; I do know that.'

Harry nodded sympathetically, took a sip of tea, then asked, 'Why do you think this portal has appeared? You said it's not supposed to be here, you're supposed to meet Ceriddwen beside the portal near your Aunt Gwynnie's? Does this mean there are many portals that fairies, goblins, and all sorts can pop in and out of at will?'

'I'm not sure how many portals there are, to be honest,' answered Molly. 'I know there are portals in other parts of Sidhthean. Their locations are secret, and they are closely guarded by the fairies to avoid goblins and other creatures from "popping in and out", as you put it.'

'So, if all the other portals are in secret locations and well guarded,' Laura queried with renewed interest, 'how do you explain the appearance of *our* portal?'

'I can't.' Molly shook her head. 'The only thing I can think of is that the goblins are constantly searching for new portals, and it looks as though they've almost succeeded if Harry's assertion is correct.'

Molly looked warily at the sinkhole entrance as if she expected Lord Nudd to leap through at any minute. 'The thought terrifies me. Lord Nudd is a cruel and ruthless man!'

'He sounds fascinating,' Laura said tactlessly.

Harry glared at her, and again asked gently, 'But surely, it's no accidental discovery if the portal is on a ley line that runs straight through your garden? What makes you think Lord Nudd is coming after you? I thought you said it was Ceriddwen who was coming?'

'I really don't know, I still can't remember everything — I think it may have something to do with Xander, but I do know there's not supposed to be a portal here, and that's why it really worries me.'

'But that doesn't really make sense.' Harry sounded perplexed. 'Xander and I live in Glastonbury. Surely Stonehenge or even Avebury would be nearer. And people believe West Kennet Long Barrow is a portal, too.'

'Even I knew that,' affirmed a somewhat subdued Laura. 'I'm sorry I was tactless, Molly, I... I'm just so wound up over all this.'

'But don't you see!' exclaimed Molly. 'I am the link to Xander. I know you are his father, Harry, but in Ceriddwen's world, the matrilineal line takes precedence. It must be because I am the direct link to him, not you. And another thing, Lord Nudd is in for a shock if he intends to send dragons through, because I'm very good with dragons, at least I think I am.'

'Dragons?' howled Laura, horrified. 'Nobody said anything about dragons!'

'Be quiet, Laura!' snapped Harry. 'Haven't you been listening at all? If you'd stopped mooning over your Australian friend for five minutes, you might have heard Molly telling us about Fafnir, the goblin king's pet dragon.'

'Oh, he's not a pet,' countered Molly, 'he's just a poor abused creature at the mercy of those awful goblins — they torment him and the other dragons and feed them poisonous minerals to make them breathe fire. They only obey the goblins out of fear. I imagine Fafnir must be in constant agony from the burns.' She began to cry. 'We must do everything we can to stop Lord Nudd and rescue Fafnir and the other dragons just as the fairies rescued the poor unicorns.' Hiccupping tearfully, she began wiping ineffectually at the tears running down her face.

'Now we're talking unicorns?'

An exasperated voice thrust itself into the conversation. Xander had wandered back into the garden.

'It'll be winged Pegasuses next! Really, Dad, this is beyond ridiculous. We should just go home.'

'Excuse me, Molly,' murmured Harry, 'while I talk to Xander.'

Harry got to his feet and firmly steered Xander towards the kitchen.

'I hope they're not going to fight,' Molly said with a sigh. 'Xander has to realise how important he is in this war.'

'War!' exclaimed Laura in a shocked voice. 'First it's dragons and now it's a war?'

'Yes, if Gwynn ap Nudd isn't stopped! He wants to capture all the portals, invade our world and rule Ceriddwen's world, too. The Arianrhod taught me that all human myths and legends of demons, monsters and strange beasts are based on actual human sightings of goblins and creatures that have breached the portals. The reason we haven't been overrun by them is down to the vigilance of the fairies. They protect both worlds from the goblins and their evil ambitions.'

Both women turned towards the kitchen as the sound of raised voices invaded the overheated atmosphere of the garden — Harry's deep soothing voice rolling over Xander's loud and angry comments.

'There has to be a sensible and logical scientific explanation for this portal thing, Dad. It must be something to do with electrical and magnetic energy; it's not magic for goodness' sake! You know I don't really believe in all your shamanic stuff, either — I came along because I thought you were doing a favour for a friend, not to get involved in all this hocus pocus!'

'I didn't bring you up to be so intolerant, Xander!' remonstrated Harry. 'Of course it's not magic, we've already had this conversation. So-called magic is just science we don't yet understand. You're the one who sensed danger, or did I just imagine that *I feel it in my blood and it's got nothing to do with Australia and Jimmy Thomson* conversation?'

A Dynasty of Dragons

'But dragons and unicorns? Fairies? Come on, Dad, even you must realise how ridiculous Molly sounds!'

'You know many animals became extinct after the comet collisions. How many people would believe in sabre tooth tigers and dinosaurs if we hadn't found their fossil remains?'

'Yeah, but what about dragon and unicorn fossils? How many unicorns have we discovered?'

At this last remark, Molly jumped to her feet and ran into the kitchen.

'Xander,' she began, 'the goblins created unicorns by manipulating their DNA — the cruelty involved is unspeakable. But the fairies rescued them and stopped the breeding programme. They are still trying to stop them from torturing the dragons. Dragons are indigenous to Sidhthean, and come from the Anunnaki Lands, but unicorns are genetically altered horses.'

Xander looked unimpressed. 'The Anunnaki Lands?' he drawled sarcastically.

Undeterred, Molly pressed on. 'Yes, that's what their homeland is called, and you and I have Anunnaki blood too, you know. You met Jimmy Thomson — how do you think he managed to get here? Your father saw him disappear in the sinkhole, he came through not once but several times, and Laura went through the portal, too! How do you explain that if I'm talking nonsense? Please, Xander, just bear with me. I'm trying hard to remember, but it's still very confusing for me also. Our presence here, you and me, has something to do with the genetic programming of the dragons.'

'Oh, so now the dragons are genetically programmed? Really? You're right, Molly, you are talking nonsense! Okay, I'm a gifted harpist, or so I'm told — so what? But now I'm a *dragon whisperer?*' He sarcastically over-emphasised the words. 'Where are you getting all this psychobabble stuff?'

Molly opened her mouth to answer, but Harry spoke first.

'My father, your grandfather, was Ceriddwen's oldest son — their crown prince. I grew up knowing nothing of this. Neither I nor your aunts displayed any signs of our fairy heritage, and my mother only told me when she was dying. My father, Prince Gwion, fell in love with her and decided to live with my mother in this dimension. By doing so, he gave up his birth right and was subject to our natural laws. In other words, instead of staying young and vigorous indefinitely, he lived a normal human life span but sadly died before you were born. Whether we like it or not, Xander, you and I are fairy royalty.'

Xander snorted in disgust. 'Next you'll be saying I'm the new crown prince!'

'You are,' replied Molly, 'and whatever happens when the portal opens is down to you and me, so please man up and let's get on with it!'

Xander looked as though he didn't know whether to laugh or cry.

'Why isn't Dad the crown prince?' he managed to splutter. Laura thought he looked more like a petulant teenager than a man of forty.

'Because Molly has fairy blood, and my mother didn't. You have more fairy blood than me,' Harry said firmly. 'So let's have no more of this intransigence, son. As Molly says, let's just get on with it.'

'All this nonsense because the allegedly utopian fairyland has the same nasty problems we have here in the real world. Surprise, surprise.'

Xander's acid tone made it clear he was anything but convinced and only staying to please his father. His antipathy towards Molly was palpable and if her plants and flowers had voices they would have been growling and snapping at him.

'I suspect it's the same in every corner of the inhabited universe,' Harry pointed out with a sigh and Xander simply rolled his eyes. 'Now, Molly, as time runs to different rules in the two worlds, I'm assuming that this war with the goblins is an ongoing thing that has been running for the last forty years of our time?'

Molly looked perplexed for a moment and then replied, 'Yes, yes, of course! It's coming back to me in fits and starts.'

'Oh goodie!' said Xander sarcastically. Harry shot him a warning look.

'It's to do with Fafnir when he comes through the portal, or is it something else? Oh, I know this is very important, I wish I could remember properly. Why don't I know anything about this?'

'I thought that was why we were here,' Xander shot back, 'to harp him to death with our music.'

'Nobody's going to kill him.' cried Molly. 'I wish I could remember all the details. Ceriddwen must be unaware of this portal!' As realisation dawned, her eyes widened in horror. 'Of course, that must be it. If she knew about it, she would have sent the Morrigan, or come herself. The shield around the garden is because of the enchantment, it's still protecting me, but I don't know how long it will last!'

'The Morrigan?' Another sarcastic remark from Xander, to which everyone ignored.

'So, what happens when the enchantment ends?' Laura looked around in shock.

'The goblin king will mount his attack at the precise moment the enchantment ends,' replied Harry. 'That's what will happen.'

'But Molly, how can we HIDE a dragon, never mind heal one?' cried a bemused Laura, still fixated on dragons.

'Well, if you remember, Laura, it was you who worked out that no one outside can see or hear what's going on in the garden. That's why nobody saw any of the Australian animals or heard Jimmy's didgeridoo.'

Laura nodded, nervously chewing her lower lip. 'Yes, of course. But how reliable is this shield? I know it kept in dingoes, but a fire-breathing dragon?'

'I've just told you, if the goblin king has his way, there will be no shield at all, and that is the danger here!' snapped Harry.

'Too much, Dad, just too much!' Xander snorted in derision. 'Keep taking the tablets, Molly, you too, Laura!'

Harry was fast losing any remnants of patience.

'If you can't say anything constructive or remotely helpful, Xander, will you just shut up!'

Xander looked mulish and opened his mouth again, but then thought better of it, and stood in sullen silence, glowering at his father. Harry gazed around the garden. He hated to admit it, but Xander was right. Something was decidedly off about Laura and Jimmy Thomson's full moon theory. He looked at the bright plant auras and the general heightened energy of the garden. As a trained druid, he knew about the energy emanated by all things, animate and inanimate, and how everything was composed of atoms all vibrating at different levels, but the energy in Molly's garden was dancing to a very different tune. Harry stood up, a thoughtful look on his face. He turned to Laura, and with a slight tilt of his head in Molly's direction, suggested that everyone could do with a break, and why didn't Laura and Molly pop down to the pub for an hour as he wanted a quiet chat with Xander. Laura took his meaning immediately and jumped to her feet.

'Great idea, Harry! I could do with a nice gin and tonic. Come on, Molly.' Before she could protest, Laura grabbed her by the arm. 'Let's get our bags,' she said, and propelled her towards the kitchen door with a knowing wink to Harry.

As soon as Laura and Molly were safely on their way to the village pub, Harry invited Xander to sit with him at the kitchen table for another cup of tea and a serious chat. Although Xander was still feeling angry and uncooperative, he reluctantly agreed and threw his tall angular frame into Molly's stylish retro Ercol chair.

Harry got straight to the point. 'I know you're not convinced by Laura and Jimmy's take on this phenomenon, and believe me, Xander, it is a phenomenon, but I am not at all convinced about this full moon theory either, in fact, I think it's plain daft!'

A flicker of interest crossed Xander's face, and he began to relax a little. 'So why are we still here?'

'Because I believe Molly's story, and before you switch off again, hear me out.'

Xander sighed theatrically. 'Okay, I'll listen, but I'm not promising anything.'

'Good.' Harry took a sip of his tea, cupping the mug between his hands, and leaning his elbows on the table, looked directly at his son. 'If you don't believe any of this, why would my mother, your grandmother, make up such a tall tale about my father? A tale that just happens to match Molly's story. And how do you explain Jimmy Thomson?'

Xander thought for a moment. 'Some sort of conjuring trick? I don't know. He's a friend of Laura's here on holiday from Australia and brought his didgeridoo with him?'

'You really think Laura would play a trick like that on her dearest friend?'

Xander was unrepentant. 'How would I know? I've only just met them, and from what I've been led to believe you haven't seen them in forty years either, so how would you know? They might be a pair of deranged sociopaths!'

Harry put down his mug, steepling his fingers towards his son as he leant back in his chair.

'Listen, Xander, please. You know as a trained druid I have been taught to recognise that things are not always as they seem and that there is much about our universe that we don't understand. Einstein believed in multi-dimensions and the String Theory posits at least ten different dimensions. May I continue?'

Xander also sat back in his chair, folding his arms defensively across his chest. 'Okay, Dad, I said I would listen, but only if you're going to be scientific and logical!'

Harry sighed, but continued: 'Our ancestors regarded Samhain, now the hugely commercialised Hallowe'en, as the most sacred time of the year. Do you know why they believed that?'

Xander shrugged. 'You know I know the answer to that — you and your cronies celebrate it every year. Something to do with, what do you call it? "The thinning of the veil", when all the ghouls and goblins are supposed to come through and scare everyone to death? That's not science, Dad, that's superstition!' He paused as Harry's face deepened into an impatient frown. 'Oh, come on, Dad, you know I've never been interested in any of that stuff, just because it's your thing doesn't mean it has to be mine!'

'I understand that, Xander, but your musical talent isn't just a matter of luck, it's *otherworldly*, whether you believe it or not. And, as Molly has been outlining in her story, the fairy folk don't bestow gifts for nothing. You inherited your gift from your grandfather, and it looks as though it's payback time.'

Xander gave a derisory snort. 'Or what? They'll steal my harp? Remove my gift? How will they do that?'

'You said you would hear me out,' Harry reminded him.

Xander gave a curt nod. 'Fire away,' he said.

'As I said, I don't believe this has anything to do with the full moon, and as this is only the end of September, it's far too early for Samhain. I think the appearance of the portal and the Australian connection was an accident. Whoever is trying to breach the portal hasn't perfected the technique and obviously doesn't have the necessary tools and skills.'

'Whoever "they" may be,' drawled Xander in a tone of exaggerated boredom.

'They are the beings who covet the secrets and skills the fairy folk have guarded for thousands of years to one…' Harry tapped his left thumb, '… prevent the evils of this world invading theirs and two…' he tapped his index finger, '…to keep the evil beings from their world from entering ours. This is a battle they've been fighting for millennia. Folk tales and myths are full of monsters and demons, goblins and fairies, and stories of people stumbling into Sidhthean. It would appear these myths and legends have been true all along.'

'Your point being?'

'My point is this: It's becoming increasingly apparent to me that Samhain was regarded as a very important time of year because the barriers between the dimensions, which are protected by the portals, and there are many of them all over the world as Molly has told us, are vulnerable for reasons unknown. Perhaps it's to do with the change in the seasons, atmospheric pressure or just some quirk of the universe that we do not yet understand.' He paused for breath, ignoring Xander's sceptical raised eyebrow. 'Whatever the reason, this goblin king is set to exploit it. Perhaps it's sheer luck or he's managed to find out that Molly's enchantment is coming to an end, and at the perfect time for his invasion plans.'

Xander gave a loud sigh, but Harry noticed the sudden ripple of interest crossing his face.

'Here we go again with fire-breathing dragons. And this is where I come in? I'm supposed to be able to calm this dragon with my music — all on my own?'

'Well, it's pretty much guess work at the moment, isn't it?' Harry gave an eloquent shrug. 'All I'm asking is that you suspend your disbelief and run with this.'

'Believe me, Dad, I'm trying, but lots of things are bothering me. For instance, you've just implied that the whole goblin army is going to come through the portal and invade the village! How are we going to deal with that? This may be a large garden, but it's a small village and I would imagine that a fire-breathing dragon is a huge animal, never mind that and an army. Don't you think people might notice?'

Harry was just about to reply when Xander went on, 'Oh, and what about Ceriddwen and her army? Are they coming through at the same time? Are these two huge armies going to have a stand-off across Molly's lawn or perhaps the village green?' His voice was beginning to rise in exasperation. 'And what about the traitor who apparently knows how to turn off the shields? Have you thought of that?'

'Calm down, son,' soothed Harry. 'Remember what Molly said — she reckons Nudd will send the dragon through first. It's supposed to cause fire-breathing mayhem and terror, clearing the way for Lord Nudd and his army, presupposing that Ceriddwen is unable to stop him beforehand. We don't even know if she knows what he's up to! He's allegedly a very wily and clever commander. Plus, Molly hasn't finished her story, we don't know yet whether they caught the traitor or not.' He paused for breath before continuing: 'I think we have to plan this for October 31st and stay in the garden all day and through the night; into the next day if necessary. And during this time, we will be ready to start playing music and help Molly with whatever is necessary as soon as we sense any activity from the portal.'

He took another gulp of tea then added, 'And I'm still not sure about any of this, in case you think I have all the answers. I'm actually pretty much as confused as you are!'

Xander regarded his father thoughtfully. Although he had been raised mainly by his grandmother, Chrissie, Harry had been a good father throughout his childhood: he did all the regular Dad things like school sports days, parents' evenings, helping with homework and taking Xander on holiday during school breaks. But he was away a lot too, building up his herbal apothecary shop and therapy business in Glastonbury and, being a trained druid, he was regularly called upon to perform solstice and festival rituals as Glastonbury became an increasingly popular New Age spiritual haven from the 1970s onwards, thanks to the annual Glastonbury music festival and the Arthurian connection to the Abbey and Tor. Xander had never been spiritually inclined in any way. His grandmother and aunts encouraged his music and nurtured his talent. His grandfather was seldom mentioned and all he really knew about him was that he had died when Harry and his sisters were quite young. Xander was considered very precocious musically and regarded as a child prodigy on the harp.

Xander wasn't stupid, either. He knew he was being deliberately pig-headed about this portal business, but he was genuinely worried. He had not only found out that this rather odd woman was the love of his father's life AND his mother, but he was also expected to believe that his grandfather was a fairy prince, and because Molly also had fairy blood, that made him the Crown Prince of *Fairyland*, or whatever it was called. Try telling that to the lads down the pub!

He hated to admit it, but he agreed with Harry that the portal breach was more likely to be at Samhain, as his father insisted on calling Hallowe'en. He still couldn't shake off or explain the all-pervading sense of fear and unease he had experienced when they pulled up outside Molly's house. He still found it hard to admit to himself that he really had felt some sort of connection when he entered the garden, something had stirred his blood (*that blood thing again*, he thought irritably). The rational part of his brain agreed that it was all total nonsense, but his primeval gut instincts were telling him something completely different.

His mind was in turmoil and surrounding himself with a protective shield of denial was the only way he could cope with it for now. He knew he couldn't keep it up.

'Dad, if you don't mind, I'm going to take my tea into the garden. I need a few minutes to clear my head. Okay?'

Harry nodded. 'Of course, take all the time you need,' adding enigmatically, 'I think I need to make a phone call.'

ELEVEN

The Reckoning

Morven sighed and finished unpegging a towel from the washing line as the shrill ringing of the telephone invaded the quiet September evening. Gwynnie was deep in conversation with her herb garden beside the beehives and oblivious to everything else. Tossing the towel into the basket, Morven stomped irritably through the kitchen into the front hall. 'Yes?' she barked into the receiver.

A deep voice replied, 'May I speak to Mrs Gordon, please?'

'Whoever you are and whatever you're selling, I'm not interested. Goodbye and don't call this number again!'

As she was about to bang down the receiver, the voice quickly said, 'It's about Molly — please don't hang up.'

Morven was instantly alert. 'Who is this? What about Molly?'

'Is that you, Mrs Gordon? It's Harry Bamford — I need to speak to you about Molly.'

'Harry? Is that really you?' Morven sank into the old-fashioned telephone seat, clutching the phone to her ear. 'Is…is

Molly okay? I don't understand why you should be calling... Why, it must be forty years?'

As soon as she uttered the words, Morven's heart fluttered like a frightened bird. 'Of course, forty years! Something's happening, isn't it? Gwynnie said it would. What is it, Harry?'

Harry took a deep breath, visualising the cottage in his mind's eye. He didn't imagine it had changed very much over the years — the lovely country garden, its orchard, vegetable plot and herb gardens, the ramshackle greenhouse, and the glorious profusion of flowers. The little house nestling in the depths of the Wye Valley always seemed like a pocket of heaven. He loved it almost as much as he had loved his old cottage on the moor. He always regretted selling it, but suddenly having a young baby to feed and look after required money, so the cottage had to go, and Harry moved back in with his mother to help look after Xander.

'Yes, Mrs Gordon, something's happening, and I need you to tell me everything you know about Molly's experiences with Ceriddwen and the fairy folk. And Molly's fine, please don't worry about that,' he added reassuringly.

Morven's heart sank. She had been dreading this moment. Not because she knew what was going to happen, but because she had absolutely no idea. She and Gwynnie had decided not to dwell on it, but that permanent sense of unease had been at the back of their minds for decades. She remembered how terrified she'd been. She had thought Ceriddwen monstrous and was still of the same opinion, shuddering at the memory of that day in the forest.

'Well, as long as you promise me that Molly's okay,' she said in a rush, 'I'll go and fetch Gwynnie. I'm not the best person to talk to; I was terrified and made a bit of a fool of myself. I've never been good with all this fairy blood stuff...' She paused for a moment and Harry heard her take a deep breath as though trying to calm herself. 'As you know, Harry, I did what I had to do for you and the baby, but most importantly, I did it for Molly. Perhaps it wasn't the right thing to do, but there it is, though now's not the time to discuss it. Please hang on while I call Gwynnie.' Harry heard a clunk as Morven put the receiver down, and waited patiently for Gwynnie to arrive.

Morven made her way into the garden, heart thumping. So, it was finally happening, Ceriddwen was calling in her favour. She felt sick with fear for Molly. Gwynnie hurried to the phone and they both listened intently as Harry relayed what was happening.

'There's not really much we can actually tell you,' admitted Gwynnie. 'It sounds as though everything's going according to plan.'

'What plan?' Harry asked, frustrated now.

'Well, we don't know, cariad, only Ceriddwen knows.' Gwynnie sounded surprised at Harry's apparent naivety.

'So, how do you know there is a plan?'

'Because,' Gwynnie replied patiently, 'we were promised that nothing would happen for forty years. Molly's baby would be...'

'His name is Xander,' Harry interrupted in exasperation.

'Really? That's a nice name, cariad, a bit unusual but...'

'You were telling me what was going to happen?' Harry interjected.

'What? Oh yes, Ceriddwen. Well, we were promised that Molly would be allowed to get on with her life and that baby Andrew...'

'Xander!' Harry was gritting his teeth by now.

'Sorry? Ah, righty oh, Xander then, would be allowed to reach full manhood before being advised of his birth right. Have I got that right, Morven? That's what happened, isn't it?'

'I think so. I didn't like that fairy queen at all!'

Harry was almost beside himself with frustration. Gwynnie and Morven were the last people he would have expected to turn into dotty old ladies. He fumed for a moment, and then felt ashamed of himself. He had just delivered a tremendous shock to two elderly women who must have been living in dread of this conversation for years. He took a deep breath and gently asked Gwynnie, 'Didn't the fairies give you any idea at all what would happen after forty years?'

'No, nothing at all. Just that the Queen would decide what she wanted from us when the time came.' Gwynnie sighed. 'We were just so relieved to have Molly healed and back with us again.'

'Although,' put in Morven, 'she was never the same Molly, I don't care what anyone says, she was different!'

'Different? In what way?' queried Harry.

~

Back in 1972, the three women returned for Molly later as directed by Morfan and, sure enough, found her waiting patiently on the same fallen log. She greeted them with a wan smile.

'Did you enjoy your walk? I'm glad I stayed here — it's so peaceful and relaxing just sitting listening to the trees and the birds. I bet you went to that little tearoom!'

Remembering Morfan's admonition to betray nothing of Molly's absence and to act as normally as possible, Gwynnie quickly replied, 'Yes, we did! It was lovely, but you must be starving, let's head home for dinner.'

'Yes, I am a bit hungry,' agreed Molly and jumping off the log, linked arms with her mother and allowed herself to be led back to the car.

After dropping Nan off, they spent a perfectly normal evening in front of the television watching *Coronation Street* and *Are You Being Served?* and Molly sat with them instead of staying in her room. Although a bit subdued, she displayed no signs of depression or anxiety and spoke about whether she should do another year at Hereford or return to university and finish her degree. And the following morning, she went into Hereford with Gwynnie for a chat with the college administrator and signed up for another year. Morven was relieved by this; less chance of Molly accidentally bumping into Harry and running the risk of triggering unhappy memories. Morven didn't trust the fairy assurances that she wouldn't fret, so least said soonest mended, and staying with Gwynnie for another year was the best way forward. And indeed, it was.

Molly sailed through her second year at Hereford and returned home the following year to complete her arts degree, and, as luck would have it, secured a position as Fine Arts Curator at the big museum in town. She continued to stay at home with her parents, and outwardly appeared to live a normal life, but she wasn't the same joyous, free-spirited young woman she had been. She was quieter and much less flamboyant and artistic.

'My work is my art, Mum,' she would tell Morven when asked why she no longer pursued creative outlets.

'But that's other people's art!' Morven objected, but her gentle remonstrations fell on deaf ears. Molly appeared content, and she would have to accept that. Her father, on the other hand, was cock-a-hoop at his daughter's career. He loved hosting dinner parties where he would boast about Molly's career, how important her job was and how many wonderful works of art were owned by the museum thanks to Molly's good eye and recommendations.

Around 1975, Laura appeared back on the scene. She was teaching English at a Secondary Modern in Torquay and had come home after securing the promotion of Deputy Department Head at the local grammar school. Molly and Laura were thrilled to be together again, and swiftly renewed their friendship. Both women were footloose and fancy free. Laura loved to play the field and enjoyed being squired around town by a string of highly unsuitable young men. She loved every minute of it and showed no signs of settling down. Molly's father, however, deeply disapproved.

One warm summer's evening, after a great deal of excitement and hard work on Molly's part, the museum held an exhibition celebrating Female Abstract Impressionists featuring works on loan by Lee Krasner and Joan Mitchell — well known American painters. It was a glittering occasion followed by a lavish cocktail party stuffed with well-heeled local celebrities, politicians, and several well-known British painters, plus the usual crowd of critics from the art world. Molly's parents were guests of honour and her father had invited some of his friends and colleagues from the oil business. The museum's director, hoping for a generous donation from Shell or Texaco, fluttered around like a butterfly on speed.

About halfway through the evening, Molly's father put his arm around her shoulder and pushed his way through the other guests towards a young man chatting with her mother.

'Darling,' he said, in his most charming voice, 'allow me to introduce Fred Colman, an erstwhile colleague of mine, now moving onto bigger and better things!'

'You flatter me, James,' Fred said, bashfully, whilst holding out his hand to Molly. 'Delighted to meet you, Molly! James...I mean, your father, has told me lots about you.'

Molly raised her eyebrows. 'Really?' she exclaimed, throwing her father a dark look.

'Oh, just run-of-the-mill stuff about the gallery, nothing too personal,' her father flashed back. 'I'm proud of you, Molly, I like to brag!'

'Don't I know it!' said Molly ruefully. 'Sorry, Fred.' She grinned apologetically. 'Pleased to meet you, too, I'm sure.'

'You don't have a drink, Molly,' Fred observed. 'Can I fetch you something?'

'Yes, please, that would be lovely. Brandy and Babycham.'

As Fred made his way to the bar, Molly turned to her father.

'Would you be matchmaking, by any chance?'

'Who, me?' he replied with an air of studied innocence. 'I wouldn't dare!'

'Ha!' snorted Molly and rolled her eyes at her mother who smiled and mouthed, *He is!*

'I'll choose my own boyfriends if you don't mind!' she warned her farther tartly.

'Fred's a good sort,' he persisted, 'brain like a computer — I'm sorry to see him go, but we all knew he had prospects. Been made Chief Accountant at the Metropolitan Bank here in town — you could do worse, Molly!'

Molly wasn't so sure, but as is so often the case, found herself being swept along by events. Before the evening was out, she'd agreed to have supper with Fred after the party at a bijou and very expensive little bistro in town.

She decided she liked Fred. He was good company and fun to be with, so she ignored the little inner voice that kept telling her they had very little in common. He was also very good looking, which helped a lot. Medium height with a fit, athletic body from all the sport he played, velvety brown eyes and thick dark hair. Her female colleagues at the museum were beside themselves with envy. Laura loathed him on sight.

'I don't know what you see in him,' she complained. 'You have absolutely nothing in common. He's a first class bore!'

'No, he's not,' defended Molly. 'He's fun to be with and I like him!'

'You're people pleasing again,' said Laura darkly. 'I've warned you about that before.'

'No, you haven't!'

'What about the trip to Seville with your selfish colleagues?' Laura retorted. 'You knew they wanted to go to a *bullfight*, but you didn't want to let them down after they'd paid for the trip.' Then she added, 'They would've latched onto someone else if you'd had the sense not to go!'

'They were depending on me,' Molly protested, but Laura was outraged.

'Depending on you to get them back to the hotel when they were too drunk? Depending on you to get them to the airport on time, to look after their money? You had nightmares for weeks after that trip, as I recall.'

Despite Laura's dire warnings, Molly continued to date Fred, besotted by his charm and *bon viveur* attitude to life. She was so bowled over she failed to notice that he never consulted her or asked her opinion on holidays, day trips, where they should eat and what films they should see. He assumed she was happy to comply with his wishes and she did. For a long time.

Molly, who had very little interest in sport, found herself travelling all over the world for the Six Nations Rugby Championships and Grand Slams, sweating in the midsummer heat at Wimbledon for endless tennis tournaments, The Oval or Lords for cricket, and endless trails around windy Scottish golf courses listening to drunken golfing anecdotes at the nineteenth hole. Worst of all were the sailing regattas. Fred loved sailing and found Molly's constant bouts of seasickness highly amusing as his yacht was buffeted around various islands on stormy seas.

No one could ever say Molly wasn't well travelled. The only problem was she wasn't travelling to places she wanted to visit — she just trailed around after Fred, working on her tan, smiling, and making sure she looked elegant at cocktail parties.

While they were dating, Fred maintained a polite interest in Molly's career at the museum but was too wrapped up in his own meteoric advancement at the bank to really care. Things began to change, however, when he proposed. He went the whole hog — booking the most expensive restaurant in town, hiring two virtuoso violinists to serenade them, and going down on one knee in front of everyone. He presented Molly with a beautiful two carat diamond platinum engagement ring. Overwhelmed as usual, Molly's people-pleasing instincts went into overdrive, and she immediately said, 'Yes.'

Her father was delighted, her mother a bit more circumspect and Laura, of course, absolutely horrified.

'You aren't serious!' she wailed. 'He's already stolen your life; he'll steal your soul if you marry him, Please reconsider, Molly!'

But Molly was not for turning. She was swept along in the wedding preparations, booking the venue, choosing a dress, sorting out bridesmaids and the number of guests.

Fred was in his element, engaging in endless meetings with Molly's father about their speeches amid lots of whisky drinking, jokes and backslapping. Fred, of course, decided where they were going on honeymoon. He chose India because they could take in some good cricket, and he could also check out the bank's latest branch in Bombay.

He took Molly to see a pretty, double-fronted Edwardian house in Heathervale Avenue. To her delight the house had a beautiful garden, but she was dismayed to hear Fred say the garden was a mess waiting to be sorted. He'd already bought the house and told Molly any renovation work and decorating would be finished in time for the wedding.

One evening, over dinner at Fred's favourite restaurant, he casually asked Molly when she planned to give up work.

Astonished, she replied, 'What do you mean? We haven't even discussed having a family yet so why would I be thinking of giving up my career?'

Fred put down his knife and fork and looked steadily at Molly. 'I didn't say anything about children and you're quite right, we haven't discussed having a family.' He wiped his mouth with his napkin. 'I asked you when you planned to leave your work because that's what women do when they get married, isn't it?' Molly stared at him.

'Yes, that was the done thing a few years ago, but this is the 1970s, Fred, women aren't expected to leave their jobs anymore just because they're married!'

'Do you plan to honour your marriage vows, Molly?' he asked quietly.

'Of course I do! What kind of question is that?' she demanded.

'Well, as my wife, you will be promising to love, honour and obey me, won't you?' He wasn't looking at her as he spoke, and was instead concentrating on cutting his steak into precise bite-sized pieces. Molly was astounded.

'What exactly are you saying? You won't marry me if I don't "obey" your every whim?' You do know that word is no longer used in wedding vows, don't you?'

'Well, I do expect you to enter into the spirit of things and not go against my wishes just for the hell it!' His words were quite measured, but his tone was steely. Molly glared at him.

'And one of these wishes I apparently don't know anything about is that I give up my career?'

'I earn plenty of money — there's no need for you to work outside the home at all — in fact, it wouldn't reflect very well on me professionally to have a working wife.'

'And you are obviously unconcerned about how ditching my career would affect me professionally!'

'I didn't have you down as one of those Germaine Greer bra-burning feminist types, Molly,' he chided.

'Maybe not, but I am one of those Shirley Conran *Life's-too-short-to-stuff-a-mushroom* types!'

'Stuff a mushroom?' he asked, a puzzled expression on his face.

'Yes, life's too short! What I really mean, Fred, is don't you think we should have had this conversation before we got engaged? I had no idea you wanted me to give up my career.'

'I just assumed you would — it never occurred to me...'

'You seem to assume quite a lot, Fred,' Molly cut in before he could finish. 'In fact, it has just occurred to me that you never ask my opinion on anything, you just assume.'

Fred gazed at her in astonishment. They had never quarrelled before, and Molly had certainly never displayed anything remotely resembling assertiveness. He tried what he thought was a more persuasive tack.

'Look at it this way, Molly, you don't need to work, we don't need your earnings, and...' he couldn't keep the triumphant tone out of his voice, 'if you remain at work, you'll be doing someone who does need the money out of a job. Surely you can see that?'

'You really are a patronising pigheaded so and so, Fred Colman!' she shouted, standing up and throwing her napkin onto the table. Several people turned to look and the maitre'd bustled over, wringing his hands in concern. Fred thrust him a handful of notes and waved him away before rushing after Molly, who was halfway to the cloakroom in search of her coat.

'Molly, wait!' he called desperately, weaving in and out of tables and waiters as he tried to catch up with her. He could have sworn that two large potted palms on each side of the lobby doorway physically bent over to block his way. He managed to push past them in time to see Molly hail a cab and speed off into the night.

'I've just had a terrible row with Fred!' Molly burst out, pushing past Laura into the room beyond as soon as she opened the door.

'Well, hello to you and yes, I'm fine, thanks for asking,' replied a bemused Laura, following Molly into her sleek, Habitat furnished sitting room. Molly didn't like to say, but she found the white wooden sofa and matching armchairs very uncomfortable, and the op art wallpaper hurt her eyes. Laura's Sony Trinitron colour television blared from atop a white cuboid unit in the corner. Laura believed in keeping up with the trends, although she would be livid if she knew that Fred thought her taste was vulgar, as he put it.

You can't beat G-Plan or Ercol, was one of his favourite mantras.

'I'm watching *The Onedin Line*,' Laura announced accusingly. 'You *would* have to fall out with him tonight!' Then added, 'I hope you've dumped him?'

Molly was unoffended. 'Don't be silly, Laura, of course I haven't dumped him. He just sprang something on me tonight, and I'm very angry with him!'

Laura stomped over to the television and switched it off with a dramatic flourish. 'This had better be good. I'm missing my favourite programme for you!'

'I thought *Rich Man, Poor Man* was your favourite programme,' Molly retorted — Laura was always contradicting herself.

'Never mind that, tell me what's happened!'

Molly relayed the evening's conversation to a stony-faced Laura.

'Don't tell me you had no idea he wants you to be the little stay-at-home wife and homemaker?' she asked 'He's Head of International Funding — he'll also be expecting you to travel the globe with him. For goodness' sake, Molly, you've been all over with him already. Surely you must have considered the possibility?'

Molly shook her head emphatically. 'No, I absolutely did not. I just assumed I'd carry on with my career and Fred would get on with his. We've managed fine as we are up 'til now, I don't see why it has to change!' A little furrow creased her brow as she frowned in exasperation. 'I assumed…'

'Sounds to me like you've assumed quite a lot,' Laura cut in scathingly.

'You know, that's exactly what I said to Fred.' Molly stared thoughtfully at her hands, the diamond ring twinkling merrily on her finger.

'Molly, all this assuming is why you didn't discuss these matters before you decided to get married and I'm not prepared to go over old ground. You know I think you're making a mistake, and whatever you decide to do is your decision. I don't really see how I can help you.'

Laura tried to keep the irritation out of her voice. She was desperate to mention Harry, but for some reason the subject was totally off limits, and she knew if she pursued it, she would jeopardise their friendship. It was a mystery she couldn't get to the bottom of. It was easier to blame Molly's over-bearing father, and now her over-bearing fiancé.

'So,' she paused to take a breath, 'what are you going to do? Dump Fred or dump your career? And what about children? Have you discussed having babies?'

A certain froideur descended on the room as soon as Laura mentioned the word "babies".

'We haven't discussed children.' Molly's tone was cool. 'I don't particularly want any, and from tonight's conversation, I get the impression that Fred's not too keen, either. Not that it's really any of your business.'

It was Laura's turn to be astonished. Apart from Fred perhaps wanting Molly to accompany him on business trips, Laura had felt sure the main reason her friend would be giving up her career was to produce babies. Fred was the sort of man who would employ an au pair or a nanny to look after the children when he and Molly were away. And now Molly was sitting here telling her that she didn't want children and she was going to marry a man who would like her to be a housewife for the rest of her life. Whatever happened to Women's Lib and burning your bra? Molly had changed a lot and Laura couldn't put her finger on the cause of it all. The university years had changed her, and a part of the old fun-loving, free-spirited young woman seemed to have been lost along the way.

'So did you just come here to annoy me and lick your wounds?' she grumbled. 'You're going to let him sweat a bit and then forgive him tomorrow and carry on being his doormat?'

Molly lifted her chin. 'I'm nobody's doormat and I'm certainly not giving up my job!' she declared, a defiant look on her face. 'I know you think Fred and I aren't suited, and the funny thing is, Laura, deep down I know that, too. But something's telling me this is my path. I can't explain it. I just know that I do love him despite his funny ways.' Laura suppressed a shudder.

'His funny ways? He's a control freak and a dinosaur. You're meant for far better things than making Fred Colman's dinner every night!'

'I am meant for better things,' Molly agreed enigmatically, 'I know this deep down, too. I can't define it, I don't understand it, but that's just how it is.'

Laura shook her head. 'I'm sorry, Molly, I think you're talking nonsense. You're an intelligent woman and my best friend. I can't believe you're going to throw your life away like this.'

'It's my life,' Molly said mildly. 'I'll throw it away however I like, and as my friend, I expect you to respect my decision.'

TWELVE

The Cauldron Speaks

As soon as Tanith announced Molly's presence, Ceriddwen dismissed her with a curt nod and took Molly's arm. 'Come, child, there are people you must meet,' she murmured, proceeding to usher Molly past the huge table and through a narrow door beneath another magnificent tapestry. This door opened into a large room comfortably furnished with cushioned chairs, low tables, and the rich, jewel-coloured rugs Molly had become familiar with throughout the palace. The room was crowded with people who all bowed as Ceriddwen and Molly entered. Ceriddwen waved her arm, indicating for them to rise before introducing Molly. She then invited each in turn to step forward and introduce themselves. One by one they approached, bowing, and speaking their names. The Morrigan was first to approach; tall like Ceriddwen, with an intricately plaited auburn braid and dressed in a black leather jerkin, trousers and boots, with two crystal wands strapped in holsters across her back and a sword in a tooled scabbard around her waist. She had a narrow severe-looking face with the usual feline fairy eyes.

The introductions seemed to go on forever. The Morrigan was followed by all manner of military personnel and palace officials. Molly's head was beginning to spin until finally she was introduced to the last in line, Andraste, the Elfin Queen. She was as tall as Molly with sparkling blue eyes and strands of fair hair escaping from a tight-fitting leather headband. She wore a body-hugging green jumpsuit and bristled with glittering pointed wands and a strange shimmering coil of rope hanging from a belt slung around her hips.

Once Andraste had introduced herself, Ceriddwen invited everyone to sit, as attendants bustled around placing glasses and carafes of water on tables. She then called for attention, explaining she had called the Council of War because Nudd's behaviour was becoming untenable. Several people began speaking at once until she silenced them by banging her staff on the floor.

'Silence!' she thundered. 'I understand you are shocked and infuriated by Lord Nudd's latest impudence — none more so than I, but protocol must be observed! You will be allowed to speak in turn, if necessary.' She glowered around the room, eyes finally lighting on the Morrigan. 'Lady Morrigan, you wish to speak?'

The Morrigan rose to her feet. 'Thank you, my Queen. As you are aware, I have recently been engaged in several skirmishes with the goblins. Since the loss of Prince Gwion, they have become emboldened to leave the lands beyond the Northern Gate, making incursions further afield, causing much damage to property and making off with livestock. We are especially perturbed by the raid on the hospital stud. The situation is becoming grave indeed.' She paused, looking around the room, then continued: 'Of particular concern is the knowledge that we have a traitor in our midst, a traitor who knows how to void our shields. May I ask, Your Majesty, what steps are being taken to discover who this traitor might be?' Ceriddwen held up her hand to silence the murmurs of agreement, and raised an eyebrow.

'You did not notice my cauldron in the middle of the council chamber? The Ladies of Astarte are tending it as we speak, awaiting the return of Lord Lleu with the goblin prisoners so ably captured by the Epona and Princess Molly.' Molly squirmed, hugely embarrassed by the fact that she had done nothing, she was present, that was all, but royal protocol prevented her from acknowledging that publicly. The Queen would have been fully briefed by Morfan, and Molly didn't have the nerve to contradict her. 'If the goblins know who the traitor is, the cauldron will have it from them!'

An official then entered the room, bowed to Ceriddwen, and whispered something in her ear. She nodded then stood up, announcing that Lleu had arrived with the captured goblins. Everyone trooped back into the hall amid much concerned chattering. Lleu, Cernunnos and Tabitha were standing by the great table waiting for Ceriddwen to be seated on her carved ebony throne. Lleu and Morfan sat on either side of her with Cernunnos next to Lleu. Molly was seated next to Morfan and, as Lady Morrigan and Andraste took their seats, Molly was surprised to see the Arianrhod sitting with Tabitha. The three hapless goblins were standing by the cauldron, bound together by a shimmering rope like the one carried by the Elfin Queen. The room was full of army officers, dignitaries, guards, and officials all talking at the same time. Ceriddwen's staff banged imperiously, silencing the noise immediately.

'How went the questioning?' she demanded.

'They appear to know nothing of our traitor,' Lleu replied grimly. 'We have questioned them at length to no avail.'

'Ha!' spat the Morrigan. 'Give them to me, and I will make them eat the fire mineral they feed the dragons. That should focus their minds!'

'It may well focus their minds,' Morfan observed drily, 'but how will they talk with their vocal cords burned out?' The Morrigan glowered at him but said nothing.

'Perhaps we should begin by hanging them one by one from the battlements,' piped up Andraste in her high fluting voice. 'The sight of their comrade choking to death should loosen the other tongues!'

Molly shuddered inwardly. She hadn't considered violence or torture, although it was obvious the goblins themselves had no such scruples and were capable of great cruelty.

'Enough!' snapped Ceriddwen. 'I will not countenance such talk! We are superior to these creatures and do not stoop to their tactics, no matter how tempting, and believe me, when I think how my beloved unicorns died, I have malign thoughts of my own. But we must rise above such barbarity. Protecting ourselves in the heat of battle is one thing, but we must treat prisoners as we would hope to be treated ourselves.'

Andraste and the Morrigan looked askance at each other but remained silent, while Molly marvelled at Ceriddwen's ability to ignore her own fearsome and unbridled temper tantrums. She had no doubt that Ceriddwen would boil the goblins alive in her cauldron or hang them from the battlements if she really felt like it. Molly fervently hoped not.

Ceriddwen rose to her feet, magnificent in her high-necked purple gown with a jewel encrusted girdle encompassing her waist. Her hair was bound with a silver and amethyst diadem and her trademark slash of white curls tumbled around her face. Her throat was encased in a huge diamond and ruby collar and her fingers were adorned with glittering rings. She looked every inch the powerful autocratic ruler she was. The goblins had the decency to look terrified.

'Ladies of Astarte, prepare the cauldron! Lord Taliesin, bring the prisoners to the table.'

As Tanith and her colleagues busied themselves around the cauldron, Molly watched as Lord Taliesin unbound the goblins from the shimmering rope and urged them towards the table and into three chairs facing Ceriddwen. She had forgotten all about meeting Lord Taliesin at the hospital and hadn't really paid him much attention. She was now shocked to feel her pulse quickening and her heart beginning to thump in her chest — he was the most attractive man she had ever seen in her life! He noticed Molly staring and gave her a nod and a little bow. Embarrassed, Molly nodded back, and, hoping no one else had noticed her blushing furiously, forced her attention back to the goblins who were now seated and watching Ceriddwen with wary, ashen faces. Ceriddwen regarded them with undisguised contempt.

'So, you dared invade my territory, burn my property, kill my unicorns and steal my yearlings?' she spat at them.

'We were acting under orders,' responded one of the prisoners defiantly. 'Would your subjects have disobeyed an order from you, Fairy Queen?'

'How dare you question me!' blazed Ceriddwen. 'You forget yourself, goblin!'

The goblin prisoner, though visibly terrified, held Ceriddwen's glare. 'I repeat, Queen, we were acting under orders.' An angry buzz erupted as outraged fairies reacted to the goblin's bravado. Ceriddwen thumped her staff on the table to silence the commotion.

'Enough! Ladies of Astarte, is the cauldron ready?' Lady Tanith stepped forward and curtsied. 'It is ready, Your Majesty.'

'Fill the cups and bring them to the prisoners.'

Ceriddwen sat and waited as three women filled cups with a bubbling red liquid and placed them in front of each goblin. The goblins stared sullenly at the steaming liquid. Lord Taliesin stood behind their chairs and ordered them to drink from the vessels, and the hall was silent in hushed expectation as everyone waited for their response.

'We refuse to drink your poisonous filth!' snarled one of them. Lord Taliesin strode forward and thrust the point of his crystal wand into the goblin's back. 'Drink!' he growled.

The goblin yelped and jerking his arms up in pain, knocked his cup over, spilling the contents. The liquid sizzled and streamed into the centre of the table where it pooled for a few seconds, then began forming into little rivulets casting around the table's surface as though searching for something or someone. Molly held her breath in appalled fascination as she realised the liquid was now streaming towards her. It stopped in front of her and began to form itself into two very distinct shapes: a dragon and a flower. She stared at the shapes, and then looked up at the Arianrhod's gasp of shock, amid a rush of murmurings from the others around the table. The goblin responsible for the spillage gazed in disbelief at her before uttering hoarsely.

'Anunnaki, it's not possible! We killed you all! My father said you were all dead! This is a trick! A lie!' The other two goblins began to babble incoherently, and Molly clearly heard one of them saying *dragon queen*.

Uproar broke out as guards rushed to restrain the goblins, especially the one who had identified himself as Lord Nudd's son. Lord Taliesin indicated to Lady Tanith that she should remove the remaining cups as it was obvious this line of questioning was over for now.

Ceriddwen sat, whitefaced with shock, as Lleu whispered urgently to her and then turned to the Arianrhod. Molly felt a great sense of foreboding as she realised all eyes were on her, including the goblin prince, who glared at her balefully, silenced only by the threat of another blast from Lord Taliesin's wand.

'I...I don't understand,' she whispered to Morfan. 'What did he mean? What is he talking about?'

Morfan held her hand in a comforting grip. 'My father is about to speak; let us hear what he has to say.'

Lleu thumped the table and called for order before he turned and bowed to Ceriddwen.

'Your Majesty, may I speak on your behalf?' Ceriddwen gave a slight nod and Lleu turned to face everyone. 'Lord Taliesin, remove the prisoners. What I have to say is not for their ears. We shall return to our interrogation presently.'

Lord Taliesin bowed and signalled to the guards, who then unceremoniously hauled the goblins out of the room. As soon as the great double doors were closed, Lleu continued.

'My Lords and Ladies of the Tuatha de Danann, and other honoured guests, you have heard with your own ears the admission of genocide from the lips of the accursed goblins who sat in our midst.'

Voices were raised again in furious outrage including calls of *execute them*, and Lleu held up his hand for quiet.

'You will be aware that Princess Molly joined us after her human family requested our Queen help them with a great sadness. After agreeing in the usual way, our Queen crossed into the human dimension with the cauldron, intending to heal the human child and nothing else apart from receiving the usual tribute or gifts. However, the cauldron revealed that the princess not only has our blood, but that her child is the grandson of our beloved Prince Gwion.' He paused as various murmurings rumbled around the hall, then continued: 'When I met the princess, I was very aware of the essence of Prince Gwion, but I also detected another scent which, at that time, I could not identify, and now the cauldron has revealed the mystery. The princess and her son are the only remaining link to the Anunnaki which, I understand, comes directly from her mother's line.'

The hall buzzed with gasps and exclamations of amazement. Again, Lleu called for order and turned to Molly, who stared at him in bewilderment.

'This must be very confusing for you, Princess Molly,' he stated formally, fairy protocol still in place amid all the turmoil. 'Will you allow me to explain?'

'Yes, please do, my Lord,' Molly replied as calmly and formally as she could. Lleu gave a little bow and continued.

'Many years ago, the goblins committed a great crime against the Anunnaki people. To gain control of the dragons they abuse so cruelly to help wage their wars, they systematically hunted down and killed every member of the Anunnaki House of Dragon. The Anunnaki Lands are many miles from here and by the time word was received, the deed was done. The goblin king has consistently denied responsibility, shamelessly blaming the gnome people. Now we have the truth, and we also have the goblin king's son. It would appear at some time in the past that one or more of your ancestors had children with dragon fairies. You also have the blood of the House of Blodeuwdd, the flowered ones, which means you have power over plants and trees. The Epona told me how the trees bent to hide you when you rescued the yearlings and captured the three miscreants. The House of Blodeuwdd also hails from the Anunnaki Lands, and sad to say, they were also murdered in the goblin king's determination to gain control of the dragons.'

Molly glanced guiltily around the room, again reminded that it was Tabitha, Rollo and Paris who had captured the goblins, but resigned herself to the omnipotent power of fairy protocol.

'This is a momentous revelation for us, Princess, and it alters the balance of power in these kingdoms as our loose-lipped goblin prince knows full well. I don't imagine he will be in any hurry to inform his father of his slip of the tongue!'

A ripple of nervous laughter ran through the company. Lleu smiled at Molly.

'Is there anything you would like to ask, Princess Molly?'

'Yes, there is,' she replied, sounding braver than she felt. 'If I really do have Dragon...Anunnaki blood, how does this alter the balance of power?'

The hall fell silent as Ceriddwen rose to her feet. 'I shall explain this to the princess.'

Lleu bowed and sat down. Ceriddwen's eyes glittered as she began to speak in icy measured tones.

'The cauldron is never wrong, and the cauldron never lies, despite the impudent assertions of Lord Nudd's son, and he shall pay dearly for his insults. There are no *ifs* about it, granddaughter — you are Anunnaki, a dragon fairy, which means only you and your children have power over all species of dragon. That is why the balance of power has changed and will be changed forever once we relieve Lord Nudd of his captured dragons.'

Molly's mouth had fallen open in shock, and she quickly closed it as the Arianrhod held up her crystal staff to catch Ceriddwen's eye.

Ceriddwen nodded to her. 'You may speak, Mother Arianrhod.'

'Thank you,' she replied graciously, rising to her feet. 'My Queen, Lords and Ladies of the Tuatha de Danaan, and honoured guests, this is indeed a momentous and joyous discovery. Our beloved dragon family has been restored to us, but I am afraid I must be a cautious voice in all our rejoicing.' She paused for breath as concerned murmuring rippled around the room, trailing off as she continued.

'Unbeknown to many of you, this Council of War was initially arranged many months ago following Lord Nudd's uninvited foray into our palace when, taking advantage of the sad loss of Prince Gwion, he challenged the Queen to mortal combat. He was not convinced then, and he will not be convinced now. His incursion into the hospital is a timely reminder that we acted correctly, and we must deal with him swiftly. However, we must tread carefully. All the omens seem to be with us, and that is to be celebrated, but again I urge caution. We have a traitor amongst us. We must find this person or persons quickly, for even as we speak, they could be relaying all that has transpired today to the goblin king.'

You could hear a pin drop now, and this was Molly's first experience of how important the Arianrhod was. All attention was focused on this tall, dignified woman standing in her simple woollen robe with her pure white hair encased in a filigree net of crystals and silver stars, her face a web of fine lines as she spoke quietly, yet with great authority.

'Lord Nudd will not give up his dragons as easily as he gave up the unicorns. He will have them well hidden from prying eyes. This will be a long and arduous battle, and I fear many lives will be lost. Guard his son well. He may prove to be an important bargaining tool, but do not be surprised if our goblin king favours dragons over his son. I understand he has many sons, so the prince may yet prove to be expendable as far as his father is concerned. Finally, if I may be so bold, Your Majesty, I suggest that you continue questioning the goblins and then all those connected to the hospital as soon as possible. We must maintain the integrity of our shields at all costs.'

Another moment's pause ensued, before finally saying with heavy emphasis, 'And unfortunately, if this information is relayed to Lord Nudd by our traitor, it could place Princess Molly in great danger. He will do everything in his power to rid himself of the princess and her son to maintain control of the dragons!'

The Arianrhod sank into her chair, looking strained and worried.

'Thank you, Mother Arianrhod. We benefit greatly from your wisdom, and we shall do everything in our power to keep the princess safe.' Ceriddwen smiled at her before turning her attention back to the other members of the council. 'It has been a long day, and everyone is tired and overwrought. The council is adjourned. We shall reconvene at 10 o'clock tomorrow morning. But,' she cautioned, 'when you leave this hall, there will be no discussions with each other, or anyone else for that matter, concerning all that has passed here today. Not one word. Do I make myself clear?'

Everyone murmured assent, bowing respectfully, as Ceriddwen turned and made her way into the anteroom behind the table. The excitement in the chamber was palpable, and as soon as Ceriddwen left, the room exploded into a cacophony of excited voices as the company began to form into chattering groups that quickly fell silent as they made their way into the corridor and beyond in search of rest and refreshments. No one wished to incur the Queen's wrath.

'Are you hungry?' asked Morfan. 'Would you like to eat before retiring?'

Molly realised her stomach was growling. 'Won't the kitchen staff be finished by now?' she asked doubtfully. Morfan gave her a wide grin. 'Who says we need to be served by kitchen staff? Follow me!'

Molly followed him along the corridor and through double doors that opened into the military yard outside. He led her up a flight of narrow steps onto the wall walk where they paused, looking down on the assembled tents and pavilions belonging to the Morrigan and Andraste. Men were gathered around cooking fires and moving up and down lines of horses and unicorns, filling hay nets and feed bags. Colourful flags and pennants fluttered in the cool evening breeze, carrying the sounds of voices and horses snorting and whinnying up to Morfan and Molly high above.

'So many people,' said Molly fearfully. 'Has Ceriddwen summoned all these warriors to fight Lord Nudd now?'

Morfan shook his head. 'No, lots of them would be here at this time anyway. Lady Morrigan and Lady Andraste bring their troops every year for the Samhain celebrations.'

'Samhain?' Molly asked curiously.

'Summer's end,' Morfan explained. 'I think you would call it Hallowe'en.'

'You celebrate Hallowe'en? You wear fancy dress to disguise yourself from ghosts and ghouls? Really?' Molly laughed in disbelief.

Morfan smiled. 'No, our Samhain is nothing like the human celebration of hiding from dead people. We don't hold with such nonsense, anyway. I understand it has some sort of religious connotations for humans. We are not a religious people.'

'I know you aren't religious, I learned that at the Crystal Tower — but why do you celebrate this Samhain or Hallowe'en thing?' she asked, intrigued.

'We have eight celebrations throughout the year to mark the turning of the seasons, the solstices, and the equinoxes. These are times of great pleasure for us and a chance for people from the towns and villages to come together. Many of us find our one true love at the festivals.'

'But surely these are pagan festivals? You must be sort of religious, then?'

Morfan laughed out loud. 'Molly, you do know that the word "pagan" means *people of the country*? Humans have a predilection for religion, and each so-called religion thinks their beliefs and deities are better than everyone else's.'

'I don't need a lecture on religion,' Molly said huffily, picking at some moss growing on the wall.

'I'm sorry, I don't mean to patronise. It's just that you humans seem to insert religious beliefs into everything. Your ancestors turned my ancestors into gods and goddesses because they were too backward to understand what we were trying to do after the Great Catastrophes.'

'I know all that!' Molly still sounded peeved, studying her fingernails, now stained green by the moss. 'Mother Arianrhod is teaching me your history. I just haven't been taught very much about your celebrations, yet. I suppose I haven't been here long enough.'

'Well, let's not fall out about it,' Morfan soothed. 'My mother must have had good reason for keeping you away from the celebrations last year. She probably felt you had enough to contend with. The celebrations can be very boisterous!'

'Yes, I dare say you're right,' Molly conceded. 'Although I do remember Brighid saying it was a pity I missed out on the Lammas parties a few weeks ago.'

They continued their stroll along the wall until finally, they came to another flight of stairs leading down to another stone corridor, and at the end of this passage Molly found herself once more in the kitchen courtyard she had passed through that morning on her way to the stables. Was that just this morning? She recalled her tumultuous day and all that had happened with a sense of disbelief, so much having happened in the space of a single day!

The courtyard was still and quiet as they crossed to the huge kitchen doors and slipped inside. The kitchen was warm and cosy — Molly admired the array of gleaming pots, pans and various kitchen utensils and appliances hanging in neat rows along the walls.

They were enjoying some bread and cheese Morfan found in one of the pantries, when he suddenly held a finger to his lips, pointing to a window overlooking another courtyard. Molly's eyes widened as she saw a shadowy figure heading towards a tall windowless tower at the far end of the yard.

Morfan frowned. 'Now, who could that be, I wonder? Anyone heading for the tower should have an escort, especially at night, so obviously this is someone who doesn't want to be seen.'

'What's inside the tower?' Molly asked.

'It's the palace prison — where the goblins are being held.'

'Do you think whoever that is could be our traitor?'

'I don't know — there could be more than one. Stay here and keep watch — I'm going to fetch the palace guard!'

Molly peered through the window as Morfan swiftly exited the kitchen. She couldn't see anything, but oddly enough, thought she could hear trickling water. Although the sky was cloudy, it hadn't rained at all that day, and Molly couldn't see a well or any horse troughs in the courtyard. The sound was drowned out by keys noisily jangling and gates being flung open as the palace guard rushed through. Molly slipped through a door beside the window and joined Morfan in the yard. They followed the guard to the prison tower and waited as the captain unlocked the massive iron-studded door. She grabbed Morfan's arm as her feet suddenly slipped on the cobblestones.

As they both looked down to see what had caused her to slip, she exclaimed, 'Look, the ground's wet — I thought I heard trickling water, but it hasn't been raining, are there any wells or water containers out here?'

Morfan shook his head. 'No, none.'

'Do you think someone was bringing the prisoners something to drink or wash in?'

Morfan laughed. 'Molly, we're not barbarians! The prisoners are well cared for; no one needs to bring them anything and certainly not from the palace kitchen area. The tower has its own separate facilites.' Then he added in a more serious tone, 'But you're quite right to bring this to my attention.'

By now they were inside the tower, and as soon as the prison warders had checked the prisoners were still safely inside their cells, Morfan told the captain about the wet cobbles.

'Don't like the sound of this,' he muttered as he headed outside to check for himself. 'Are you thinking what I'm thinking?' he asked Morfan as he rubbed his wet fingers together.

'Unfortunately, I think I am.'

The two men looked at each other. 'The Queen must be informed immediately. See to it, my Lord!' He gave Morfan a curt little bow before turning to bark orders at his men.

THIRTEEN

The Goblin Queen

The following morning, an air of nervous anticipation rippled through the council chamber with people conversing in low, subdued voices, as they waited for Ceriddwen's entrance. She swept into the room, waving everyone to their seats and calling for silence as she settled into her chair. The chattering ceased immediately and, without preamble, Ceriddwen called for the prisoners. The cauldron, already bubbling in the centre of the room, was again being carefully tended by the Ladies of Astarte. The three goblins were dragged back to the table, protesting loudly, trying to resist being forced into their chairs.

'The cups, Lady Tanith!' Ceriddwen called imperiously. The goblins glared mutinously at Ceriddwen as three goblets were once again placed in front of them. She fixed them with a hard stare. 'Resistance is futile. If you do not drink willingly, you will be restrained, and the liquid forced down your throats through a funnel.'

The goblins remained silent as Ceriddwen continued, her voice icy with contempt. 'A process you are familiar with I'm sure, for that is how you force feed fire minerals to the dragons, is it not?' The goblins shifted uncomfortably in their chairs, the youngest visibly trembling. 'As their leader, Prince Jasper, and yes I know who you are thanks to your little slip of the tongue yesterday,' Ceriddwen said, her voice now taking on an almost conversational tone, 'I think you should set an example to your men and drink first.' Her tone hardened as she finished the sentence.

Prince Jasper, throwing Ceriddwen a look of pure hatred, grabbed his goblet and gulped the liquid down, gagging as he swallowed. He threw the vessel onto the table and contemptuously wiped his mouth with the back of his hand. Molly thought Ceriddwen looked like a cat playing with a box of mice.

'Who's next?' she purred, looking at the other two in turn. The younger goblin, looking fearfully at Prince Jasper as though he expected something dreadful to happen to him, reached for his goblet and managed to drink it down, despite also gagging and choking, immediately followed by the third goblin, who made a great show of holding his nose and swallowing the liquid with no apparent problem.

'That wasn't so hard, was it?' Ceriddwen was on her feet now with both hands on the table, leaning towards the goblins. 'Now we shall attempt to get at the truth,' she said grimly. 'The cauldron begins its work.'

To Molly's surprise, the three goblins were no longer looking angry or frightened; they looked relaxed and comfortable, not in the least upset. Ceriddwen began by asking their names, where they lived and other mundane and rather innocuous questions about their day to day lives. The goblins readily answered and when Ceriddwen was sure the potion had taken full effect, the serious questioning began.

Molly realised the potion the goblins had ingested was a truth drug that rendered them incapable of lying. Again and again Ceriddwen questioned them about the shields, what did they know about them, and who was providing Lord Nudd with information. It soon became obvious they knew nothing of importance. They had simply been ordered to raid the hospital and steal the yearlings by whatever means possible. Ceriddwen finally ordered the prisoners back to their cells.

'A pointless exercise!' she snapped irritably as they were led away. 'They know nothing, probably because Lord Nudd knew there was a good chance they'd be caught.'

'My Queen,' interjected Lord Taliesin, 'may I be so bold as to voice an observation?'

'Of course, Lord Taliesin, speak.'

'Thank you.' Taliesin bowed to Ceriddwen. 'I find it strange that Lord Nudd should risk his son being caught.'

'What are you getting at?' Morfan asked, frowning.

'I may be entirely wrong, but in view of last night's developments, I think Lord Nudd hopes that his son, aided by his spy, might facilitate an invasion of the palace.'

'What developments? What happened last night?' A rush of concerned voices sped around the hall until Ceriddwen banged her staff on the table.

'Silence!' she barked. 'We have too much business to deal with this morning for such undisciplined behaviour! We shall discuss last night after a short break. Leave, all of you, apart from senior council officers, and return in forty minutes.'

Once most of the delegates and officials had left, Ceriddwen and the others retreated into the ante-toom for more privacy.

'My Lords and Ladies,' Ceriddwen began immediately, 'some of you will know I have instructed the Morrigan to take a squadron beyond the Northern Gate to advise Lord Nudd we have his son. We know he is aware of the situation, but let's see what he has to say. Any questions?' She scanned the room. 'Good, we're settled on that course of action, then.' She then murmured, 'Thank you,' as a servant handed her a cup, pausing for a moment to drink before carefully placing the cup on a side table. 'Now, following last night's disturbing events at the prison, I have also sent Queen Andraste and just a few of her troops, as we have no wish to appear threatening, to request that Lord Llyr attend the palace for urgent talks. Again, are there any questions?'

Molly held up her hand, feeling like a foolish schoolgirl. 'I'm sorry, Your Majesty, but who is Lord Llyr, and what does he have to do with last night?'

Ceriddwen grimaced. 'Yes, Molly, I'm sorry, you're quite right to ask. You haven't been appraised of the situation.' She turned to Morfan. 'Please explain why we have summoned Lord Llyr.'

'Of course, Lady Mother,' he replied, with a quick bow, and turning to Molly said, 'The Captain of the Guard knew immediately, as did I, why you heard trickling water last night and why the cobblestones were wet. We think our spy is a water fairy. In fact, we're sure of it.' Molly's eyes widened in shock.

'A water fairy? But they're everywhere! Will the cauldron have to test them all?'

'Unfortunately, that will not be possible,' Ceriddwen was forced to admit. 'The cauldron, by its very nature, relies on water as its main ingredient.'

Molly was perplexed. 'But why is that a problem?' she asked.

'Because, by their very nature, water fairies spend their lives manipulating water to their will. Should the spy be tested by the cauldron, he or she will simply distort the water molecules and render their properties useless.'

'I'm sorry if this is a silly question, but why did I hear trickling water and why was the ground wet?'

'Water fairies can also shapeshift into water. To gain access to the prison tower, all a water fairy has to do is change into a trickle of water and flow beneath the door or through a crack.'

'Why aren't your doors and walls watertight, then?' Molly thought she might have been a little over-assertive, but a few rueful nods reassured her that she had been within her rights to ask.

'They should be,' agreed Lleu, 'but we are imperfect beings, and sometimes the little things go unnoticed.'

'Especially when you don't expect to be betrayed by those whom you trust!' fumed Tabitha.

'The palace builders and stonemasons are working flat out checking the whole palace,' Morfan reassured, 'but the question is, what do we do in the meantime?'

'What can you do?' asked Molly.

'Not a lot,' admitted Lleu, 'that's why we've summoned Lord Llyr.'

'You still haven't told me why he's important,' Molly reminded him.

'Ah…umm…yes…' Lleu seemed terribly discomfited by the whole situation.

'The truth is, Molly,' Morfan interrupted hotly, fairy protocol forgotten, 'we can't function without the water fairies. Apart from the obvious fact that they supply a great deal of our food, they also control the water supplies to the entire realm. If they withdraw their co-operation, we will also be without clean drinking water or sanitation. I could go on, but I'm sure you get the picture.' Molly looked aghast as Morfan continued: 'Lord Llyr is Tribal Chief of the Water Fairies. He is, in theory, responsible for them and all their actions. He is also subject to our Queen, and that is why he has been summoned to answer this charge.'

'Do you think he knows anything about it?' Molly was curious to learn why it would be in a water fairy's interests to betray Ceriddwen.

'I would be very surprised,' answered Ceriddwen, 'but then we do not know what they have been bribed or threatened with, or if we are dealing with a lone wolf.'

'Lord Nudd can be very charming and persuasive,' added Tabitha. 'He once offered me a lot of gold from his mines if I would sell him Merrily and Poeme. He was desperate for unicorn mares at the time as his were all dead.' Tabitha shuddered at the memory. 'I had to keep reminding myself who and what he is. I finally threatened him with the palace guard before he gave up and left. I submitted a full report, if you remember, Your Majesty?' she said to Ceriddwen, who nodded in agreement.

'I remember, Epona. It was just before we lost Prince Gwion.'

Fortunately, just as an oppressive gloom began to descend, Meyrick, the major domo, appeared to advise that the rest of the council members had returned from their break.

Molly was relieved to learn her presence would not be required for a while. Ceriddwen had decided she would delay any official announcement of Molly's newly discovered heritage until the traitor was identified. The only members who knew what the goblins had revealed were those seated around the table, plus Lord Taliesin. Protocol forbade them to discuss the matter with anyone else without the Queen's express permission.

Ceriddwen decided the current codes for the shields should be revoked and new codes issued to a trusted few. This would be inconvenient for a short while until a better system was devised and it also ensured that no water fairies would have access to the codes until Ceriddwen met with Lord Llyr.

'We were complacent,' Ceriddwen admitted bitterly. 'It shall not happen again!'

Tabitha was also excused as she was required at the hospital stud along with several grooms from the royal stables while the hospital staff were being questioned by Ceriddwen. Molly asked permission to accompany Tabitha, and to her delight, it was granted. Ceriddwen was far too preoccupied with the questioning to worry about Molly's lessons with the Arianrhod or business procedures with Holda.

'I don't think you should be gallivanting all over the place when we've a traitor in our midst and Her Majesty is conducting a Council of War,' grumbled Brighid as she bustled about laying out Molly's riding clothes.

Molly laughed. 'I'm not gallivanting, Brighid, I'm going to help Tabitha look after the hospital while the staff are up here being questioned. And the stud is well guarded now.'

Brighid just harrumphed further disapproval. 'It's not fitting for a royal princess. Mucking out stables indeed! You could be injured or captured by a roving band of goblins!'

Molly rolled her eyes. 'Oh really, Brighid, don't be so melodramatic! I can look after myself. Jarol and the other stable grooms will be there, too,' she pointed out, pulling on her riding boots as Brighid held out her padded jerkin. 'And besides, I need the exercise and distraction before my head explodes trying to process everything that's happened.'

Brighid shook her head and continued to tut her disapproval as she ushered Molly out of the door and along the palace corridors. In her opinion, royal princesses should be concerning themselves with beautiful gowns and jewels and dreaming of fairy princes to sweep them off their pretty little feet. Princess Molly certainly had a mind of her own.

Molly and Brighid arrived to find the stables amid frenetic activity. Several stable hands were loading supplies onto large wagons, and Jarol and Paris were tacking up Merrily and Flambeaux. Their own mounts were already tacked and waiting patiently, dozing in the autumn sunshine. Tabitha came out of the yard office wielding a sheaf of documents and issuing instructions to the groom trotting at her side.

'Send pigeons if you have any problems, don't bother sending a rider, pigeons are faster!'

The groom nodded. 'Of course, Epona.'

A Dynasty of Dragons

Molly noticed pigeon baskets being loaded onto one of the wagons. Telephones were another form of technology Ceriddwen's world had shunned. Molly hugged Brighid goodbye, much to the housekeeper's consternation. 'Your Highness, this is most unseemly!' she protested, wriggling free from Molly's exuberant embrace. The stable staff looked away, embarrassed by Molly's lack of concern for public protocol, pretending they hadn't noticed. Tabitha handed the sheaf of papers to her deputy, dismissing her as she mounted Merrily. Jarol gave Molly a deft leg-up on to Flambeaux, checking the girth and bridle as Molly settled herself into the saddle, then, without further ado, they set off with the stable staff's goodbyes ringing in their ears.

She was unprepared for the sheer amount of hard work involved in running the hospital stud, and in just a few days discovered muscles she didn't know existed after all the mucking out, filling hay nets, grooming, exercising, and making up beds.

Several of the unicorns were injured and traumatised by the goblin raid, and during a particularly busy day when she was helping Tabitha apply a linseed poultice to a sprained fetlock, they were interrupted by the return of Oonagh, the hospital manager, and Morello, the head groom. They had been among the first to be questioned and allowed to return to their duties. They also brought news.

The Morrigan and Andraste had returned bearing intriguing messages. The Morrigan stated that Nudd had rudely refused to receive them, but her spies heard that his wife, Queen Grainne, was making her way to Ceriddwen by ship and carrying an important but unnamed cargo. Andraste reported that Lord Llyr and his wife Lady Thetis, were also making their way by ship with very disturbing news.

Oonagh dipped a quick curtsey to Molly saying, 'I am sorry, Your Highness, but you must return to the palace immediately. The Queen has sent an armed guard to escort you and the Epona.'

'Thank you, Oonagh.' Molly stretched her aching back and wondered how she would manage to persuade her complaining body into the saddle and stay put for the homeward journey. Tabitha finished bandaging the poulticed fetlock and handed the halter to Jarol.

'Return to the stables when the hospital staff come back and in the meantime, do all you can to help Oonagh.'

'Of course, Epona,' Jarol replied. 'Shall I prepare Merrily and Flambeaux?'

'Yes, at once. The princess and I will collect our belongings, and then we leave.'

Once mounted and on their way, Molly asked Tabitha how serious the messages were.

'I would say very serious. It is unprecedented that Queen Grainne should be visiting our Queen uninvited and even more unusual that she is coming without Lord Nudd. I find that aspect of her visit most intriguing.'

'Lord Nudd doesn't seem to me to be the kind of man who would let his wife do as she pleases,' mused Molly.

'Ah, but Grainne is a very powerful queen in her own right. Theirs is very much a marriage of convenience — a joining together of two powerful goblin dynasties. The intention of the match was to create a nation twice as powerful, and our Queen keeps a very careful eye on them. As you already know, they are wicked beyond belief, and Grainne is every bit as ruthless as Gwynn ap Nudd.'

'Are you saying she participated in the murder of the Anunnaki?'

'It wouldn't surprise me if it was her idea. She is much cleverer than her blustering husband,' Tabitha stated in a very matter-of-fact tone, urging Merrily into a canter as they crested the hill leading down into the valley. The citadel loomed in the distance, palace pennants and flags fluttering in the breeze, and as Molly followed Tabitha, she felt an unexpected frisson of excitement at the prospect of meeting this queen who could never be anything but her sworn enemy.

FOURTEEN

The Thinning of the Veil

When Harry hung up the phone, he felt frustrated and slightly ashamed. He also felt rather guilty, berating himself for alarming Morven and Gwynnie out of the blue, until his train of thought was pleasantly interrupted by the sound of beautiful music coming from the garden. He made his way through the kitchen to the back door and watched Xander play, the foot of the harp resting on his knees, its neck nestled on his shoulder. His eyes were closed in concentration and a smile of pure pleasure played around his mouth as the music worked its magic once more around the garden. Harry was astonished by the change in the plants as the mesmerising melodies rose and fell. Their auras were no longer desperately jumping and spiking all over the place and the garden appeared calm and peaceful. As Xander played on Harry began to understand just how hugely powerful and magical his son's gift really was. He made his way over the grass and smiled in approval as Xander finished playing.

'Have you noticed the effect your music has on the plants? They look normal again.' Xander surprised him by giving a reluctant nod as he placed the harp carefully on the grass.

'Yes, I can't deny it. I want to, but I must admit I did notice the effect it had the first time we played — I thought it was just a fluke, but it's obvious. The coloured auras and spiking have died down and the garden atmosphere has changed completely. I'm sorry about before.' He shrugged, upturning his hands in apology.

Harry let out a long sigh of relief. 'No problem,' he assured him with a grin. 'Dare I hope that we can now work together?'

'Yes,' Xander replied, 'but I think we need to know a lot more about who and what we're potentially dealing with.'

Harry nodded. 'Yes, I agree, and I think I may have a plan.' He relayed everything Morven and Gwynnie had told him about their experience in the forest with Ceriddwen and the fairies. 'I think we may have to take a trip down there and ask Morven and Gwynnie if they will take us to the forest to try and contact the fairy folk ourselves.'

Xander looked a bit doubtful. 'What if they just snatch me away and I'm marooned in fairyland forever?'

'I don't think that will happen — I think we may find that you are needed this side of the portal if Lord Nudd is to be stopped in his tracks.'

Xander still didn't look convinced. 'We don't even know if they will entertain us, do we?'

'That's why we need Morven and Gwynnie, well Gwynnie, anyway. She's the one who can speak the fairy language and knows how to make contact.' Harry was mentally crossing his fingers as he spoke, remembering Morven and Gwynnie were elderly ladies. He could only hope Gwynnie still had her skills and knowledge.

Xander knew his father was right and reluctantly agreed they should give it a try. 'I should be okay for time,' he said. 'The orchestra's going to Vienna in December and we're all on sabbatical until mid-November.' Xander played for a well-known London orchestra and travelled extensively with them. Harry nodded in agreement.

'Yes, I'll have to go back to Glastonbury and re-arrange cover for the shop and my other commitments. We should leave tonight. It's still a few weeks until Samhain, so we'll have plenty of time to prepare. Everything hinges, of course,' he added, 'on Morven and Gwynnie agreeing to help us.'

Later that evening, when Molly and Laura came back from the pub, Harry told them that he and Xander had decided on a course of action that would ensure they were ready should Lord Nudd make his move at Samhain and not at the next full moon as first thought. Harry explained that it was more likely to be at Samhain because the traditional pagan belief in the *thinning of the veil* at Samhain or Hallowe'en would appear to be based on fact. They had decided not to tell Molly they were going to Hereford, focusing instead on the need to return to Glastonbury to plan for their absence at Samhain.

Molly was reassured by the garden's peaceful demeanour and the knowledge that Xander's harp music had brought about the transformation.

'Please keep trying to remember as much as possible,' Harry urged her. 'Xander has acknowledged that he has a role to play and is confident nothing untoward can happen until Samhain, now that his music has stopped the portal from creating any further damage. We will be back in plenty of time, so try not to worry.'

Little worry lines creased Molly's forehead. 'How do you know the portal won't cause any further damage while you're away?'

Xander shrugged. 'I just know, Molly—I can't explain it—looks like you were right after all about my heritage and my musical gift.'

Molly walked over to Xander and to everyone's surprise, wrapped her arms around him in a huge bear hug which, after stiffening momentarily, he returned.

'Friends?' Molly whispered, gazing into his beautiful eyes. After just a moment's hesitation, he grinned.

'I must be mad but go on then!' Harry and Laura exchanged glances, and Laura's eyes began to fill with tears. The ice had been broken. Things promised to be so much easier now.

During his telephone conversation with Morven and Gwynnie, Harry had established that the subject of Molly's baby, her illness and the fairy involvement, had never been discussed in any shape or form during the previous forty years. The women had maintained a code of silence and secrecy borne out of fear of Ceriddwen and a fear for Molly's future when the fairy Queen came to claim her payment. Before Laura and Molly returned from the pub, Harry had phoned Gwynnie again to ask if they would object to a short visit. To his surprise, she readily agreed, thrilled at the prospect of meeting Xander.

The men hurried back to Glastonbury and after making the necessary arrangements, drove the hundred miles up to the little village, a few miles outside Hereford, in record time. When they arrived, Harry was delighted to see the little slate-roofed stone cottage looking much the same as he remembered. He turned his nose up in disgust at a few new-build houses in and around the village, but apart from that, everything looked comfortably familiar. When Gwynnie answered the door, he was pleased to see that although obviously older, she still looked similar with her thick, now-white hair caught in a bun at the nape of her neck, her weather-beaten face lined with a web of wrinkles around her still shrewd and sharp eyes. She was wearing a loose cotton top and baggy trousers, her feet encased in an old pair of Crocs.

'Harry,' she beamed warmly, 'how wonderful to see you after all these years!' Her voice trailed off as she became aware of Xander hovering behind him. 'Oh, my giddy aunt,' she cried, 'you must be Xander! You were just a tiny baby the last time I saw you. Come and let me look at you, cariad.' As she stepped forward to embrace him, she yelled over her shoulder, 'Morven! Stop hiding and come and meet your grandson!' As both men looked beyond the open door into the hall, Morven stepped from the shadows.

'Hello, Harry,' she whispered, and then looking up at Xander, burst into floods of tears. Xander was mortified as he looked at this tiny woman, so different from Gwynnie — where Gwynnie was obviously flamboyant and hearty, Morven appeared to be nervous and shy, neatly dressed in sensible slacks and a sweatshirt emblazoned, *Mrs Tiggywinkle's Hedgehog Sanctuary*. Her soft grey hair was cut in a flattering bob, and she was wearing pink trainers. The two sisters couldn't have looked more different.

Ignoring the tearful outburst, Gwynnie ushered them inside, ordering Morven to go and make the tea. 'Don't think I'm being a bully,' she explained when she caught the men's embarrassed glances, 'making tea will calm her down — she'll soon bounce back to her usual self.'

Sure enough, after about ten minutes, during which Gwynnie fired non-stop questions at Harry and Xander, Morven came bustling through pushing a tea trolley groaning with sandwiches, cakes, and a huge pot of tea.

'Right, boys,' she announced, squeezing herself between the two men on the sofa, 'dig in — Gwynnie, you can be mum!' Harry and Xander didn't have to be told twice, they were ravenous after their journey and soon made short work of the food and drink, fielding all the women's excited questions.

Once the tea things had been cleared away, Harry got straight to the point and outlined his desire to meet with the fairies. Morven and Gwynnie exchanged glances. 'I'm not sure that's a good idea,' began Gwynnie.

'She's a monster, that Ceriddwen!' Morven burst out. 'She'll steal you away and enslave you, or kill and eat you! They're not human you know!' She looked quite distraught as Gwynnie tried to calm her down.

'Let them say their piece, Morven, I'm not keen either, but they've travelled all this way, so the least we can do is hear them out.'

Morven sniffed and rubbed her eyes. 'I just can't bear to think about that horrible day!'

Harry looked at Morven, remembering the practical, capable woman she used to be, a teacher who could handle recalcitrant teenagers. This business with Molly and the fairy folk had affected her badly, and he felt a momentary surge of anger, but remembered Gwynnie telling him how they had gone into it with their eyes wide open; they knew the risks and were prepared to take them for Molly's sake. Gwynnie told him how Nan had stressed that there was no such thing as a free lunch where fairies were concerned. There would always be a price to pay.

Just as he was about to reassure Morven, Gwynnie snapped at her. 'For heaven's sake, Morven, stop being such a drama queen! Harry and Xander are Ceriddwen's flesh and blood. There's no way she'd harm them.'

'She was threatening to kill everyone, as I recall,' retorted Morven. Before Gwynnie could respond, Harry quickly made his move.

'Molly has a very different view of the fairy folk. I told you she seems to be coming out of some sort of induced amnesia, and the world she describes paints the fairies in a very different light. And this is why we've come for your help.'

'I thought you said Ceriddwen was going to come through this portal thing to fight the goblins?' Gwynnie queried with a frown. 'Can't you wait and speak to her then?'

'No, not really,' Harry replied patiently. 'Molly is having a hard time remembering everything exactly. It's very distressing for her as you can imagine. She lived a completely different life in another world and then forgot all about it for forty years. She's quite distraught.'

Morven began weeping again. 'She wasn't the same when we got her back. She stopped doing everything she loved before; her painting and drawing, design work, making things. She just threw herself into her job at the museum and then married Fred Colman and spent her life running after him!' She looked apologetically at Harry. 'James was over the moon, he thought she'd made a great match. I wasn't convinced and her friend Laura never got over it. I felt as though my daughter had been stolen away from me, and I still feel that way now.' She gulped, dabbing at her eyes with a tissue.

'For the life of me, I never understood why she married Fred,' mused Gwynnie. 'It was as if she didn't care about her life, as if marrying Fred was just a temporary inconvenience she had to put up with for a while — really, really odd!'

'Well, it looks as though that's actually true in light of what we know now,' said Xander. 'She seems to have made a marriage of convenience that would see her comfortably through forty years.'

'You make her sound very mercenary,' reproached Morven.

'I doubt very much it was a conscious decision.' Xander shrugged. 'We have to remember she was bewitched.'

Harry was anxious to move things along. 'So, ladies, will you help us?'

'I'm really not sure about this at all,' demurred Gwynnie. 'Mum always said the fairies would only honour their word if you kept to your side of the bargain. I'm afraid Ceriddwen might view any further contact from us as a breach of that contract.'

'Well,' replied Xander pragmatically, 'as far as I can see, the contract is now void — the forty-year period is up — you've kept to your promise for the allotted time, so I don't see that contacting them now would be jeopardising anything.'

'Xander's right,' agreed Harry. 'You won't be breaching any new protocols because they haven't made any, have they?' Morven and Gwynnie mulled this over for a few moments.

'You make it sound so reasonable,' Morven said in a querulous tone, 'and Ceriddwen never struck me as being remotely reasonable!'

'Well, we'll just have to hope she's as honourable and gracious as Molly says she is,' Harry responded, sounding more positive than he felt.

'Aren't you afraid?' Morven challenged Xander. 'It's you she wants after all. She made that very, very clear when she took Molly.'

'She didn't take Molly, Morven, you know that,' remonstrated Gwynnie. 'Molly went of her own free will. Ceriddwen said she had no intention of taking her; it was Molly's decision, not hers.'

Morven gave Gwynnie a mulish look and was about to reply when Harry interrupted her.

'Look, I'm sorry, but this is getting us nowhere. I don't mean to be rude, but we're all upset and to be honest, a little afraid, of course we are — this is right out of our collective comfort zones. But apart from Molly, only you have had contact with Ceriddwen and know what to do. Help us, please!'

Morven refused point blank to have anything to do with the plan, with Gwynnie eventually agreeing with a great deal of reluctance. She made it clear that, once more, she was only doing this for Molly's sake. She explained to the men that their message would have to be accompanied by a gift the fairies would consider worthy — their co-operation with any human request dependable on a favourable gift.

'So,' she asked wearily, 'what do you suggest we leave with the message?'

'Me,' Xander responded immediately. 'I am the gift! At the end of the day, isn't that what this is all about? The restoration of their crown prince?'

'You can't just offer yourself up!' Gwynnie was aghast. 'They might just take you and forget all about Molly,' she spluttered.

Xander quickly moved to calm her down. 'No, no, Gwynnie,' he said soothingly, 'I don't mean I am going to present myself personally.'

'What do you mean, then?' Gwynnie questioned, feeling somewhat confused.

'We'll put a lock of my hair inside the letter. That should flush them out,' he replied.

'I don't think you should be flippant or take anything for granted where Ceriddwen is concerned.' Gwynnie fixed him with a severe look. 'She will want to make sure we are genuine, and if she doubts us for a second, we could be in serious trouble. My mother always said we should never try to second guess Ceriddwen. So, we must tread carefully!'

Xander managed to look contrite. 'Sorry, Gwynnie, I bow to your superior knowledge.'

'Hmmph! I don't know about that,' she grunted. 'I just hope I can remember enough of their language to write this letter and talk to whoever appears.'

'Do you think the same one will come again?' Morven asked. As she spoke, she looked hard at Xander, and then, turning to Gwynnie, said, 'Do you know, I've just realised, Xander looks very like that fairy man, don't you think so, Gwynnie?'

Gwynnie looked at Xander, and after a few moments said, 'It was a long time ago, but I think you're right, Morven I should have noticed that, too!'

'Well, it's entirely possible,' said Harry at length. 'My father's younger brother, Morfan, was a great friend to Molly throughout her stay there. She's been telling us a great deal about him. I suppose it stands to reason there should be a family resemblance; Xander does look very much like my father.'

'Well, give me some of your hair then, and let's get on with it,' ordered Gwynnie, handing Xander a pair scissors produced from a knitting bag. 'The sooner this is over and done with the better!'

They headed for the forest an hour later in Harry's old Volvo. Gwynnie was relieved the earlier sunny morning had turned into a dank, dismal afternoon, explaining to the men how her mother had always said damp weather meant fewer walkers and tourists, therefore more chance the fairies would risk appearing.

They turned off the main road and soon entered the forest, bumping down the old track. Gwynnie was pleased to see the National Park authorities hadn't decided to improve this part of the forest, leaving it wild and relatively undisturbed. They parked the car and made their way along to the little clearing dominated by the stream and large rock face. Everything was more overgrown than Gwynnie remembered, but she managed to locate the cleft in the rock, and directed Xander as he clambered over wet, slippery stones, the tumbling waters of the stream rushing past him, until finally, clinging precariously to an overhanging willow branch, he tucked the rolled-up letter into the mossy cleft. When he had made his way back, they all stood nervously waiting for someone, or something, to appear. The forest was unusually quiet apart from the rattle of magpies in the surrounding trees.

'He came from behind that big oak tree beside the rock,' Gwynnie whispered, 'but the Queen and the rest of them came through the rock in a very bright light.'

'Do you think he'll come on his own this time, or with others?' Harry asked apprehensively.

'We'll soon find out...' began Gwynnie. The words were hardly out of her mouth when Morfan appeared, as before, from behind the oak tree. He greeted Gwynnie, speaking in English, bowing politely first to her, then Harry and Xander. Gwynnie returned the greeting, glad she didn't have to stumble over an unfamiliar tongue, before introducing the two men.

Morfan smiled politely at them. 'Greetings, gentlemen. I believe you are my nephews. I have been looking forward to making your acquaintance, as has my lady mother, the Queen. She is most anxious to meet you, but first you must tell me why you have contacted us.'

Gwynnie was non-plussed for a second but quickly regained her composure.

'I thought it would be obvious why we should contact you. The forty-year period is up, and my niece Molly should be released from her enchantment.'

'Princess Molly has been released, and my mother is making arrangements for her return to the Land of the Four Gates,' replied Morfan smoothly. 'Surely the princess has advised you of this? May I ask why she is not with you?' This last question was asked with a trace of anxiety.

Before Gwynnie could reply, Harry stepped forward. 'Forgive me,' he began, 'I'm not sure how I should address you?'

Morfan inclined his head graciously. 'My name is Morfan, please address me as such, we are family, after all.'

Harry grimaced and gave a curt nod. 'Very well...Morfan... Now, let me explain.'

Morfan listened impassively as Harry spoke in detail about the portal, but as soon as he mentioned Lord Nudd, he held up his hand to silence him.

'Enough! I must return and inform the Queen. This is most disturbing!' Without another word he vanished behind the oak tree, leaving Harry and the others gaping after him.

'That went well,' Xander remarked drily. 'So much for happy families!'

'This isn't the time for sarcasm!' Harry rounded on him, adding, 'I don't like this at all. He's pretty inscrutable but he certainly became rattled as soon as I mentioned Lord Nudd.'

Xander just shrugged. 'Well, what do we do now? Go home? What do you think, Gwynnie?'

'We wait,' she replied, settling herself on a mossy tree stump. 'That is if you're really serious about helping Molly?'

Harry glowered at her. 'Of course we're serious! How can you even ask that?' he snapped.

'Well, calm down and try a little patience,' Gwynnie snapped back.

'But how long do you think we'll have to wait?'

'I really don't know, Harry. My mother was the expert, and she's been dead for thirty years!'

'I just feel so useless,' he fumed, pacing back and forth, until Xander told him to sit down on a boulder next to Gwynnie.

'You're making me dizzy,' he complained. 'We've started this, so we'll just have to see it through!'

'Actually, I don't think we'll have long to wait at all,' Gwynnie soothed. 'We didn't the last time.'

'So, if Morfan's just gone to speak to the Queen, he should be back in minutes, right?' Xander reasoned. Harry seemed satisfied by this, and sat quietly beside Gwynnie, lost in thought.

Just as she'd said, they didn't have to wait long. After a few minutes, they noticed a glow of white light seeping from the bottom of the rock face, increasing in intensity as it spread upwards until Morfan, accompanied by several other figures, materialised from the centre of the coruscating brightness. Harry and Xander jumped to their feet, startled by the sight of Morfan's companions, but Gwynnie laid a warning hand on Harry's arm.

'Be careful,' she whispered, 'say nothing until we know what they want, and be polite — bow to them.' Harry eyed Morfan's companions nervously; a group of six fierce-looking warriors stood guard by the rock face as Morfan and another man approached.

They bowed as Gwynnie instructed. Morfan and his companion doing likewise.

'Gentlemen, madam, allow me to introduce Lord Taliesin, Justiciar of the Four Gates, Queen's Warrior and husband to Princess Molly.' The three companions stood open mouthed in shock, as they digested this new information. Molly's husband? They stared at the man standing beside Morfan. Obviously a warrior, strong and lithe, with a well-muscled body. Harry felt a surge of heart-stopping jealousy. He had a bold, handsome face with piercing blue eyes and the same dark hair as Xander and Morfan, hanging in an intricate plait down his back. He was an imposing figure, wearing a garment resembling a medieval chainmail hauberk, with assorted weapons in leather holsters and belts strapped about his body.

Before anyone could speak, Morfan continued: 'Lord Taliesin is very concerned about Princess Molly as is the Queen who commands your presence immediately!'

'We thought the Queen would come to us as before?' Gwynnie queried hesitantly.

'We are at war, madam!' Lord Taliesin spoke for the first time in a quiet, authoritative voice. A voice used to being obeyed. 'Her Majesty cannot leave the kingdom at such a time. You requested an audience, so let us make haste and waste no more time. My wife is in danger, and we must act swiftly!'

'You don't need me,' Gwynnie objected. 'I'm too old to traipse about!' She bowed deferentially to Morfan. 'Please allow me to stay here,' she pleaded, trying to keep the fear out of her voice.

'Very well,' agreed Morfan, dismissing her with a polite nod as he turned to Harry and Xander, ushering them towards the rock. 'Come, the Queen awaits!'

Surrounded by the armed guard, and trying to appear braver than they felt, Harry and Xander passed through the doorway of light and found themselves walking along the same stone passageway and flagstones Molly had trod forty years earlier. Morfan and Lord Taliesin strode ahead, calling for the gates to be opened as they approached the end of the passage. A large man lumbered down a flight of steps and flung open huge iron gates, allowing the party to hurry through. At the top of the stairs, as they rushed along the wall walk, Harry and Xander were astounded by what they saw: that they were in a huge, fortified castle was obvious, but they couldn't believe their eyes as they beheld the beauty of the scenery stretching for miles beyond. Rolling hills, meadows, rivers, trees, parklands teeming with herds of deer, and farmlands rich in sheep & cattle. It was breath-taking. No wonder Molly loved it so much.

They hurried up and down stairs, through tree-lined, flower-filled courtyards and along labyrinthine corridors, passing through sumptuously furnished rooms and halls hung with rich tapestries, eventually arriving in what Harry immediately realised was Ceriddwen's throne room, a huge hall with flying buttresses and large gothic-looking stained-glass windows. The room reminded Harry of some of the beautiful cathedrals he had visited. On a raised dais at the far end, beneath a myriad of colourful hanging banners, they saw a woman seated on a large ornately carved chair. A man with a long, plaited beard sat next to her.

'So, this is my grandmother and your great-grandmother,' Harry whispered to Xander. 'I hope she's friendly!'

'Me too.' Harry had heard Xander's sharp intake of breath. He was feeling completely overwhelmed by the whole experience, his previous scepticism completely forgotten, his emotions and usual rational thought processes in turmoil. Harry had been correct earlier. They were well outside their comfort zones.

The hall was noisy and crowded, busy with courtiers and officials rushing about like brightly coloured butterflies, talking and arguing, but as soon as Morfan's group made its appearance, an awed hush descended, and everyone made way, bowing deferentially, as Morfan and Taliesin led father and son towards Ceriddwen. Harry noticed the Queen reach across to grip her companion's hand tightly for a moment, before releasing it and placing her hand back on the arm of her throne.

Morfan and Taliesin bowed deeply before her. 'Lady Mother, my Queen, may I present…' began Morfan, but before he could finish, Ceriddwen interrupted him.

'My grandsons need no introductions!' She rose from the throne and stepped off the dais. Harry could see tears glittering in her eyes. He stood in shocked, confused silence, experiencing something totally removed from normal reality. He wondered if he might wake up at any moment and realise this was just an elaborate dream.

He remained frozen as this strikingly beautiful woman approached him to lay her hands on his shoulders before cupping his face, her long bejewelled fingers caressing his cheek.

'You have your father's height,' she said in a dulcet, melodic tone, 'but you must take after your mother in looks.' Harry wondered what age she must be and was suddenly very aware of his own sixty-two years. She was smiling at him, now stroking his hair. 'If your father had brought you to me, you would still be young and vigorous,' she said regretfully, as if reading his thoughts, 'but he was an honourable prince who truly loved your mother. This much I have learned.'

Xander held his breath as Ceriddwen then turned to him. 'You have your grandfather's bearing and presence, and you are as handsome as he was.' She took his hands in hers and held them to her face. Xander felt her tears on his fingers, now feeling acutely uncomfortable and embarrassed, yet wildly confused at the same time. He could feel himself being drawn to this intriguing woman — his great-grandmother! That threw him, too. What age must she be? She looked like a beautiful woman in her prime. He looked at his father, who was watching Ceriddwen with a dazed look on his face, and thought, *He looks old enough to be her father!* and realised just how totally alien this world was.

FIFTEEN

Forests and Fireflies

Later that same evening, on her own at last, Molly made herself a cup of tea and tried to concentrate on the latest episode of *Coronation Street*, but her mind was far from the antics and dramas of the Rover's Return and the underwear factory. She stared unseeing at the television screen, her head full of jumbled thoughts and memories she was trying to make sense of. At one point she began to wonder if she was having some sort of nervous breakdown, a delayed reaction to Fred's death, then reminded herself she wasn't delusional because Laura, Harry and Xander also knew about the portal. She knew she had been under some sort of enchantment and resolved to phone her mother & Aunt Gwynnie in the morning. They must have been complicit in what happened to her all those years ago. Giving up trying to concentrate on the television screen, she switched it off, ran herself a relaxing bath then went to bed, immediately plunging into a deep, dreamless sleep.

She was pegging out washing the following morning when Laura rang to suggest they go to Vigo's for breakfast. Molly readily agreed.

'Lovely! I notice they're doing scrambled egg and smoked salmon for their special this week.'

'Great! I'll pick you up in ten minutes.'

She finished hanging out the washing, and after a quick check on the garden and sinkhole to satisfy herself all was calm and peaceful, dashed indoors to brush her hair and put on a bit of makeup, leaving a note by the phone reminding herself to phone her mother. Laura arrived in her smart Fiat Punto and soon they were seated in the bright surroundings of Vigo's tucking into their Eggs Royale.

'Yummy!' Laura said.

'Sheer heaven,' agreed Molly, washing hers down with a large gulp of coffee.

'Did you manage to sleep at all last night?' asked Laura, wiping her fingers on her napkin.

'Yes, I slept like a log, believe it or not,' admitted Molly. 'I couldn't concentrate on anything, so I had a bath then fell asleep as soon as my head hit the pillow.'

'You must be exhausted by all this.' Laura's face wore an uncharacteristic, concerned look. 'I feel a bit guilty…you know… for pushing you into all this.'

'Don't be silly,' Molly said with a wry smile. 'It was going to happen anyway, whether you pushed me or not!'

'Do you want to talk about it some more, or would you rather wait until Harry and Xander come back?'

'I was thinking about calling Mum and Aunt Gwynnie today,' replied Molly. 'They must know what happened, and they've never said a word in all this time.'

'You were different after your stay at Aunt Gwynnie's,' Laura mused. 'I know we had a lot of fun when I moved back here, but you weren't the same old Molly. I thought you'd become a bit of a social climber when you got the job at the museum and married whizz kid Fred.'

'Me? A social climber?' Molly rolled her eyes. 'I just fell for Fred when I met him. How often do I have to tell you that?'

Laura gave a contemptuous snort. 'So you say!'

'Laura, let's not do the Fred stuff anymore, please,' Molly said firmly. 'You've been trotting out the same old line for years. We've got more important things to concentrate on, don't you think?'

Laura glowered at Molly for a moment over the rim of her coffee cup, then put it down, smiling ruefully.

'Sorry, I'm being a pain. Of course, you're right. I won't mention it again, so let's hear some more of your memories if you're up to it.'

They paid the bill and made their way to the park where they found a bench overlooking the river and Molly continued recounting her memories...

~

When Molly and Tabitha returned to the palace, they were whisked off to the council chamber to be briefed on the intriguing and impending presence of Queen Grainne and Lord Llyr, who would arrive in around two to three weeks.

'As far as the goblin queen is concerned,' Ceriddwen announced after greeting Molly with a kiss on the cheek, 'you will be presented as Princess Molly of the Tuatha de Danaan, Mother of the Crown Prince and Dragon Queen of the Anunnaki.'

'That's a bit of a mouthful!' protested Molly without thinking, and then noticing Ceriddwen's irritated frown, quickly added, 'But it does sound very impressive.'

'We are not about impressing arrogant goblins!' snapped Ceriddwen. 'We are about showing our strength and teaching them the error of their ways. I hope the sight of you, the Anunnaki Queen, causes her to fall from the prow of her ship and drown!'

The chamber was so quiet you could hear a pin drop. Molly looked at her feet, suppressing an urge to laugh out loud, and suspected everyone else in the room was doing the same thing. She had become used to Ceriddwen's little outbursts, and very often they were unintentionally hilarious. Realising she had been less than diplomatic, Ceriddwen glared at everyone before stalking back to her chair. Lleu raised an eyebrow, and after giving her a little bow, cleared his throat and began to speak.

'As our guests are not expected for a while since they are coming by ship,' he paused and smiled at Ceriddwen, 'our Queen has graciously decreed that the Samhain celebrations should proceed as normal, and preparations are already underway.' A loud cheer filled the room as Lleu continued.

'The usual competitions and displays of goods and animals will take place on the first day, followed by feasting and entertainments in the evening. The horse and unicorn races and the Great Truffle Hunt will take place the following day, ending with the Fire Ceremony Feast. Finally, on the third day, we will have the betrothals, and the festival will end as usual with the Masqued Ball.'

Everyone cheered and clapped as Lleu bowed and sat down. Molly's heart skipped a beat as Lord Taliesin stood up to address the room. She found herself staring unashamedly at him. *I think I'm in love*, she thought to herself.

Bowing to Ceriddwen before raising his arms for silence, Taliesin began to speak. 'Lords and Ladies of the council, as Justiciar of the Four Gates, it is my duty to guard the kingdom and keep it safe from those who would threaten us, and at this time of uncertainty, I would like to reassure you that Her Majesty's armed forces will ensure the Samhain festivities can proceed without fear of interference from our enemies.' The announcement was met with another huge round of applause.

Taliesin continued: 'For those of our people who have relatives in the security forces, please know the guard will be rotated frequently to ensure no one misses out on the celebrations.' He bowed and sat down to another round of appreciative cheers and applause.

Tabitha, who had noticed Molly's interest in Lord Taliesin, playfully elbowed her in the ribs. 'No guesses as to who you're hoping to dance with at Samhain,' she whispered. 'And just to set your mind at ease, he is betrothed to no one, so you are free to pursue him!'

'Pursue him? You think I would be so forward and obvious?' Molly retorted, trying, and failing, to sound outraged. 'I don't know what you're talking about!'

Tabitha gave a merry tinkle of laughter. 'We'll see, we'll see!' Molly, blushing furiously, pursed her lips and said nothing.

The rest of the council meeting consisted of reports on the questioning of hospital staff, all cleared and innocent, plus a long conversation about the goblin prisoners and whether they should be held in the palace prison or hidden elsewhere. It was decided that, as the prison tower had been repaired and made completely watertight and secure, it was sensible they should be held where Ceriddwen could keep a close eye on them, and a rather fractious discussion on where to house Queen Grainne, Lord Llyr and Lady Thetis. Some of the council felt they should be accorded royal status and housed in royal apartments while others took the view that, as in the case of Queen Grainne, an enemy of the state, and Lord Llyr, a potential traitor, they should be quartered in a secure area with armed guards.

Morfan pointed out that as they were coming in their ships, they may wish to stay aboard, but Ceriddwen dismissed that suggestion out of hand.

'Too easy for them to make mischief then flee under cover of darkness unless we chain their ships to the quay. No, that won't do at all.' She thumped her staff on the floor for attention. 'Enough! I have decided! They will stay in the apartments next door to those of Lady Morrigan and Queen Andraste. My word is final.'

The room fell silent as everyone digested this. It was an insult, yet not an insult. The Morrigan and Andraste were important high-born women — Andraste a queen, but not a fairy queen, elves being lower in status than fairies, and the Morrigan, a fearsome, aristocratic fairy in her own right, but not a queen. Ceriddwen was skirting the very edges of acceptable protocol, but no one dared contradict her.

Later that evening, during dinner in the Great Hall, Molly quizzed Morfan about the Samhain festivities. Brighid had already informed her she was scheduled to have several fittings with Holda's dressmakers for new gowns in time for the three-day celebrations.

'As a royal princess, you will have to outshine everyone… apart from the Queen, of course,' she added hastily. 'Why do I always have to explain this to you, Princess? You should know the festival protocols by now!'

'I haven't actually been to any festivals if you remember,' Molly reminded her. Normally, Molly baulked at the extravagance of new gowns when she already had so many — Ceriddwen was extremely generous regarding her wardrobe allowance — but this time all she could think about was how she would have to look her best in case she bumped into Lord Taliesin. The very thought of him made her go weak at the knees, and she was particularly excited at the prospect of the Masqued Ball. Brighid said it was customary for everyone to try and outdo each other with the originality of their masques and costumes. She wondered about Lord Taliesin's disguise and felt sure she would recognise him no matter how good his masque. Molly asked Mistress Holda to have her best designers produce her something extraordinary and beautiful.

'You shall have a masque like no other!' she promised.

Morfan smiled at Molly, enjoying her enthusiastic excitement.

'We'll have a wonderful time as usual, despite Lord Nudd.'

'So, will Samhain start at the usual time?' Molly asked, face aglow. She may have been kept away from previous festivals, but now she felt wonderfully alive, her new-found attraction to Lord Taliesin giving her a courage she didn't know she possessed.

'Of course.' Morfan grinned. 'The official preparations started as soon as my mother gave the go ahead, but everyone prepares weeks in advance, no one wants to miss out on Samhain. It'll be too dark after dinner, but we can go and have a look around the festival grounds tomorrow.'

Morfan kept his promise, and they went for an exploratory tour of the festival area the following morning. Preparations were in full swing; a huge pavilion had already been erected, surrounded by lots of smaller marquees, a large market area packed with stalls waiting to be stocked with enticing goods, and workers were busily raking fresh soil on a racetrack overlooked by a covered grandstand festooned in banners and bunting fluttering in the fresh autumn breeze. Molly couldn't wait!

However, despite the whirl of excited activity, Ceriddwen made sure Molly's feet were kept firmly on the ground by summoning her the next afternoon to inform her they were riding out the following morning. Molly was intrigued. She had never ridden with Ceriddwen nor, for that matter, ever witnessed her riding a horse.

Next day she arrived at the stables bright and early, bemused to see the yard full of mounted troops bristling with weapons, their horses and unicorns caparisoned in woven mesh-like armour around their chests, flanks and faces, each warrior carrying a huge shield emblazoned with Ceriddwen's insignia: a crown with four latticed points representing the Four Gates.

'What's going on?' she asked Jarol as he led Flambeaux to the mounting block.

'I don't know, Your Highness, you will have to ask Epona,' he replied, checking her stirrup leathers. Molly spotted Tabitha tightening Merrily's girth and nudged Flambeaux across the yard to join her.

'Why all the mounted troops?' she whispered to Tabitha, now in the saddle steadying Merrily who was sidestepping nervously, eyeing her snorting, amour-clad companions.

'Didn't the Queen tell you? We're going to meet Lord Dubh!'

'Lord Dubh?' Molly frowned as she tried to remember where she'd heard the name before. 'Isn't that who told Lord Nudd about Prince Gwion?'

Tabitha snorted in derision, then clucked soothingly to the normally placid Merrily, who was now tossing her head and fighting the bit. 'Lord Dubh would rather cut his tongue out than tell Gwynn ap Nudd anything! He probably got it from one of his spies.'

'But who IS Lord Dubh?' asked a mystified Molly.

'King of the Gnome people,' Tabitha announced just as Ceridwen made her appearance atop a magnificent black stallion standing about two hands taller than Flambeaux, with Morfan and Lleu by her side on their usual mounts. She saw Molly and waved her over.

'All set?' She smiled down from her huge horse, then turned to Morfan and gave the signal to leave. They trotted out of the stable yard and down the road, yellow autumn leaves swirling in their wake like beautiful golden butterflies. Once they had settled into a comfortable steady pace, chatting and laughing in the warm sunshine, Molly felt brave enough to ask Ceriddwen about Lord Dubh. The Queen was in a benevolent mood, and readily answered.

'I have asked Lord Dubh to meet us at a village called Fell Oak which is about four hours ride from here,' she explained.

'He occupies lands near the Western Gate, roughly a day's ride away, so it was reasonable to ask him to meet us halfway.'

'But why are we meeting him?' Molly persisted. Ceriddwen's skittish stallion tossed his head, shying as a startled bird flew past, and Molly found herself impressed by Ceriddwen's expert handling of her powerful steed.

'As you already know,' replied Ceriddwen, reining in her mount, 'we're probably heading for war with the goblins. I did tell you recently that we would be riding out to muster support, and as Lord Nudd grievously wronged the gnome people by blaming them for the genocide of the Anunnaki, Lord Dubh will be more than willing to rally his people to the cause.'

'Tabitha believes one of Lord Nudd's spies told him about Prince Gwion. How many spies do you think he has?' Molly ventured.

'I imagine he has many, although it troubles me greatly that he has managed to spy on us with such impunity!'

'How does he manage to recruit spies? I don't understand what fairies would have to gain from spying on their own kin. The only reason I can think of is some sort of blackmail.'

Ceriddwen gave an eloquent shrug. 'Lord Nudd is a wily and persuasive liar, Molly. He tried to spread rumours that it was I who blamed Lord Dubh for the genocides, but of course, Lord Dubh was having none of it. However, I believe you are correct — he will be using some sort of coercion to exert power over his spies, and I intend to find out exactly what he is up to.'

She then turned to chat with Lleu, and Molly sensibly refrained from further comment, concentrating on enjoying the sights and sounds of the countryside. Outriders from the vanguard were sent ahead to make sure the way was free from danger of attack and to announce the progress of the royal cavalcade. Workers called and waved to them from farms and fields filled with haystacks and ricks of straw. People thronged the roadsides through the villages, running alongside the horses, laughing, and cheering, tossing flowers and fruit, and holding their children aloft for the Queen's blessing. Some of the guards lifted children onto the front of their saddles for a ride, eliciting screams of delight. Ceriddwen smiled and nodded, waving to them all, and told Molly to do likewise.

'Messengers have been sent along the way announcing our arrival and the people will be eager to see their new princess. Hold yourself erect as Mother Arianrhod has taught you and wear the glamour of your royal blood. Never forget that you are also a queen in your own right.' Molly was astounded that the haughty, imperious Ceriddwen should accord her such favour. Ceriddwen smiled as she noticed the shocked look on Molly's face.

'Don't look so surprised, Molly. The cauldron discovered your ancestry, and it never lies. I would be no Queen if I denied a sister queen her birth right.'

Molly hoped if she really was a queen, she would be loved as much as Ceriddwen obviously was. Despite the looming threat of war, she felt that same deep sense of peace and belonging she experienced when she first crossed the threshold into Ceriddwen's domain.

To reach the village of Fell Oak, they had to travel through miles of huge, ancient forest. Molly marvelled at the size and age of the trees, their huge overhanging branches twisting up and out of the way, allowing her pass beneath them undisturbed, thickets of brambles encroaching on the pathways doing the same. The mounted troops were amazed by this, regarding Molly with even more awe and respect.

Morfan was riding with her now and told her the forests were the domain of Lord Cernunnos and the forest fairies, and although this part of the forest was ablaze with glorious autumn colours of red, gold and copper, it would soon become dark and impenetrable. Cernunnos had arranged for a guide to meet them further along the track. Molly noticed the path disappearing rapidly into the dense undergrowth and even with her power to manipulate trees and bushes, she could see pushing their way through would be almost impossible.

'Someone approaching!' called one of the troops, drawing their attention to a deer making its dainty way down the track carrying someone on its back. As the deer drew closer, Molly saw the rider was a forest fairy, who appeared to have the same bark-like skin and twiggy hair as Lord Cernunnos. Her tunic was made from some sort of woven plant fabric and her boots constructed from thick, tough-looking leaves. She had a blowpipe slung across her back and a belt crammed with lethal–looking darts. The deer stopped in front of them, ears twitching as the fairy woman slid from its back and bowed to Ceriddwen.

'I bring greetings from Lord Cernunnos, Your Majesty. My name is Birca, I am your guide to Fell Oak.'

'Thank you, Birca,' Ceriddwen acknowledged graciously. 'We are ready to follow.'

Birca bowed again, then leapt nimbly astride her deer, and headed back down the path followed by Ceriddwen and the rest of the riders, their jingling harnesses and snorting horses disturbing the silence of this deep, dark part of the forest.

The much larger horses and unicorns lumbered gamely behind the little deer as she jinked along overhanging tunnels of honeysuckle and hawthorn, and narrow trails through tightly packed hazel trees and holly bushes, her white hindquarters flashing in the gloom as she leapt across streams and fallen logs until eventually, they emerged into a large clearing. Birca stopped and turned to face them. 'Welcome to Fell Oak, Your Majesty!'

Molly's mouth fell open in wonder. She had assumed Fell Oak would be a village like any other, but now she could hardly believe her eyes. The entire village was built into the forest canopy, with pretty tree houses crowded amongst the branches high above, joined by walkways along the huge oak, beech, and chestnut branches, with spiral staircases winding around some of the massive trunks. Baskets overflowing with beautiful flowers and trailing plants hung everywhere and she could see comfortable-looking seats hanging from some of the larger branches. An over-sized pavilion tent had been erected in the clearing and a group of shaggy dun-coloured ponies were tethered nearby, contentedly munching hay. Lord Dubh had already arrived.

As soon as they entered the clearing, Lord Cernunnos emerged from the pavilion, bowing to Ceriddwen as Lleu helped her dismount.

'Greetings, Your Majesty. I trust you had a pleasant journey?'

'We did indeed, Lord Cernunnos. It was good to be out amongst my people again and to introduce them to Princess Molly.'

Cernunnos turned to Molly, who was laughing at Morfan's gallant attempts to help her dismount before she leapt from Flambeaux's back of her own accord. He was making sure he was displaying perfect protocol in front of his mother and the troops.

'Greetings, Your Highness,' Cernunnos boomed at Molly, bowing with a flourish, and after welcoming the rest of the royal party, ushered everyone into the pavilion. Comfortable cushioned seats were set out around a table amply supplied with drinking vessels and large jugs of wine, ale, water, and pots of tea, alongside beautiful crystal carafes of honey mead. Bowls of fruit & nuts were laid out beside platters of bread, cheese, cold meats, various pies, eggs, and bowls of golden, freshly churned butter. Another series of plates was filled with cream cakes, strawberry tarts, chocolate cakes and scones. Molly's stomach began to growl, and she realised just how hungry she was at the sight of the delicious-looking spread.

However, business came first, and once they were settled comfortably, Cernunnos' major domo announced Lord Dubh and his wife Lady Froya, along with several other official-looking gnomes. Lord Dubh was a squat stocky man with swarthy skin, his hair braided into innumerable plaits covering his head. His beard was braided in a similar fashion — the plaits appearing to have been stiffened with wax and splayed out in a strange fan-shape beneath his chin. Lady Froya was small and delicate with the same swarthy skin as her husband — her hair, also braided, was wound into a tall conical shape, secured on top of her head by lethal-looking bejewelled pins.

They both approached Ceriddwen, bowing and curtseying in turn, their faces wreathed in smiles. 'Your Majesty!' cried Lord Dubh. 'It has been too long. We are beside ourselves with joy to meet with you today.' At another time and place Molly may have thought the gnome king was over-egging the custard, but the couple's sheer pleasure at meeting Ceriddwen was heart-warmingly obvious. Ceriddwen clapped her hands in delight, apparently such good friends with Lord Dubh that the usual formal protocol was deemed unnecessary.

'Sit down, sit down, my friends, it does my heart good to see you both in such robust health after your trials with Lord Nudd.' Lord Dubh's face darkened slightly but Ceriddwen made a dismissive gesture with her hand saying, 'Tsk! Do not fret, Lord Dubh. We shall make merry and plot his downfall, for we have his undoing in our midst!'

'How so, Your Majesty?' Lord Dubh asked, frowning through a mouthful of bread and cheese.

'I take it the great news hasn't reached the gnome kingdom yet. I felt sure Lord Nudd's spies would have spread the glad tidings quickly, but then, considering how it exposes his evil doing, perhaps it is not surprising he keeps it to himself!'

'The lands around the Western Gate are fortunately far from Lord Nudd,' murmured Lord Dubh, frowning again. 'But what is this great news?'

'My dear friend,' Ceriddwen turned and gestured to Molly with a flourish saying, 'allow me to introduce you to my granddaughter, Princess Molly, one of only two surviving carriers of the Royal Blood of the Anunnaki, living proof that Lord Nudd's attempted genocide has failed.'

Although still acutely embarrassed by the attention her new-found status generated, Molly assumed her royal expression, smiling, and nodding politely as the gnomes regarded her in open-mouthed astonishment. After a few moments, they bowed in unison, still staring in amazement.

'But, if I may be so bold, who is the other survivor, Your Majesty?' asked Lady Froya, in a surprisingly deep voice for such a little woman.

'Princess Molly has a son who is residing with his human family until he comes of age. We must wait until then before he claims his birth right.' The gnomes nodded sagely.

'Very wise, Your Majesty,' agreed Lord Dubh, 'although hopefully not too long, for time moves capriciously between the worlds. Do we know what age he is at present?'

'We are not at liberty to disclose such information,' Ceriddwen replied smoothly. 'I do hope you won't take offence, my friend, but the utmost secrecy is required.'

'We understand all too well,' Lady Froya cut in before her husband could reply. 'The matter will not be spoken of again until we have your leave to do so.'

'Thank you for your discretion.' Ceriddwen rewarded her with a dazzling smile. 'Now, let us relax and enjoy the delicious food Lord Cernunnos has provided before we get down to the business at hand.'

Molly sat impassively throughout this exchange. If she had any vestige of maternal feelings or instincts, they were firmly buried by Ceriddwen's enchantment. Molly was completely oblivious to this. She listened politely to the talk of her son — she knew who he was, and that Ceriddwen would send for him eventually, but until that happened, the enchantment kept her firmly detached and unconcerned. She was living in the present moment, not the past or the distant future.

When they finished their meal, the discussions of an alliance against Lord Nudd began in earnest with officials and notaries from both parties taking notes and drawing up lengthy contracts for signing. Although they were good friends, Ceriddwen and Lord Dubh took their affairs of state and security seriously, leaving no room for misunderstandings or breaches of protocol on either side.

Molly and Tabitha were excused from these protracted discussions, and spent a pleasant afternoon with Lady Flidais, Lord Cernunnos' wife, a charming hostess who took them on a guided tour of the tree-top village. They enjoyed meeting and chatting with forest fairy families in their cosy homes until the negotiations were finally over and it was time to mount up and follow Birca through the forest again. Darkness was falling as they left the forest, and Molly was delighted and dazzled by hundreds of beautiful little fireflies, summoned by Lord Cernunnos, to light the way and ensure their safe return. Morfan told her they were so bright that they were also employed to light up the Samhain evening festivities.

When an exhausted and happy Molly finally collapsed into bed that night, she fell asleep immediately, and dreamed of Samhain and Lord Taliesin.

Sixteen

Maps and Ley Lines

After the initial emotional meeting and introductions with Harry and Xander, Ceriddwen quickly regained her composure, announcing that they must address the council members immediately, and appraise them of their concerns. Without further ado, Harry and Xander were whisked along another corridor towards huge double doors flanked on either side by two enormous guards who stood aside to allow them entry. They were then confronted by a large group of fairy men and women seated around a large circular table. To one side, beneath glorious stained-glass windows, several maps were laid out on long trestle tables. On the other side, a group of fairy women stood in a circle around a large cauldron. Harry shivered involuntarily; he was more afraid than he cared to admit. He was also discomfited by the fact he couldn't understand a word being spoken and had no idea what was going on. Once the meeting and introductions were over, the fairies had lapsed into their own language. He was also unnerved by Xander's sudden ability to converse with Morfan and Taliesin in the fairy tongue.

'How come you can suddenly speak the lingo?' he hissed to Xander, who looked at him in surprise.

'What do you mean?'

'You're chatting away to them in their own language — I haven't a clue what's going on!'

'No, I'm not...' began Xander, then stopped with a puzzled look on his face. 'Yes, I am! I just wasn't aware of it; that's really weird!' Before he could say anything else, a door behind the table was thrown open.

'Please be upstanding for Her Majesty the Queen!' announced an official from the open doorway.

Everyone around the table rose and bowed as Ceriddwen swept through the door, waiting until she had settled herself into an elaborately carved ebony chair before sitting down again. After a quick word with Ceriddwen, Lleu stood up and began to address the council. To Harry's relief he spoke in English.

'My Lords and Ladies of the Council, please allow me to introduce our beloved Prince Gwion's son, Harry, and his son, Xander, blood princes of the Royal House, here to bring news of Princess Molly.'

Harry stood rooted to the spot, feeling deeply uncomfortable, as they were subjected in equal measure to applause, gasps of amazement, and a few frowns of mistrust. He pondered wryly for a moment on Xander's initial scepticism of Molly's tales of Sidhthean as here he was, taking it all in his stride, apparently far more at ease than his father. The room was a cacophony of noise as everyone absorbed the news, calling excitedly to each other across the table and around the room until Ceriddwen rose to her feet and thumped her staff on the floor.

'Silence!' she thundered, a ferocious expression on her face. 'I will not countenance such bad manners in front of our guests!'

As the room fell silent, Harry and Xander had a glimpse of just how fearsome Ceriddwen could be and resolved to watch their step. Harry was becoming more afraid by the minute, although Xander still appeared annoyingly relaxed.

Turning to face them, Ceriddwen demanded, 'Which of you will address the council?'

Taking a deep breath Harry stepped forward, palms sweating. 'I will, Your Majesty.'

Everyone listened intently as he told them about the portal and Molly's gradual emergence from her enchantment, along with her abject terror at the imminent arrival of Lord Nudd and his dragon.

'We are also concerned by the fact Prince Morfan indicated this is not something you were expecting to happen?' It was a question and Harry sounded braver than he felt as he asked it, but to his relief, Ceriddwen nodded in agreement.

'Yes, we are concerned,' she conceded. 'The princess appears to have genuine and unforeseen fears as she comes out of the enchantment, but we do have an unfortunate theory. Come, let us show you.' Ceriddwen rose to her feet, and with Lleu and Taliesin behind her, strode in a rustle of swishing silk, across to the tables where the maps were spread out. Harry and Xander stared at them in confusion. That they were maps was obvious, but not the kind of maps they were familiar with.

'I assume you are familiar with ley lines?' Taliesin challenged Harry. The suppressed hostility between the two men was palpable. Harry bit down an angry retort. His rival exuded all the potent strength and virility he no longer possessed — the testosterone was positively fizzing as they eyed one another. Harry wisely decided discretion was the better part of valour.

'Yes, as a matter of fact I am,' he said through gritted teeth.

Taliesin gave him a long, cool stare before saying, 'In that case, have a look at this.' He pointed to a map with a series of lines joined into geometric shapes, with identical lines directly above. 'These are maps of all the known ley lines in our realm.'

He traced a finger along the bottom lines. 'The lower lines are our ley lines and the lines above are the corresponding lines in your world.'

'And how are these relevant to what is happening to Molly?' asked Harry.

Again, Taliesin gave him that long, cool stare. 'I am just about to explain,' he replied with exaggerated patience. Harry felt like punching him on his very straight patrician nose. 'As I am sure you know, ley lines are caused by geopathic stress beneath the earth's crust.' Harry inclined his head in agreement as Taliesin continued: 'This stress can be caused by any number of reasons, underwater rivers and streams or underground caverns and mineral deposits. In your world, geopathic stress is also caused by sewer pipes, electrical cables, underground railways and so on, but most importantly,' he paused to emphasise the point, 'geopathic stress can be caused by portals.'

Ceriddwen swept an arm across the maps. 'These are all the ley lines we are so far aware of, and, as I am sure Lord Taliesin was about to say, none of them represent the portal in Princess Molly's garden. That fact is causing us great concern!'

Harry's eyes widened in horror. 'Are you saying that Lord Nudd has tracked the co-ordinates of an area of geopathic stress unknown to you and discovered another portal?'

'Yes, that would appear to be the case,' admitted Taliesin.

'Were you aware that he had the means and skill to carry out such an exploration?' demanded Harry, barely attempting to keep the accusatory tone out of his voice.

Taliesin glared at him with barely suppressed fury. Sensing the ever-mounting tension between the two men, Lleu quickly took control of the situation.

'Pure luck, I would say, on Lord Nudd's part,' he cut in smoothly. 'We are far more technologically advanced than goblins. I would imagine they came across it by accident in one of their mines.'

'You may be more advanced than the goblins, but that doesn't alter the fact that Lord Nudd is in control of a portal you know nothing about and plans to use it to murder Molly and gain access to our world!' Harry was dangerously close to losing his temper and he fumed beneath Lleu's sympathetic gaze. He couldn't believe how jealous he was of Taliesin and how afraid he felt.

'And what exactly is *my* role in this fiasco?' Everyone turned to look at Xander, who had been listening quietly to all that was being said. 'Molly seems to think I am vitally important to the cause, and the sooner you tell my father and I what we need to do,' he said, glaring angrily around the room, 'the sooner we can leave here and take the necessary steps to try and stop this goblin and his dragons!'

'Dragons are the least of our problems!' Ceriddwen retorted. 'The princess can communicate telepathically with all dragon species — if any dragons come through the portal, all she has to do is tell them to lie down and sleep and they will do so. It's what she herself might do that worries me.'

'And what might that be?' Xander shot back. Ignoring him, Ceriddwen paced up and down the floor, swinging her staff ominously to and fro, causing people to duck as she passed.

'No, the question is this — how do we stop Lord Nudd before he attempts to go through the portal?' She stopped in mid stride, whirled about, strode over to Xander, and without any warning, yanked some strands of glossy black hair from his head.

'Ouch!' he yelled. 'What are you doing?'

'You will see,' Ceriddwen answered enigmatically. 'Ladies of Astarte, prepare the cauldron!' she barked, sweeping back to her ebony chair. 'Lady Tanith, give these to the cauldron.' Tanith collected Xander's hair and gently laid the strands on the surface of the liquid gently bubbling in the large pot.

Harry and Xander watched in fascination as the circle of attendants began to pour herbs from little pouches, and liquids from phials into the cauldron, as another stirred it with a long crystal ladle. With no outward signs of heating, it continued to bubble and simmer, as the women continuously chanted a strange song while they worked. Ceriddwen drummed her fingers impatiently on the table until finally, Tanith presented her with a little jug of the steaming liquid. Another fairy woman brought a large crystal bowl of water and placed it in front of Ceriddwen.

'Ceri, my dear,' Lleu said nervously, 'are you planning to ask the cauldron where the portal is?'

'I am,' Ceriddwen replied. 'And why shouldn't I?'

'You know the cauldron will think it unethical if the portal is in Lord Nudd's kingdom. It would only feel obliged to tell you if Lord Nudd had invaded a portal that belonged to you.'

'He plans to invade Princess Molly's garden. She is our princess, therefore, he invades our territory!'

'I must admit I hadn't thought of it like that.' Lleu appeared somewhat reassured. 'I suppose it's worth a try.'

Harry and Xander looked at each other. 'Totally surreal!' hissed Xander. 'They're going to ask a pot of boiling soup to tell them where Lord Nudd's portal is and Lleu's worried the pot might think it's unethical!'

'Molly did tell us about the cauldron, though,' Harry reminded him.

'I know,' groaned Xander. 'How on earth did we get ourselves into this?'

'Well, that's just it,' whispered Harry with a rueful smile, 'we're not on Earth — we're in an entirely different dimension of time and space!'

'Why do you think she wanted my hair?' Xander asked, wincing as he rubbed his head.

'I don't know,' Harry whispered back, 'but I'm going to ask right now.' Drawing himself up to his full height, Harry cleared his throat. 'Your Majesty, may I ask why you have given Xander's hair to the cauldron?'

Ceriddwen gave him an irritated look as though he should already know the answer, then realising that Harry and Xander had no idea what was going on, flashed them an indulgent smile. 'The cauldron will extract DNA and genetic information from Xander's hair. By chemical analysis it will also be able to identify what part of your world you come from and what areas you have recently visited. Given that information, it will deduce what your nearest ley lines are, including any we have not yet mapped, and the corresponding ley lines in our world. It's very simple, really.'

'I understand what you are saying about the DNA and chemical analysis, but the manner of obtaining it doesn't seem very scientific,' Harry responded dubiously.

'It is "very scientific", as you put it, my child, but you will soon learn that our ways are very different from yours,' Ceriddwen replied patiently. 'And from what I have learned, you are more interested in the natural world than the scientific world. You are a trained druid, are you not?'

'I am, Your Majesty, and I have to say I do find the cauldron fascinating, if a little unorthodox, to our way of thinking.'

'Then I am sure you will find this most interesting. Approach and learn!' Harry and Xander stood beside the Queen and watched as she poured liquid from the jug into the crystal bowl. 'The crystal activates the properties in the liquid and breaks them down into groups belonging to ley lines in all geographical areas. If an unfamiliar ley line is detected, it will pinpoint the exact area.'

As they watched, the contents of the crystal bowl began to swirl about in separate little whirlpools until finally, they coalesced into a single whirlpool that reared out of the bowl in a swirling liquid column. Harry and Xander stared in horrified fascination as the shape of a woman wrapped in a black hooded cloak gradually appeared in its midst. The men realised instantly that they were looking at a hologram.

'The Cailleach!' breathed Lleu. 'The portal is in the Cailleach's lair!'

'How did the goblins manage that?' Morfan appeared mystified. The black-shrouded figure in the hologram faded as the column of watery liquid gradually began to subside. After a few moments of shocked silence, everyone began to talk and shout at the same time.

'How can I think when you are all gabbling like a gaggle of geese?' Ceriddwen erupted furiously. 'I'll throw the next person who speaks out of turn into the tower, so think on that before you open your prattling mouths again!'

Harry and Xander wondered if they were included in the threat, which did nothing to alleviate Harry's fearful feelings. They were keen to find out who this Cailleach was and listened intently. Lleu, ever courteous and observant of protocol, whispered something to Ceriddwen, who nodded, and turned to speak to them directly, all signs of fury now erased from her smiling face. Harry decided his grandmother had more faces than the town hall clock.

'My dear grandchildren, I am aware you are strangers in our world and unfamiliar with our ways. You have witnessed my cauldron in action and now I shall explain to you what has been revealed.' Everyone waited in hushed expectation. 'It appears that Lord Nudd has discovered a portal, and therefore a ley line, within the Cailleach's domain. It would appear he has dug a mine deep into her territory, and, as we thought, come across the portal by accident.' She paused a moment to let this information sink in. 'The Cailleach is a most spiteful and venomous creature who rules her people, the trolls, harshly. Her land is mostly swamps and bogs, very little grows there as the air is toxic to most other living beings.' Ceriddwen looked apologetically at Lord Taliesin. 'As Justiciar of the Four Gates, it falls on you, Lord Taliesin, to venture into her den and find out if she is aware of Lord Nudd's activities. Take Lord Varik and your best men with you. We are all fearful for Princess Molly's safety, none more so than you. Impress upon the Cailleach's black heart that she will incur the full force of our wrath should she impede you or fail to cooperate in any way. Make sure you show her the Royal Seal!'

'At once, Your Majesty!' Taliesin leapt to attention, saluted Ceriddwen, and swiftly left the room.

Feeling like a gauche schoolboy, Harry held up his arm. Ceriddwen noticed immediately. 'Speak, Harry.'

'Forgive me, Your Majesty,' he began, feeling flustered and uncomfortable, 'but we still have questions that need answering.'

Ceriddwen gave him a level gaze before nodding. 'Proceed. I will answer if I can.'

'Thank you.' Harry took a deep breath and ploughed on. 'The portal in Molly's garden caused great distress to the plants and I couldn't figure out what was causing that, but now I'm wondering if it might have something to do with where this new ley line is situated. You say the Cailleach's land is mostly swamp and bogs with a toxic atmosphere?'

Ceriddwen nodded. 'Yes, that is so; Lord Taliesin is aware of that and will spend as little time with the Cailleach as possible.'

'And very little plant life exists there?'

'Yes, that is also correct, mostly mosses and specialised fungi.'

'So, not only do we have the prospect of Lord Nudd and his army invading us, but we also have the all-too real threat of our atmosphere being polluted by poisonous gases from the Cailleach's bogs and swamplands?'

'I see what you mean,' mused Ceriddwen. 'We must take this into careful consideration.' She creased her brow in thought for a few moments before replying, 'The goblins breathe the same air as we do, yet they appear unaffected, I wonder why that should be?'

'Why were the plants soothed by my harp music if it's the toxic air from this dimension that's harming them?' Xander put in quickly.

'You healed the plants with your music?' Ceriddwen and Lleu exchanged glances.

'Yes — when Molly's friend asked us to help, she told us the only thing that would close the portal was music. My father did tell you about Jimmy Thomson!' Xander was beginning to feel exasperated.

'Indeed, but I dismissed that as mere human superstition, which it is, and I'm not convinced it's toxic air doing the damage, either,' Ceriddwen continued, a worried frown darkening her face. 'It seems you have inherited your grandfather's musical gift, which has been enhanced by the blood of the Annunaki and the Flowered Ones inherited from your mother. This explains the importance of your presence when Lord Nudd makes his move.'

'But I only came along to help my father,' protested Xander. 'We didn't know anything about Lord Nudd, or you, for that matter, so how would anyone know my presence was essential?'

Ceriddwen was unperturbed by Xander's outburst. 'Obviously, you have inherited the strong sixth sense inherent in all members of the fairy tribes, something most humans have forgotten about. That would explain why you so readily accompanied your father. You have much to learn about us and our ways.'

Harry tried to keep his voice steady, his heart thumping, fit to burst, in case he said the wrong thing. He felt as though he was tiptoeing through a minefield.

'But much as we would also love to learn more about you and your people, Your Majesty, time is of the essence. We don't know how advanced Lord Nudd's invasion plans are. That is why we are here, to try and head him off at the pass, so to speak.'

Ceriddwen gave him a quizzical look, but before she could answer, Lleu said, 'We are all tired and overwrought. Lord Taliesin and Lord Varik will reach the Cailleach's lands by nightfall. As soon as they make contact, they will send word if there is anything they think we need to know urgently.'

'How will they do that?' asked Xander.

'We have very swift pigeons,' answered Lleu.

'Pigeons!' cried Xander in amazement.

'For sure,' replied Lleu smoothly. 'It's the quickest way!'

'Not that fast, surely?' scoffed Xander, instantly regretting his outburst at the sight of Ceriddwen's deepening scowl.

'That is because they are creatures of this world, not yours,' Lleu snapped back before Ceriddwen reacted

'As opposed to a telephone,' sighed Xander.

SEVENTEEN

Samhain (Summer's End)

Molly woke on day one of the long-awaited Samhain celebrations with a shiver of anticipation. Light streamed through the gauzy embroidered curtains at her bedroom window, casting little spots of dancing sunlight around the room. She yawned and stretched, then hugged herself in excitement until Brighid tapped on the bedroom door telling her she would be late for breakfast if she didn't get a move on. She slid out of bed and padded into the bathroom, giving herself a quick wash; she would have a long luxurious bath before tonight's feasting and entertainments.

'Hurry, Molly!' Brighid chided. 'You know how the Queen hates tardiness.'

'Oh, Brighid!' Molly said, laughing and grabbing hold of the startled fairy's hands and whirling her into a dance around the room. 'I'm so excited! I can't believe Samhain's finally here!'

'Princess,' spluttered Brighid, 'the Queen is waiting. Enough of this tomfoolery, if you please!'

Still laughing, Molly released her flustered and unwilling partner, and pulled on her boots. 'I'm ready now. Sorry, Brighid!'

Brighid shook her head, smiling and out of breath, as Molly skipped through the door and along the maze of corridors to the breakfast room, her glorious russet curls tumbling down her back in abandoned glee.

'Of course, you will be expected to perform some little duties today,' Ceriddwen advised over breakfast, adding in response to Molly's puzzled expression, 'the children will be thrilled to receive prizes from their princess. There is no question of disappointing them, so please be sure to check the games list with Taranis — he will let you know what games you should attend.'

Taranis was events manager for the eight festivals celebrated every year and took his position very seriously. He made sure everything ran effortlessly and ruled his staff with a rod of iron, including royal princesses who were expected to pull their weight. When Molly presented herself, he handed her the list of children's morning events.

First off was the pet show. As Molly made her way through the market thronged with happy, smiling people, she met Morfan strolling arm-in-arm with a handsome young man whose hair was dressed in the braided style Molly now understood meant high warrior status.

'Morfan,' she cried delightedly, 'I missed you at breakfast — I hoped you weren't ill today of all days.'

Laughing and ruffling her unruly curls as he wrapped her in a huge bear hug, he said, 'I'm not ill and I do like your hair loose like this, it suits you!'

'Thank you, but aren't you going to introduce me to your friend?' Molly replied archly. Morfan's companion smiled and bowed politely, and Morfan immediately became contrite.

'Of course, of course. My apologies! Allow me to introduce Lord Varik. Lord Varik, Princess Molly.'

'Delighted to finally meet you, Princess,' Lord Varik murmured, brushing Molly's proffered hand with a light kiss.

'Please, call me Molly,' she pleaded, 'unless the Queen is listening,' she added with a giggle. 'But you must excuse me, gentlemen — I have a very important engagement and I must fly.' She started to hurry away then turned, calling over her shoulder, 'You didn't tell me why you missed breakfast!'

Morfan laughed. 'Tell you later!' he said, throwing his arm around Varik's shoulders before disappearing into the milling crowd.

Molly's morning flew by; she held kittens and puppies, and all manner of cuddly and not so cuddly pets; she laughed herself silly at the antics of the donkeys in their race and had enormous fun joining in the sack and three-legged races. Fairy children enjoyed the same fun and games as humans, and when Brighid came to find her at lunchtime, she was appalled to find a muddy and dishevelled Princess Molly surrounded by a crowd of besotted children.

'Your Highness, your appearance is most inappropriate for a royal princess!' she cried in dismay, attempting to brush some of the mud from Molly's bodice.

'How am I supposed to get to know the children if I remain aloof and unapproachable?' Molly laughed, tucking stray curls behind her ears. 'We had a wonderful time, didn't we, children?' Little heads nodded enthusiastically, but shrank from the sight of Brighid's frowning face.

'Shoo, be off with you, the princess has to leave!' Brighid flapped her hands at them and they fled in terror, after begging Molly to come back and play with them soon.

'You'll have to change into a fresh gown for lunch,' grumbled Brighid. 'We'll have to hurry, or you'll be late.'

Molly sighed. 'Brighid, I'm not changing into a clean dress just to get it filthy during the truffle hunt!'

'But...but the Queen will notice and think I am neglecting my duties. Molly...I think...'

Molly cut her off. 'Leave the Queen to me. I'll wash my face and hands and brush my hair. That will have to do. Go and have your own lunch and I'll see you later.' Brighid wasn't convinced, and gave Molly a dark look before stalking off, back ramrod straight in affronted indignation.

Lunch was served in the Royal Pavilion, and if Ceriddwen noticed Molly's mud-splattered gown, she made no comment. Molly sat with Tabitha and Oonagh, all chattering excitedly about the truffle hunt and who was favourite to win. People came from all over to compete, bringing their best pigs to sniff out the pungent fungi, and competition was fierce. Each truffle hunter and his pig were accompanied by a pair of monitors to ensure fairness, no undue damage to the forest floor and no cheating.

'I thought it was natural for pigs to forage in the forest,' stated Molly. 'Why do we need to monitor them?'

Tabitha explained that monitors were introduced because pigs, if unchecked, cause a great deal of damage. A different area was designated each year so that the pigs could uproot the denser undergrowth, allowing seeds and other forest plants room to grow and flourish. Constant disturbance damaged flowering bulbs and other spring plants so access was limited, and Taranis handpicked each monitor himself.

'It all adds to the madcap fun!' she said, laughing, and looking Molly up and down added, 'and so will the sight of you traipsing around in that gown! Why didn't you wear breeches?'

Tabitha and Oonagh were wearing their usual riding breeches with sturdy padded jerkins over woollen tops. Molly looked down at herself and let out a peal of laughter.

'I suppose I do look ridiculous dressed like a princess to go chasing after pigs!'

'You could always tuck it up,' suggested Oonagh, pointing to Molly's skirt. 'Pull the back between your legs and tuck the front and back into your belt.' As Molly obediently did as she suggested, Tabitha and Oonagh nodded in approval.

'You look as though you're wearing fancy breeches.'

'Quite fetching really!'

Molly couldn't quite decide whether they were laughing at her or not and giving a dismissive shrug said, 'Too late to change now, this will have to do. Let's go and see these pigs!'

The competing pigs were held in pens at the forest edge and the noise was deafening with people shouting to each other over the relentless squealing and grunting, and the overpowering smell made the women's eyes water. Tabitha introduced Molly to a jolly little fairy called Tuke and his enormous red boar, Soffo. Tuke was a veteran competitor and the current reigning champion. Molly scratched Soffo's ears. He was quite the ugliest boar she had ever seen, with his little beady eyes and huge betusked snout, but he was endearingly friendly, and Molly wished Tuke the best of luck as they moved on to check out the other competitors. It was customary for spectators to follow the hunt and people queued up behind the monitors in charge of their favourites. Her heart skipped a beat as she spotted Morfan and Varik with Lord Taliesin. Tabitha had also seen them and with a mischievous gleam in her eye, propelled Molly towards them.

'Let's go and find out who Morfan's following this year!'

Morfan gave them a welcoming grin as they approached, raising an amused eyebrow at Molly's attire as he swept them a bow, the other men following suit.

'Your Highness.' Varik smiled before giving way to Taliesin, who touched Molly's hand to his lips.

'A great pleasure, Your Highness,' he said, fixing her with a long smouldering look. With her eyes glued to Taliesin's face, Molly was oblivious to the meaningful glances exchanged by the others. Tabitha broke the spell by asking Morfan who he was following this year.

'We were going to follow Iken Faria and his Blue Spot sow,' he replied wistfully, 'but Lord Varik has been recalled for duty. Lord Taliesin has come to fetch him.'

Just about to say what a shame it was, Molly instead found herself nodding, remembering her royal training and etiquette. 'The security of the celebrations must come first,' she said. 'We thank you and look forward to your return soon.'

Unable to keep the twinkle from their eyes, Varik and Taliesin saluted her, bowed to Tabitha and Oonagh, and made their smiling way towards the citadel.

'See you at the Fire Festival tomorrow,' Morfan called to their retreating backs, Varik raising his arm in acknowledgement.

Tabitha and Oonagh decided they would follow Tuke and Soffo, and in the absence of Varik, Molly said she would accompany Morfan following Iken Faria. Mayhem descended as soon as the starting horn was blown. Scores of people and pigs raced through the forest in search of the prize—the biggest and tastiest truffles. The winner would have the honour of presenting the truffles to the Queen and be known thereafter as "Royal Truffle Hunter to the Crown"—a coveted title as the owner enjoyed rich patronage and trade throughout the entire realm. Tuke had held the title for several years and was widely tipped to win again. Soffo had an uncanny nose for rooting out the best truffles in the shortest time, but there were plenty of younger rivals snapping at his heels.

At first, Molly gamely kept pace with Morfan, puffing and panting with the exertion of climbing over fallen logs and splashing through pools and streams. Her arms and legs were scratched and bleeding from crashing through brambles and thick blackthorn bushes—somehow the bushes never quite managed to pull themselves out of her way in time, and an exasperated Molly hurled unladylike expletives at some of the worst offenders. She cursed herself for being so inappropriately dressed. Brighid would have a fit when she saw the state she was in and Morfan wisely decided not to mention Ceriddwen's reaction if she caught sight of Molly's bloodied arms and legs. After a two-hour headlong, exhilarating and ultimately exhausting charge through the forest, several resounding blasts from the finishing horns signalled the hunt was over, and the competitors had to return to the pig pens with their baskets of truffles to await the announcement of the winner.

Her breath coming in great gasps, Molly sank gratefully onto a grassy tussock and put her head between her knees. Her hair was damp with perspiration, hanging around her face in lank ropes, and her heart was pounding fit to burst. Morfan perched himself on a tree stump, looking relaxed and amused. To Molly's disgust, he was hardly out of breath.

'You look as though you've been pulled through a hedge backwards,' he remarked.

'Actually, I've been diving headfirst through hedges, as you very well know!' she retorted.

'Ooh, we are touchy!' Morfan laughed, adding slyly, 'Your bad temper wouldn't have anything to do with a certain Lord Taliesin, would it?'

Beneath her curtain of messy hair, Molly blushed deep crimson. 'What's it got to do with Lord Taliesin?'

'Quite a lot, I would say, judging by the colour of your face!' replied Morfan with a chuckle. 'Worried you're not going to look beautiful at the feast tonight with all these cuts and scratches?'

'I couldn't care less what I look like, because...'

'Because he isn't going to be there.' Morfan finished the sentence for her, adding sadly, 'And neither will Varik, so we can sit and mope together!' Molly's eyes narrowed as she gazed at him with renewed interest. 'You seem very attached to Lord Varik. Is he your best friend or what?'

'Or what.' Morfan smiled. 'He is my beloved; my life partner, and I hate it that his work with my mother's army takes him away from me so much.' He turned away as his eyes filled with tears and Molly, feeling acutely embarrassed, immediately jumped up and threw her arms around him.

'I'm sorry, Morfan, I didn't mean to be insensitive, I just didn't realise how much he meant to you.'

Morfan returned the hug and kissed the top of her unkempt curls. 'It's alright, and your feelings for Taliesin are safe with me,' he murmured into her hair. 'Although he made his feelings for you perfectly obvious today, we all noticed!'

'I...I just thought he was being polite.' She looked up at Morfan, a stricken look on her face. 'I mean, how could someone like Taliesin find a *Plain Jane* like me attractive?'

Morfan gave her an incredulous look. 'Plain Jane? What are you talking about? Who told you that?' Seeing Molly's look of consternation, he cupped her face between his hands and said softly, 'You are one of the most exquisite creatures I have ever seen, and Lord Taliesin has never, to my knowledge, looked at another woman the way he looked at you this afternoon.' Molly's heart did a double somersault as her face flushed red again and then turned pale with shock.

'Please don't say things that aren't true just to spare my feelings, I know I'm plain and uninteresting.' Now it was Molly's turn to be tearful. Morfan gave an exasperated grunt.

'Molly, you are beautiful. Our bards will be writing songs and poems about your gorgeous russet curls and your emerald-green eyes forever more. Whoever made you think you weren't beautiful must have been blind!'

As Molly opened her mouth to protest, another memory from her previous life pushed itself uninvited into her brain — she was holding her father's hand and he was looking down at her fondly as he was saying to someone else, 'Yes, she's a funny wee thing. Pity about the ginger hair — not very attractive — my Scottish genes, unfortunately!' And then it was gone.

Before she could speak, Morfan held up his hand to silence her. 'No, Molly, not another word. You have caught the eye of the most eligible man in the kingdom and it's not because you are ugly!'

'People shouldn't be defined by their looks,' Molly persisted mutinously. 'Many so-called unattractive people are beautiful on the inside. You know what they say, *Beauty is only skin deep.*'

'Well, then, you have the best of both worlds,' Morfan told her crisply. 'Beautiful on the inside and the outside!'

Before Molly could argue further a smart little pony trap drew up beside them with Jarol in the driving seat. He dipped them a bow, announcing that he had been sent to bring the princess home. Morfan waived the offer of a lift, saying he had things to do, and would see Molly later at the feast.

Despite the absence of Taliesin and Varik, Molly and Morfan decided to enjoy themselves anyway, feasting and attending the various entertainments. Molly was dazzled by the colours and extravagant costumes of the revellers and was secretly relieved she had allowed Brighid to override her initial reluctance to wear new gowns, as the beautiful aquamarine velvet dress she was wearing hid all her cuts and bruises. Brighid was outraged by her injuries, immediately insisting Molly wear something that completely covered her arms and decolletage. Ceriddwen had presented her with jewels to compliment her new gowns and Molly was subsequently decked out in a stunning pearl collar with matching drop earrings and bracelets. Morfan let out a long whistle of admiration as she glided down the steps into the outer bailey of the citadel.

'Lord Taliesin will be in for stiff competition tonight,' he whispered wickedly as she took his arm, and she blushed scarlet as usual.

'Shhhh!' she hissed furiously. 'Someone might hear you!'

'You'll be fighting off suitors all night — I shall guard your honour with my life!' he cried, bowing extravagantly.

Molly couldn't help giggling. 'You always make me laugh, Morfan. Let's go and have a wonderful time!'

The feast was traditionally held in the large pavilion once the Truffle Hunt Champion had received his sash and certificate of honour. Tuke had won again, narrowly beating Iken Faria, and was gracious enough to concede that this was most likely his last year as champion. Ceriddwen placed the sash over his head to loud cheers and a stamping of feet — Tuke was extremely popular, and as he held his certificate aloft in triumph, Ceriddwen called for the evening's feasting and revelry to begin.

Molly didn't have time to fret over Taliesin's absence; she was the centre of attention just as predicted by Morfan, surrounded by a buzzing throng of admirers, well-wishers, and the plain curious who were anxious to check out their half-human princess for themselves. Her royal status was further emphasised by Ceriddwen's insistence that four palace guards hover in discreet attendance, the goblin threat always a priority.

She was enthralled by the seemingly endless stream of performers on the pavilion's huge stage: a troupe of elfin acrobatic tumblers from Andraste's army performing a series of impossible-looking stunts, each one more vertiginous and daring than the last. The Morrigan's cavalry thrilled everyone with an energetic Cossack-style dance, leaping and whirling around the stage, and the Infantry Male Voice Choir had the audience cheering and whooping as they sang a succession of rousing battle songs.

When Molly mentioned to Morfan that the performances reminded her very much of something she had seen before, he just smiled and remarked, 'Well, you know where they got it from!'

At that moment, an attendant approached and whispered something into his ear. Dismissing the man with a nod, he turned to Molly saying enigmatically, 'I'll be back soon,' before standing up to shoulder his way through the crowd of rollicking choristers tumbling down from the stage amid cheering and back-slapping, dodging the sloshing tankards of ale being passed to them by an appreciative audience.

As Morfan disappeared, Molly noticed Lleu threading his way through the crowd, patting children's heads, shaking hands, nodding and smiling at everyone until he managed to slip into the empty seat beside her. 'Ah, that's better!' he remarked with a heavy sigh, settling himself comfortably. 'And how are you enjoying the entertainment, my dear?'

'It's amazing!' she enthused. 'Everyone's so talented. I had no idea it would be this good.'

Lleu nodded in agreement. 'Yes, we are extremely blessed.' Then, placing his finger to his lips, he murmured, 'But hush, the next performance is about to begin.'

To Molly's surprise, the curtains opened to reveal Morfan sitting centre stage with a beautifully carved clarsach on his lap as a cloud of brilliant fireflies danced above his head in a dazzling fiery halo. The lights were dimmed, and the noisy pavilion fell silent. As Morfan began to play, the room was enveloped in the most beautiful, ethereal music Molly had ever heard. She closed her eyes and leant against Lleu, allowing the sublime sounds to wash over her, surrounding and filling her with that familiar sense of intense peace and happiness. However, as Morfan played on, she began to feel a bit odd, as though the music was reaching deep into her body and plucking at her insides. Startled, she pulled away from Lleu and sat up straight, rubbing her stomach. Lleu gave her a concerned look.

'What is it?' he asked. 'Are you feeling unwell?'

'I think something I've eaten has given me terrible indigestion,' she replied, wriggling uncomfortably in her seat. 'I could do with some of Brighid's peppermint tea!' She laughed shakily.

Lleu beckoned to one of Molly's guards. 'The princess is feeling unwell, fetch the pony trap!'

'At once, my Lord.' The man bowed and hurried off.

'Oh Lleu, I don't want to make a fuss, I'm sure it'll pass, and I'll be fine soon, really.'

Lleu raised his hand to silence her, a grave look on his face.

'Molly, we're leaving now. This is something that, foolishly, we did not consider. We thought we would have more time before telling you.'

'Telling me what, Lleu?' Molly was beginning to feel quite sick. 'Is there something here I'm allergic to? Do you think I've been poisoned?' Her voice became shrill as she started to panic. Beads of sweat were beginning to form on her forehead and upper lip, and she began to shake uncontrollably. 'What's happening to me, Lleu?' she cried.

Lleu wrapped a comforting arm around her and barked at the other guards. 'Where is the pony trap? The princess must leave immediately!'

The three remaining guards who had been trying to keep curious onlookers away, looked considerably relieved when their colleague came rushing back to tell them Jarol was waiting outside. As the guards cleared a path through the crowd, Lleu swept Molly up into his arms and hurried after them to the waiting pony trap. They set off at a fast gallop and very soon she was lying in the palace hospital.

Ceriddwen had been summoned, and Morfan, who had been oblivious to the commotion during his performance, arrived hot on her heels. The doctors bowed and made way for Ceriddwen as she hurried to Molly's side.

'Is it what we feared?' she asked Lleu as she smoothed Molly's hair from her pale, sweating face. By this time, Molly was semi-conscious and delirious.

'The dragon stirs, and I am afraid she is not strong enough yet.' The fear in Lleu's voice was palpable. The two doctors in attendance quailed as Ceriddwen turned on them, furiously demanding their opinions.

'Well, Your Majesty, we...we...think the fact that she has human blood means her system c...c...cannot cope...' one of them stuttered.

'On the other hand,' the younger doctor cut in smoothly, 'because the dragon has manifested so soon, it could mean she is a very powerful Anunnaki!' The smug look disappeared from his face as Ceriddwen prodded him violently in the chest with her staff, fear for Molly launching one of her fearsome rages.

'So why are you just standing here like the useless fool you are?' she raged. 'Why has she not been put into the crystal monitor?' She prodded him again with the staff, causing him to stumble backwards into Morfan, who caught him with a rueful smile.

'Mother, please, it's not Master Heka's fault, it's mine! I should never have agreed to play tonight. I had no idea it would affect Molly so soon.' Lleu laid his hand on Ceriddwen's arm before she could attack the terrified doctor again.

'Ceri, calm yourself. Morfan speaks the truth. We are all at fault here. We have completely underestimated the Anunnaki power.'

'Molly may die,' Ceriddwen spat our harshly, her voice raw with anger and fear, 'and these fools just stand about doing nothing!'

'Your Majesty,' pleaded the older doctor, a tall, spare man with unruly grey hair and kindly eyes, 'if I may be allowed to offer an opinion?' Ceriddwen's knuckles whitened as she gripped her staff, giving the man a curt nod. He swallowed nervously before continuing: 'I fear the Anunnaki gene is too powerful for our conventional medical expertise, but I understand the gene was originally detected by the cauldron?'

A glimmer of understanding flickered in Ceriddwen's eyes. 'Of course! The cauldron! Thank you for your insight, Master Lenus.' Lenus bowed politely and busied himself, checking Molly's vital signs as Ceriddwen yelled at her attendants, 'Instruct my Ladies of Astarte to bring the cauldron immediately!'

The attendants scurried away and Ceriddwen turned to Molly, who had now lapsed into unconsciousness.

'She's not moving, Lleu,' she said hoarsely. 'Please let us not be too late!' Lleu wrapped her in his arms as she burst into tears. 'It's all my fault! I should have warned Morfan not to play.' She then spun around to face Morfan. 'What melody did you play, anyway?' she demanded.

'A tune Gwion taught me years ago — we couldn't read the script, only the music. He said he found it on a market stall — the stall holder said he bought it from an itinerant goblin who had a bagful of weird and wonderful stuff. The goblin said it was an ancient Anunnaki tune called *Moon Dragon*.'

Understanding began to dawn on Morfan's face. 'Anunnaki,' he repeated, 'it's Anunnaki dragon music!'

'Do you still have the music sheet?' Ceriddwen asked urgently.

'Gwion kept it. He said he wanted to eventually try and translate the script, and as soon as I memorised the tune, he took it back to his quarters.'

Lleu and Morfan exchanged glances. Ceriddwen had decreed that no one should enter Gwion's rooms again after his departure and they had remained firmly locked ever since.

She took a deep breath to try and compose herself. 'Very well,' she said steadily, 'we shall have to unseal Gwion's apartments and search for this music and take it to the Arianrhod. Someone at the Crystal Tower may be able to translate the script.'

She began pacing up and down, berating herself again. 'I should have foreseen this! How could I have been so careless? So complacent?' she cried, smashing her fist into her other hand with such force she cut her palm with the large ruby on her finger.

'No one could have foreseen this, Ceri,' Lleu replied soothingly, beckoning Master Heka over to tend Ceriddwen's bleeding hand. 'We know little of Anunnaki power. The only thing to blame is our failure to understand exactly why the goblin king murdered them. He must have understood their power and how it stood in his way.'

'But why were we unaware of it?' Ceriddwen grabbed a proffered napkin from a hovering attendant and wiped her face. 'We thought they were fairy like us, but we don't even understand their written language, yet a wandering goblin could apparently understand it. I can't bear it!'

'The goblin didn't understand it — he just repeated what he had heard, that's all.' Morfan tried in vain to reassure his mother.

'They were like us,' said Lleu, 'but thousands of years living alongside the dragons must have altered them. We didn't notice because we considered them our kin, and they had no need to use their dragon power against us.'

'Nudd and his network of spies!' Ceriddwen hissed. 'They're everywhere. They must have told him the only way he could gain control of the dragons was to kill the Anunnaki!'

'Hush, my dear, you're becoming much too overwrought. We must remain calm for Molly's sake.' Lleu guided Ceriddwen to a nearby chair. 'You must prepare yourself for the arrival of the cauldron — it will be here soon. Sit, meditate and ready yourself. We shall worry about the music sheets later.' Lleu's calm and measured tone soothed Ceriddwen as she settled herself into the chair, closing her eyes, trying to block out the music and sounds of merriment drifting up from the on-going celebrations.

EIGHTEEN

The Cailleach

Lleu knew he would have to entertain Harry and Xander, keeping them busy and distracted until Taliesin and Varik's return. Ceriddwen had already arranged a private meal in the royal apartments instead of the usual evening meal in the Great Hall — she was keen to find out as much as possible about her grandchildren, and she was determined to quiz Harry about Gwion. Harry and Xander were also shown to their overnight quarters, each given a sumptuously furnished suite of rooms with huge balconies overlooking the countryside beyond.

Xander let out a long whistle of appreciation as he gazed around his opulent surroundings. 'If only the orchestra could afford accommodation as luxurious as this — I wouldn't mind the travelling so much!'

'You won't be so keen on basic three-star hotels after this,' Harry said. 'You'll be spoiled for life now.'

With a few hours to spare before dinner, Lleu and Morfan decided to take them on a whistle-stop tour of the palace and surrounding township, finishing up at the royal stables where

Xander would have the opportunity to meet Tabitha and the unicorns whose existence he had so scornfully denied.

Morfan made the introductions. 'My Lady Epona, allow me to present Princess Molly's son, Xander, and his father, Harry.'

Harry and Xander bowed politely to this jolly-looking woman who waved them up after a quick bow in return, greeting them enthusiastically. 'Please call me Tabitha, my title is too formal for the princess's family. I am so delighted to meet you. I understand you would like a tour of the stables?'

'Yes please!' replied Harry. 'I'm afraid my son has difficulty believing in unicorns.'

'Perfectly understandable,' said Tabitha. 'They are, if you like, manufactured animals.' By now they were crossing the yard to the stable block.

Harry nodded. 'Yes, Molly told us they're actually horses with manipulated DNA.'

'Exactly so,' agreed Tabitha. 'The goblins designed them as weapons of war. Fortunately, we have managed to rescue most of their unicorns, but they may yet have breeding facilities we are unaware of.'

Before either of them could reply, she opened the stable doors to reveal a huge airy barn lined on each side with roomy looseboxes. The air smelled of horses, hay and sawdust, and they had their first breath-taking sight of unicorns. Harry had a soft spot for horses, and he gasped as he glimpsed the beautiful creatures, regarding them curiously, heads hanging over their loosebox doors, ears pricked expectantly. Again, Harry was struck by the total feeling of *otherness*. He could hear the blacksmith's hammer clanging on the anvil inside the forge on the other side of the yard. They could be in any stable yard at home, apart from the fact that instead of looking at horses, they were gaping, open mouthed, at a dozen or more surreal-looking unicorns, all whickering eagerly as Tabitha produced a bucket of apples, inviting her guests to take one. They wandered along the looseboxes, handing out apples, stroking velvety muzzles and laughing as soft, whiskery lips tickled their palms as the unicorns gently picked up the sweet tasting fruit, but most of all, they were awed by the spiralling horns in the centre of each animal's forehead. They came in all lengths and colours. Some were short and stubby, others long and tapering, and a large, black unicorn sported a sharp, gleaming white horn.

'I don't know what to say.' Xander was dumbfounded. 'It's all a bit much to take in. I feel as though I'm an actor in some sort of science fiction movie, and someone will shout *CUT!* at any moment.'

Tabitha obviously had no idea what a science fiction movie was, but she smiled sympathetically. 'Princess Molly adjusted very quickly, but unlike you, she was under the auspices of the Queen's healing, and had very little memory of her own world. We must seem very strange to you.' As she spoke, she led the black unicorn from his loosebox. He stood patiently, eyes closed in pleasure as Tabitha gently scratched his ear.

'What a beauty,' breathed Harry, running his hand along the unicorn's gleaming flank. 'I've never seen such a magnificent animal!

'Yes, he's very special indeed,' replied Tabitha. 'This is Flambeaux, Princess Molly's mount, and he misses her very much, as we all do.' She patted his sleek neck, crooning gently into his luxurious mane. Just as she was leading him back to his box, Lleu stuck his head around the barn door.

'Sorry to interrupt, Tabby.' He smiled apologetically. 'But I fear we must leave and prepare for dinner. Wouldn't do to keep the Queen waiting!'

'Of course,' she replied. 'I do hope you have enjoyed meeting our unicorns, my Lords.' She gave them a little bow and waved them off as they reluctantly made their way back to the palace.

'So, we're lords now?' Xander said, with a slight sarcastic edge to his voice as they passed through the bustling kitchen, breathing in the delicious aromas. 'I'm certainly no lord; anything but!'

'Yes, you are,' replied Lleu. 'You are both members of the royal family, your human blood doesn't invalidate that.' Xander pursed his lips and rolled his eyes, but said nothing.

Looking back, father and son wondered how they managed to survive the nerve-wracking wait for Taliesin and Varik's return, but finally, on the second morning of their stay, the queen received word they would arrive within the hour. The council was immediately reconvened and just as they were all seated, the dusty, travel-stained warriors strode into the chamber, bowing low before Ceriddwen who greeted them warmly.

'We are delighted by your safe return, my Lords. Please be seated and have some refreshment before you give us your news.' She waved both men into waiting chairs with a large jug of ale beside each seat and waited patiently as they settled themselves. After a refreshing drink, Taliesin advised they had entered the Cailleach's lands unchallenged and were surprised to be made very welcome.

'She did not send her troll guard to attack you?' Ceriddwen sounded sceptical. 'A ruse, surely?'

'Not at all, Your Majesty.' Taliesin shook his head. 'We also thought it was a trick and kept our arms at the ready, but the lady herself rushed to greet us. She was overcome with joy by our arrival. She thought we had come to rescue her!'

'Rescue her? From whom?' Ceriddwen was intrigued. 'Please continue, Lord Taliesin.'

Taliesin and his men were surprised to encounter a large forest upon entering the Cailleach's northern territory. They had assumed the entire land would be a barren, toxic wilderness. The last thing they expected was miles of thriving broad-leaf forest alive with plants and all manner of wildlife. The air was pure and clean with streams of fresh water gurgling and splashing beneath the verdant greenery, but, as they ventured further, they began to come across clearings where great swathes of trees had been systematically felled. They also noticed hundreds of recently planted saplings. Someone was obviously making valiant efforts to replant. After a while the air had become increasingly noxious as the trees began to thin out and they found themselves at the edges of a foul-smelling, pestilent swamp. Taliesin, deciding it wasn't safe, doubled back along the east side of the woods where, after a few miles, they spied, to their good fortune, the Cailleach's fortress hidden deep amongst the trees. They knew the Cailleach had been alerted to their presence by the flurry of activity on the battlements, and readied themselves for attack, raising the Tuatha de Danaan flags. As soon as the flags were aloft, they could hear the creaking and clanking of rusty chains as the drawbridge was lowered, and the huge, studded fortress doors slowly opened, allowing three riders to thunder across the drawbridge towards them. Taliesin recognised the Cailleach immediately, flanked on each side by two fierce-looking troll guards.

Taliesin and Varik pushed their horses forward to greet them. The Cailleach pulled her horse up sharply, drawing her cloak around her face. They could see she had once been a great beauty, but now her face was sunken and wrinkled, etched with lines of grief and worry.

'Greetings, my Lady Cailleach,' announced Taliesin. 'I am Lord Taliesin, Justiciar of The Land of the Four Gates. We come in peace to speak to you at the behest of Queen Ceriddwen of the Tuatha de Danaan and would ask that you admit us for a parley.'

She answered with a sad smile. 'I welcome you with all my heart, Lord Taliesin! I have prayed that Queen Ceriddwen would come to our aid, and it seems my prayers may be answered.'

Taliesin and Varik exchanged mystified glances and Taliesin nodded, saying, 'If we may partake of your hospitality, then we can talk. My men and horses are hungry and weary.'

'It will be my pleasure, my Lords,' she replied. 'My home is at your disposal, although our fare is poor.' She signalled to her guards, instructing them to lead the troops to the fortress barracks to feed and bed down the horses, then show the men to the mess hall where they could eat and rest.

'Follow me,' she said to Taliesin and Varik, 'we shall dine and talk in my private quarters.' As they clattered over the drawbridge into the bailey, Taliesin noticed that this once magnificent, well-appointed castle was fast becoming a crumbling ruin in urgent need of costly repairs.

'Forgive the state of my humble abode,' the Cailleach spat harshly. 'That accursed goblin Nudd has almost driven me to ruin!'

'He wishes to bring us all to ruin, I fear,' replied Varik.

After a meagre dinner, seated in the Cailleach's shabby, sparsely furnished solar, Taliesin and Varik listened intently as she told her story. She was the eldest daughter of the powerful troll king, Jontar. She refused to marry the man her father had chosen and, to punish her, he had her lover executed, forbidding any other man in the kingdom to marry her on pain of death. He then banished her to this toxic wasteland at the farthest reaches of his kingdom. She was given the fortress and a small allowance. Her faithful retainers were allowed to remain in her service should they wish to do so. As soon as she arrived, she set about trying to heal the poisoned land, beginning with a very successful tree planting programme which started to reap huge benefits after only a few years. Life was very hard, and many of her friends died, but they carried on until one day the Cailleach was visited by Lord Nudd. He came to tell her he had *accidentally* mined into her lands in his search for gold and precious minerals, stating his intention to purchase the land from her. She advised him that the land was not hers to sell, but her father's, and given the animosity between goblins and trolls, it was unlikely that her father would ever sell. Lord Nudd had flown into a ferocious rage, ordering his soldiers to round up as many people as possible. Despite her guard putting up a brave fight, they were outnumbered, and many of them killed or seriously injured. The prisoners were then dragged off and forced to work in the goblin mines. He refused to feed or clothe them unless she paid him vast amounts of tribute, hence the parlous state of her home and finances. Part of the tribute he insisted upon receiving was wood from her forests. He used the stolen lumber to shore up his mines and to sell as timber for fuel and building. His treasury was growing fat at the Cailleach's expense.

When Taliesin paused for another drink of ale, Harry quickly asked, 'Surely the toxic air from this Cailleach's lands must affect your borders? How do you protect the people who live near them?'

'The Cailleach's lands are many thousands of miles from here and do not affect this part of our world at all,' answered Varik.

'But how is that possible?' Harry was incredulous. 'You were gone less than forty-eight hours!'

'We went through the Eastern Gate,' explained Taliesin, once again fixing Harry with a look of barely concealed dislike.

'The Eastern Gate?' asked a puzzled Harry.

'What you would probably think of as a portal.' Taliesin took another long draught of ale.

'You're talking about a wormhole, aren't you?' Xander said excitedly, although secretly relieved they hadn't said they'd made the journey on flying horses. He preferred the scientific approach.

'What's the difference between a portal and a wormhole?' Harry wondered out loud, then felt foolish as he knew very well the theories regarding wormholes and the universe.

'Portals allow us to travel between dimensions into your world, and wormholes allow us to travel great distances throughout our own world,' explained Lleu. 'Our kingdom is known as the Land of the Four Gates because we have three portals and a wormhole. All gates are heavily guarded and supervised — Lord Taliesin is responsible for their protection.'

Varik suddenly cut into the conversation, his voice shaking with fury. 'We digress! We're not here to speak of portals and wormholes, we must focus on crushing Nudd and his infernal ambition.' Morfan laid a steadying hand on Varik's arm as he continued.

'Do you know he took mothers with babes in arms from the Cailleach? Most of the babies died, and he sent their little decomposing bodies back to her, all tossed into a huge basket like unwanted rubbish! He is an unspeakable monster!'

He swallowed hard, obviously making a supreme effort to control himself. Everyone in the chamber stared at him in shocked silence. 'This lady has suffered unimaginable horrors and I beg Your Majesty to intervene before he turns on us.' Ceriddwen stood up, her face white and grim.

'It would appear we have been very much mistaken in our opinion of Lady Cailleach. Our assertions that she was in league with Lord Nudd are unfounded, and in the light of these revelations, we must decide upon an appropriate course of action. Please continue, Lord Taliesin.'

As the council waited expectantly, Taliesin cleared his throat and resumed the harrowing tale.

Sitting in front of the blazing fire he knew his careworn hostess had only provided in the name of hospitality, he asked carefully, 'Surely you have sent word to your father, my Lady. I cannot imagine he would tolerate a goblin invasion of his realm.'

'My father is a very proud man,' she replied. 'He would consider it weakness on his part to offer me assistance.'

'So, he is unaware of Nudd's incursion?'

She nodded. 'Yes, there is no way he could know, we are too far away.'

'You haven't seen him since your banishment?' Varik found it hard to believe a father could abandon his child in such a fashion. 'People can change, and many years have passed.'

'There has been no contact, I was abandoned to my fate along with my faithful retainers, and none of my father's subjects would dare to venture over the wall anyway.'

'The wall?' asked Taliesin and Varik simultaneously.

'Many, many years ago, my people built a great wall to try and prevent the poison from the swamp spreading into the fertile lands. Of course, we now understand a wall can't stop it, only careful land management and husbandry, but the wall has symbolic meaning, and is carefully maintained and guarded as a reminder of what lies beyond.' The Cailleach tossed another precious log onto the fire, staring moodily at the burst of sparks erupting as it hit the glowing embers. 'As far as my father is concerned, he no longer has a daughter. I have forgiven him for what he did to me, but I am afraid he remains intransigent.'

A storm began to brew outside, and a chill wind blew through the cracks in the solar windowpanes, lifting the threadbare curtains and flaring the flames of the fire. Taliesin looked around at the room's faded elegance amid the crumbling plaster and damp walls hidden by worn tapestries. He felt an enormous surge of rage. This unfortunate woman in the shabby, patched gown was a princess in her own right, and the abuses she had been subjected to from her own father, and now the goblin king, deeply offended his sense of chivalry and fair play.

'Forgive me, my Lady, but do you know why the goblins wish to buy the land they have mined beneath?'

She turned from the fire, a puzzled look on her face. 'I thought it was just a ruse to gain access to the castle and enslave my people for his mines. You don't believe that was the reason?'

'Absolutely not!' snorted Taliesin. 'He has discovered a portal into the human world beneath your land. A ley line runs through your land into his. This ley line runs parallel to a ley line in the human world, and if he can work out the logistics, he is going to open the portal and bring disaster to us all!'

She palmed her face in horror. 'How do you know this? Is this why Queen Ceriddwen has sent you?'

'We know because he is trying to breach the portal but hasn't quite worked out the correct procedures for determining specific destinations.'

'But how do you know this?' the Cailleach persisted.

Realising that this was becoming difficult for Taliesin, Varik answered for him. 'Through Lord Taliesin's wife.'

The Cailleach raised a questioning eyebrow. 'What has this to do with your wife, Lord Taliesin?'

'The Princess Molly is Queen Ceriddwen's granddaughter,' replied Varik. 'She is human with fairy blood, but most importantly, she and her son, who is Prince Gwion's grandson, are the sole surviving heirs of the Anunnaki.'

Now both Cailleach's eyebrows shot up. 'So, he didn't manage to wipe them out completely, after all,' she said softly, turning to Taliesin. 'And now he wants your wife and her son dead because of the Anunnaki power.'

'You knew about the Anunnaki power? You knew more than the Tuatha de Danaan!' Taliesin was finding it difficult to maintain his disciplined warrior composure.

'They supported our people in a war against the goblins many years ago.' The Cailleach smiled sadly. 'We saw them use their dragon powers. We thought the goblins had killed them all.'

'As did we until Ceriddwen's cauldron identified Princess Molly as Anunnaki,' stated Varik.

'But why did you think I could help you?' The Cailleach sounded genuinely puzzled.

Taliesin and Varik had the grace to look ashamed. 'We thought you may have been colluding with Lord Nudd,' admitted Taliesin. 'We had no idea he was persecuting you.'

She glared at them. 'Because I live in a foul, benighted land, everyone thinks I must be an equally foul creature! It would appear my father has well and truly traduced my reputation.' She spat contemptuously into the fire. 'You think I am lying to you about the goblin king?'

'Lady, please calm yourself,' pleaded Varik. 'We can see for ourselves that you speak the truth. We shall make that very clear to Queen Ceriddwen.'

The Cailleach stood up abruptly, her tattered gown hanging loosely on her thin, bony frame. 'Come,' she commanded. 'I will show you something.'

They made their way down the crumbling stairs into the main hall and through to the kitchen area, where several people, including small children, lay huddled around the hearth. A woman scrambled to her feet in alarm. 'Are you ready for sleep, my Lady?' she asked, looking doubtfully at Taliesin and Varik. The Cailleach shook her head, lifting her cloak from a peg.

'Not now, Dala, I will return later. Go back to sleep and try not to waken the children.'

'You all sleep in the kitchen?' queried a shocked Varik.

'It's the warmest room in the castle,' retorted the Cailleach. 'Would you have children sleep in cold, damp beds?'

The men were appalled. Even during the harshest campaigns, their battle-hardened warriors were bivouacked in better conditions than these poor forsaken souls. They followed the Cailleach down a stone flagged corridor into a small courtyard and through a wrought iron gate. The moon shone a pearly light through the storm-tossed clouds, and they realised they were standing in a large garden full of young trees. Each tree was planted within a circle of stones, and every stone had a letter painted on it. The men could see that each stone circle bore a name.

'All our beloved babies sleep beneath these trees,' whispered the Cailleach. 'Twenty-four little bodies tossed in a basket and returned to us like so much rubbish.' She turned to look at them, tears gleaming on her ravaged cheeks. 'And you thought I was a monster like him?' she said bitterly. 'We shall never cease grieving for our lost children.'

Taliesin stared at the stone garlands around the trees in horrified silence. They weren't in a garden after all, they were in a babies' graveyard. An owl hooted mournfully and the Cailleach wrapped her cloak tighter around her skinny body, stumbling slightly as she was buffeted by the intensifying wind and rain.

'I think we've seen enough, my Lady,' said Taliesin quietly, offering her his arm for support. 'Come, let us return to the castle and take shelter from the storm.'

Before leaving the following morning, Taliesin promised the Cailleach he would fully appraise Ceriddwen of the situation, with a recommendation that troops be sent immediately, including a full regiment of sappers to repair and refortify the castle, temporarily replenish her guard, and help with the urgent replanting of trees. Tears of joy and relief streamed down her face as she bade them goodbye, surrounded by the rag tag remnants of her faithful retinue.

As he leant from his horse to kiss her hand in farewell, Taliesin asked, 'My Lady, you are known as the Cailleach, a fearsome title for such a gentle woman. Tell me please, what is your given name?'

'My name is Velecia,' she replied, proudly drawing herself up to her full height.

'A beautiful name,' replied Taliesin, wheeling his horse around. 'Adieu, Lady Velecia, we shall meet again soon.'

Taliesin then paused to take another drink from his cup before addressing Ceriddwen. 'I trust I acted in accordance with Your Majesty's wishes?'

'You acted correctly, Lord Taliesin, and we must plan our next move swiftly.'

Xander could contain himself no longer. 'Is the goblin mine far from the Cailleach's borders?' he asked. 'Does this mean you will have to invade his territory if there is no entrance to the mine on her lands?'

'I was just coming to that,' replied Taliesin with an irritated look on his face. He felt he had enough to contend with, without overwrought humans muddying the waters, royal blood or not. 'Lady Velicia's foresters discovered a cave behind a waterfall a few miles into the forest. All the streams and rivers had silted up before she arrived. Any water was just seeping into the poisonous swamps. The tree planting programme began to revive the air and the environment, and once they had cleared out most of the streams and riverbeds, water began to flow again. When Lady Velecia's workers were clearing accumulated debris to allow the water to flow freely once more down a rocky ridge, they stumbled upon the cave. This cave may extend all the way into the goblin kingdom. If Lord Nudd is aware of this, I doubt he is troubled by it. He knows Lady Velecia has no effective defences.' He paused as the Morrigan indicated she wished to speak, saying graciously, 'Go ahead, Lady Morrigan.'

'Your Majesty, I propose that I take a task force of my best warriors and cryptanalysists and investigate this cave. If we can work out the co-ordinates before Lord Nudd, and he is obviously having some difficulty, we may be able to stop him in his tracks by blocking his signals.'

Ceriddwen got to her feet, a resolute expression on her face, and spoke urgently. 'Thank you, Lady Morrigan, and thanks again to my Lords Taliesin and Varik for your excellent reconnaissance of the situation. However,' she paused and looked around the room, 'we are extremely aware that time is of the essence and therefore we must act swiftly. This is what we are going to do.' Everyone sat with bated breath, waiting for the Queen's command. 'Lord Taliesin, your services are required here, as I am sure you understand.'

'Of course, Your Majesty.'

'Lord Varik, you will return to Lady Velicia with my royal engineers and a battalion of men at arms. Take all the supplies you need for rebuilding her castle and reinforcing her defences. Take food, clothes and bedding for her people, and livestock to replenish her herds. You will also investigate the cave and take Lady Morrigan's cryptanalysists with you. You may leave now to begin preparations'

'At once, Your Majesty.' Varik gave a swift bow and left the chamber as Ceriddwen turned to the Morrigan and Queen Andraste.

'Queen Andraste, you will take a squad of your most experienced warriors and make a reconnaissance of the area around the mine inside the goblin territories. We need to know how many troops he has on standby for the opening of the portal, and how many dragons he has. If he thinks he's almost there, he'll have everything in position. As soon as we know how many troops he has, we can work out our best strategy for attack.'

Queen Andraste laughed and tossed her elfin head. 'We are on our way, Your Majesty. They will never know we were there.' She bowed, turned on her heel and strode out of the room, her glittering crystal ropes shooting sparks of light in all directions as she went.

'Lady Morrigan, I am despatching you and a large contingent of troops to King Jontar. You will advise him that his cruel treatment of his daughter has come to our attention, and he has incurred our displeasure. Abandoning her to the mercies of the goblins has resulted in OUR children and kingdom being placed in imminent danger. If he does not wish to further risk our wrath, he will pay serious attention to what we have to say. Show him the Royal Seal and advise him that our allies are standing shoulder to shoulder with us to maintain the peace and harmony of this world, and those who wish to destroy it will be shown no mercy. You may remind him I killed his traitorous brother in fair combat, and I shall do the same to him, if necessary.'

The Morrigan nodded in agreement. 'We shall be ready to leave within the hour, Your Majesty.'

Xander wasn't surprised to hear that Ceriddwen was a warrior, she terrified him, and he nearly jumped out of his skin when she turned her attention to him and his father when the Morrigan took her leave. 'Harry, Xander, my dear grandchildren, you must return to Molly immediately. Please be assured, she will be in no danger if you act correctly, but I fear you are ill-prepared for what you may witness.'

She focused all her attention on Xander as Morfan handed her a bundle of parchment sheets.

'We know why your presence is essential, but you must understand that no matter what happens, no matter what you see, keep playing your harp. This is vitally important for you and for Molly. You must keep playing, and you must play the music written on this sheet.' She extracted a sheet from the bundle and held it out.

Xander took the sheet from Ceriddwen and studied it carefully. It was written in a strange script, but to his amazement, he found he had no difficulty understanding both the words and the music.

Ceriddwen and Lleu exchanged glances. Breaking the seal on Gwion's apartments had been an emotional trial, and rummaging through his belongings, lying just as he had left them, was almost unbearable. The music sheets had been despatched to the Crystal Tower for translation, but no one could decipher the strange language. Ceriddwen felt a tremor of excitement as she realised Xander could read the sheets and handed him the rest of the bundle. 'You can read the script as well as the music?'

'Yes, Your Majesty, it is called *Moon Dragon*.'

'This is more than I had hoped for — you are truly a prince of both bloods. Do not falter as I have instructed, and all should go well.'

She held out her glittering, beringed hand. Harry and Xander bowed and kissed it in turn.

'Now go! Protect our princess and return her safely to us,' she ordered, her voice cracking with emotion.

NINETEEN

A Dangerous Cargo

'So, you didn't get to the Masqued Ball after all?' mused Laura. By now, she and Molly had continued their walk through the park, kicking up the crunchy red and gold autumn leaves as they strolled.

'No, I didn't,' Molly replied with a wry smile. I don't really remember very much about it, but I do know I was very ill for a while.'

~

Molly's beautiful Samhain dresses hung unworn in her bedroom as her life hung in the balance, torn between two worlds, her human immune system desperately trying to overpower the once dormant Anunnaki DNA. Masters Lenus and Heka fretted and fussed over her inert body until Tanith and her ladies rushed in, wheeling the cauldron and a long, low crystal bath on two separate trolleys, followed by a distraught Brighid. Tanith shooed the protesting doctors, along with Lleu and Morfan, out of the room. This was ancient, traditional fairy work, and required ancient, traditional methods.

Brighid quickly stripped Molly while the Astarte ladies filled the bath with liquid from the cauldron. When it reached the correct level, Molly was gently immersed. Ceriddwen, meanwhile, stirred the cauldron with her staff, murmuring incantations as Tanith sprinkled various herbs and powders into the roiling contents. The women bathed Molly's entire body, ensuring her hair was also thoroughly soaked. Every part of her body, even the most intimate parts of her anatomy were washed in the pungent fluid. After a few minutes, Ceriddwen withdrew her staff from the cauldron and approached the crystal bath. Two women gently raised Molly's head as Brighid prised open her mouth. Ceriddwen positioned the point of her staff over Molly's mouth as, very slowly, drops of the liquid dripped down her throat. This task had to be performed very carefully to avoid Molly choking, and Ceriddwen stood resolutely until she had ingested every drop. She was kept floating in this magical soup for another half-hour, the Ladies of Astarte constantly checking her pulse and the temperature of the water. When she was finally removed from the bath, she was dried in soft fluffy towels laundered in the cauldron's liquid. Her bed gown, blankets and pillowcases were also replaced with others previously washed in cauldron liquid. Ceriddwen was taking no chances — Molly had to receive all the protection the cauldron had to offer.

Morfan and Lleu were pacing up and down outside the room when a frowning and worried-looking Taliesin strode down the corridor. He clasped Lleu's arm in greeting, then Morfan's. 'What has happened to the princess?' he demanded, face stricken.

'Try not to worry, cousin,' Lleu replied soothingly, 'she is being well cared for.'

'But what's wrong with her?' Taliesin repeated. Lleu and Morfan looked at each other. Taliesin was no longer trying to hide his feelings for Molly. Morfan decided to own up and admitted it was his fault.

'Stop speaking in riddles!' snapped Taliesin. 'What do you mean it's your fault?' He was glaring furiously at Morfan. Lleu, fearing that Taliesin's notoriously short fuse was about to be ignited, quickly explained what had happened.

'And, of course, it's not Morfan's fault,' he added, as Taliesin's expression became even more ferocious. 'None of us expected this reaction, or for it to happen so quickly.'

'But what does the Queen hope the cauldron will do?' Taliesin asked desperately.

'Ah, that's a very good question,' sighed Lleu. 'You were present when the cauldron recognised Molly as Anunnaki?' Taliesin nodded. 'Well,' continued Lleu, 'Ceriddwen believes the power of the cauldron will enhance and strengthen Molly's human DNA, enabling it to merge safely with the Anunnaki DNA, which presently is the stronger of the two.'

'And what if the Queen is wrong?' Taliesin said roughly, his face now pale with dread.

'We must hope that she isn't,' whispered Morfan, 'for if my mother *is* wrong, Princess Molly will die.' Masters Lenus and Heka chose that moment to emerge from a side room and were immediately blindsided by a truculent Taliesin.

'Ah, the palace doctors!' he growled. 'Have you decided to come out of hiding and run for cover? Why aren't you in that room trying to find a cure?'

'I...I...we don't know what you mean, Lord Taliesin,' quavered Master Lenus. 'We did our best for the princess, but Anunnaki physiology is outwith our area of expertise.' Taliesin growled even louder, but Lenus gamely carried on. 'We thought the Anunnaki race was extinct, so had no reason to study it, not that we had any reason to study it before,' he finished defiantly, staring nervously at Taliesin clenching and unclenching his fists in fury. Taliesin made a sudden lunge at Master Lenus, who made a surprisingly deft sidestep out of the way, just as Molly's door was flung open.

'Lord Taliesin!' Ceriddwen stood in the doorway. 'What is the meaning of this boorish behaviour?' Summoning immense self-control, and ignoring the smug look on both doctors' faces, Taliesin turned and bowed low before the Queen.

'Forgive me, Your Majesty. I should learn to control my temper.'

Ceriddwen was unimpressed. 'How many times have I heard you express that same sentiment, my Lord Justiciar?'

Taliesin managed to look passably contrite as she continued to berate him. 'You come to the hospital wing and cause a scene when the princess lies in her sickbed? Explain yourself at once!' Observing the doctors' lack of protocol by arrogantly listening to the conversation when they should have been about their duties, she dismissed them with an imperious wave of her hand. When they had reluctantly plodded out of sight, she fixed Taliesin with an eagle eye and pointedly demanded, 'Well, I am waiting — why did you cause such a scene?'

The proud Taliesin looked like a chastened schoolboy as he bowed his head and admitted in a quiet voice, 'Your Majesty, forgive me, but I have fallen quite hopelessly in love with Princess Molly, and my fear for her safety has made me unreasonable and bellicose.'

Ceriddwen studied him for a moment and then announced, quite pleasantly, 'Yes, I thought as much.' Three mouths fell open in surprise. 'Don't look so shocked,' she admonished them, 'I am your Queen — nothing escapes my attention! Now, be off with you. We will know nothing for a while, so there is no point in remaining here. That is my command. Go!' With a final glare, she retreated into the room, closing the door firmly behind her.

A Dynasty of Dragons

Ceriddwen leant against the door with a sigh. She had been aware of the growing spark between Molly and Taliesin since the day of the initial goblin questioning. It would, of course, be the perfect dynastic match, and there was no denying that they would make a handsome couple. Molly's sweet disposition would be the perfect foil for Taliesin's mercurial nature. Unless, Ceriddwen suppressed a shudder, the Anunnaki gene changed Molly's temperament, though they would have no way of knowing this until she regained consciousness. Ceriddwen would not countenance any other outcome. The cauldron would work its magic, and all would be well. Anything else was inconceivable. Giving herself a mental shake, she issued instructions to the Ladies of Astarte, and as the women loaded the bath and the cauldron back onto their trollies and wheeled them out of the room, she busied herself by tucking the blankets ever more firmly around Molly, ignoring Brighid's affronted look that the Queen should be performing such a menial task.

As the three men left the hospital, Morfan asked Taliesin how he had heard of Molly's illness so quickly. 'I thought you and Varik were checking the northern perimeters?' he queried in a puzzled tone.

'I came back initially with important information. Let's find somewhere to talk—I could do with a strong drink to steady my nerves!'

Lleu laid an encouraging hand on his shoulder. 'Splendid idea! We could all do with one. We'll go to the pavilion—no one will pay any attention to us with all the merry-making going on.'

Seated in a secluded corner at the back of the pavilion, drinks in front of them, Taliesin began to speak in low urgent tones. 'We have received a message from Lord Llyr—he fears there is something seriously amiss with Queen Grainne's mission.'

'How so?' queried Lleu.

'As you know, Lord Llyr's ships are always escorted by dolphin pods — they act as lookouts and navigators.' Morfan and Lleu nodded in agreement. 'Well, it seems they spied Queen Grainne's ship, and it's not a cruiser, it's a man of war, apparently fully armed with a huge contingent of men, plus something that sounds a lot more sinister.' He took a long draught from his tankard.

'What does Lord Llyr mean by *sinister*?' Lleu frowned.

'Sinister enough for his dolphin pod to have fled in terror!' snapped Taliesin. 'He sent a scout to investigate and when he returned, he told Lord Llyr he didn't encounter any marine life at all within a two-mile radius of the ship.'

'I don't like the sound of that,' demurred Morfan, chewing his bottom lip nervously.

'No, it doesn't bode well at all!' growled Taliesin.

'We'll have to tell the Queen.' Lleu sighed wearily. 'This couldn't have happened at a worse time.'

'But the goblin queen hasn't actually threatened anyone,' reasoned Morfan. 'There could be any number of reasons why the dolphins fled and maybe the goblins have just eaten all the fish around their ship if they have a large crew on board.'

Taliesin curled his lip contemptuously. 'Complete nonsense, and you know it, Morfan — you've already said you don't like the sound of this!' He slammed his fist down hard on the table causing several revellers to turn and stare at them in alarm. Unperturbed, Taliesin continued, glaring furiously at his companions. 'No marine life within a two-mile radius of the ship? What does that suggest to you?' he hissed.

Lleu glanced surreptitiously around the pavilion to make sure no one was still listening before whispering incredulously, 'You think Queen Grainne has a sea dragon on board?'

'I don't doubt it for a minute. The scourge of the oceans — no wonder Llyr's dolphins fled. Sea dragons eat anything and everything that lives in the sea!'

'But they only live in the waters surrounding the Annunaki lands!' protested Morfan. 'The Sirens make sure they stay there. They control them and keep them small because they're so rapacious.'

Taliesin stood up and pushed his chair back, jabbing his finger at them. 'If the goblins are capable of subjugating winged dragons, they're capable of anything, but we've no way of knowing they have a sea dragon until the ship arrives, so we'll have to be prepared!'

Morfan and Lleu followed suit, jumping to their feet, drinks half finished.

'How soon before she arrives?' Lleu quickened his pace to keep up with Taliesin's long, powerful strides.

'I estimate three or four days. Both parties are due to dock at the same time.'

'Where are you going?' panted Morfan. Keeping up with the unstoppable force that was Lord Taliesin was exhausting.

'To find Admiral Sulis and advise her to prepare a naval blockade. The goblin queen must not be allowed to enter our harbour!'

'But there won't be enough time,' gasped Lleu, who was now seriously out of breath, 'The fleet is docked at the Western Gate.'

'I am aware of that!' snapped Taliesin. 'That's why time is of the essence — I'm leaving right now. Please advise the Queen immediately!' He strode away from his puffing companions without a backward glance.

~

Ceriddwen sat slumped in her ebony chair, her beautiful face drawn and weary as council members streamed in for the meeting. Many were chattering loudly, although some lowered their voices respectfully at the sight of Ceriddwen's morose demeanour. No one had seen her looking this upset since the

Prince Gwion business. Above all, they were intrigued and concerned that such an emergency meeting had been called, especially during the Samhain festivities. Many of them were still wearing their celebratory finery, having had no time to change.

Lady Tanith dipped a goblet into the cauldron and handed it to Ceriddwen. She swiftly drained the vessel and returned it to Tanith who slipped quietly back to her place amongst the Ladies of Astarte. Revived and refreshed by the cauldron's potion, Ceriddwen got to her feet with her usual aplomb, banging her staff on the table.

The room fell into a fitful silence, and firstly, Ceriddwen sombrely advised everyone of Molly's sudden indisposition, reassuring them that she had been treated by the cauldron, and would hopefully make a swift recovery. She spoke with a confidence she didn't really feel, but the alternative was unthinkable. Murmurs of concern and sympathy rumbled around the room, but soon all were focused on the Queen's next statement.

'Lord Taliesin has advised us that the goblin queen, Grainne, does not appear to be visiting us in peace after all, but is, in fact, arriving in a fully crewed and armed man of war.' Councillors gasped in outrage.

'And where is our fleet!' a voice demanded from the back of the room, with many more voices joining in unison, until Ceriddwen once more slammed her staff onto the table, bellowing for quiet.

'My Lords and Ladies,' she cried 'where are your manners? We are in our hallowed council chamber, and we shall proceed with respect! Any more interruptions and the culprits shall be stripped of council office. Do I make myself clear?' She glared around the room, a ferocious frown darkening her features. 'Good! Then let us continue. Lord Taliesin is riding hard to warn Admiral Sulis of the situation, but as the fleet is currently docked at the Western Gate, he asked that we also send our swiftest pigeons — they will get there first and hopefully Admiral Sulis will have readied the fleet by the time Lord Taliesin arrives to give her a fuller picture.'

'What exactly do you plan to do, Your Majesty?' asked a councillor from the middle of the room, carefully observing correct protocol after Ceriddwen's warning.

'A very good question, Lord Ruka,' Ceriddwen replied grimly. 'First of all we will have to form a blockade to prevent Queen Grainne from entering our harbour.'

'But, Your Majesty,' Lord Ruka persisted, 'what about Lord Llyr? He is due to arrive at the same time. Is he friend or foe? Do we blockade him or send him an armed escort?' Ceriddwen explained it was Lord Lyr who had alerted them to the clear and present danger of the goblin ship.

'Your Majesty, surely we are not afraid of the goblins on board this ship? We are more than a match for one man of war, so why go to the lengths of a blockade?' Ruka sounded genuinely perplexed.

Ceriddwen threw herself back into her chair, indicating to Lleu that he should continue. He got to his feet and placing both hands on the table, took a long hard look around the room. 'You are quite correct, Lord Ruka,' he said finally. 'Under normal circumstances we would flick away these irksome goblins as a horse flicks flies with its tail, but these are not normal circumstances, and I am afraid we cannot flick away what lies hidden in the bowels of that ship.' A murmur of disquiet rippled around the room

'And what might that be, my Lord?' a quiet voice gently asked; the venerable Arianrhod had risen to her feet, leaning on her crystal studded staff for support. 'What new weapons are the accursed goblins going to unleash upon us now?'

'They have a sea dragon,' Ceriddwen announced wearily from the depths of her chair.

'What?' cried an aghast Arianrhod. 'Surely there must be some mistake! Sea dragons cannot leave the waters around the Annunaki lands — they cannot pass the...'

A look of utmost horror transfixed the Arianrhod's face as she collapsed into her chair in shock. Tanith rushed to her side and thrust a goblet into her shaking hands. 'Please drink, Mother Arianrhod, it will calm you,' she urged in gentle, soothing tones. You could hear a pin drop, such was the silence in the chamber, as everyone digested the meaning of the Arianrhod's unfinished sentence.

While Tanith fussed over the stricken Arianrhod, Ceriddwen once again took control of proceedings. 'If it is true that the goblins have a sea dragon, then I am afraid we have to conclude that they have either killed or captured the Sirens.' The entire council reeled in shock as Ceriddwen's words sank in.

'What can we do?' whispered Lord Ruka, bravely voicing the thoughts of the entire assembled council.

'We must hope that Princess Molly makes a full recovery!' The Arianrhod, also revivified by the magical properties of the cauldron, had risen to her feet again. 'I am afraid she is our only hope!'

'I will not have the princess placed in danger,' retorted Ceriddwen. 'We shall have to think of something else.'

'There is nothing else,' the Arianrhod insisted obdurately.

'Are you suggesting that the princess be carried from her sick bed and offered up as some sort of sacrifice?' Ceriddwen was outraged.

'Of course not,' the Arianrhod continued, unperturbed. 'You say the princess has been subjected to the cauldron?'

'So?' replied Ceriddwen.

'You also said the goblin queen is not due to arrive for another few days. The princess may be sufficiently recovered by then!'

'It's not an exact science,' Ceriddwen cried furiously. 'We are dealing with an unknown quantity — we don't know how the princess's system will react to the Anunnaki DNA!'

'Well, what we do know, Your Majesty, is that we have to fight fire with fire, or to be more accurate, dragon with dragon.'

'I refuse to listen to any more of this nonsense!' screamed Ceriddwen, rapidly descending into one of her monumental rages, council protocol forgotten. 'Council is dismissed apart from Lady Morrigan, Queen Andraste and Lord Ravenna.' She snapped her fingers imperiously at the three hapless victims who obediently hung back as the other council members scrambled for the doors. The Arianrhod hovered by her seat, unsure what to do. Important decisions were seldom made without her wise input and guidance. Catching sight of her from the corner of her eye, Ceriddwen rounded on her. 'You may leave too, Mother Arianrhod,' she ordered with icy politeness. The Arianrod's eyes momentarily widened in shock, but she quickly composed herself, bowed and made a slow and dignified exit.

As soon as the chamber doors were closed, Ceriddwen began to issue orders. The Morrigan and Queen Andraste were each to move a contingent of their troops in and around the harbour areas, effectively sealing them off. Lord Ravenna, Ceriddwen's frigate captain, was ordered to leave immediately and sail out with four frigates, fortunately docked in the palace harbour, to provide a safe escort for Lord Llyr's ship. Lleu and Morfan sat tight lipped, their faces etched with worry. Everyone was used to Ceriddwen's tantrums and outbursts, but her rudeness towards Mother Arianrhod was unprecedented. Usually her judgement was faultless, but her concern for Molly, and the Arianrhod's insistence that only Molly could deal with the fearsome sea dragon, appeared to have clouded her normal sangfroid.

'Permission to speak, Your Majesty.' The Morrigan stepped forward, dipping a bow to Ceriddwen, who nodded curtly.

'I fear the sight of so many armed warriors will alarm everyone, and perhaps alert the goblins, especially as we still haven't apprehended the spies working for Lord Nudd.' She stepped back respectfully, bearing herself proudly in the face of Ceriddwen's malevolent glare.

'How many more times do I have to repeat myself?' she snarled. 'I will take all necessary measures to protect the princess. She will not be presenting herself anywhere near these abominable goblins, and it is your duty, Lady Morrigan, to protect her if I order it, and even if I don't!' Flecks of spittle flew from her mouth as she spat out the words. The Morrigan stood unflinching as saliva landed on her face and hair. Lord Ravenna now cleared his throat and nervously held up his hand.

'What now?' screamed Ceriddwen at the cowering captain. 'Are yet more of my orders to be questioned?'

'No, not at all, Your Majesty,' he ventured. 'I was just wondering about the blockade. Do we know if it will be in place before our...er...guests arrive? The Western Gate is many miles from here, as you know,' he added hastily.

He blanched under Ceriddwen's baleful look as she hissed at him, 'I do not know whether the blockade will be in place or not. That is why I am ordering the harbour area to be sealed off, and the longer you stand here prattling with your inane questions, the nearer the goblin queen gets. If you do not obey my command immediately, captain or no captain, I shall see you hanged from your own ship's yardarm. Now get out!' As Lord Ravenna scuttled away, Ceriddwen turned her attention to the Morrigan and Queen Andraste, who were standing rooted to the spot. 'Are you still here?' she screeched, her face contorted in fury. The two warrior women swiftly bowed and hurried after Lord Ravenna.

'Bah!' she yelled, throwing her staff across the huge carved council table. 'I am surrounded by fools!'

TWENTY

To The Western Gate

Taliesin tried to let the steady rhythm of Luath's galloping hooves soothe his turbulent thoughts as they made their headlong flight towards the Western Gate. The stallion's powerful neck was lathered in white foamy sweat, but he never faltered as his huge heart powered him onwards. The fastest and most powerful of Taliesin's mounts, he lived up to his full name — Luath Chasach, meaning "swift footed". If any horse or unicorn could get him there in time, it was Luath.

As they travelled ever further west, the weather began to change, with dark clouds bubbling ominously over the horizon, a sure precursor of stormy weather. Taliesin let out a furious curse. Western weather was notoriously unpredictable and if a storm blew up it could prevent the fleet leaving harbour for days. By now they were on the coastal road, still many miles from the Western Gate, and the sea was already pounding the shore with huge crashing waves throwing up great spumes of foaming water, as sea birds wheeled and screamed in the storm-bruised sky.

He knew he would have to stop for the night as Luath needed food and rest. The courageous animal would gallop on until his heart burst, but Taliesin was too good a horseman to let that happen. They were approaching a coastal village and Taliesin decided to stop at the inn. As soon as he clattered into the courtyard an ostler appeared, bowing to him, as he surreptitiously cast a critical eye over Luath's heaving flanks and lathered coat. Taliesin handed him the reins, instructing him to give Luath a good rub down and to make sure he received the best quality oats and hay before being bedded down in a comfortable loosebox. The ostler looked pained at the insinuation he might do otherwise but nodded quickly at the sight of Taliesin's glowering face. Luath taken care of, Taliesin made his way towards the inn's warm and cosy parlour. It was a pleasant room with a blazing fire and furnished with comfortable tables and chairs. Colourful festive bunting hung from the ceiling, but it was apparent the dismal weather had put paid to any meaningful Samhain celebrations. The enticing smell of cooking filled the air, and several people were seated enjoying a meal. The diners looked up as Taliesin's tall figure framed the doorway. As soon as they noticed his warrior's braid and Justiciar's badge of office, chairs scraped across the floor as everyone jumped to their feet, bowing respectfully. The innkeeper and his wife immediately bustled over to introduce themselves.

'My Lord Justiciar, Samhain blessings to you and welcome to our humble inn!' The stout innkeeper could hardly contain his pleasure. 'I am your host, Luca, and this is my wife, Muirin.' Muirin dimpled prettily at Taliesin and urged him over to a cosy table and chair by the fireside.

'We are serving stew and dumplings tonight, my Lord, or freshly caught sea trout.'

Taliesin decided on the stew and asked for a room. He was tired, travel-stained, and desperate for a long hot bath and a soft bed.

'I will prepare our best room for you.' Muirin fussed over him, laying the table before bringing a tankard of ale. 'Would you like me to draw your bath while you eat?'

'Yes, very good, thank you,' he replied wearily. He was in no mood for conversation and couldn't wait to eat, retire to his room and sleep. After what turned out to be a very good meal, he thanked his hosts and after checking that Luath was bedded down and settled for the night, he sank gratefully into bed after a welcome hot bath.

He tossed and turned before falling into an uneasy sleep where his dreams were filled with visions of Molly on the day of the truffle hunt. He was kissing her hand again and gazing into her beautiful green eyes, but the dream soon turned into a nightmare of her lying ill and helpless as a monstrous sea dragon ravaged the palace searching for her. He woke, drenched in sweat, to the sound of rain hammering against the window, and wind howling through the sleeping village. He could hear the relentless roar of the sea as the storm gathered in strength and intensity and he tried to fall asleep again for the remaining few hours until sunrise, but his mind raced with thoughts of Molly. He could hardly believe he had fallen in love again. This beautiful, russet-haired, fairy blood human was melting the lump of ice that encased his heart. After Morgaine, he had vowed never to allow his heart to be stolen again.

He met Morgaine at Scatha's Warrior School on the Isle of Clouds far out in the Western Sea. Scatha was a famous warrior and teacher, only ever bested in combat by Ceriddwen. Fairy children identified as potential warriors were chosen for the school only after passing rigorous training and tests. Only the toughest and best qualified were sent to the island, where they stayed for seven years to learn the necessary skills required for a warrior and guardian of the realm. It was a hard life for children, and to help them cope with the hardships involved, they formed close relationships with their comrades, relationships that often blossomed into intense love affairs as the children matured into young adults. Not only was Morgaine beautiful, but she was also an accomplished horsewoman who could shoot arrows while standing on the back of a galloping horse, swing down and shoot them from under the horse's belly, and vault from the back of one galloping horse onto another. In fact, there was very little involving horses she couldn't do, and Taliesin loved her for it. Their combined love of horses made them an ideal couple and they planned to join the Morrigan's prestigious cavalry. Their future seemed set as their student days came to an end and they prepared to take their oaths as fully trained warriors entitled to wear copper armbands, with their hair in warrior braids.

Everything was going to plan until Nuada broke the spell. Nuada was a fairy aristocrat, also in love with Morgaine and determined to win her from Taliesin by fair means or foul. He wormed his way into their company at every opportunity, pretending he wanted Morgaine to help him improve his riding skills. He constantly flattered her and encouraged her to teach him some of her more outlandish feats. Taliesin tried to talk Morgaine out of encouraging him, because, as he pointed out, Nuada was already a very skilled horseman, and he was being disingenuous in maintaining he needed her help. It fell on deaf ears until one day, they were practising driving horses through fires whilst standing astride them. Morgaine's horses sailed through, expertly guided and controlled, but when it was Nuada's turn, Morgaine noticed, too late, he wasn't maintaining the correct tension on the left-hand horse's rein and instead of going straight through the fires, it veered to the left and panicked as it almost blundered into the flames. This caused the other two horses to panic in turn, and Nuada was thrown into one of the fires, seriously burning his hand and forearm. His hand was crippled and had to be amputated, which meant he would never be able to fulfil his warrior ambitions. All his training was for nothing, and Morgaine took the blame, berating herself for not noticing the erroneous rein sooner. No amount of reasoned argument from Taliesin or anyone else could change her mind. She became very cold towards Taliesin, implying it was partly his fault because his hostility had affected Nuada's concentration. Taliesin hotly denied this slur, horrified and heartbroken by her changed attitude towards him.

The final blow came when Morgaine announced that she and Nuada were to be betrothed. She was going to look after him for the rest of his life in atonement for her part in his injury. Taliesin pleaded with her, he even persuaded Scatha to intervene, but Morgaine was adamant, and there was nothing more he could do. He hardened his heart and threw himself into his career, working his way through the warrior ranks until he was promoted to his current position as Queen's Warrior and Justiciar of The Four Gates. A prize worth waiting a lifetime for. But that was before he met Molly.

Yawning, he finally woke from his troubled dreams, light beginning to filter reluctantly through the shutters on his window. The dawn sky bruised and yellowed by heavy storm clouds and a strong wind blew squalls of driving rain. He groaned inwardly as he pulled on his boots. The inclement weather would slow his progress and the lowering sky indicated it could become a lot worse. He made his way downstairs and signed Luca's guest sheet to enable him to claim provisions in return for his bed and board. He requested a quick breakfast and Muirin hurriedly brought him freshly baked bannocks, butter, and cheese, with a mug of hot tea. He ate quickly, thanking Luca and Muirin for their hospitality, before making his way to the stables. The ostler had already groomed and tacked Luath, assuring Taliesin his mount had been fed and watered as instructed, and the farrier had checked his feet. The last thing needed was for Luath to throw a shoe. Taliesin checked Luath's bridle and girth, and nodding to the ostler, mounted up and cantered out into the howling wind.

Luath snorted, tossing his head and laying his ears back as the driving rain hit him full in the face, the wind blowing his luxurious mane over his eyes. 'Steady boy,' soothed Taliesin. 'You've dealt with worse than this.' Calmed by his master's familiar voice, the stallion settled into a steady gallop as Taliesin urged him up the hill and out of the little seaside village. Luath's long swift strides began to eat up the miles as they careered along the vertiginous cliff edge track, constantly buffeted by howling gales with the angry, roiling waves roaring and pounding below them as they galloped through the unforgiving weather.

At last, as the gloom of a thick, swirling mist began to lift, Taliesin could make out the huge dry dock sheds of the Western Gate Harbour and, as they drew nearer, the shingled roofs and gables of the little town hunkered in the shadow of the dockyard. He slowed the exhausted and blowing Luath to a trot as he approached the yard gates. The town was quiet, battened down and shuttered against the ferocity of the storm, but the dockyard was alive with the sound of sawing and hammering and the creaking of hulls being tossed around in their moorings by the wind and waves. He looked at all the naked masts lined up and his heart sank even further into his boots. It was obvious Admiral Sulis was not putting to sea in this weather.

At the sight of Taliesin's badge of office, the gatekeeper opened the gates immediately, and as Taliesin dismounted, called for someone to attend Luath, who stood, head down, trembling with exhaustion. A young woman quickly scurried over from a nearby barn. Taliesin handed her the reins, instructing that his steed be rubbed down and fed a warm bran mash before hurrying across the busy yard to find Admiral Sulis. He was just approaching the quaint little office building when he was surprised to bump into Lord Cernunnos supervising a team of huge draught horses hauling a wagon of massive oak trunks.

'Cernunnos,' he cried, 'what brings you here at Samhain and in this accursed weather?'

Clasping Taliesin's arm in greeting, Cernunnos boomed back, 'I could ask you the same question, brother!' He took in his friend's tired face and travel-stained clothes. 'Trouble?' He raised a quizzical eyebrow.

'Aye,' came the reply. 'The worst. You need to hear this too. Come, I must find Admiral Sulis immediately!'

As Taliesin started to head towards the small office building, Cernunnos stopped him, saying, 'The Admiral's in the sawmill checking my oak trees — that's why I'm here, delivering these beauties for the gnome king's galleon — he's making our Queen a gift of one so long as we call it *The Lady Froya* after his wife!'

Despite his tiredness and the urgency of the mission, Taliesin couldn't help but laugh.

'Sounds like Lord Dubh right enough! Nothing's too good for his lady.' As soon as the words were out, his heart wrenched. *Yes, nothing's too good for my beautiful lady, either*, he thought, before snapping back to reality. 'Ok, brother,' he forced a smile, clapping Cernunnos on the shoulder, 'lead me to the sawmill.'

The water-powered sawmill was set back from the main dockyard and the shrieking and grinding of saws was deafening. Cernunnos and Taliesin entered from the front, skirting a huge sawpit where two burly men were cutting a large piece of timber with a whipsaw. The top sawyer, who determined the thickness of the plank, was working on top, gleaming with sweat, the other man toiling below in the pit. Sawdust covered every surface and clouds of it hung in the air. Cernunnos led Taliesin through to the rear of the building where Admiral Sulis and several personnel were examining a load of freshly delivered timber.

'The Admiral likes to check the quality of the merchandise personally,' Cernunnos whispered as they approached the group.'Oh, and by the way, she likes to be called Lady Sulis.'

Seeing Taliesin's raised eyebrow, Cernunnos shrugged. 'She's only called Admiral when she's at sea. Don't ask me why.'

Cernunnos coughed politely to herald their arrival, and Lady Sulis turned to greet them. She was covered from head to foot in a layer of fine sawdust; it was stuck to her hair, eyelashes and face and seemed not to bother her in the slightest.

'My Lords.' She bowed politely, the men bowing in return. 'I have been expecting you, Lord Taliesin. The Queen sent pigeons ahead of you, they arrived a few hours ago — a miracle they made it through this storm. Grave news indeed!' She turned to Cernunnos saying, 'Splendid timber, Lord Cernunnos. This will build Lord Dubh a very fine galleon indeed. However, my Lords,' she said without missing a beat, 'back to business. Walk with me, please.'

As they followed Lady Sulis out of the sawmill and down to the harbour where the bulk of the fleet was docked, Taliesin quickly outlined the reason for his mission. Cernunnos was horrified, but before he could say anything, Lady Sulis held up her hand for attention. 'I don't suppose I have to tell you, Lord Taliesin,' she shouted, trying to be heard above the howling wind, gesturing towards the creaking ships, their hulls banging into each other as they rolled about in the thrashing waves, 'there is no question of taking the fleet out in this. It's far too dangerous. This is the worst storm I've seen in years!'

Taliesin knew he was defeated. He had suspected this would be the outcome almost as soon as he encountered the first taste of bad weather the day before. 'If the storm abates, the soonest we can set sail will be tomorrow noon,' Lady Sulis continued. 'If the storm persists, who can say when we will arrive at the Queen's harbour.' She stood facing them, all traces of sawdust blasted out to sea by the gale force winds, her hair streaming behind her, and her weather-beaten face set in a defiant expression as though she expected Taliesin to argue with her. But Taliesin wasn't a trained seaman, nor was he a fool. If the admiral said the fleet could not sail, then that was that. She had the final word. 'Let's get inside out of this maelstrom. I don't know about you, but this wind is freezing my bones!' she added, shivering.

They headed into the office where a young midshipman served them hot spiced wine and plates of bread, cheese, miniature cakes, and savouries. Ravenous, Taliesin wolfed into the food to settle his growling stomach. He knew he couldn't afford to relax for long in the warmth of the snug little room and soon advised the others he would have to leave and return to the Southern Gate.

'No need to worry, my Lord,' said Lady Sulis briskly, 'I have already sent pigeons to explain the situation. You may rest a while longer.' Taliesin's thoughts raced. He couldn't very well tell them he wanted to rush back as quickly as possible to check on Molly. He was Queen's Warrior and Lord Justiciar, he wasn't supposed to let personal matters cloud his judgment. He was in an agony of indecision. 'Furthermore,' continued Lady Sulis, 'you must let that wonderful stallion have some rest. He's certainly earned his oats bringing you here so swiftly.' She smiled at him before answering his unspoken question. 'I can see you wondering how I know about your horse!' She gave a little laugh. 'He's the darling of the dockyard, being petted to death as we speak, if Master Jax is to be believed.' The midshipman blushed scarlet as Taliesin gave Lady Sulis another uncomprehending look.

'The stable girl from the dockyard barn who took him from you has been singing his praises all over the yard. No one believes he got you here in less than two full days. Quite the hero!'

Taliesin grunted. 'He's my best mount. The Epona bred him herself.'

Lady Sulis nodded. 'Ah, that explains it!' she said.

Cernunnos chuckled. 'Tabby always had an eye for a fine piece of horse flesh!'

Taliesin began to feel a stir of irritation. 'Lady Sulis, Cernunnos, I beg your pardon, but we really shouldn't be sitting here talking about horse bloodlines when the goblins may have murdered the Sirens and are about to unleash the unspeakable!'

'What do you mean "they may have murdered the Sirens"?' gasped Lady Sulis, laughter forgotten as her face turned pale.

Cernunnos said nothing — he just stared at Taliesin, open-mouthed. 'Admiral,' said Taliesin stiffly, 'are you telling me it didn't occur to you to wonder how the goblins managed to capture a sea dragon? And didn't you wonder how a sea dragon managed to get past the Sirens?'

'But...but you may be wrong,' spluttered Lady Sulis. 'The Queen's note only said there was something sinister in the hold of the goblin ship, and Lord Llyr suspected it might be a sea dragon, there was nothing definite about it.'

Taliesin sighed in frustration. 'Believe me, Lady Sulis, when a pod of dolphins flees its post in terror, when there is no marine life to be found within a two-mile radius, you can be sure there's a sea dragon in the vicinity!'

Cernunnos nodded in agreement. 'Aye, that would be the case.'

'Well, sea dragon or no sea dragon, the fleet can't sail until this storm blows itself out. If you want to leave, Lord Taliesin, be my guest, but the death of that fine animal will be a shame, and on your conscience be it,' Lady Sulis retorted tartly. Taliesin winced. He knew she was correct, but every fibre of his being screamed to be on his way.

'Yes, my Lady, you're quite correct. It would endanger Luath's life if he made the journey again with insufficient rest, but I must return one way or another,' he said desperately.

Lady Sulis appeared to be deep in thought for a few seconds, then jumped to her feet. 'I think I may have the answer,' she said, pulling her admiral's cloak around her shoulders. 'Follow me!'

With heads down against the blustering wind and rain, they battled their way across the yard to the barn where Luath was stabled with the rest of the dockyard horses. As Lady Sulis and Cernunnos made their way through the huge building, Taliesin quickly checked in on Luath. He was housed comfortably in a warm loosebox with a cosy straw bed, contentedly pulling hay from a bulging net. He pricked up his ears and whickered softly at the sight of his master. 'Good boy,' Taliesin murmured. 'Enjoy your well-earned rest.' Then he gave Luath's sleek neck a quick pat before following the others.

The barn was L-shaped, and Taliesin hurried to catch up as they turned left and proceeded down a passageway lined with more looseboxes. Lady Sulis stopped halfway down, now accompanied by one of the stable grooms. By the time he caught up with them, the groom was in the loosebox clipping a lead rein onto the biggest unicorn Taliesin had ever seen. He stood about eighteen hands high, with a powerful chest and hindquarters, huge, feathered hooves and a vicious-looking horn in the middle of his forehead. He snorted and stamped, tossing his head in agitation as the hapless groom tried to coax him out of the box. Finally, he stood trembling in the passageway, wild-eyed and obviously terrified.

'Meet Storm,' said Lady Sulis without a trace of irony.

'Appropriate under the circumstances.' Taliesin muttered under his breath, casting an experienced eye over the huge unicorn.

'He won't be as fleet-footed as your magnificent stallion, but with that chest he'll have the stamina to get you home quickly,' continued Lady Sulis. 'Some of my men were on cross-country exercises when they came across a group of goblins who were about to bludgeon him to death.' She grimaced at the memory. 'He was down on his side with his legs and head tied. They arrived just as the goblins were about to deliver the killer blow.' She reached out to stroke the animal's muzzle, but he jerked his head back in fear. 'Poor boy,' she crooned, 'another victim of goblin cruelty.'

'Why do you think they wanted to kill him? He looks every inch a war horse, and that's what their unicorn breeding programme is all about, isn't it?' Cernunnos said, frowning. 'I suppose they found him completely intractable. They like their animals to be obedient and submissive. I don't think they were able to break his spirit, so they were just going to dispose of him.'

Lady Sulis shrugged. 'Who knows? Animals, people, they're all expendable as far as goblins are concerned!'

'Can he be ridden?' Taliesin cut in sharply.

'Yes, he's broken, probably by cruelty and force, but he can be ridden, although only by a strong and experienced horseman.' Lady Sulis gave Taliesin a long, appraising look. 'Someone of your stature, Lord Taliesin, Queen's Warrior and Justiciar!' She emphasised his titles, hard-won through his strength and fitness. Not titles handed to someone who couldn't control a feisty, powerful warhorse or unicorn in the heat of battle or anywhere else.

'I don't fancy taking him out in this weather for a first attempt. Do you have somewhere inside where I could try and put him through his paces?'

The young groom piped up to answer: 'Yes, we have an indoor school where we train the draught horses. This way,' and he dragged a very reluctant Storm along with him.

Taliesin was surprised to find the dockyard barn boasted a very fine indoor schooling arena. The floor was covered in thick sawdust and the guard rails were padded to prevent injury to animals and trainers alike. Unlike the goblins, who broke their animals with cruel force, fairies understood the nature of horses; they were herd animals and needed to belong and feel accepted by the herd, and this was the secret to gaining their confidence.

The others sat on benches as Taliesin led Storm into the arena, holding the lead rein loosely and just walked around slowly, randomly changing direction, never pulling on the rein and always keeping his shoulder near Storm's head. He would stop occasionally, just standing, then move off again. Gradually, the unicorn began to mirror Taliesin's every movement, turning when he turned and stopping when he stopped. By now, Taliesin had dropped the rein and Storm could gallop off to the opposite end of the arena if he chose, but instead he stuck to Taliesin's shoulder. Eventually, he laid a gentle hand on Storm's neck, then moved along his back and down his flank. The unicorn didn't flinch. Taliesin then walked over to where the others were seated, with Storm calmly plodding beside him.

'I think he'll do,' he said to Lady Sulis.

'Well done, my Lord!' she replied, her face wreathed in smiles. 'He is yours. Consider him a gift.'

Taliesin nodded his thanks. 'Has he been measured for a saddle and bridle?' he asked brusquely, eyeing Storm's huge bulk.

'Not yet,' admitted the groom, 'but if you're having him shod before your journey, we can measure him up while the farrier works.'

Lady Sulis looked discomfited. 'I forgot he would need shoeing. I don't know how he'll react to that!'

'He'll be fine if I'm there to steady him,' Taliesin reassured her. 'I just hope you have a saddle big enough or I'll be riding bareback!'

Lady Sulis laughed. 'Don't worry about that,' she said. 'Have you forgotten about our dockyard horses? They're not just draught horses, we do ride them occasionally, so there will be suitable saddles in the tack rooms.'

'Excellent.' Taliesin was itching with impatience. 'If we could just make our way to the farrier, and have the unicorn fitted for tack while he's being shod, I can be on my way as soon as the farrier is finished.'

'Of course,' replied Lady Sulis frostily, thinking to herself that Taliesin really didn't have to make it so obvious that he wasn't bowled over by her charm and hospitality. She preferred her men to be more amenable and appreciative; she would have liked to add him to her list of conquests. Her mouth watered at the thought of running her hands over his hard, muscled body and kissing his beautiful mouth…*Ah, well, perhaps another time,* she thought ruefully.

An hour later, Storm was tacked up and sporting a new set of shoes. The dockyard farrier was a jolly, affable man with a gentle, easy-going manner, ensuring the big unicorn stood calmly throughout. Tacking Storm up with a suitable saddle and bridle proved to be equally uneventful, and despite much quivering, eye-rolling and side-stepping, he allowed Taliesin to mount and settle himself into the saddle.

'Take care, brother,' warned Cernunnos, shaking Taliesin's hand. 'Word tells there's a band of goblins marauding around these parts. When all's done here, I've to update the Queen on the galleon's progress, so I'll bring your horse with me when I come down.'

'Thank you, my friend,' said Taliesin gravely, 'but I fear this blasted weather has done for us. There's no telling what damage will be wreaked if the goblin queen enters our harbour unchecked!'

Cernunnos maintained a more cheerful outlook. 'Ach, you worry too much. The goblins are no match for the Morrigan, and

Andraste's elves will be all over the goblin ship like a plague of mosquitos!'

'And no one's a match for sea dragons!' retorted Taliesin, reining Storm in as he snorted and pawed at one of the many puddles covering the rain-sodden yard, impatient to be off.

'Safe journey, then!' Cernunnos called into the driving rain as Taliesin urged Storm through the dockyard gate and clattered along the village street.

TWENTY-ONE

A Surreal Experience

Harry and Xander found Gwynnie waiting patiently, still seated on the same tree stump. She rose to greet them as they materialised through the coruscating light. 'You've been here all this time?' Xander asked sceptically. Gwynnie raised an eyebrow and laughed.

'You've only been gone about twenty minutes!'

'Don't be ridiculous!' scoffed Xander. Then, realising his mistake said, 'Of course. Sorry, how stupid of me. I forgot about the time conundrum. It's very confusing!'

Gwynnie smiled sympathetically. 'I know how you feel. Molly was away for a few hours, and you told us she'd been with the Fairy Queen for years. Hard to believe!'

'Really disorientating,' admitted Harry, 'and a totally surreal experience, but let's not discuss it here. I could murder a cup of tea — nothing like homemade cake and a brew for grounding the spirit!' He linked his arm through Gwynnie's as they hurried back to the car.

Back at the cottage, after filling Gwynnie and Morven in

with most of the details, both men checked their phones for messages. The best laid plans of mice and men are often waylaid by everyday life and Harry found he had a message from Sue, who was minding the shop in his absence, saying her mother had fallen ill and she'd had to close and drive straight to Exeter. Xander also had a message telling him that, although technically still on sabbatical, he was being recalled because the orchestra had been invited to hold a week of recitals at Wells Cathedral.

Morven and Gwynnie were aghast. 'But how will Molly cope if this goblin creature arrives and you're not there to protect her?' cried Morven, clutching at Gwynnie's arm. 'We'll have to go to her, we can't leave her on her own!'

'Ladies, please,' soothed Harry. 'Molly's not on her own, Laura's with her. The portal has been temporarily secured by Xander's music, and we've learned the goblin king will most likely wait until Hallowe'en before making his move.' Morven and Gwynnie didn't look convinced, saying they would phone Molly as soon as the men left just to reassure themselves she was fine.

'Please don't phone her,' begged Xander. 'She doesn't know we've come to see you, and it would only worry her further.'

Morven looked mutinous, but Gwynnie nodded. 'Yes, you're right, we have to trust you know what you're doing, but please don't keep us in the dark.' She smiled sadly at them. 'It's been so lovely to see you. We'll miss you when you've gone.'

'Speaking of leaving,' said Harry, 'we really must be on our way. Thanks for everything; you've both been marvellous, and we'll be in touch soon. Promise.' They hugged the women and said their goodbyes before climbing into the Volvo to head for the motorway and home.

Xander stared moodily out of the window as they sped up the M5.

'Feeling alright? asked Harry. 'You're very quiet — this whole thing getting to you?'

'It's the noise,' replied Xander. 'I can't get used to the noise.' As if to emphasise the point, a huge articulated lorry thundered past, overtaking several other cars as it hurtled on down the motorway.

'I can feel a but coming on.' Harry looked in the mirror as he overtook a motorhome.

'But…I mean…to be honest…did all that really happen or are we just having some sort of collective delusion?'

Moving smoothly back into the inside lane, Harry lifted an eyebrow. 'A delusion? Go on…'

'One week I'm plodding along with my pleasant but not terribly exciting life…you know…just drifting, I suppose.' Xander ran his hand through his hair, a confused, exasperated look on his face. 'And then, before I know it, I meet my long-lost mother and travel through a portal into another dimension of space and time and, you know what, it seems to me that this was always the plan!'

'Always the plan? I thought we were having a delusion?' Harry gave him a sidelong glance. 'What makes you say that? You knew nothing about Molly or who your grandfather really was. Hell, I knew nothing about him until my mother was dying! Do you think she was delusional as well?'

'No, that's not what I'm saying! I…I don't really know how to explain any of this…whatever it is. You know I've never wanted to settle down, do the whole getting married, have children thing. I never felt the need. I always made my career the excuse, but plenty of my colleagues are married. I've never felt comfortable, always felt as though something was missing, but the minute I went into Molly's garden and looked at all those flowers and plants, I knew something weird was going on, and I knew I was supposed to be there.'

'Well, you could have fooled me!' Harry quipped.

Xander heaved a great sigh. 'I didn't want to admit to myself that there might be some truth to Molly's story — you have to admit, it sounded mad.'

'Well, Molly always did have strange powers — the way plants reacted to her was always weird, but she just laughed it off, and I suppose we just accepted it. We were young and naive. Looking back, maybe I should have paid more attention.'

'Well, she's certainly got our attention now and...Would you look at that idiot!' he yelled angrily as a bag of take-away food cartons and cups was ejected from the window of a car in front of them. The bag hit the road, bursting open and strewing the contents across three lanes of motorway. 'You know, I fully understand why the fairies guard their world so ferociously against us. This is what we would do to it. Destroy it with pollution, litter, wars, weapons of mass destruction...'

Harry interrupted him in full flow. 'They have plenty of wars of their own, I believe, why else have all these armies of warriors? Molly's husband being an example, not to mention Lord Nudd.'

'You're missing the point,' retorted Xander. 'They have no pollution, no litter, the place is quiet, for goodness' sake! No traffic noise for a start. They care about their environment — they see what we've done to ours and they want no part of it. It was one of the first things Molly told us she was taught.'

'They have their ways, we have ours.'

'You mean it doesn't bother you?' Xander was incredulous. 'I thought you of all people would know exactly what I'm talking about!'

Harry shrugged. 'If I'm honest, I'm glad to be home, I felt totally out of my depth, and I'm not a big fan of Molly's *husband*.'

'You mean you're jealous!'

'Don't be ridiculous!' snapped Harry, colouring slightly. 'Molly was married to someone else for years. We were over a lifetime ago!'

'If you say so.'

Harry ignored the remark, saying, 'I take it the delusion theory is out the window, then? So, what else is bothering you?'

'You'll probably think I'm overreacting, but although we were only there a short while, and the Queen absolutely terrifies me, by the way, I felt oddly at home, and I'm a bit depressed that we had to leave.'

'Coming back to reality is a big anti-climax and you're probably having a bit of an emotional hangover.' Harry gave him a sidelong glance. 'Plus, for what it's worth, I think your double dose of fairy blood made it easier for you to adapt. You started speaking the lingo almost immediately, after all, and it transpires you can read ancient scripts that even their best brains couldn't decipher. So, no,' he said with a shrug, 'I don't think you're overreacting at all, and Ceriddwen wants you back. You're the heir apparent, after all!' Xander didn't reply and just continued to stare morosely out of the window.

'Those sheets Ceriddwen gave you are on the back seat — why don't you look at them to pass the time?' suggested Harry. 'You never know what you might find.'

'May as well.' Xander sighed, turning to reach for the plastic bag Gwynnie had given them for the documents. 'At least it'll take my mind off the traffic for a while.' He spent the next fifteen minutes carefully scanning the ancient parchment sheets before finally exclaiming, 'Every sheet has instructions for casting different sonic spells!'

'Remember, spells and magic are just science we don't yet understand,' Harry responded mildly.

'Whatever,' grunted Xander, 'but it explains why Ceriddwen told me to keep playing the music, no matter what I see happening, and you need to hear this right now. Ceriddwen may have been unable to read these sheets, but her intuition was spot on!' He went on to outline in detail what the spells were about, emphasising one in particular. Harry visibly paled and his knuckles whitened as he held the steering wheel in an ever-tighter grip. 'And as if that isn't hard enough to believe, what about this,' Xander continued, 'I thought I was making up the music I played in Molly's garden, but here it is on this sheet, note for note.'

'As I said, a double dose of fairy blood. It's obviously embedded into your DNA. Your playing is instinctive,' Harry said tightly, never taking his eyes off the road. 'So, we'd better hope you get it right at Samhain!'

'That's okay for you to say,' Xander protested defensively, 'when all the pressure is on me!'

Harry was immediately repentant. 'Sorry, son, I'm still trying to process the enormity of this, I didn't mean to get at you — it's almost too much to take in — there's so much we don't understand and I never for a moment imagined...' His voice trailed off miserably.

'I know, Dad — we'll just have to put our trust in Ceriddwen and hope these sonic spells work.' As he put the sheets back into their bag he added, 'I can't believe my life has changed forever in just a few days — I don't even know why I'm bothering with these recitals at Wells.'

'Because we must remain grounded and focused. Doing normal everyday things will help us to do that.'

'I suppose you're right,' Xander agreed doubtfully as they turned off the motorway onto the familiar country road that would take them home.

As they drew nearer to Glastonbury, the Tor rising in the distance like a welcoming beacon, their conversation was desultory to say the least, both men lost in their own thoughts. Xander was troubled by the fact that he had no interest whatsoever in the week of recitals ahead of him. Under normal circumstances, he would be looking forward to it enormously, the adrenalin rush of his solos, the camaraderie of his fellow musicians and the inevitable after-concert parties full of gorgeous women. He just wasn't interested anymore, and if he was completely honest, all he wanted to do was rush back to the Welsh borders, summon Morfan, and go back to do battle with Gwynn Ap Nudd. He felt altered, not himself at all, and when he reflected on the events of the last few days, he had to concede that he had become a different person with a new set of priorities. You don't find yourself in a real-life science fiction story in another dimension of space and time without it having some effect on your sense of self. The fact that he couldn't discuss it with any of his friends didn't help either — they would think he had lost his marbles! He just hoped he had the strength of character to deal with it.

Harry was also deeply troubled. He wasn't lying to Xander when he said he was glad to be back, but he *was* lying when he said he wasn't jealous. He just didn't know how to cope with his feelings. He thought he was well over Molly, even when he first saw her after all that time. She hadn't changed much; older, of course, like him, but when she started to tell that story, he began to remember why he had fallen in love with her. There was something about her, the strange effect she had on trees and plants. She'd laughed at him, but there was no denying it had been hiding there in plain sight all the time — Molly was different and so was he; he had simply been unaware of it for most of his life. Now she was lost to him because she had another love, a love that apparently transcended her feelings for him and more than that, her feelings for Fred, the man she had spent almost forty years of her life with. Taliesin strode relentlessly through Harry's thoughts — strong, handsome, invincible, Queen's Warrior and Molly's husband. He remembered his shock at that announcement. It punched him full in the solar plexus and he had almost gasped out loud with the force of it.

After dropping Xander off at his cottage in Manor House Road, Harry made his way to Benedict Street and headed upstairs to his flat for a welcome shower and change of clothes. They had arranged to meet in Hawthorns at 6pm for a curry and perhaps work out some sort of plan for Hallowe'en.

He found a note from Sue telling him she had arranged shop cover for the next week while she was in Exeter, but if she wasn't back the following week, Harry would have to arrange help himself. He groaned in frustration. Of all the times for this to happen! He would worry about it later; if he had to close the shop for a while, so be it, what they were dealing with was far more important.

Hawthorns was quiet and they managed to find a secluded table where no one could listen in to their conversation. After their meal, the men sat back with a couple of beers and tried to formulate a plan. At least that was Harry's intention. Xander had other ideas.

'Dad,' he began, 'I've come to a decision, and I don't want you to get upset or try and talk me out of it, okay? Will you just listen and let me explain?'

Harry shrugged, gulping down a long draught of Best Bitter. 'Okay, fire away,' he urged, eyeing Xander warily as he put down his glass.

Xander took a deep breath and plunged in. 'No matter what happens at Hallowe'en, if I'm still alive...' Harry's eyebrows shot up indignantly. 'Oh, come on, Dad!' Xander snapped in exasperation, 'it must have crossed your mind that, potentially, this is an extremely dangerous situation?'

Harry opened his mouth to answer, but Xander cut him off. 'At one point I thought we should inform the authorities. It doesn't feel right that we know what a monster this goblin is and the havoc he could wreak, and that we're trying to deal with it on our own.' Seeing Harry's look of utter horror, he gave a humourless laugh and said, 'But don't worry, I soon disabused myself of that notion when I remembered that we're not on our own, we have the entire armed forces of the Fairy Realm at our disposal, notwithstanding the odd dragon or two.' Harry suppressed a shudder as he thought about the possible consequences of the goblin attack. 'Let's hope and pray we can stop Nudd, and the authorities never find out. You know what would happen — our world would invade, exploit, and ultimately destroy Ceriddwen's world. People like us, with our fairy blood, would be regarded as aliens, freaks to be examined and probably feared. It would be like the Spanish Inquisition all over again, only more sophisticated.' After swallowing a mouthful of beer, Xander gazed thoughtfully at the frothy, amber liquid he was swirling in his glass. Harry waited patiently.

'To get back to what I was saying, and we really need to inject a touch of realism into the subject, Dad, it could get very nasty and people may die. What I want to make clear to you is this: If all goes to plan, and we manage to stop the goblin king, then I am going back through the portal for good. That's where my future lies, a fact that has become clear to me very quickly.' Harry stared at him for a moment, then shook his head in consternation.

'But Xander, you just can't walk away from your entire life. I didn't think you meant literally disappear off the face of the earth when you mentioned it earlier!' Harry could barely keep the frustration from his voice. 'You have commitments, a career. What about the family, your friends? What about me? What am I supposed to say to everyone if you simply vanish?'

'Why not?' Xander argued. 'Apart from my job and my mortgage, I don't have any commitments. I'm a free agent and surely, in that respect, I can do as I please?'

'Don't you think, in all probability, you're still in shock? I know I am. I don't know if I'll ever recover from this revelation.

My father was a fairy prince, my son is a fairy prince, my sisters and I are fairy royalty and my mother kept it to herself for years. The whole thing is quite a shock, wouldn't you say?' He paused with a concerned look on his face. 'I don't think this is the time to make rash decisions.'

'Maybe you're right,' conceded Xander, 'but I don't think I'll ever feel the same about my life here again.'

'Just give yourself a bit more time,' Harry pleaded.

'I just wish I was there in the thick of things with Ceriddwen, Lleu and the others, helping with the preparations to try and stop that monster!' Xander's eyes blazed with conviction and passion.

'Yes,' mused Harry, 'I just hope things are going to plan.'

TWENTY-TWO

The Troll King

Once Harry and Xander were gone, Ceriddwen swung into action and issued an urgent call to arms to every ally. They were now on a war-footing with Lord Nudd. This put previous skirmishes and confrontations well and truly in the shade. Nudd was a thorn in everyone's side, not just Ceriddwen's. He had been thoroughly humiliated by the collective opprobrium of the Queen's allies regarding the long-suspected truth of the Anunnaki genocide and the shattering discovery that the line survived through Molly and her son. This revelation meant he could no longer legitimately challenge Ceriddwen for her kingdom, and as he could not countenance such a loss of face, it made him an extremely dangerous foe. Ceriddwen knew that far from lying low and licking his wounds, hoping no one would declare war on him, he had spent his time seeking revenge and fate had been kind — she had delivered a gift beyond his wildest dreams — a portal! Not just any old portal, either. A portal he hoped would enable him to exact absolute vengeance by killing Molly and invading her world.

He craved power above all else. He was much more dangerous than anyone imagined.

When he gate-crashed the dinner party welcoming Molly into Sidhthean, he was backfooted by the discovery that Gwion had fathered children with a human. Never one to accept defeat graciously, Nudd began trying to find out as much as he could about Ceriddwen's mysterious grandchildren. It took his network of spies a long time to glean the necessary information. Kidnap, torture, and murder were his preferred tools of persuasion, although occasionally a large bribe worked just as well until, eventually, he discovered the location of Molly's home. He couldn't believe his luck when his engineers told him that not only was her home built on a ley line but was also the site of a new and unknown portal, and joy of joys, it was sited within one of his mines. Nudd could hardly contain his glee. Once in possession of this knowledge he had thrown all his resources into trying to work out the co-ordinates and best time for opening the portal. Yes, fate appeared to be on his side.

Ceriddwen constantly berated herself for underestimating him, warning her ambassadors not to make the same mistake on their various missions. Her allies swiftly reaffirmed their allegiances, with Lord Dubh and Lady Froya coming personally to pledge their unstinting support. Other allies promised transport, weapons, ships, food, and clothing as well as troops. Ceriddwen was known to be a fair and just ruler, her capriciousness and towering rages forgiven because her loyalty and commitment to the people were unconditional, and all understood the dangerous depths of the goblin king's ambitions. Their world and the human world would change forever if his invasion plans succeeded, and the thousands of years the Tuatha de Danaan had spent keeping the two dimensions apart would have been for nothing. The ensuing chaos and destruction didn't bear thinking about.

The Morrigan's second in command, Lady Keres, was despatched with a large brigade to liaise with King Ossian. His Fianna kingdom was on the other side of the Northern Gate and had the misfortune to share a border with the goblin kingdom. Ossian was an old hand at skirmishing with the goblins, both on sea and land, and he was more than happy to join forces with Ceriddwen. Queen Andraste had already brought him up to speed. She passed through his kingdom on her sortie into goblin territory and, on her way back, shared with King Ossian the disturbing news she had for the Queen.

Thousands of goblin troops were bivouacked around the mine and at least three dragons chained up in makeshift enclosures hidden in a nearby wood. The goblins obviously intended to push a huge invasion force through the portal as soon as they had the correct co-ordinates and conditions. Ceriddwen instructed Lord Varik to send her a full briefing on the cave leading to Nudd's mine, and soon an exhausted courier arrived with a detailed report. The cave ran for several miles before being eventually blocked by an electro-magnetic force field. This was caused by the energy fields of both dimensions coming together at the ley lines, facilitated by huge deposits of quartz, thus creating the conditions for the portal. But no one knew if the portal was on the Cailleach's side or Nudd's. The force field was preventing the goblins from pushing through, and there was no doubt that they would keep trying until they accessed the portal. Varik concluded his message by stating it was only a matter of time before the goblins managed to work out the co-ordinates and open the portal. He believed they were hoping to access it around Samhain when the portal skin was at its atmospheric seasonal weakest. The reports from Varik and Andraste convinced Ceriddwen she would have to take immediate action.

King Jontar, however, was unimpressed by the Morrigan's incursion into his territories, despite being told she was on urgent business. He refused to receive her for several frustrating hours, insisting she camp well away from his sprawling, colourful city with its magnificent buildings and towering spires, while he decided whether to receive her or not. By the time an armed escort arrived, the Morrigan's temper was at boiling point — it was abundantly clear that Jontar had no intention of observing normal diplomatic protocol.

'So be it, if that's how he wishes to play it!' she fumed.

As soon as Jontar's unsuspecting, smirking men trotted nonchalantly into the camp, they were swiftly surrounded, hauled off their mounts, trussed, gagged, and tossed back over their saddles. The Morrigan and her troops then galloped across the lush, green plain, scattering herds of grazing animals in their wake, dragging the hapless escort behind them. Jontar was waiting in a lavishly appointed pavilion outside the gleaming limestone city walls. He sat on a high dais surrounded by courtiers, officials, and a group of flamboyantly dressed women, all chattering and fanning themselves with large ostentatious feathered fans. Complacently expecting little or no complaint from the Morrigan, Jontar had carelessly placed just a handful of guards around the pavilion, and now looked up in alarm at the sound of dismayed shouting and, more ominously, the thunder of galloping hooves. He jumped to his feet in shock as the guards at the entrance fled to avoid being trampled by the Morrigan's huge war horse as she charged straight into the pavilion, skidding to a halt in front of Jontar, followed by several of her cavalry. The rest of her troops surrounded the pavilion outside.

Jontar was a large man with close cropped hair, an aquiline nose and shrewd, deep-set eyes, his face now contorted in fury as he screamed in vain for his guards. 'Silence, King Jontar!' The Morrigan's clear, authoritative voice cut through his outraged protests. Jontar stared at her in disbelief. He couldn't remember anyone ever speaking to him in such a disrespectful manner. Before he could respond, the Morrigan launched into another verbal attack. 'How dare you keep a messenger from the High Queen waiting!' She glared at him contemptuously as Jontar's face purpled in apoplectic fury, his eyes bulging as he tried in vain to get a word in edgeways. 'This is no time for your petty game-playing. I have been sent here in friendship to discuss an extremely important matter. Your intransigence and disregard for diplomatic protocol have wasted hours of valuable time, and I will have no more of it!'

Jontar's women hissed at her, making the sign of evil. 'Ha!' The Morrigan threw back her head and laughed mirthlessly. 'You'll be meeting evil soon enough and not through me or Queen Ceriddwen! I am the Morrigan,' she stated with haughty self-assurance, raising her voice above the loud hissing. 'Commander of *High* Queen Ceriddwen's armies, and I come bearing the Royal Seal. I act with the express authority of the High Queen herself.'

Jontar snorted rudely, although the Morrigan's sharp eyes detected an uneasy shift in his demeanour at the mention of the Royal Seal. He knew he had blundered but didn't wish to lose face. 'I know who you are, Lady Morrigan!' he spat. 'It still does not give you the right to invade my territories and abuse me to my face.'

Ignoring him, she continued. 'It has come to the attention of Queen Ceriddwen that your ill-treatment of Princess Velecia, your own daughter, known as the Cailleach, has resulted in her being attacked and abused by Gwynn ap Nudd, King of the Goblins. He has plundered and ravaged her territories and people, murdering many of them, including babes in arms.'

The Morrigan noticed Jontar's courtiers shifting uncomfortably at the mention of the goblin king. 'How dare Ceriddwen interfere in another kingdom's business!' roared Jontar. 'This is insufferable!'

Unperturbed, the Morrigan stared him down. 'Lord Gwynn Ap Nudd interferes in your kingdom's business, not the Tuatha de Danaan. Lady Velecia appealed directly to Queen Ceriddwen because she knew you would refuse her. This incurred my Queen's displeasure because your lack of paternal care for your daughter and her people, your *subjects*, has resulted in the goblin king becoming a clear and present danger, not only to your daughter, but also to the people of Queen Ceriddwen's realm and beyond.'

'How am I responsible for the actions of that accursed goblin?' Jontar blustered angrily, clearly rattled.

'By leaving your daughter undefended! She had no means of preventing him from mining beneath her land, your land, and when she found herself and her people on the brink of starvation and death because of the goblin king's cruelty and oppression, she reached out to Queen Ceriddwen, who was appalled to discover Nudd's interest in your daughter's estates.'

'His interest?' squawked Jontar. 'Who would be interested in that foul pestilential swamp?'

'Certainly not you,' replied the Morrigan coldly, 'otherwise you would have been aware that Lady Velecia has transformed the land, re-planting its forests and meadows and restoring sweet water and fertility to the entire estate.' Jontar stared at her in disbelief. 'Nudd has cut down her forests and plundered the wood. He uses it to shore up his mine and the surplus he sells, leaving your daughter to starve. He has enslaved her people and mined deep into her territory.'

As Jontar digested this, the Morrigan paused, then asked, 'Are you not curious as to why the goblins are mining beneath your land?'

Some of the courtiers who'd gathered around Jontar began to mutter nervously as the Morrigan waited for an answer. A vein began to pulse in Jontar's temple as he glared at her. 'Well, do enlighten us, Commander Morrigan,' he snarled sarcastically. 'We are all ears!'

'Indeed,' replied the Morrigan, 'there is no need for coyness on our part. The goblins are searching for another portal into the human world and this portal appears to be on Lady Velecia's land, or, should I say, *your* land!' The pavilion erupted with furious shouts and foot stamping. The court was outraged.

'Silence!' roared Jontar. 'I would hear more of this!'

The noise subsided into angry mutterings as the Morrigan continued. 'We believe he intends to invade the human world, first to destroy the Anunnaki bloodline once and for all, and then try to take control of as much territory as he can.'

'Anunnaki? What Anunnaki bloodline?' Jontar sneered. 'They're all dead!' Jontar's eyes narrowed suspiciously, and he drummed his fingers impatiently while the Morrigan calmed her horse as it pawed the ground and tossed its head, excited by the shouting.

Settling back into her saddle, she said, 'By deliberately cutting off diplomatic ties, King Jontar, you fail to keep up with important information. Prince Gwion fathered children with a human, and his son fathered a child with a human with Anunnaki blood. This human is an Anunnaki dragon queen who defeated the goblin queen, Grainne, and executed her son, Prince Jasper. It is this queen whom Lord Nudd seeks to destroy, along with her son, our crown prince. She is presently in the human world, preparing for Nudd's invasion.'

'Apart from mining under my land, you still haven't explained what this has to do with me!' Jontar growled impatiently, ignoring the gasps of disbelief and shock from his people. 'I grow tired of this!'

The Morrigan smiled wryly. 'All descendants of the survivors of the Great Catastrophes have worked together for thousands of years to protect our world from being contaminated, and I make no apologies for using such a strong word, by the human world. All of us, apart from the goblins, that is. They will do anything for power and influence. Their cruelty and wickedness mar our world, but we have contained them thus far. We have deliberately avoided much of human technology because, as we have observed over aeons, they ultimately misuse many of their inventions for personal power, war, greed, and glory. They have no respect for their environment, or the creatures that co-inhabit it. They have the capacity to destroy their world with nuclear weapons — their invention of weapons of mass destruction is foolish beyond belief. Under no circumstances can we allow Nudd to succeed. The humans will annihilate his armies in the blink of an eye with their superior weapons if it gets that far; we are, by our own choosing, primitive by their technological standards.'

She paused for a moment to allow Jontar and his courtiers to absorb this information. They regarded her with growing horror. 'Ultimately, Nudd is not the problem. The problem is humans finding and gaining access to the portals. That must never be allowed to happen, or our world and our way of life will be destroyed forever by human colonisation and greed. Nudd must be stopped to prevent that happening. What say you, King Jontar? Are you with the Tuatha de Danaan or against us?' Again, the pavilion erupted in fury and consternation.

Jontar raised a hand for silence, resting his forehead on the other, digesting the Morrigan's words. Although he was proud and brutal, ruling his kingdom with a rod of iron, Jontar was no fool. He knew their world owed a huge debt to the Tuatha de Danaan. They had policed and protected the portals for thousands of years. No one would be here in this world at all if it hadn't been for the ancient Tuatha de Danaan civilisation. They worked tirelessly, saving thousands of people during and after the catastrophes.

A woman, whom the Morrigan assumed to be his wife, stepped forward and whispered into Jontar's ear. He patted her hand and, as she withdrew, stood up abruptly and announced, 'Tiya, my queen, has wisely suggested we discuss this in a more convivial manner over dinner. Our meal is about to be served if you would care to join us with your senior officers.'

The Morrigan inclined her head politely. 'Very well, but I must remind you, time is of the essence. Queen Ceriddwen must be informed of your decision very soon.'

'You have made your point most eloquently, Commander. You shall have my decision over dinner.'

Jontar's dinner party proved to be business-like and straight to the point. Several of his army officers were present, and during the meal he agreed to put several thousand troops under the Morrigan's command, plus send a company to boost the troops already sent by Ceriddwen to the Cailleach's aid. He also decided to send two platoons of engineers to dismantle part of the infamous wall incarcerating his daughter. This drew shocked looks from the other trolls present, but no one contradicted him. He had wisely decided to heed Ceriddwen's summons, and his mind was made up. When the meal was over, the Morrigan tarried as briefly as etiquette allowed, before thanking her host and his queen for their hospitality and taking her leave.

TWENTY-THREE
Siren Song

Meanwhile, Molly was continuing her painstaking attempts at piecing together the jigsaw of another life she had forgotten about for forty years. The initial shock was beginning to wear off with each succeeding day, but sometimes memories would whoosh into her consciousness, bludgeoning her with an intense ferocity. When Laura dropped her off after breakfast at Vigo's, she decided she would clean her oven, a chore she normally disliked. She thought the mind-numbing boredom would soothe her jumbled thoughts, but her subconscious had other ideas and sure enough, another huge memory assaulted her senses with startling clarity...

~

The storm having prevented Admiral Sulis from putting to sea in time to blockade the huge river harbour, Grainne's man-of-war now squatted in the water like an enormous toad, dwarfing Lord Llyr's ship, now securely anchored and tied up thanks to Lord Ravenna's safe escort. Lord Llyr and his wife, Lady Thetis, were still onboard. Ceriddwen refused to allow them to disembark for the time being. She trusted no one. The Morrigan's troops lined the quayside, Andraste's elves manned the harbour walls, bristling with weapons, while scores of archers stood ready behind the citadel walls. Lord Varik and his men evacuated the worried townspeople and villagers to the safety of the citadel, explaining it was just a safety precaution, as they had never been visited by a goblin man-of-war before. It wasn't a lie, but Ceriddwen had made it clear, in order to avoid utter panic, that the people should be kept in the dark about Grainne's suspected cargo.

Ceriddwen was taking no chances, providing a reassuring and impressive sight as she rode along the quay on her huge black stallion, Arien, eventually taking up position in front of the troops, flanked by Lleu, Morfan, the Morrigan and Andraste. The Arianrhod was there too, seated in a high carriage, accompanied by Lorien, Chief Bard. He insisted his presence was required as the unprecedented arrival of the goblin queen would surely require a lengthy poem. He was in his usual state of polite inebriation through his constant consumption of hazelnut wine, justifying his drunkenness as unavoidable, caused by the necessity of consuming hazelnuts for their known wisdom-producing properties. The Arianrhod sat with a slightly pained expression on her face as he droned on in slurred tones, about his latest treatise on Prince Gwion's exploits.

Ceriddwen was in full battle dress, wearing a tooled leather cuirass and greaves, her hair pulled back in the warrior braid. She was wearing a tall glittering crown with latticed points at each corner representing the Land of The Four Gates and sporting an array of crystal weapons holstered about her person, crystal darts in a belt around her waist and a lethal-looking blowpipe hanging from her saddle. She stared impassively at the goblin ship, as Lleu, in the absence of Lord Taliesin, ordered the Queen's herald to sound the challenge to Queen Grainne. As soon as the goblin herald responded, hundreds of goblin warriors materialised, manning every side and deck of the ship. Grainne stood haughtily on the quarterdeck, dressed in a thick, quilted jerkin tightly belted over calf-length leather culottes and sturdy boots. A bull whip and two lethal looking daggers were thrust into the belt. Her hair was hidden beneath a head-hugging leather cap, although the wind had teased out some blonde strands, and she pushed them away impatiently as they blew about her strong, square-jawed face.

A huge brazier stood behind her blazing furiously, the flames leaping high in the air, almost licking a large hessian-covered bundle hanging from the yardarm above. Grainne glared contemptuously at the armed forces arrayed before her.

'My presence seems to alarm you, Queen Ceriddwen!' she boomed in a loud guttural voice.

'We are not alarmed by goblins guilty of war crimes against us.' Ceriddwen's rich, melodious voice carried effortlessly across the harbour waters. 'We merely make ready to arrest you!'

Grainne's face contorted in fury. Ceriddwen had deliberately insulted her by not referring to her as Queen and recognising her as an equal. 'I am not here to bandy words with arrogant fairies!' she spat. I demand you release my son and his two cousins immediately!'

'You mean the three goblins captured red-handed in an act of war? Impossible, I'm afraid.' Ceriddwen's tone was reasonable, her face implacable.

'Very well.' Grainne smiled maliciously, tugging on a rope hanging from the covered bundle above the blazing brazier. 'You leave me no choice!' The hessian fell away, tumbling into the flames to reveal three trussed figures tangled in a tight net. A collective howl of shock and outrage erupted from the quayside as the full horror of goblin cruelty was laid bare.

The Arianrhod stood up and shouted in a surprisingly strong voice, 'You have no idea what you are about to unleash upon yourself, Goblin Queen!' Ceriddwen turned and gave her a sharp look, but the Arianrhod ignored her. 'If you harm the Sirens, there will be unspeakable consequences,' she continued.

Grainne laughed harshly. 'Their famous singing didn't stop me from capturing them, and it's not going to stop me killing them, either!'

Ceriddwen's troops growled in helpless fury as Grainne sent one of her men scrambling up the rigging. Once he reached the yardarm, he crawled along the beam with a dagger between his teeth, reached inside the net and unceremoniously sliced off the gags tied tightly around the Sirens' mouths. As soon as the gags were removed, the Sirens began to sing, an unearthly, heartbreakingly beautiful sound that echoed around the harbour and beyond, causing everyone, goblins included, to fall into stunned, awe-struck silence.

'Why are they singing when she's going to burn them alive?' Tears were pouring down Morfan's face.

'They sing their Death Song. It will last until they are consumed — it will be the last part of them to die.' The Arianrhod's voice cracked with grief. 'Your Majesty,' she pleaded, 'fetch the princess!' Ceriddwen steadfastly ignored her, staring resolutely ahead, preparing to give the archers the command to attack. The Arianrhod shook her head in disbelief.

Grainne then turned her attention to Lord Llyr's little ship with its seahorse figurehead and pretty, blue sails. 'Hear me, water fairies, lest you be considering directing the river waters to quench these flames, I have a little something that may make you wish to reconsider!' She reached into a basket held by her first officer and pulled a baby out by the ankles. The baby screamed in terror and pain as she held it aloft. A loud, anguished cry came from behind Ceriddwen, and pushing herself through the mass of armed men, Melusine flew to the harbour's edge and threw herself on the ground, sobbing incoherently.

'Please, please don't harm him,' she babbled. 'You promised you wouldn't harm him if I did as you asked.'

Grainne smirked as she held the wailing infant closer to the scorching fire. 'Yes, you were useful, if incredibly stupid, water fairy, but why should I care about your puling child when my child is a prisoner of your accursed Queen?' The assembled crowd listened in horrified outrage.

'I think we have just found our spy,' Lleu whispered grimly to Ceriddwen.

Ceriddwen's face paled in shock. 'Who could blame her?' she replied, tight-lipped with fury. 'Her child's life threatened by that monster?'

Lleu raised his eyebrows. 'Surprisingly magnanimous of you, my dear.'

Grainne watched their reaction with relish. She obviously enjoyed torturing her victims and had no intentions of giving any of them a quick death, but despite the hideous fate about to befall them, the Sirens' mesmerising singing never faltered. The song made its way along the quay, up the harbour steps, into the citadel and through every corridor, room, and magnificent hall, immersing the palace in its haunting melody, until finally, the ethereal refrain found its goal.

Brighid, meanwhile, quietly sewing by Molly's bedside as usual, was trying not to feel irritated by the gossipy Ladies of Astarte. Despite the protocol of not discussing council business outside the chamber, they constantly whispered and gossiped about the goblin queen just out of Brighid's hearing. She was further frustrated by the appearance of two enormous amarok hounds on the other side of the door. Lady Tanith, noticing

Brighid's bemused frown, gleefully asked her why the Queen hadn't bothered to tell her the hounds were coming,

'Surely,' she simpered maliciously, 'someone as important as you would have been informed beforehand.' She turned to her giggling companions and said, sotto voce, 'Obviously not as important as she thinks! '

Gritting her teeth, Brighid tried to ignore them. She had always found Tanith and her ladies irritating and self-absorbed. As if carting the cauldron around and mixing potions made them extra special. Brighid's Aunt Clodagh had been an Astarte Lady. Brighid's connections were impeccable, a fact lost on the current incumbents. Why else would she be looking after a royal princess, trusted completely, and considered to be utterly indispensable, unlike the empty-headed Ladies of Astarte whom Ceriddwen would sacrifice in an instant if she had to?

Silly, gossipy ladies were one thing, huge amarok hounds were quite another. Amaroks were serious competition for truffle hunting pigs, but the fairies seldom used them for that purpose, training them as guard and war dogs instead. Normally loyal, gentle, and wonderful with children, they could become ferocious killers on command. Their appearance outside Molly's room filled Brighid with foreboding, as to place such fierce animals outside Molly's door could only mean that Ceriddwen must have serious fears for her safety. Lost in these thoughts, she looked up in surprise as the Siren song crept into the room. The effect on Molly was startling. She began to mutter and toss her head from side to side, the singing swelling to a desperate crescendo as she became increasingly agitated. Just as Brighid was about to call Tanith for help, Molly opened her eyes, and Brighid's hand flew to her mouth in shock, her sewing tumbling to the floor. Molly's lustrous green eyes revealed vertical, reptilian irises, and, as she turned to Brighid, nictitating membranes flicked across them. Brighid stood frozen to the spot, watching

Molly rise from the bed, step out of her bed gown, and point to her aquamarine dress, now staring in horror at the line of green reptilian scales running the length of Molly's spine. She stood with her arms outstretched, waiting to be dressed, and numbly, Brighid drew the dress over her head then helped her into the matching leather shoes.

Molly appeared to be in a trance, moving like an automaton, guided by the insistent call of the Sirens. Ignoring Brighid, she left the room and made her way along the palace corridors, the amaroks padding silently by her side. Brighid flew after her, noticing the guards shrinking back, allowing Molly and her terrifying hounds to glide past them. She grabbed one of them by his tunic and shook him roughly, hissing furiously, 'Go and tell the Queen!' then she pushed him down a flight of narrow steps into another corridor, as he gawped at her open-mouthed. Having dealt with the guard, Brighid managed to catch up with her as she made her way down the broad steps to the heavily guarded Citadel Harbour gates. Again, the guards made no attempt to stop her, rushing instead to open the massive gates, eyes popping in terrified wonder. Molly paused for a moment, confused by the tumultuous din of weapons being clattered on shields by furious troops. The noise gradually trailed off as they stared at the strange sight of Molly and her amaroks making their way along the wharf towards Ceriddwen and the others, Molly's thick russet hair billowing behind her like a glorious autumn cloak.

As the warriors' loud, outraged shouting and shield banging trailed into awed silence, curiosity got the better of Ceriddwen, and she urged Arien forward to gain a better view. She gasped at the sight of Molly's determined progress along the quay flanked by the amaroks. Grainne, also noticing the sudden hush, coupled with Ceriddwen's interest, turned to see what they were looking at. Unexpectedly, she felt a frisson of alarm, and unceremoniously dropped the squalling infant back into its basket. Ignoring Melusine's anguished screams, she reached into her skirt pocket and produced a small telescope, training it on Molly as she drew closer. She lowered the telescope in consternation.

'Who is this woman?' she muttered. 'Is this the half-human mother of their new prince my fool of a husband was babbling about?'

While musing on these thoughts, she was astute enough to notice a change in the cadence of the Sirens' song and raised the telescope again to take another look. This time she almost dropped the telescope in shock, clutching it tighter before screwing up her eye for another look. None of this had gone unnoticed by Ceriddwen, who sat grim-faced and silent, just as shocked as Grainne, but still unaware of the change in Molly, a change that Grainne had noticed and found extremely worrisome. Paying no attention to Melusine sobbing hysterically on the ground, Molly stood in front of the goblin vessel, gazing up at the unfortunate Sirens. Ceriddwen began to push Arien forward again, but the Arianrhod held out a restraining arm as Morfan and Lleu began to follow.

'No, Your Majesty, you must not interfere. This is Anunnaki business. As I said, Grainne does not know what she has unleashed upon herself.'

Ceriddwen furiously shook off the Arianrhod's arm, but reluctantly moved her stallion back, watching in helpless, impotent rage. Molly stood silent for a few moments before calling to the Sirens in a strange language. 'She is speaking to them in the Anunnaki tongue,' breathed the Arianrhod, scarcely able to contain her excitement. 'The alchemy is working!'

Ceriddwen shot her a venomous look but said nothing, steadying Arien instead. The troops were muttering uneasily, and Morfan wished that Taliesin and Varik were with them.

'I know Varik is protecting the township and villagers,' he whispered to Lleu, 'but surely Taliesin should have returned by now?'

'He sent word. He is on his way,' murmured Lleu, watching the proceedings in nervous trepidation. He leant towards Ceriddwen. 'I think now is the time to fetch the goblin prince, my dear.'

'Not until Lord Taliesin returns. Protocol demands that the Justiciar deals with valuable prisoners,' Ceriddwen replied impatiently. 'Why isn't he here? He had no right to rush off like that without my permission!'

Lleu rolled his eyes with a sigh. 'The small matter of a sea dragon possibly about to be unleashed on us from that ship? Surely it hasn't slipped your mind.'

'Of course not!' Ceriddwen snapped. 'And I'll thank you not to take that tone with me! You forget yourself, husband.'

'I apologise, my Queen,' Lleu replied soothingly. 'We mustn't let Grainne think we are quarrelling amongst ourselves, now do we?'

Grainne eyed Molly uneasily. Her goblin instincts were screaming danger, but her pride and arrogance would not let her believe what she was seeing. 'It's a trick,' she told herself. 'We killed them all, right down to the last child.' Having convinced herself, she decided to try and regain the upper hand, pointedly ignoring the restless mutterings coming from her sailors, who were becoming increasingly unnerved at the sight of this strange fairy woman.

'How dare you address my prisoners without my permission, fairy woman!' she screeched. 'Don't you know how to address a queen?' And drawing herself up even more haughtily, said, 'I am Queen Grainne, wife of Gwyn ap Nudd, goblin king. And who, may I ask, are you?'

Molly reverted to the fairy tongue. 'I know very well who you are, goblin! The Siren song told me all I need to know!'

Grainne's lips tightened in fury at the insult and reaching into the basket to retrieve the unfortunate baby, she began to swing him to and fro, edging nearer to the burning brazier. 'Have you come for a better view of the execution?' she sneered. 'Who shall we despatch first? This snivelling infant, or the three screeching harridans?'

Molly stared her down, ignoring Melusine's frantic pleas. 'You will release my subjects immediately,' she told Grainne in a reasonably calm tone.

'Your subjects?' Grainne glared at her haughtily, trying to suppress a most unwelcome feeling of deep unease. 'These squawking wretches are MY subjects — *I* rule the lands of the Anunnaki — the lands these creatures are supposed to guard!' She laughed harshly. 'Who are you to question my authority, fairy?'

'I am their Queen, goblin, and you displease me at your peril!' Molly stood tall and unafraid, flanked on each side by her huge amaroks, as Grainne's sailors whispered nervously among themselves at this revelation.

'Stay at your posts or I'll have you all flogged,' Grainne snarled as some of the sailors began to draw their weapons and mill about the decks, taunting the warriors behind Molly. She turned her attention back to Molly as the ship's officers forced the recalcitrant sailors back to their posts.

'I don't take orders from fairy nonentities. Tell your Queen to stop hiding behind her warriors and bring me my son! I've had enough dissembling and procrastination,' she continued defiantly, then screamed, 'I want my son and just to make sure your minds are focused on that fact, I'm going to treat you all to a bonfire. Are we too late to call it a Samhain bonfire? I know how you fairies love your little celebrations!'

With a nasty chuckle, she turned to her first officer and ordered him to loosen the rope holding the Sirens above the blazing fire. Before he had time to react, huge green clumps of waterweed erupted from beneath the harbour waters, dousing the brazier flames in a hissing blanket of dripping weed, a separate clump gently creating a cradle for the baby. Water weed stems snatched it from Grainne's startled grasp, before wrapping themselves firmly around her wrists, imprisoning her on the quarterdeck. Everyone on the quay stood open-mouthed as Molly appeared to direct the water weed in much the same way the water fairies controlled water.

Grainne quickly tried to regain control, screaming, 'Man the oars, man the oars!' Almost at once the huge ship tried to back out of the harbour, but the waterweed, rooted deep in the riverbed, held it firmly in place. At a nod from Ceriddwen, Andraste ordered her elves into action. They rushed to the harbour's edge and began hurling their shimmering ropes at the straining ship. As soon as the ropes gained purchase, the elves swung themselves aboard, and as some began fighting in earnest with the goblins, others untied the gangplank and swung it into place enabling more elves to swarm onto the ship. Some of the goblins jumped overboard and others tried to rush down the gangplank towards Molly as Grainne struggled to free herself, hurling screaming curses at her men, ordering them to kill Molly. The snarling amaroks crouched protectively beside her, and Ceriddwen watched with satisfaction as one of them seized a knife-wielding goblin by the throat, killing him instantly, blood spraying everywhere. It stood, blood dripping from its jaws, defying another goblin to approach. Molly turned to Ceriddwen, who stared in shock at the sight of her strange saurian eyes.

'Your Majesty, I must board this ship and attend to the Sirens and my dragon.' Ceriddwen, who could see that Molly was in thrall to a different personality, and not her usual self at all, hesitated for a moment, unsure what to do.

The Arianrhod leant forward and whispered urgently, 'Do as she asks, my Queen, and quickly. She is not yet strong enough for this and will weaken quickly once the Sirens stop singing. She has drawn strength from their music, but it will not last. Her body hasn't had time yet to fully assimilate the alien DNA.'

Ceriddwen turned and motioned to the Morrigan, who was itching to join the affray. 'Clear the way for the princess, kill them all if necessary, but bring that goblin hag to me in chains!'

The Morrigan didn't have to be told twice, and letting out a terrifying ululating battle cry, charged up the gangplank on her enormous war horse, her warriors rushing behind her screaming their own war cries as she laid into the goblins with lithe ferocity, scything through them, a weapon in each hand. Molly stood on the harbour, protected by her amaroks and the four guards Ceriddwen had ordered to her side, watching the fighting with detached interest. She seemed unconcerned by the noise, the agonised screams, the triumphant battle cries and the metallic smell of blood and fear permeating the air. She glanced at the Sirens and called encouragingly to them in the strange Annunaki tongue. Their constant singing could only just be heard above the battle melee. Ceriddwen rode furiously along the harbour, barking orders to the elves on the walls and the archers high on the battlements. All bows were to be trained on Grainne, still held fast by the waterweed. Ceriddwen was taking no chances that she might manage to free herself and flee.

As she galloped back towards the ship, she saw Morfan trying to move his horse towards Molly. He was arguing with the Arianrhod who obviously wanted him to stay put. 'Don't be ridiculous,' Morfan cried, 'I'm not letting Molly climb aboard that ship on her own!'

'She's not on her own and she won't want your help, my Lord,' protested the Arianrhod. 'At this moment, she does not recognise you as her kin.'

'Well why is she allowing our troops to help?' Morfan retorted furiously.

'To clear the way for her! She must attend to the Sirens. She knows the warriors will release them, but then they must leave.'

'Why?' persisted an ever more truculent Morfan.

'Because she has to deal with the dragon!'

Ceriddwen pulled Arien up and laid her hand on Morfan's arm.

'My son, have you ever seen a sea dragon?'

'You know I haven't, Lady Mother,' he admitted.

'Well, soon you shall.' Removing her hand from his arm, she dismissed him with a peremptory gesture, and he reluctantly moved back beside Lleu, helplessly fuming.

The Arianrhod nodded her gratitude. 'Thank you, my Queen. Soon we shall see the power of an Anunnaki dragon queen.'

TWENTY-FOUR

Retribution

The goblins were also, of course, seasoned warriors and fought ferociously with more and more of them emerging from the depths of the ship, armed to the teeth, and screaming defiance at Ceriddwen's men; their prime aim to try and free Grainne still securely tangled in the waterweed. The first officer, along with several men, had rushed to her side in a vain attempt at rescue, but were cut down by Ceriddwen's sharp-eyed archers, and the unfortunate officer was despatched by a head blow from the Morrigan's rearing war horse. Despite this, the goblins seemed prepared to die for their queen, and continued to fight back with astonishing tenacity as the Morrigan repeatedly attempted to gain access to the quarter deck to remove Grainne.

Amid the noise and confusion, Ceriddwen saw Molly whisper something to one of the guards standing stoically beside her, weapons drawn in readiness. He seemed unsure and looked nervously at the fighting warriors, but nodded reluctantly, and began fighting his way up the gangplank.

'What's he doing?' Ceriddwen demanded, ordering one of her bodyguards over to find out. He came back a few moments later, bowing low.

'He has gone to fetch the baby, my Queen!'

'The baby?' Ceriddwen frowned.

'Melusine's baby, my dear,' prompted Lleu. 'The reason she was spying on us, remember?'

Ceriddwen nodded. 'Yes, of course! I'd forgotten about the baby, but how is one warrior going to bring it safely ashore?'

'That remains to be seen,' Lleu replied grimly.

What they hadn't noticed was the amaroks Molly sent with the guard. They slashed, ripped, and tore throats and flesh in a snarling, blood–drenching fury from any goblins who dared challenge them. Amaroks were trained to track and kill goblins and these hounds were living up to their fearsome reputation. They circled the area beneath the quarterdeck and the guard positioned himself below the waterweed cradle holding the baby's basket. Molly made a deft hand movement, and the waterweed released the basket, dropping it neatly into the guard's waiting arms. As goblins fled the ferocious amaroks, he quickly made his way back down the gangplank and handed the basket to Molly, who then sent him across to Ceriddwen, sitting impatiently on her horse as the battle raged in front of her.

Shocked by what she heard, the Queen quickly turned to consult the others. The Arianrhod leant over the carriage to hear what was being said while Lorien lolled drunkenly in his seat, garrulously reciting passages from the battle saga he was composing, oblivious to the actual reality as Lleu, Morfan and the Arianrhod digested Molly's message. Ceriddwen was still infuriated by Taliesin's absence.

'It's untenable that he should be absent at such a time of crisis!' she fumed, and turning to Lleu, snapped, 'I thought you said he was on his way?'

'Yes, I did say that,' Lleu replied mildly. 'About an hour ago, if you recall. Patience, my dear, patience.'

'I don't have time for patience!' Ceridwen retaliated furiously. 'Molly wishes a decision now!'

'Well make one, you are the Queen after all. We are here to advise, but the final decision is yours.'

'Remember what I said, Your Majesty,' the Arianrhod reminded her. 'You must let her use her power. This is Anunnaki business.'

Ceridwen glared furiously at the three faces calmly waiting for her to make her move, then raised her arm imperiously and signalled to the waiting trumpeter, who, after a somewhat startled hesitation, sounded the retreat.

Trained to obey instantly, the fairy and elven warriors turned and streamed off the ship, slipping and sliding down the blood-soaked gangplank. The Morrigan turned in surprise, weapons held aloft, a look of disbelief on her face, before urging her mount down the gangplank behind the bemused troops, his nostrils flaring and ears laid back in battle-lust, goblin jeers and insults ringing in their ears.

Meanwhile, although most people were shocked that Melusine had been coerced into spying for the goblins by the kidnapping of her baby, her offence was still extremely serious, and once Molly appeared on the scene, she was whisked away and placed under arrest. Lord Llyr and Lady Thetis watching helplessly from their little ship as their daughter was bound in shimmering crystal rope and surrounded by four stone-faced guards.

Despite the uproar and confusion caused by the retreat, angry warriors milling around, some calling for their wounded comrades to be attended to and others jostling for position behind the reformed shield wall, Molly gently lifted the whimpering baby out of the basket and carried him across the harbour towards Ceridwen, her strange eyes glowing with an alien fervour.

'The child needs his mother, Your Majesty,' she announced, facing Ceriddwen confidently, queen to queen. Ceriddwen was struggling to balance her love and fear for Molly with the need to reassure her people that, as their Queen, she was in full control of events as normal, but this situation was something outwith her normal scope of expertise.

'Yes, I can see that,' she agreed, nodding to Morfan who turned to the carriage and beckoned Brighid, who was now sitting with Lorien and the Arianrhod. Brighid climbed down from the carriage and, after a quiet word with Morfan, took the baby from Molly's arms. Molly seemed to recognise her and relinquished the baby without question. Brighid pushed her way through the press of warriors and horses to the harbour wall where Melusine was being held. Once the guards had untied her hands, she placed the baby in her arms then made her way back to the carriage to the sound of Melusine's sobs of joy and relief.

Molly returned to the harbour's edge and faced the howling mob of goblins who believed they had beaten off Ceriddwen's warriors of their own accord. They hurled insults at her, but were wary of launching another attack, aware of the archers high on the citadel walls itching for the order to fire. To Ceriddwen's horror, Molly began to climb the gangplank preceded by the amaroks and followed closely by her guards. Grainne was still trussed in waterweed, screaming curses, her face contorted by a mixture of fear and defiance. Again, Molly summoned the waterweed and great green, dripping ropes reared out of the water onto the ship, flinging the goblins against any surface they could find, snaking after them wherever they fled, imprisoning them behind strong, slippery stems as thick as a man's arm.

Molly made her way onto the quarterdeck and ignoring Grainne, ordered two of the guards to lower the net containing the Sirens who were still bravely singing, although noticeably weaker. The guards gently sliced the net from around the exhausted creatures. They were tiny little things, only as high as Molly's waist, with strange bird-like feet and humanoid faces. Their eyes were huge with terror, and they clung to Molly's gown as she spoke soothingly to them in the strange Anunnaki language, at the same time indicating the guards fetch them water, which, after reassurance from Molly, they drank in great desperate gulps. Molly's words seemed to soothe them, and they allowed themselves to be gently lifted and carried off the ship, safely wrapped in the guards' cloaks.

Molly waited until they were back on the harbour, then turned to Grainne, who glared at her defiantly. 'I shall now retrieve my dragon, goblin,' she said, strange eyes watching, unblinking, as Grainne visibly blanched. 'Do you think she will wish to reacquaint herself with you?' Grainne said nothing. 'You are strangely silent for a change,' Molly taunted her. 'Very well, let's see if she remembers you!'

Grainne's eyes bulged in fear as Molly left the quarterdeck and made her way to the huge trapdoor over the hold at the steerage end of the ship. She had her guards release four of the goblins, forcing them to haul the trapdoor open. A rush of fetid air escaped from the dark, dank interior, but even those watching from the harbour who had had the misfortune to previously encounter sea dragons, were unprepared for the nightmare about to emerge.

The four goblins fled in terror as an ophidian head with large bulbous eyes furtively crept over the entrance, blinking in the unfamiliar light. This head was followed by another five heads, each on a long sinuous neck, but as the creature's eyes became used to the light, it let out a startled hiss, lifting all six heads for a better look. The watching crowd gasped in horror as it began to change shape, swelling and metamorphosising into a huge scale-covered body with long lethal claws sprouting from its front limbs. The now powerful, muscular shoulders supporting the six heads were enclosed in a circle of strange nubbly protuberances, and the horrified onlookers watched in appalled fascination as long spikes began to emerge, surrounding the dragon's necks and heads in a fearsome, impenetrable ruff. The heads grew elongated snouts accommodating ferocious teeth as long snake-like tongues darted in and out, scenting the air.

From her vantage point on the harbour, Ceriddwen's acute fairy instincts told her this enormous, fearsome beast was terrified, and she held up her hand to stay any over-enthusiastic archers who might let fly in the heat of the moment. The creature began casting its heads about as though searching for something. Fortunately, just as it was about to rear up to its full gargantuan height, the Sirens began to sing from the enveloping depths of the guards' cloaks. The dragon located the direction of the singing and tried to move its enormous bulk forward, but collapsed with an agonised groan, before again trying to haul itself painfully out of the hold.

Molly whispered something to one of the two guards still with her, who, after a moment's surprised hesitation, nodded and rushed along the ship, down the gangplank and towards Lord Llyr's ship. As the Sirens continued singing to the dragon, Molly began to move towards it, crooning softly.

Ceriddwen tried to suppress a mounting sense of panic. 'What's she doing?' she asked no one in particular.

Her mounted personnel were having difficulty controlling their normally well-trained mounts, but the sight and smell of the dragon terrified them. One of the younger, more skittish horses had already bolted, galloping headlong towards the harbour gates after throwing its hapless rider. Even Ceriddwen's faithful steed, Arien, tossed his head and sidestepped in obvious distress. Ceriddwen kept expecting Molly to collapse in a heap following the Arianrhod's pronouncement, and when the Sirens stopped singing on their release from the net, she was prepared to forget protocol and jump from Arien's back to rush to Molly's side. Molly hadn't collapsed, of course, but time was marching on, and Grainne was still screaming from the quarterdeck. Ceriddwen felt like ordering an archer to shoot a bolt through her black heart to silence her. She turned and asked the Arianrhod, 'Do you understand what she's doing? I can hardly bear to watch. I'm terrified that beast will devour her!'

To Ceriddwen's intense irritation the Arianrhod seemed unconcerned. 'She is receiving instructions through the Sirens' singing. They have also told the sea dragon who Molly is. It won't harm her, quite the contrary, as we shall soon see, Your Majesty.'

As Molly moved closer to the dragon, it swung its heads from side to side, the fearsome spiny ruff rearing up menacingly then lying flat against its body as it tried at first to move away from Molly's advances, withdrawing five of its heads to hide in the hold. Eventually, it placed the visible head on the deck and allowed Molly to touch it. Everyone on the harbour held their breath, anticipating a dreadful finale to this horrible spectacle. What happened next was astonishing. As soon as Molly began to stroke the dragon's hideous head, it seemed to fall into a stupor, apparently calmed by her presence. She reached behind its head and deftly plucked one of the vicious spines from its ruff, slipping it into the pocket of her gown. As she continued stroking, the creature began to shrink smaller and smaller until it was the size of a small cat, reabsorbing the five extra heads and allowing Molly to gently lift it and place it on her shoulder whereupon it wrapped itself around her neck, hiding its head in her hair. Still stroking the emaciated little body, Molly walked back to the quarterdeck and faced Grainne.

'Think yourself lucky, goblin, that this poor animal is so sick and hungry, it doesn't have the energy to deliver you the fate you so richly deserve. But fear not, Queen Ceriddwen will be delighted to do the honours instead.' She turned to the guards behind her. 'Make ready to take her to the Queen!'

The guards surrounded Grainne, each holding a shimmering rope, and Molly made a quick upward movement with her hand. The waterweed released Grainne as the guards deftly bound her in a coil of unforgiving liquid crystal before bundling her down the steps towards the gangplank and the waiting Queen. While all this was going on, Morfan was gabbling incoherently to his father about what they had just witnessed. Lleu was equally astounded.

'I had no idea they could do that!' exclaimed Morfan. 'Or did Molly do it? Can she control their size like that? Do you think that's its real size? Who would have guessed they could be that small!'

'Yes,' agreed Lleu. 'Tiny when you consider the size of winged dragons.'

'I wonder if the giant size is a glamour it puts on to terrify its enemies?' commented Ceriddwen, never taking her eyes off Molly and Grainne, until she was distracted by a commotion at the main harbour entrance. Urging Arien forward, she saw a huge grey unicorn thundering towards her, with a horse on a lead rein galloping behind. Ceriddwen was bemused by the combination of loud cheers, shouts of recognition and outright insults flying from the troops and warriors watching. As the unicorn drew closer, Ceriddwen saw that Taliesin had finally arrived, having apparently decided to first make a detour via the prison tower, for on the horse behind him sat the trussed and furious figure of Prince Jasper.

The unicorn skidded to a halt in front of Ceriddwen as Taliesin leapt from the saddle and bowed low. She raised her hand to silence the noisy, cheering troops, delighted that their Justiciar had returned, and fixed Taliesin with a hard glare.

'How good of you to grace us with your presence, Lord Taliesin,' she said coldly. 'Fortunately, Princess Molly rose to the occasion in your absence.' Before Taliesin could reply, she added, 'And I mean that literally; she rose from her sickbed to deal with that creature's mother!' She gave a dismissive nod in Prince Jasper's direction as he was unceremoniously hauled off the horse and roughly forced to his knees in front of her.

Taliesin looked over to the harbour's edge and cursed aloud when he saw Molly. She was now feeding the starving sea dragon with tiny minnows from a bowl provided by Lord Llyr and Lady Thetis.

'Forgive me, Your Majesty,' he muttered apologetically, 'I did not expect to see the princess — I thought she would still be in hospital.'

'And that's where she should be, my Lord!' Ceriddwen snapped. 'I am afraid you have missed most of the excitement, if that is an appropriate description.'

'And what of the sea dragon, Your Majesty?' he asked quickly, looking nervously at the huge goblin ship. 'Has it been dealt with?'

'Oh yes, my Lord Justiciar!' Ceriddwen laughed mirthlessly. 'It is wrapped around the princess's neck, like one of my cats!'

Taliesin snorted in puzzled disbelief, surveying the battle scene; the wounded warriors being tended by fairy medics and the three Sirens still wrapped in the guards' cloaks. This was an unprecedented situation. Normal protocol seemed to have been abandoned, Her Majesty seeming to act in a most un-queen-like manner. He could hardly believe he had allowed that thought to materialise, and instantly dismissed it. He had the intelligence and experience to realise something monumental had occurred in his absence, and the crux of it seemed to be Molly.

He noticed Grainne, securely imprisoned in the shimmering ropes, just as she noticed her son kneeling in front of Ceriddwen.

A Dynasty of Dragons

She began to scream at him. 'Jasper, my son! You are a prince! Get off your knees! Goblins don't kneel to snivelling fairies!' She then turned her attention once more to Ceriddwen, howling at the top of her voice, 'If you dare harm my son, the goblin nation will rise and destroy you as we destroyed the Anunnaki! And your little Anunnaki pretender doesn't frighten me!'

'Ha!' retorted Ceriddwen. 'I rather think she does!' Grainne struggled helplessly against the ropes, continuing to shriek curses at all and sundry.

At the mention of Prince Jasper, Molly froze, minnow in hand, slowly turning to look at the kneeling prince, then back to Grainne. Grainne stopped shrieking and watched Molly in wordless horror as she gave the minnow to the dragon, handed the bowl to a guard, and began to walk towards Jasper. Ignoring everyone else, including the horrified Taliesin, she reached into the pocket of her gown, and before anyone could stop her, thrust the sea dragon's spine deep into Jasper's neck. He gave an agonised scream before collapsing onto the ground.

Molly gave him a derisory glance, nodded to Ceriddwen, and returning her attention to Grainne, called out, 'Retribution, goblin! Let that be a warning to those who have laid claim to Anunnaki lives and lands!'

A shocked stillness befell the seething mass of bodies and restless animals until Lleu broke the spell by snapping his fingers for medics, who swiftly bore the unfortunate prince away as Grainne resumed her shrieking and wailing, promising to wreak vengeance on everyone, and on Molly and Ceriddwen in particular.

'Is he dead?' asked Morfan.

'I would say most likely,' replied Lleu. 'I have never heard of anyone surviving sea dragon venom.'

Despite being desperately worried about Molly, and appalled by her actions, Taliesin had no alternative but to quickly assume his normal role of command regardless of his own feelings. He began to issue orders, holding a quick meeting with the Morrigan and Queen Andraste to assess their casualty numbers and decide what to do with the goblin prisoners. Lord Ravenna was summoned to take charge of the goblin ship. Once the goblins were removed, he was to sail it downriver to a breaking yard until Ceriddwen decided what to do with it.

After a short consultation with the Arianrhod, it was decided the goblin prisoners be held in the Crystal Tower's Correction Centre, a formidable prison built into a hill behind the tower, where they were to be held until the outcome of Grainne's trial. There was no confusion as to Grainne's fate. She would be formally charged with genocide, kidnapping, warmongering and threatening the lives of sister queens, being arraigned for trial as soon as possible. Fairy law decreed that all their allies be present, which meant the trial would be delayed until all concerned had arrived. In the meantime, Grainne would be securely incarcerated in the palace prison where the unfortunate Prince Jasper's cousins still languished. Standing in front of Ceriddwen, she maintained a defiant demeanour despite the denouement of her plans and demise of her son. Ceriddwen almost felt sorry for her.

'We shall not meet again until your trial, Queen Grainne,' said Ceriddwen, obeying protocol and addressing Grainne by her title, although it almost choked her to do so.

'I do not recognise your authority, fairy,' Grainne sneered, pointedly ignoring protocol. 'My husband will wreak vengeance and havoc upon you and your snivelling people!'

'That remains to be seen,' Ceriddwen replied, without rancour, knowing that would further infuriate her prisoner. 'Captain,' she called, 'remove the prisoner to the tower.'

Grainne held her head high, attempting to throw off the guards' restraining hands as they propelled her towards the citadel's huge gates and through numerous courtyards before being swallowed by the grim windowless tower.

A Dynasty of Dragons

Amid all this drama, as the sinking sun sent pink streaks across the sky and lengthening shadows began to play hide and seek amongst the ships' hulls, Morfan noticed Molly and her entourage making their way towards Lord Llyr's little blue ship.

'What's she doing now?' Morfan asked anxiously, watching Lord Llyr's gangplank being slowly lowered.

Lleu frowned. 'I'm not sure,' he replied. 'The guards carrying the Sirens are following her. It looks as though she's going to give the Sirens to Lord Llyr!'

'But the Queen hasn't allowed that. Lord Llyr can't do anything without Mother's express permission.' Morfan was horrified at Molly's total disregard for proper protocol. 'I'll have to alert the Queen, there's still the matter of Melusine to deal with, too!'

Lleu pushed his mount through the milling throng of warriors, goblin prisoners and medics just as Ceriddwen's bodyguard was helping her remount following Grainne's departure. As she settled into the saddle, Lleu quickly told her what he thought Molly was doing. She nodded curtly, trying to gather her thoughts, steadying Arien as he pranced and fought the bit impatiently. She knew she had to regain control of the situation, aware that Molly's strength could give out at any moment.

'Lord Taliesin,' she called imperiously, trying to make herself heard above the cacophony of noise around them, 'I would speak with you now.'

Hearing her call, Taliesin, who had also remounted, quickly made his way to the Queen's side, Storm's formidable horn instantly clearing the way as people dived for safety.

'I don't have time to explain fully, Lord Taliesin,' said Ceriddwen as he drew alongside, 'but the princess is not, how can I put it, exactly herself just now.' Taliesin nodded; he had already worked that out for himself. 'She is very weak, her constitution hasn't had time to fully assimilate the Anunnaki

DNA and, according to Mother Arianrhod, she is only being sustained by the Sirens' singing, and they are also weakened by their ordeal. They cannot support the princess for much longer. The situation is becoming untenable.'

'What do you wish me to do, Your Majesty?'

'Take Lleu and Morfan and find out what she is up to. You know how to deal with the amaroks, they will not attack you, but you must be careful of the sea dragon. If it thinks you mean harm, it will become aggressive and that doesn't bear thinking about.'

Taliesin swallowed. He was a brave man, afraid of very little, but dragons terrified him, especially sea dragons. The fact that one was now draped innocuously around Molly's shoulders terrified him even more.

Noting the flicker of concern, Ceriddwen leant over and laid her hand on his arm. 'I know I am asking much of you, Lord Taliesin, but if you love Princess Molly as much as I think you do, you know you must do this, and do it well.'

Taliesin, Lleu and Morfan rode along the quayside towards Lord Llyr's ship, dismounting a few yards away. As they walked towards the group, Molly turned in surprise as Taliesin called to her, bowing politely.

'Princess Molly, forgive the intrusion, but the Queen asks what business you have with Lord Llyr.'

As soon as Lleu, Morfan and Taliesin made their appearance, the guards immediately stood to attention, including those cradling the Sirens. The amaroks slunk back at Taliesin's snapped command, snarling and growling, eyeing the newcomers warily. Molly stared at them, exhaustion etched on her face, her strange reptilian eyes glittering feverishly.

'Is it not obvious? I am sending the Sirens home! They must return before the web is further broken by their absence and the other sea dragons come looking for them.' As if to emphasise the point, the dragon hissed threateningly from behind the curtain of Molly's hair. She began stroking its head reassuringly until the hissing subsided.

Taliesin looked at the shadows beneath Molly's eyes, her parched, cracked lips and her expression showing exhaustion, and he wondered when she last ate or drank. She looked as though a puff of wind could snatch her away.

'I know the Sirens must be returned, Princess, but Lord Llyr cannot just up anchor and leave without the Queen's permission. He has been summoned here for important business reasons.'

At that point, Lleu called out, 'Lord Llyr, the Queen commands that you raise your gangplank at once. You have not been granted permission to lower it.'

'No! No! They must leave now!' Molly cried out in anguish. 'We cannot delay any longer!'

'Princess, I am afraid we must,' Taliesin replied gently.

Sensing Molly's agitation, the sea dragon emerged from beneath her hair and, clinging to her shoulders, reared up and began to sprout spines from the knobbly protuberances along its back and shoulders, the former hissing becoming an ominous growl. The spines continued to form the poisonous ruff as its body began to swell inexorably.

'Princess, I beg of you, calm the dragon, we mean you no harm!' Taliesin could feel beads of sweat forming on his forehead as all three men, plus Molly's guards, began to back away.

Her knees began to buckle under the ever-increasing weight on her shoulders and just as everyone thought she was about to be crushed beneath the expanding dragon, the Sirens began a gentle rhythmic hum, hypnotising and calming the dragon into lowering the spiny ruff and shrinking back to its former size. As she struggled back to a standing position, the Sirens began to sing another song, this time directed at Molly. She stared at them in confusion, then to Taliesin's relief, and the guards' horror, unwound the dragon from around her shoulders and placed it into the open arms of one of the Sirens.

'She won't harm you while she is with the Sirens,' Molly managed to whisper to the terrified guard just as she was beginning to lose consciousness, the Sirens and the little dragon chattering in distress as she slumped onto the hard, unforgiving harbour cobbles.

TWENTY-FIVE

Melusine

Molly was confined to hospital, sleeping most of the time, but eating and drinking a little when awake. She was very weak as her body fought to assimilate the alien DNA and prevent it from completely overwhelming her human physiology. Ceriddwen provided potions from the cauldron, enriched with specially chosen healing herbs, but otherwise took a step back, leaving Molly in the care of Masters Lenus and Heka. It was Brighid, of course, who was really in charge, bustling in and out the room, bullying the doctors and issuing orders to the indignant Ladies of Astarte.

'That'll teach them to look down their pretty little noses at me!' she grumbled to herself.

Queen Grainne's trial came and went very quickly. It was held in the State Law Courts, situated deep within the Crystal Tower, and the magnificent courtroom was packed to capacity. Ceriddwen, enthroned upon a high dais, had an uninterrupted view of the proceedings. The cauldron stood nearby with Lady Tanith in attendance. Ceriddwen would not hesitate to force

Grainne to drink from the cauldron should its truth-inducing properties be required.

Ceriddwen's allies turned out in force. As well as her own Tuatha de Danaan fairy folk, silver-haired mountain fairies, forest fairies in their foliage clothing, water fairies, with their glorious fin wings on display, plus elves and gnomes sat shoulder to shoulder, all watched over by towering crystal statues of long-gone kings, queens, and heroes, glowering down from their niches and pedestals.

If Grainne was concerned Lord Nudd hadn't attempted to negotiate her release or mount an invasion to rescue her, she appeared somewhat blasé, maintaining a calm and inscrutable demeanour. Ceriddwen had provided a clothing allowance plus ladies to dress her hair and attend to other needs. She continued to look and behave as a queen throughout, unrepentant, haughtily maintaining she was within her rights to try and rescue her son by whatever means to hand.

'All's fair in love and war,' she asserted to a stony-faced courtroom. She was unconcerned by the charges of kidnap and proof of genocide, advising the court her son's eventual murder, by what she believed to be an Anunnaki fraudster, justified her every action. When the prosecution pointed out her son was very much alive when she kidnapped the Sirens, captured the sea dragon, and blackmailed Melusine, she simply shrugged and said the end justified the means.

The court was presided over by three grim faced judges drawn from the Tuatha de Danaan, elves and forest fairies, and when the excoriating guilty verdict was handed down, loud, triumphant cheers echoed around the high vaulted, crystal faceted ceiling. Grainne stood ramrod straight, her previous calm appearance belied by the look of pure venom on her face when the sentence of life-long incarceration was handed down.

A Dynasty of Dragons

As she was led away, she turned to Ceriddwen. 'This is not over,' she hissed. 'My people shall destroy you all! My son will be avenged!' She was still screaming defiant threats and curses as she was escorted back to prison. She would languish there until a date was set for her removal to the island of Coira, far out in the Western Sea, hidden from prying eyes by Ceriddwen's enchantment.

The questioning of Lord Llyr and Lady Thetis was a much more muted affair. The court accepted they knew nothing of their grandchild's kidnapping, nor of Melusine's subsequent blackmail, and found they had no case to answer.

Melusine, on the other hand, was a different matter. The court sympathised with her dilemma, and understood her actions were driven by fear for her baby, but nevertheless, the prosecution made much of the fact that valuable property and livestock had been destroyed, lives put at risk, particularly emphasising the fact that Princess Molly's life had been placed in considerable danger when she became embroiled in the attack on the hospital stud. They gave no quarter, calling witness after damning witness.

Why had she been at the stud on the day of the attack? Her excuse, when Oonagh questioned her appearance that day, was that she had agreed to meet a gnome fish merchant and deliver some packages of smoked fish as it was a convenient halfway point on his journey home. But Oonagh, when called to testify, pointed out that there had been no unexpected visitors that day, apart from the goblin raiders. Upon reflection, she thought it odd that Melusine didn't appear to have any large packages with her. Proof, asserted prosecuting counsel, Master Jarox, that Melusine's only purpose for being at the stud was to obtain the codes for the shields, and turn them off.

'And how, may we ask,' pressed Master Jarox, 'were you able to gain the codes?' Meulsine looked like a crushed water lily, huddled in the witness box, illuminated by a pool of dappled light streaming through an open blind. She replied in a frightened, hesitant voice.

'I hid amongst a shower of raindrops and followed Morello when he brought the mares in from the meadow. I looked over his shoulder when he keyed in the code.' A collective gasp of horror came from the water fairies in the court room. Lord Llyr bore the shame stoically, staring impassively ahead, but Lady Thetis sat, head bowed, sobbing uncontrollably, her daughter's dishonour and undoing laid bare before the world.

To shapeshift without express permission or good reason was betraying a sacred vow all water fairies were expected to honour without question, and to break that vow to further betray Queen Ceriddwen and the Tuatha de Danaan, was unconscionable. The courtroom descended into uproar until the senior judge furiously banged his gavel, threatening to clear the court unless everyone settled down.

Ceriddwen sat in shocked silence. She had often thought Melusine a flighty piece, but capable of this level of betrayal? Never! *I have become complacent*, she thought. *What did Lleu say to me about her? That was it, magnanimous; he thought I was being magnanimous!* She drummed her fingers on the arm of the chair, silently fuming while prosecuting counsel continued their questioning.

'How did you really come to be at the stud during this convenient shower of rain?' Jarox demanded.

'I brought Morello some rainbow trout. I know he likes them, he likes me too, if you know what I mean.'

'No, we don't know what you mean,' snapped the prosecutor. 'Please explain.'

'Objection!' cried Melusine's defence lawyer, Master Loran. 'My learned friend is badgering the witness. We know what she means.'

'Objection sustained,' agreed the judges. 'Ask another question, Master Jorax.'

'Sorry, my Lords,' Jorax apologised. 'I will rephrase the question. Apart from the facts that Morello enjoys a rainbow trout and there were no packages of smoked fish either, please tell the court your real reason for going to the stud on that particular day.'

Melusine broke down in tears. 'They had my baby,' she sobbed. 'I had to do it! I had to!'

'Just answer the question, please.'

Melusine crumpled further into her seat. 'To turn off the shields so that the goblins could get into the stud,' she whispered, almost inaudibly.

'We didn't quite hear your reply, could you repeat it, only louder this time?'

'Objection! Please, my Lords,' protested Master Loran. 'Master Jorax is harassing the witness!'

'Objection overruled,' replied the frowning forest fairy judge. 'The witness will give her answer again, and please speak up this time.' Melusine repeated her answer in a marginally louder voice and Jorax turned to the court, crowing triumphantly, 'There we have it, from her own lips. She went to the stud to turn off the shields to grant the goblins access!' A murmur of anger rippled through the room. 'And,' he announced theatrically, 'speaking of shapeshifting, you will remember Prince Morfan's testimony that he suspected a shapeshifting water fairy had entered the prison tower the same day Prince Jasper and his cousins were captured. May we now assume you were that shapeshifter?'

Melusine blinked at him miserably. 'We are waiting!' Jorax pressed relentlessly. 'Was that you?'

Melusine gulped and croaked, 'Yes,' in a strangled tone.

Again, Jorax turned to the court, making an exaggerated sweeping movement with his arms. 'Will you please tell the court why you visited Prince Jasper so surreptitiously that evening!'

'To tell him that his mother was coming to rescue him with a sea dragon.'

Lady Thetis let out a great wail of anguish, rocking back and forth in her seat, as once more the court erupted. All three judges banged their gavels this time, shouting over the commotion,

'Silence! Silence in court!' It took the court officials a few minutes to settle things down, and only after several particularly enraged individuals were forcibly ejected.

The air thrummed with tension as Melusine was led out of the witness box back to the defence benches. The defence and prosecution then made their closing statements, after which the court was adjourned until the following morning. The three judges were expected to have completed their summation by then with verdict and sentence prepared.

After a few minutes of desultory conversation, Taliesin slipped from the courtroom and made his way to the main entrance where Storm stood patiently tethered to a hitching post. He gave the unicorn's nose an affectionate rub before mounting and cantering along the broad tree-lined avenue to the palace hospital wing a mile distant. He visited Molly at every opportunity. As soon as he was off duty he was at her bedside, and his required presence at the trials meant he could visit her more often than usual. Brighid scolded him for getting in the way and for tiring Molly if he visited when she was awake, but she didn't mean a word of it — she noticed how Molly's eyes brightened and the colour came to her cheeks whenever Taliesin was there. He encouraged her to eat more, tempting her with tasty titbits, delicate pastries and delicious cheeses, her favourite dried fruits and divine little chocolates made especially for her by Ceriddwen's chocolatier. Day by day her strength returned, and day by day Taliesin became ever more determined to ask Ceriddwen for permission to marry Molly.

Fairy betrothals were often fraught with complications due to the omnipresent protocol. A fairy could not marry beneath their class. A warrior married another warrior, fairy royalty married fairy royalty, water fairies married water fairies, and so on. Although he was from aristocratic royal blood, Taliesin hesitated because Molly was half-human, and he was uncertain as to the correct protocol in such a situation. He knew Ceriddwen had already noticed their mutual attraction and had no qualms at all about it being a great match.

As he trotted up to the hospital entrance, he spied Cernunnos' tall figure approaching the wards. Handing the reins to a waiting groom, he hurried after him and the two friends greeted each other enthusiastically.

'Taliesin, my brother!' boomed Cernunnos. 'I was just on my way to find you. Morfan said I would likely find you here visiting the princess.'

Taliesin laughed. 'And he was correct,' he said, slapping Cernunnos on his leafy green back. 'Were you in court this afternoon? I didn't see you.'

'Only for a short time this morning — my turn to give evidence. You gave yours yesterday, I believe?'

'Yes,' replied Taliesin with a deep frown. 'It's a bad business. I fear for Melusine's future. It didn't go well for her this afternoon, I'm afraid.'

'Poor lass. A terrible predicament to find herself in.' Cernunnos shook his head ruefully. 'Let's hope the judges treat her leniently. Who knows what any of us would have done in her situation?'

'Indeed,' agreed Taliesin. 'You said you were on your way to find me?'

'Just to tell you I've brought that fine beast, Luath, back to you,' he cried jovially, good humour restored. 'I left him with the Epona until you could collect him. I think she's going to ask you if he can cover some of her mares. He's a magnificent specimen!'

Taliesin nodded in agreement. 'He is that! Heart like a lion. The Epona mentioned a while back that she thought he would throw good foals. I'll speak to her later. Thanks for bringing him back.'

'Not a problem.' Cernunnos shrugged. 'I had to come and see the Queen anyway, as I told you,' he grimaced. 'Not that this is the most auspicious time to update the Queen on Lord Dubh's galleon when she has a goblin man o' war and its crew to deal with.' They paused in the corridor outside Molly's room.

'What's to be done with the goblin crew?'

'Well, I know what I'd like to do with them,' growled Taliesin, 'but as they're prisoners of war, some sort of deal should be negotiated.'

Cernunnos snorted in derision. 'Ha! Good luck with that!'

'Don't remind me!' Taliesin knew that Lord Nudd regarded his troops as expendable, and he would rather see them rot in prison than strike a meaningful deal with Ceriddwen or any of her allies. 'I think the Queen will dose them all with potions from the cauldron and keep them at the Correction Centre for debriefing and re-programming.'

'And then what?'

'And then send them back to Nudd. What else can she do? Keep them here, eating us out of house and home, adding insult to injury? No, let him deal with a crew of useless deprogrammed sailors!'

'He'll probably send them to the mines!'

'As their Queen said at her trial, all's fair in love and war!'

'And speaking of love,' Cernunnus laughed with a salacious wink, 'I shall leave you to your princess.' Lowering his voice, he added, 'I hope to be a guest at your betrothal feast very soon!' He set off back down the corridor, chuckling to himself, before Taliesin had time to reply.

Just as Taliesin was about to knock and enter, the door opened and Brighid stepped out, closing it quietly behind her. She motioned him a little further down the corridor out of earshot. 'Has something happened?' he asked anxiously, taking in Brighid's angry expression.

'Lady Tanith came bursting into the room about ten minutes ago, she must have galloped the dog cart here at full speed as soon as the trial stopped.' Brighid's voice was shaking with fury. 'She didn't even look to see if the princess was awake before she started gossiping and laughing with the others about what's going to happen to Melusine when the verdict's announced tomorrow.'

Taliesin put his hands on her shoulders to steady her. 'What about the princess? Has she started to remember what happened?' he asked urgently.

'Oh, those little minxes and their gossiping!' cried Brighid. 'I could box their ears, every one of them!' She sank unhappily onto one of the corridor benches. 'I'm not sure what she remembers, but she heard every word, and now she's in a right state, demanding to see Melusine and her baby. I had to call Master Lenus to give her something to calm her down, but she's refusing to take it. She's insisting we fetch Melusine and tell her what Lady Tanith is talking about. Oh, Lord Taliesin,' she wailed, 'I don't know what to do!'

Taliesin let out an exasperated sigh. 'Leave the princess and Lady Tanith to me. Go for a walk in the gardens for ten minutes and calm yourself.' Brighid pursed her lips in irritation, but obediently made her way towards the gardens as Taliesin let himself into the room. As soon as Molly saw him, she shot out of bed and threw her arms around him and he instinctively hugged her close, breathing in her perfume as she babbled incoherently about Melusine and her baby.

Master Lenus coughed discreetly, and Taliesin gently unwound Molly's arms from around his neck and led her back to the bed.

'You may leave us for now, Master Lenus,' he said quietly to the hovering doctor. 'I wish to speak to the princess in private.'

'Of course, my Lord.' The doctor bowed politely and left. As soon as the door closed, Taliesin turned to Tanith and the other Astarte ladies who were gathered by the window at the other end of the room, all ears, intent on listening in to what they hoped would be more gossip. Taliesin fixed them with a steely gaze.

'Lady Tanith, it has come to my attention that you seemed to be in a great rush to return to the hospital after today's trial. I believe the poor pony pulling the dog cart is quite exhausted after the effort he must have made to get you here so quickly.'

A slight flush spread across Lady Tanith's elegant cheekbones. 'I...I don't know what you mean, my Lord.' She managed to sound haughty. Taliesin ignored her protest.

'Have you become tired of your cauldron duties and serving the Queen?' His tone was deceptively mild, a fact not lost on the now slightly discomfited women.

'No, of course not!' snapped Tanith. 'Why would you ask such a thing?'

'Why indeed?' He smiled pleasantly. 'Everyone in the Queen's service is expected to be loyal and discreet. Their behaviour must be exemplary and beyond reproach, eyes downcast and lips sealed when it comes to official business. Am I correct?' The women nodded, open-mouthed. Their fitness for office had never been questioned before.

'Yet,' his voice now carried a hard edge, 'you think nothing of coming into a sickroom, a sickroom occupied by a royal princess no less, to laugh and gossip at someone else's misfortune as though it were a great joke?' The women's eyes widened. They didn't like the sound of this at all. 'But apart from the fact that such gossip is cruel and dangerous, you are breaking your vows, aren't you?' They stared at him, speechless, as he continued. 'And my problem is this, what am I going to do about it?'

One of the women, Lady Rowan, burst into tears. 'We meant no harm, Lord Taliesin. We…we just a get a bit bored sometimes and chattering eases the monotony.' She rubbed at the tears running down her pretty face.

'You get bored?' thundered Taliesin. 'Bored? How bored do you think sentries and guards are protecting you every day and night? How bored were the warriors standing behind the shield wall for hours protecting you from the goblins two weeks ago? Do they leave their posts and play boules and cards because they're bored and can't be bothered obeying orders anymore?' The women shrank from his rage, huddled together like terrified rabbits, unable to flee as he glowered at them.

'You should be humbled that you are accorded such privilege, yet you behave as though you are greater than anyone else and above the laws and protocols the rest of us live our lives by. You demean the honourable Order of Astarte. You are a disgrace!'

He paced up and down the floor, his face creased in a ferocious frown. They stood white-faced, waiting for his next onslaught. 'I've decided not to tell the Queen this time,' he barked at them, 'but get one thing through your arrogant, self-centred, empty heads; your future lies squarely in the hands of Mistress Brighid, and should she report the slightest digression from your named duties, make no mistake, the Queen shall be fully appraised of your behaviour.' He glared at them contemptuously. 'Now leave us!' The women scuttled from the room like frightened mice. When the last lady closed the door behind her, Taliesin turned and sat beside Molly, who had been listening, open-mouthed. Gently, he took her hands in his.

'Now, my love.' There, he'd finally said it, horrified for a second in case he'd been picking up all the wrong signals and now faced rejection. 'Tell me what's wrong.'

He needn't have worried. Molly threw herself into his arms again, whispering, 'Help me, please! I'm starting to remember. I keep having these terrible flashbacks and I'm still trying to understand what's happened, but most of all, I'm frightened for Melusine!' She burst into floods of tears, sobbing into his shoulder.

Although outwardly, Molly seemed to be recovering from her ordeal with Queen Grainne, she was still finding it extremely difficult to process her emotions. Days merged into nights, nights when she was plagued by strange dreams of different worlds. Worlds where sometimes she was happy with people she knew well and loved, living a life wildly different from her life as Princess Molly. She would wake in the morning deeply troubled and try as she might, she could never remember the faces of those who invaded her dreams. At other times she was lost in a dark world filled with screaming and the sound of fighting and the roaring of dragons, and through the swirling mists, the haunting songs of the Sirens. Again, in the morning, only fragments of the dreams remained. Despite this, Master Lenus advised Ceriddwen that Molly's system was assimilating the Anunnaki DNA extremely well and that physically she was almost back to normal, although her emotional state might take rather longer.

'Help Melusine, Taliesin. Don't let anything happen to her. I couldn't bear it. They tried to kill her little baby, I know that much, and now something terrible is going to happen to her!' Again, Taliesin gently extricated himself from her embrace and looked at her gravely.

'You do understand Melusine committed a very serious offence? An offence which caused much distress and loss of life?'

'But they stole her baby and threatened to kill him!' Tears now forgotten, Molly's eyes blazed. 'I would have done the same,' she said fiercely.

'I believe you would,' he murmured, pressing her hands to his lips. He was resisting the urge to pull her into his arms and make wild, passionate love to her. His senses swam as his breath quickened and his heart pounded furiously. 'Let me think for a moment...'

He stood up and turned away from her, fighting to bring his emotions under control. This was the first time he had ever been alone with Molly, and he was behaving like a testosterone-fuelled teenager! Mercifully, there was a light tap on the door as Brighid returned from her sojourn to the gardens.

'Ah, Brighid.' He smiled at her, glad of the distraction as she bobbed a little curtsey. 'There will be no more nonsense from Lady Tanith and her ladies. They have been warned and they know there will be no second chances.'

'I am glad to hear it.' Brighid nodded her head in approval. 'Thank you, my Lord.'

'But what about Melusine?' Molly queried, and Taliesin realised she was going to be like a dog with a bone unless he could come up with a solution very quickly.

'Forgive me,' he said, lifting her hand and kissing it once more. 'I must cut my visit short. I have an idea, but first I must discuss it with the Queen. Time draws on, and she shall be at dinner shortly unless I leave now.'

'I knew I could rely on you!' Molly exclaimed, throwing her arms around him, and planting a luscious kiss on his lips in front of Brighid, who tried in vain to look scandalised.

Taliesin touched his forehead to Molly's and whispered, 'Wish me luck, my love!'

TWENTY-SIX

The Queen is Magnanimous

The following morning, the courtroom was even more packed than usual. Everyone, it seemed, wished to witness Melusine's fate. The court was evenly split between those who hoped her sentence would be lenient, and those who wished to see her bear the full brunt of the law.

Water fairies weren't universally popular. Many people believed they were fickle and untrustworthy, an opinion Molly frequently heard but decided to ignore. She liked Melusine, although she had noticed she could be slightly irreverent regarding protocol. Molly didn't think this prevented them being friends and had continued to laugh and chat with her whenever they met.

Everyone bowed as Ceriddwen swept into the room and settled into her chair. She was dressed in a gown of chartreuse silk, lavishly embroidered with silver thread. It had a sweetheart neckline which displayed, to great effect, the magnificent green diamond pendant resting on her splendid bosom. Her glorious hair was piled on top of her head and held in place with a matching diadem. The outfit was set off by a dazzling tourmaline wand that glittered and sparked off great shards of light every time she moved.

Taliesin had been fortunate on two counts the previous evening. As he hurried through the palace to the Great Hall, hoping to catch the Queen before dinner, he was intercepted by a page requesting that he dine with Ceriddwen, not in the Great Hall, but in her private apartments. He couldn't believe his luck.

When he arrived, Morfan, Lleu, Cernunnos and the Arianrhod were already present, chatting and sipping pre-dinner drinks. Taliesin was pleased to see the Arianrhod obviously restored to favour after the unfortunate council chamber spat. His next stroke of good fortune was the fact that Ceriddwen was in considerable good humour because Master Lenus had earlier informed her that Molly was physically ready to be discharged from hospital. He believed that doing normal things again with people she knew and loved would help her deal with any emotional problems arising from her ordeal. Ceriddwen was delighted by this news, welcoming her dinner guests with a dazzling smile, and Taliesin felt quietly confident.

Conversation around the dinner table consisted mainly of Grainne's banishment and whether Lord Nudd would retaliate or not. It was well known their liaison was a matter of political expediency rather than a love match. 'I wouldn't even say it was a meeting of minds,' opined Cernunnos, 'it's always been obvious to me that she's the brains behind the operation.'

'Perhaps so,' countered Ceriddwen, 'but is he so reliant on Grainne? It doesn't explain why he didn't attempt to rescue her or negotiate a deal.' She turned to Taliesin. 'What do you think, Lord Taliesin?'

He frowned. 'Perhaps she has outlived her usefulness. Nudd is certainly not the sentimental type, and he has never liked the power sharing aspect of their relationship.' The others nodded in agreement as he counted off reasons on his fingers.

'Firstly, he no longer needs her for dynastic reasons. Princess Molly may have killed Prince Jasper, but their second son, Prince Idris, is now the heir apparent. Grainne may have given birth to him, but unlike Jasper, Idris is Nudd's son through and through, and from what my spies tell me, there is no love lost between mother and son. Secondly, should anything happen to Idris, Nudd has at least ten other children by various goblin princesses. Thirdly, Grainne's followers may be loyal and prepared to fight for her, but they are vastly outnumbered by Nudd's people. He is a charismatic ruler, and his subjects adore him. And lastly and most importantly,' he looked around the table to emphasise the point, 'they are also terrified of him. Goblins are a cruel and ruthless race, and they know Lord Nudd is their king because he is crueller and more ruthless than anyone else, so they toe the line, no matter what!'

'I have to agree with you, my Lord.' The Arianrhod sat between Lleu and Morfan. 'He has achieved what he wants. The manpower and riches provided by Grainne plus a compliant heir, and with her out of the way, he has free rein to pursue his own agenda without Grainne's restraining hand.' She put down her fork and took a sip of wine before continuing: 'I think Lord Nudd engineered the attack on the hospital stud knowing there was a reasonable chance that Jasper might get caught. From what I know of him, he wasn't particularly bright, and I think Nudd was exploiting that. He obviously had no interest in his son's fate otherwise he would have sent an envoy demanding his release for a ransom or a deal.' She paused, allowing Lleu to speak.

'Grainne must have realised she would have to rescue Jasper herself and was hoping to secure a military victory at the same time by kidnapping the Sirens and threatening us with the sea dragon.'

'She must have already had the dragon and the Sirens,' reasoned Morfan. 'She couldn't have sailed to and from the Anunnaki lands that quickly!'

'But what I don't understand,' cut in Ceriddwen, 'is that Melusine was already spying for them before Jasper was captured, therefore Grainne must have been involved in the goblin raid. Why would she allow her son to be put at risk of capture?'

'Forgive me, my dear,' Lleu smiled at her apologetically, 'but a mother's love is a wondrous thing to behold. Grainne would see no fault in Jasper, he was her shining star and it almost certainly never occurred to her that he wasn't up to the task. He probably went with her blessing.'

'Speaking of sea dragons, how goes it with Lord Ravenna, Your Majesty,' asked Cernunnos.

'Ah yes, Lord Cernunnos, thank you for reminding me.' Ceriddwen smiled. 'He should be on his way home by now. We received word that the Sirens have been safely reinstalled on their island and the sea dragon has been released into calm waters just off the Anunnaki coast.' She paused as an attendant began filling their glasses with a golden liqueur. 'Thank you. Perfect timing!' She beamed at him, raising her glass. 'Come everyone, let us toast Grainne's defeat and the safe return of the Sirens and the sea dragon — let us hope never to see any of them again!'

'May we never see them again,' the others cheerfully chorused, clinking glasses, and downing their drinks.

'This is a fine liqueur, Lady Mother,' remarked Morfan, swirling the golden liquid around his glass.

'A gift from Lord Cernunnos,' said Ceriddwen, raising her glass in his direction. 'He sent it with this year's Yule log.'

'And we raise our glasses again, my friend,' added Lleu. 'To Cernunnos for growing such very fine hazelnuts!'

'To Cernunnos!' they cried. Cernunnos' hearty laugh boomed around the room as the attendant recharged their glasses.

'I fear if Lorien hears you are in possession of such a fine vintage, he will swiftly seek to entertain you with an epic poem, which will require much pausing for imbibing refreshing drink,' voiced the Arianrhod with a chuckle, 'and he will not hesitate to tell you he has heard of your wonderful liqueur!'

Ceriddwen laughed. 'You have a wicked sense of humour, Mother Arianrhod. Poor Lorien!'

The Arianrhod was unrepentant. 'Poor Lorien, my foot! He is in a permanent state of inebriation, and pretends he needs to drink any hazelnut liquor he can get his hands on, for wisdom and inspiration!'

'You have to admit he does come up with wonderful stories and poems, though,' said Morfan. 'He keeps us spellbound!'

'He did say,' mused the Arianrhod, 'he is now thinking of composing a poem about Melusine and Grainne, but he can't start until after tomorrow's verdict.'

'Ach,' sighed Cernunnos, 'I was just saying to Taliesin this afternoon, I feel a bit sorry for the lass, she was in a no-win situation, for sure.'

'I doubt the judges will be feeling sorry for her,' Ceriddwen said tartly. 'They will apply the law, leaving emotions out of it. She committed a terrible crime, whether she was being blackmailed or not.'

'But surely, they must take the extenuating circumstances into account, ma'am?' protested Cernunnos.

'I do feel for her, despite what she did,' admitted Ceriddwen. 'I'm afraid my husband thought I was being *magnanimous*, and I'm afraid my feelings do vacillate between absolute fury and great pity.'

'I didn't mean anything by it, Ceri,' protested Lleu, 'I was just surprised that you didn't...'

'Fly into an uncontrollable rage and order her executed on the spot?' Ceriddwen said drily. 'Oh, for goodness' sake, don't look so shamefaced. I know that's what you were all thinking! I might be a queen, but, as you have already reminded me, husband, I am also a woman and a mother. I know what losing a child feels like.'

They all nodded sympathetically, momentarily distracted, as another attendant handed round a plate of delicious-looking cakes.

'So, what's the best outcome she can hope for?' asked Morfan through a mouthful of sponge.

'It's not for me to second-guess the verdict,' Ceriddwen replied, somewhat testily, 'but, if pressed, I imagine it will be life imprisonment or banishment.'

'Surely that's a bit harsh under the circumstances!' Cernunnos was aghast.

'The circumstances are very serious, as well you know, Lord Cernunnos,' admonished Ceriddwen. 'Have you a better solution that would satisfy the court?'

Cernunnos sighed, shaking his head. 'She was only protecting her child, and what will happen to the little one? Will he be torn from his mother's arms again?' Before anyone could reply, Taliesin seized his chance.

'I may have a solution. If it pleases Your Majesty, of course.'

Everyone looked first at Taliesin, then expectantly at the Queen. She settled back in her chair, an amused smile playing about her mouth. 'We are all ears, Lord Taliesin, do continue.'

Taliesin took a deep breath and plunged straight in. 'Thank you, ma'am. I could use someone with Melusine's talents on my estate.' Taliesin looked after his family's large estate, Tigh Falloch, and spent as much time there as he could, but his duties as Queen's Warrior and Justiciar kept him away, often for long periods, and he felt that the work involved was becoming too much for his incumbent manager, Arden, to cope with on his own. He had plenty of estate workers and retainers, but he needed someone with Meulsine's skills.

'And what particular talents do you have in mind?' asked Ceriddwen.

'Her obvious fish husbandry skills,' said Taliesin. 'My lakes and rivers are well stocked, but, unfortunately, poorly managed. I have also heard that she is an exceptional fish tanner.'

'She is indeed,' interjected Morfan. 'Mistress Holda buys a lot of her leather from the artisan traders.'

'Mistress Holda who testified against her in court?' said Cernunnos tetchily.

'Gentlemen, please,' Ceriddwen snapped. 'Lord Taliesin has the floor, not you!'

'Thank you, ma'am,' Taliesin acknowledged. 'Actually, it was Mistress Holda who told me Melusine's talents were wasted providing fish for the, ahem, royal tables.' He looked apologetically at Ceriddwen, who smiled thinly, inclining her head slightly. 'Mistress Holda felt she would be better employed improving breeding stock and being given free rein to develop her considerable artistic tanning skills.'

'Praise indeed from someone who obviously has no love for her!' Cernunnos snorted.

'Mistress Holda is a shrewd judge of character,' the Arianrhod said mildly. 'She doesn't have to like someone to recognise their talents. She deals in facts, and Melusine's talent is a fact.'

'Speaking of facts,' Taliesin continued, 'these talents will be lost forever if she is imprisoned or banished, for she will be treated as other prisoners, and no special allowances will be made for her skills. She will also have her child taken from her. If you allow me to take her under my supervision and protection, she will be unable to leave my estate without permission, and I will make sure she and her child become useful and productive members of our society.'

Ceriddwen gazed thoughtfully at Taliesin. 'There are those who might regard such an outcome as a reward rather than a punishment, you must know that.'

'And who would challenge me, Your Majesty?' Who would dare suggest that my word is other than my bond? Who among our people would consider themselves more fit for the challenge than I? All said and done, she will still be very much a prisoner.'

'A prisoner in a gilded cage, some might say,' mused Ceriddwen.

The others said nothing, for they knew Taliesin was correct. No one would challenge him. Next to the Royal Family, he was the most powerful man in the kingdom, a position well-earned. He was also well-liked and trusted, fair minded and never abused his position. Ceriddwen knew those who disliked water fairies would object, but most of the population would favour Taliesin as Melusine's jailer, for want of a better expression. She would just have to be careful in her choice of words when the judges asked her to ratify the verdict.

~

As soon as Ceriddwen was settled comfortably, the three judges took their seats. Melusine sat beside Master Loran, looking pale and wan, her eyes red and puffy from weeping. Lady Thetis sat behind, leaning forward slightly to place a comforting hand on Melusine's thin shoulder. Master Jorax sat on the prosecution benches with a slightly smug, confident air about him. The verdict was not in doubt.

At a signal from the judges, the clerk of the court stood up, bowed first to Ceriddwen, then to the judges. Master Loran and Melusine then stood up as the clerk was handed the verdict. He turned to face the court and began to read from the sheet.

'Having heard all the arguments from the prosecution and defence, the testimonies from witnesses, and taking all relevant circumstances into consideration, we, the undersigned, appointed to judge this case on its merits, have no alternative but to find the defendant, one water fairy named Lady Melusine, daughter of Lord Llyr and Lady Thetis, guilty as charged. The sentence is life imprisonment or banishment, whichever, if any, should please Her Royal Highness, Queen Ceriddwen.' He paused to allow the court to absorb this. No one was rude enough to cheer, but some people murmured *Shame* while others began clapping to show their agreement. One of the judges banged his gavel for quiet as the clerk now approached Ceriddwen, bowed, and handed her the verdict sheet. You could hear a pin drop and everyone held their breath as Ceriddwen scanned the sheet. What would it be? Life imprisonment, or banishment to some barren island? Only the Queen could decide. Finally, Ceriddwen put down the sheet and turned her attention to Melusine, her rich melodic tones ringing around the courtroom.

'Lady Melusine, my court has found you guilty of very serious charges.'

Melusine stood like a frightened deer, trembling as her mother stood behind, supporting her, fearing she might collapse. *A mother's love is truly a wondrous thing*, Ceriddwen thought as she watched Thetis comforting her daughter.

'As is our custom, I will make the final decision regarding your sentence. However, the court should be aware that someone has made representation to me regarding your fate. It is in my gift to allow this petition, whether it pleases the court or not, and after much consideration, I am minded to allow it.'

The silence was palpable. The more vindictive members of the court room were hoping for a life sentence in some grim prison or banishment to a harsh barren island. The more tender-hearted felt sorry for her, but all were now sitting with bated breath, waiting for the Queen to reveal all.

Ceriddwen looked sternly at Melusine's white, stricken face. 'Lady Melusine, from this day forth you shall carry out your life sentence under the supervision of Lord Taliesin at his estate,

Tigh Falloch. Your son shall be allowed to accompany you, but when he is of age, he shall be free to do as he pleases with his life. You, however, shall spend the remainder of your life under the auspices of our Lord Justiciar.' She looked from Melusine to the rest of the courtroom and added, 'Anyone unhappy with this decision, please feel free to take it up with Lord Taliesin.' The room remained silent. Apart from the fact everyone knew the Queen's decision was law and final, no one, as discussed the previous evening, would challenge Taliesin. 'Do you have anything to say, Lady Melusine, before you leave the court?'

Master Loren whispered to Melusine, who was swaying unsteadily with a bewildered look on her face. Lady Thetis held her shoulders in a tight grip as Melusine answered in a quiet, tremulous voice. 'I thank Your Majesty and Lord Taliesin from the bottom of my heart. I thought I would never see my son again.'

Ceriddwen nodded. 'You may have a few moments alone with your parents before Lord Taliesin's carriage comes for you. Do not disappoint me, for any further betrayals of trust will not go well for you, Lady Melusine.'

With that, she stood up, causing the clerk of the court to hastily cry, 'All rise,' as she stalked from the room. Lady Tanith scuttled after her, the cauldron left to the ministrations of the other Astarte ladies, and the members of the courtroom to their various mutterings and grumbles.

Ceriddwen had instructed Brighid to find a suitable nurse who would be willing to stay at Tigh Falloch in the long term to look after Melusine's baby boy, Luss, while Melusine went about her duties.

Mistress Tansy, a recently widowed, motherly fairy woman, gladly volunteered, and she sat in the carriage nursing Luss as Melusine and her parents made their tearful goodbyes.

Taliesin had decided to travel to Tigh Falloch the following day having already sent instructions to Master Arden and the estate staff regarding Melusine's arrival. He had requested a private audience with Ceriddwen later that evening, but first he intended visiting Molly before she left the hospital to ask her a very important question...

TWENTY-SEVEN

A Declaration of Love

Molly was feeling ridiculously happy. She had made a good recovery and Master Lenus was only too happy to discharge her from hospital now that her memory, as well as her strength, was returning. The Anunnaki and human DNA were fully integrated, with her system showing no apparent ill-effects. In fact, she appeared to be glowing with health; back to normal weight, feeling energetic and full of life. Only one small niggle marred her happiness — would Melusine really be safe now?

She had burst into tears of relief when Taliesin told her the good news. Brighid, busily packing up Molly's belongings now that she had been discharged, tutted loudly, and frowned at Taliesin, scolding him for upsetting the princess.

'I'm not upset, Brighid,' Molly said through her tears, 'I'm just so pleased Melusine hasn't been sent to some horrible prison or deserted island.'

'It's her husband who should be banished, if you ask me!' Brighid retorted primly.

'It never occurred to me she had a husband!' Molly sounded surprised.

'Well, she has, and he's every bit as fickle as all water fairies.' Brighid sniffed, wrinkling her nose at the thought. 'He was working at the Western Gate dockyard and took up with some flighty mermaid. Melusine had just given birth to that poor baby boy, too. Absolutely shameful!'

'A mermaid?' Molly's eyebrows shot up in surprise 'Are they classed as water fairies, too?'

'Well, what else would they be?' demanded Brighid, carefully packing one of Molly's gowns into a large trunk. Taliesin had been listening quietly to this exchange with a wry smile on his face.

'Well, it's good to have the benefit of your expertise on water fairies, Mistress Brighid,' he cut in before either woman had the chance to speak, 'but I wish to speak to the princess in private, if you would leave us, please, and make sure we are not disturbed until you are sent for.'

Brighid looked up indignantly, about to protest, but the look on Taliesin's face changed her mind. 'Of course, my Lord.' She nodded hastily. 'Ring when you need me, Princess,' and bobbing a quick curtsey, left the room. Taliesin locked the door firmly behind her.

'This all sounds very serious.' Molly began to feel a little worried. 'Is everything all right?'

Taliesin smiled at her, clasping her hands and pulling her over to the bed. 'Come and sit down.' Molly obediently sat, heart pounding. Was this going to be some not-so-good news about Melusine? Had he just given her the best part first to soften her up for whatever was really going to happen? Her mind was in a whirl as she watched his face nervously. 'Molly,' he was still holding her hands, 'I have something very important to ask you.'

'About Melusine?'

Taliesin smiled and shook his head 'No, not about Melusine. She's safe, and always will be at Tigh Falloch. No, I want to talk about you,' he paused, squeezing her hands, 'about me... us.' He was looking deep into her eyes now, and Molly felt her stomach lurch as her heart turned over.

'Us?' she said weakly. The light danced and shimmered in a corona around his head as she tried to focus on his face.

'Yes, us,' he murmured, letting go of her hands to gently cup her face, before leaning forward to kiss her very softly on the lips. He could feel her quivering like a frightened bird. 'I love you, Molly,' he said simply. 'You took my breath away the first time I saw you.' Tears of happiness filled her eyes and spilled down her cheeks and Taliesin brushed them away as she gazed helplessly into his eyes. 'Would I be correct in thinking that we were both hoping for great things at Samhain? That we had an unspoken understanding?' She nodded, remembering her excitement when he gave her that long smouldering look of promise, her hopes for the great Masqued Ball, all her dreams in ruins because of an unforeseen illness. Until now.

She stared at him in wonder, scarcely daring to breathe, as he continued. 'I have a private audience with the Queen tonight,' he said, smoothing her hair back from her face, running its lustrous strands through his fingers, 'and before I meet with her, I...' he stumbled nervously over the words, 'I would love to know if you would do me the honour of becoming my wife?'

Molly's heart skipped another beat as she said faintly, 'Will the Queen not expect us to...' and searching for the appropriate words, she added, '... date each other for a while first? To get to know each other better?' She then began to feel a bit foolish as Taliesin looked at her curiously.

'Dating?' He sounded puzzled. 'I don't understand what that means? Are you unsure about becoming my wife after all?'

'No…no, not at all!' Molly replied hastily. 'There's so much I can't remember about my previous life, but I do remember dating someone. In the human world it's something we do to find out if we really like someone or not.' Watching Taliesin frown slightly, she quickly added, 'But you must explain to me how betrothals work here, because I want to become your wife more than anything else.'

His face brightened as he smiled at her. 'We don't "date", as you call it, our fairy instincts usually guide us unerringly to our beloved. I knew it the first time I saw you, and it is many years since I have known that feeling. I thought it would never happen again.'

'Do you think the Queen will allow it?' Molly asked anxiously.

'I have a feeling she will. She knew about my feelings for you almost before I did myself. Her intuition is usually infallible.' He kissed her tenderly once more before releasing her and standing up. 'Wish me luck, my love. I must bathe and change before my audience with the Queen.'

'Taliesin!' Molly gripped his hand to stop him as he headed for the door. 'You know I am changed? I am Anunnaki now and capable of terrible things! I killed Prince Jasper, and I don't feel the slightest remorse.' She held his gaze earnestly. 'Are you not concerned that, for better or worse, I am a dragon queen?'

'I love you even more for it,' he replied. 'You are fierce and loyal with a great sense of justice. You are every inch a queen, and I will never stand in your way should you ever be called to protect your people again. My love for you is unconditional.' He kissed her fingertips, bowed, and left the room.

Taliesin was hardly out the door when Brighid bustled back into the room, immediately noticing Molly's flushed, happy face. Protocol forgotten for the first time in her life, she couldn't stop herself from bursting out, 'Dare I ask? Has Lord Taliesin finally asked you to be his wife?'

'Yes, he has!' Molly cried joyfully, throwing her arms around the delighted Brighid, who, for the first time ever, hugged her right back.

'He has an audience with the Queen tonight and he thinks she will agree. Do you think she will, Brighid?'

'I have no doubt about it,' Brighid replied firmly. 'You couldn't make a better match, nor have a better husband. Her Majesty holds Lord Taliesin in the highest regard, as do the people. And he is very handsome, too!' she added mischievously.

Ceriddwen's enthusiasm for the wedding wasn't entirely altruistic. Molly's Anunnaki ancestry changed everything as far as she was concerned. That discovery now paved the way for the perfect dynastic marriage, a marriage that would join the Houses of Tuatha de Danaan and Anunnaki forever, eventually creating a formidable alliance that would prove extremely difficult for the goblin kingdom to overthrow. Taliesin was Ceriddwen's cousin, pure-blooded Tuatha de Danaan, and any children he and Molly produced would be the beginning of a powerful new generation of fairy blood.

Although Ceriddwen gave Taliesin her blessing, she was at first reluctant to let him take Molly on a visit to Tigh Falloch, wishing him instead to oversee the clearing up of the Grainne debacle, dealing with the prisoners of war, finalising the details of Grainne's banishment, and, although it pained Ceriddwen to even think about it, deciding what to do with Prince Jasper's body, currently preserved in a bath of cauldron liquid.

'I know you are anxious for the princess to visit your estate and meet your parents, but I can't rest easy until all these loose ends are dealt with,' she complained.

'Your Majesty, my deputy, Lord Varik, is more than capable of dealing with these matters, I have every confidence in him. He is a man of many talents and great integrity.'

'Yes, yes, I know — he is a fine warrior, but he's not you, is he?' she retorted petulantly. 'It was bad enough that you weren't here when Grainne arrived, and now you wish to absent yourself from her leaving?'

'You know perfectly well why Taliesin wasn't here when Grainne arrived.'

A calm voice quietly joined the conversation. Lleu lifted his head from some paperwork. 'And you also know, my dear, how unseemly it will appear if you prevent the princess from visiting Lord Brude and Lady Adwena, very unseemly indeed.'

His point made, Lleu turned his attention back to his papers, turning his head slightly to hide a little smile. Ceriddwen stared at him, open-mouthed, and just before launching an angry reply, she realised he was quite correct as usual. She could not agree to the betrothal without involving Taliesin's family. She might be Queen, but Taliesin's parents were also fairy royalty, and to prevent Molly from visiting them immediately for their blessing too, would be an unforgiveable breach of protocol.

Taliesin assumed a bland expression as she turned, without missing a beat, to fix him with a dazzling smile saying of course Lord Varik should take charge of events while Taliesin and Molly visited Tigh Falloch. 'Lord Varik can disperse the prisoners and deal with the sale of that accursed goblin ship; I will not have it anywhere near my fleet. Perhaps the Fianna would be interested in having it? I've heard they've had quite a few sea skirmishes with the goblins. Is that not so?'

'Quite true, Your Majesty,' agreed Taliesin. 'The goblins have become rather a nuisance in the Northern Sea. Admiral Sulis advised me that King Ossian complains often about goblin piracy.'

'Hmm.' Ceriddwen pursed her lips in disapproval. 'Lord Ravenna did mention something to me but said he and the admiral weren't unduly worried.'

'The goblin ships are no match for our fleet, and they know it, Your Majesty,' Taliesin said stoutly, Lleu nodding in vigorous agreement.

'Nevertheless, before you leave for Tigh Falloch, I would have Lord Varik inform Admiral Sulis and Lord Ravenna that I must be kept informed of any goblin sea-going activities, no matter how trivial. Under no circumstances will I allow the goblins to become a sea power, especially considering our recent debacle. And on that subject, I have decided that Queen Grainne will remain under our supervision until you return. I also wish you to be present when we decide what to do with Prince Jasper's remains. That is all, good evening, Lord Taliesin. Give your parents our regards.'

Thus dismissed, Taliesin bowed and made his retreat, relieved and very, very happy.

TWENTY-EIGHT
Tigh Falloch

Back in Heathervale Avenue, Molly put away her ironing and began to prepare dinner for two. She didn't feel like spending the evening alone with her ever-burgeoning memories — it helped having someone to share them with and Laura was the perfect companion.

As she scraped potato peelings into the food waste bin, the door to the attic stairs caught her eye. She froze in mid-scrape as something gradually dawned on her. She hadn't been up those stairs for years. One of the quirks of her lovely old house being it had two sets of attic stairs, the short flight on the upper landing leading to the lumber room at the far end of the house, and this longer, narrower flight off the kitchen. She disposed of the potato peelings and placed the dish on the counter. Wiping her hands on her apron, she reached out to grasp the attic door handle, then changed her mind. *No*, she thought, *I'll wait until Laura comes. I don't really want to go up there on my own.*

After a dinner of shepherd's pie followed by rhubarb crumble and custard, Laura and Molly sat sipping cups of tea. 'When I was preparing dinner,' began Molly, 'I remembered something else.'

Laura swallowed a mouthful of tea. 'About your fight with the goblin queen?'

'No, something entirely different, well, not entirely different, just different, if you know what I mean.'

'Not really, just tell me what you've remembered!'

'It's probably best if I show you, and then you'll understand. Finish your tea first.'

'Okay,' said Laura, draining her cup. 'Lead on!'

Laura followed Molly up the narrow stairs, waiting impatiently while she fumbled nervously with the door at the top. Once inside, Laura found herself standing in an artist's studio, with huge north-facing skylights. Stacked all around the walls were dozens of canvases. She gazed around the room open-mouthed.

'I...I...we thought...well, I thought you'd given up painting. You never said a word!'

Molly shrugged, almost apologetically. 'I only painted when Fred was away — it helped pass the time.'

Laura took in the large canvas standing on an easel in the middle of the floor, covered by a sheet, as she inspected the others along the walls, running her finger along the top of one — it was thick with dust.

'So why are you showing me this now, what's different about this room, apart from the fact it's obviously been kept secret?' She looked over her shoulder at Molly, standing white-faced in the doorway.

'It wasn't a secret; I just didn't know,' she said softly. 'All this time and I didn't know!' She gestured round the room. 'I created all this, and I thought I was just illustrating Nan's stories from my childhood, straight from my imagination, but it was all true!'

'What was all true? What do you mean...' Laura began, feeling mystified, but stopped in mid-sentence as she turned over a dusty canvas. The painting revealed two men with their arms around each other's shoulders, one obviously a warrior of some sort and the other bearing an uncanny resemblance to Xander. Glancing at Molly again, she began to flick through other canvases — beautiful fairy creatures with jewel-coloured, fin-like wings, a smiling fairy woman holding a chubby child waving a webbed-fingered hand, a strikingly beautiful woman, this had to be Ceriddwen, with a glorious mane of dark hair punctuated by a slash of white curls. Laura went through canvas after canvas, each one more exquisite than the last, beautifully and lovingly crafted, a glorious record of Molly's other life. She was a talented artist, and Laura could make an educated guess as to the identity of every character; she felt as though she knew them all personally, thanks to Molly's returning memories.

'I haven't been up here for years,' Molly said slowly. 'Fred stopped going abroad about five years before he retired, he wanted to concentrate on preparing for retirement, you know, playing more golf and tennis, and that's when he joined the gardening club...' she trailed off lamely.

'And became best friends with Dolly Dimpleknees at Number 11,' Laura said drily. Molly laughed in spite of herself.

'I forgot you used to call her that!'

'Anyway, back to reality,' Laura said briskly. 'These paintings are fabulous! It looks as though, despite Ceriddwen's enchantment, your subconscious was well aware of your life in Fairyland.' She wandered over to the painting on the easel, indicating to the sheet. 'May I?' she asked.

Molly's hand flew to her mouth. 'I...I don't know if I want to see that painting, not right now, anyway...'

'Why ever not? You were happy enough for me to look at the others.' Laura glanced back at the canvases, frowning for a moment. 'Wait a minute, it's just dawned on me — where are your paintings of Taliesin?' Molly just stared at her as tears began to trickle down her face.

'I'm a traitor — an adulteress! And a wicked mother, too!'

'You might be many things, Molly, but wicked was never one of them.' Laura smiled, trying to lighten the mood.

'What must they think of me?' sobbed Molly. 'If they even think of me at all!'

'Who are you talking about? Who are *they* and why would anyone think ill of you?'

Molly took a deep breath and gulped through her tears. 'They must think ill me. My husband and my children.' She crossed to the easel and yanked the sheet from the canvas. Laura gazed in shock at the painting of a stunningly handsome man with brilliant blue eyes, black hair pulled back in the warrior's braid Molly had so eloquently described. He held a laughing, dark-haired baby boy in his arms and a little girl with russet hair like Molly's, peeked shyly from his side.

'You have children?' she asked incredulously.

'I did have,' whispered Molly. 'Who knows what has happened to them since I left. How could Ceriddwen be so cruel? How could she do that to me?' She flung herself onto a battered sofa covered by a colourful patchwork throw. 'I thought she loved me!'

Laura sat down and took hold of her hand. 'Let's not get this out of all proportion,' she said soothingly. 'This has been a tremendous shock for you, goodness knows, I can't remember the last time I've felt so overwhelmed, either.' Squeezing Molly's hand reassuringly, she continued: 'Let's think straight and get our ducks in a row here. You've told us repeatedly that time moves differently in Ceriddwen's world. When you came back in 1972, you'd only been away for a few hours, but according to what you've told us, you believe you were there for years. Correct?'

Molly nodded miserably. 'Yes, that's true, but look at me now, I'm old!' she wailed. 'How can I go back now?'

Laura got to her feet and wandered back to the stack of canvases, flicking through them, pulling out paintings that caught her eye. She studied a pretty, half-timbered cottage, beautifully decorated with timbered murals and, just behind it, a tantalising glimpse of a long, quaint-looking house with turreted towers and leaded windows.

'Tell me about this,' she said, handing Molly the canvas. 'Looks like somewhere I would love to visit!'

'That's Tigh Falloch,' replied Molly, gripping the canvas tightly, 'where Taliesin was born and where I lived for a lot of the time.'

Laura nodded, looking at the painting on the easel. 'And you have beautiful children. When we were walking in the park today, you told me that Taliesin had asked you to marry him if the Queen would allow it. Can you remember what happened after that, or is it still too vague?'

Molly placed the painting at the side of the couch and smiled wistfully at Laura through her tears. 'I remember every second of it.'

~

Ceriddwen decreed the Betrothal Feast be held at Yule and be the centrepiece of the celebrations. Molly was swept up in a maelstrom of frenzied activity as she juggled preparations for her visit to Tigh Falloch with organising endless dress fittings and helping Ceriddwen compose the all-important guest lists. Once the lists were finalised and her betrothal garments in the capable hands of Holda's dressmakers and tailors, the happy couple finally set off for Tigh Falloch, Taliesin and Molly taking the lead, followed by Brighid and Rollo in a pony trap, plus a

A Dynasty of Dragons

baggage wagon and four of Taliesin's most trusted warriors. At Ceriddwen's insistence, Lady Kiya, the kennel mistress, had released the amaroks into Molly's care and they frolicked joyfully by her side.

The previously mild autumn weather had embraced a decidedly winter chill, and sharp easterly winds buffeted the travellers, gusting great swirls of crunchy copper and gold leaves around them as they set off beneath a chilly cerulean sky. Taliesin had presented Molly with an early betrothal gift of a beautifully tooled leather bridle and matching chest strap for Flambeaux, both decorated with little silver bells that tinkled merrily as the cavalcade trotted through the frost-rimed shires.

Tigh Falloch was some thirty miles north-east of the Southern Gate, an eight-hour ride, and Molly sat back and enjoyed the glorious scenery, marvelling at the beauty of windswept moors scattered with huge, brooding tors, the road winding along the edges of deep, rugged ravines where nimble mountain goats watched them warily from precarious cliff-edge perches. Spectacular waterfalls thundered down the steep slopes in blue-grey torrents, hurtling themselves into pellucid pools before continuing their headlong rush towards the distant sea. Early snow capped the tops of the distant northern mountains, gleaming in the sunlight, as they descended from the moors to wind their way through narrow lanes bordered on each side by holly, hawthorn, and beech hedges, bright with red berries and gleaming green and bronze-coloured leaves. Taliesin called the group to a halt beside a sturdy wooden gate enclosing a grassy clearing beside the tumbling river.

'We'll stop here for lunch and rest,' he announced, dismounting to open the gate. Molly and the others followed suit, and once their mounts were happily munching oats from their nosebags, they sat themselves on fallen logs conveniently arranged around a well-used fire-pit. They were sheltered from the icy winds by high hedges on one side and a dense screen of willow and alder thickets on the opposite riverbank.

'This is obviously a popular resting place,' Molly commented, hungrily shelling a hard-boiled egg, as Brighid bustled about handing out more eggs, bread, cheese, and elderberry wine.

'Yes, it is,' agreed Taliesin, taking a welcome gulp of wine. 'It's about halfway between the Southern Gate and Tigh Falloch. It's a wonderful place to swim and cool off in summer.'

'Hard to imagine on a chilly day like this,' Molly said. 'But you can bring me back for a swim next summer.'

'Try and stop me,' Taliesin agreed, giving her one of his heart-stopping, smouldering looks.

After their meal, while the others chatted and flirted with Brighid, who was trying and failing to look outraged, Taliesin suggested he and Molly take a stroll to stretch their legs. Molly whistled the amaroks, and they set off along the riverbank, Taliesin smiling to himself as low-hanging branches lifted themselves above Molly's head and sprawling bramble bushes cleared themselves from the path. Molly chattered on, oblivious to it all.

She was bundled up in a thick woollen riding coat, snuggled into its soft, fleecy hood, her cheeks rosy from the biting wind, hands warm, one snug in her coat pocket, and the other in Taliesin's strong, calloused grip. She looked up at him, so handsome in his Justiciar's greatcoat, emblazoned with badges of office, but the one that caught her eye was the badge she most associated with him: two white cows with foliage entwined between their enormous curving horns.

'Is the white cow badge your family crest?' she asked, rubbing her fingers over the smooth embroidery.

'Yes, it is.' He smiled down at her, tucking her hand through the crook of his arm. 'But once we're married, it will incorporate your crest, too.'

'I don't have a family crest.' Molly frowned.

'Then you shall have one! Your status demands it.' You're an Anunnaki dragon queen, and you have flower fairy blood, too. The cauldron told us that, if you remember.' Molly nodded, recalling her shock at the revelation. 'Plenty of scope there for an excellent crest.' Taliesin smiled indulgently, adding, 'Don't you think?'

'There is,' agreed Molly, 'and you're right, everyone else has their own crest, so, yes, we'll have one, too!'

Taliesin nodded. 'When we return to the Southern Gate, we'll go to the Crystal Tower and consult the genealogists. We must make sure we don't accidentally use another family's crest — there are thousands, and the experts at the tower know them all. They'll even help us design it unless you already have something in mind?' He gave her an enquiring look.

'I do have a few thoughts of my own, but obviously, we'll have to have them checked out — something with dragons and flowers incorporated with your cows.'

Taliesin snorted. 'As long as it's not a sea dragon!'

'What's wrong with a sea dragon?'

'What do you know about sea dragons other than the one Grainne captured?' Taliesin couldn't keep the distaste out of his voice.

'Why, what do you mean?' Molly's voice rose indignantly. 'She almost starved the poor thing to death — it was terrified!'

'Molly, sea dragons are amongst the most feared creatures in our world. That is why they are guarded so carefully by the Sirens, and another reason why Grainne deserves her harsh punishment. She was about to unleash hideous death and destruction upon the Southern Gate and beyond!'

They paused to watch a little brown dipper dive in and out of the fast-flowing river, flashing his white breast as he hopped on and off rocks in his search for tasty titbits, as the amaroks snuffled through the undergrowth searching for rabbits.

'I don't understand — how can it be more fearsome than the other poor dragons captured by the goblins?' Molly remained unconvinced.

'When they are hunting, they hunt with six heads — six heads full of ferociously sharp teeth on very long necks. They are monstrous, shape-shifting creatures!'

Molly stared thoughtfully into space. 'I vaguely remember her having a lot of heads before I calmed her down. You know she sounds just like Scylla in Homer's Odyssey.'

'There are sea dragons in your world?' Taliesin looked at her incredulously.

'No, not at all, the sea dragon I am talking about is a monster in a mythological story, and if I remember my Homer correctly...'

'Homer?' interrupted Taliesin. 'What's a "homer"?'

Molly frowned in concentration; Ceriddwen's enchantment still had a powerful amnesiac effect on her memory. 'Not a *what* — Homer was a person. A famous Greek poet — you know, like a bard.'

'Ah, yes, I see. At least I think I do.' Taliesin bent to pat one of the amaroks as it bounded to his side and sat, tongue lolling happily.

'Anyway', continued Molly, 'Homer wrote two epic poems called the Iliad and the Odyssey, and Scylla, the six-headed monster, was in the Odyssey. Mother Arianrhod teaches that all myths are based on distant memories of actual events, and I'm wondering if Scylla is a myth based on a sea dragon that stumbled through a portal.'

'Very possibly, although it would never have been allowed to stay in your world — the Sirens would have noticed its disappearance and summoned help to call it back.'

'Summoned who?'

'An Anunnaki dragon queen, just like you. You command all dragons. Why do you think you were able to handle Grainne's captive dragon with ease?'

Before Molly could reply, he glanced beyond the treeline; the wind had sharpened into a vicious howling gale, and the sky was taking on a dark, purplish, bruised look as ever-darkening clouds massed ominously above them.

'Time to mount and head out; there's a storm brewing.' He whistled the other amarok to heel and ushered Molly quickly back along the riverbank.

Brighid and Rollo were already packed and waiting in the trap, the little dapple-grey pony snorting and rolling its eyes, sensing the approaching storm. Taliesin's men had already tightened Storm and Flambeaux's girths, and once Molly was safely mounted, Taliesin leapt into the saddle and led them off at a brisk canter, heads down as heavy rain began to slash at them, driven by the fierce, relentless wind, reminding Taliesin of his fruitless dash to the Western Gate in his attempt to head off Grainne's attack.

After about twenty minutes or so, the amaroks growled a warning as they noticed another group of riders approaching them through the curtain of relentless rain. As the riders drew nearer, Molly realised they were forest fairies, recognising Birca astride her little doe. The others were mounted on larger deer, leading others loaded with panniers.

The leader of the group bowed and raised his hand in greeting, calling above the roaring wind.

'Greetings, Lord Taliesin!'

'Greetings to you, Lord Pan!' Taliesin's powerful voice cut across the gale. 'And well met! Allow me to present the Princess Molly, granddaughter to Queen Ceriddwen, and my future wife.' Turning to Molly, he said formally, 'Princess Molly, allow me to present Lord Pan, eldest son of Lord Cernunnos.'

'A great pleasure to meet you at last, Lord Pan.' Molly, smiled, inclining her head politely. Pan's bark-like features creased into a wide smile, his twiggy hair blowing about his face as he swept an extravagant bow.

'A great pleasure, Your Highness, I have heard much about you from Birca here.' Birca grinned, lightly touching her doe's neck, and to Molly's delight, the deer bent her foreleg in a pretty bow.

'Birca,' Molly cried, 'how lovely to see you again. But what are you doing out in this storm?'

'Delivering hazelnuts to the palace winery, Your Highness.'

'Aye, we weren't expecting this storm, it's come up suddenly,' said Pan, 'but it's fortuitous we've met, my Lord.'

Taliesin raised a questioning eyebrow. 'How so?'

'The white wolf pack has pulled down an old stag further into the forest, and if you don't mind me saying, I think you should leash your amaroks.' He looked apprehensively at the hounds as they stood, ears pricked, alert and watchful, growls still rumbling in their throats.

Taliesin nodded. 'Yes, we'll do that,' he said, calling to Rollo who produced two long leashes from somewhere in the pony trap, and proceeded to fasten them to the hounds' collars. 'Thank you. Even two fully-grown amaroks would be no match for a wolf pack guarding its kill!'

'Better to be on the safe side, my Lord. If the amaroks scented the kill, they'd be off into the forest looking for it!'

'Indeed,' Taliesin agreed. 'Well, we won't keep you, this storm shows no sign of letting up, best we be on our way. Safe journey to you all!'

Waving their goodbyes, the two parties took off once more into the driving wind and rain. Molly was glad when they eventually left the forest, fighting down a primeval fear every time she heard the wolves' eerie howls reverberating through the closely packed trees. Wolves weren't persecuted in Ceriddwen's world — they were seen as part of the natural order of things, the precious symbiotic balance of nature, keeping the deer herds in check, culling the sick and the old, eating what nature intended, living in harmony with the fairy folk. Despite this knowledge, Molly still suppressed a shudder as they trotted out of the forest, emerging into a sodden landscape of rolling hills, woods, and meadows.

'Welcome to Tigh Falloch!' Taliesin announced. 'Soon you will be mistress of all you survey!'

Molly peered through the rain and fading light — it looked beautiful, and she thought if it was beautiful in foul weather, it was bound to be much more so in glorious sunshine. She smiled at Taliesin, reaching for his hand and smiled. 'So, my love, I am home!'

He kissed her hand and murmured, 'At long last.'

They skirted the curving edge of a lake, wind whipping the water into white crested waves that splashed against rocks, sending great flumes of water across their path, their steeds' hooves throwing up divots of muddy turf as they dashed towards the twinkling lights of what Molly assumed to be Tigh Falloch Grange. She could see two turrets on either side of the main part of the building and a massive double door in the centre. A curtain wall surrounded the house, and Taliesin was heading towards gates on the right-hand side. A stream exiting the lake ran along the front of the grange and they clattered over a little hump-back bridge, drawing closer to the great arched gateway. A figure high on the wall waved to them and called to someone below. Almost immediately, the huge wooden gates swung open, and the exhausted group cantered gratefully through.

Molly found herself in a large courtyard, its cobbles slick with rain, glistening in the arching overhead crystal solar lights, as grooms ran forward to relieve them of their mounts, retainers quickly taking charge of the baggage wagon and the pony trap. Others, carrying bags, scurried down a stone flagged corridor followed by Brighid exhorting them to be careful with Princess

Molly's belongings. The curtain wall surrounded the sides and back of the grange and housed stables, a smiddy, a barn, a bakehouse, and various outhouses with what Molly assumed to be staff living quarters above them.

After calling someone to take the men to be fed and dried out, Taliesin led Molly down the same corridor Brighid had vanished into, and after a few steps, opened a door, showing Molly into a large stone flagged hall, thickly carpeted in warm rugs, its wood panelled walls hung with family portraits and beautiful tapestries. A large quartz crystal radiator took up most of one wall, projecting comforting heat.

Two elfin women, carrying towels and bedding, were being merrily chivvied up a wide, carved wooden staircase in the centre of the hall by a jolly, plump fairy woman, followed primly by Brighid who was relishing her position as Molly's maid and companion.

'The princess will require a warm bath before she retires,' she called out imperiously to the elven backs. 'Please make sure it is ready.' The words were no sooner out of Brighid's mouth when Taliesin cleared his throat and took Molly's hand.

'Molly, may I present my father, Lord Brude, and my mother, Lady Adwena.' His announcement was formal, protocol strictly observed, albeit through an enormous smile. His joy in his bride-to-be was obvious to all. Molly, who hadn't noticed Taliesin's parents quietly making their appearance, was overcome with embarrassment at Brighid's pomposity, and stuttered apologetically as they watched Brighid's ramrod straight back disappear along the first landing.

'I'm sorry about that — Brighid's rather...er...overprotective, I'm afraid.'

Lady Adwena laughed merrily. 'And so she should be! She's accompanied by Enya, Taliesin's nurse — a formidable lady who now rules the staff with the same rod of iron she ruled Taliesin with,'

Taliesin snorted. 'Lady Mother, a rod made of feathers would be more truthful!'

Lord Brude chortled. 'You got that right, son! You had Enya wrapped around your little finger, your Lady Mother misremembers, I fear!'

Lady Adwena regarded them with mock severity. 'You were both terrified of her, as I recall. I most certainly haven't misremembered that.'

'We forget ourselves,' said Lord Brude, bowing deeply.

'Welcome, Princess. We are delighted to welcome you to Tigh Falloch and even more delighted to welcome you into our family.'

'We are indeed,' agreed Lady Adwena, curtseying prettily.

Molly's trepidation at meeting Taliesin's parents was soon dispelled. Lord Brude was a jovial man, tall and broad like Taliesin, who had obviously inherited his father's good looks. Lady Adwena was about the same height as Molly, with huge brown eyes and auburn curls tumbling around her shoulders. With the famous fairy longevity, their ages were indeterminate, and they could easily have passed for Taliesin's siblings rather than his parents. The butler, Finlas, chose that moment to announce refreshments were ready.

'Poor things,' fussed Lady Adwena, 'you look exhausted, cold, and hungry. Come through to the parlour where we can eat by the fireside and chat. I want to know all about you, my dear.' She smiled warmly, tucking Molly's hand under her arm and leading her into the comfortable sitting room. Molly was happily looking forward to becoming further acquainted with her very charming future in-laws.

Taliesin's parents no longer lived at Tigh Falloch. Lord Brude was Legion Commander of the Eastern Gate Garrison, which was now their permanent home. Because of the wormhole, the gate was in constant use, most travellers preferring that to long overland or sea journeys, and the constant flow of traffic meant it had to be heavily guarded twenty-four hours a day.

Ceriddwen granted Lord Brude and Lady Adwena a few days leave to return to Tigh Falloch to meet their future daughter-in-law and prepare for the forthcoming celebrations. They were thrilled their son had fallen in love again as they feared he would never get over Morgaine's betrayal, and as the years passed, had almost given up hope of Taliesin ever finding true happiness.

Molly fell in love with Tigh Falloch. The quaint, turreted, half-timbered grange with its façade smothered in rampant wisteria, almost obscuring the massive, iron-hinged front doors, and the magical, coruscating effect the next day's wintry sunlight had on the roof's crystal solar flashings, simply enchanted her.

'We're going to be so happy here,' she confided to a very relieved and happy Taliesin.

Their short visit flew by. Taliesin was anxious to show Molly as much as possible of the estate and introduce her to the staff who ran it in his absence. Molly, meanwhile, anxious for news of Melusine, was delighted to find her happy and well-cared for. Although she had only been there a short while, she had been warmly welcomed by everyone on the estate, no one cared about her past. If Lord Taliesin trusted her, that was good enough for them, and she was soon happily settled into her pretty, thatched cottage with baby Luss and his doting nurse, Mistress Tansy.

Melusine took Molly on a short tour of the lakes and fish stocks, showing her the little tannery where she worked with a couple of helpers when she wasn't tending the fish. After showing Molly around and explaining some of the tanning processes, she shyly presented her with an exquisite, iridescent purse, its cross-body strap decorated with gleaming freshwater pearls.

'You saved my baby's life, Your Highness, and gave me a chance to redeem myself. Lord Taliesin told me I am here thanks to your intervention.'

Her eyes glittered with unshed tears as Molly took the jewel-like purse from her hands. 'We would do anything for our kin, Melusine, I should know, I killed Prince Jasper in retribution for his parents' crimes and for the crimes he himself would have committed had their plans succeeded.'

Melusine nodded miserably. 'And I can never forget the number of people who died, but all I could think of was...'

'It's over, Melusine.' Molly touched her shoulder gently. 'This is your life now. Enjoy it, and enjoy watching your son grow in safety and, ultimately, in freedom. We shall see more of each other after the wedding. I suspect I shall be spending a lot of time here.' Melusine smiled her gratitude, curtseying as Molly made her way over the little bridge and back to the grange.

The estate was enormous, and employed many workers, each performing their own specialised tasks, but coming together as one during important times like ploughing, planting, and harvest. Molly noticed several forest fairies working with teams of horses hauling enormous logs, their forestry skills unsurpassed throughout the kingdom, and Melusine had a small team of water fairies maintaining the lakes and rivers. Tigh Falloch was well-known for its magnificent herds of aurochs and their flocks of sheep, producing best dense, high-quality wool, famous throughout the land. Molly felt a bit overwhelmed by the size of the estate and the sheer number of people needed to maintain its output of high-quality produce.

'What will my duties be as Mistress of Tigh Falloch?' she asked Taliesin tentatively as they rode through a hazel grove and down a little lane beside a large pasture where a herd of white aurochs grazed peacefully, several looking up, swinging their wide curving horns to gaze placidly at the passers-by.

'You will supervise the staff, ensure the estate is managed efficiently, check the accounts, greet and entertain visitors, and...' He stopped, his face creasing into a wide grin at the horrified expression on Molly's face. 'Your face is a picture!' His eyes twinkled merrily. 'My love, all that is required of you is to be my loving partner and my soul mate. Your time will be your own. Take all the time you need to familiarise yourself with the house, the farms, the villagers. And maybe, if you have time, we can make babies to share our love!' His voice was husky as he reached for her hand and tenderly kissed her palm. 'Your wish is my desire, and I hope my desire will be yours also.'

Molly felt as though her heart would burst. That this sometimes taciturn and laconic man, Queen's Warrior and Justiciar of the whole land should be in love with her, and show such a gentle, loving side to his nature, made her want to shriek with joy. Instead, she hugged her happiness to her heart, where it sat, glowing like a precious ruby.

'We shall make beautiful babies!' Her eyes sparkling and her face flushed with desire, she leant over and drew him into a passionate kiss, deaf to the sounds of aurochs lowing in the pasture and rooks scolding from the treetops.

TWENTY-NINE

A Winter Betrothal

'Brrr!' Laura gave an exaggerated mock shiver. 'Sounds like awful weather. I had the impression it was always fine and warm. I didn't realise Sidhthean had such horrible weather!'

'You mean normal seasonal weather?' Molly raised a questioning eyebrow. 'I think you've forgotten what that is. Sidhthean has proper seasons, spring, summer, autumn, and winter, regular as clockwork. No climate change to worry about there.' She frowned at the mention of Planet Earth's bête noir. Laura and Molly fancied themselves as eco-warriors and tried to do their bit, recycling and avoiding waste as much as possible, but most of the time they just felt helpless. 'I did tell you about the terrible storm Taliesin had to ride through on his way to the Western Gate?'

'When he was trying to head off Grainne?' Laura nodded in agreement. 'Yes, I'd forgotten about that.'

'And there was an enormous snowstorm the day before our betrothal feast. It was quite magical.' Molly settled further into the couch, hugging a cushion and gazing into space as she continued her story.

Fairy betrothals are the main event in a partnership agreement between two Fae. The marriage ritual may or may not take place later depending on how the relationship between the couple develops. A betrothal can be dissolved if one half decides they don't wish it to continue, as with Taliesin's previous betrothal to Morgaine, or if they are unable to have children together. Fairy folk love children and this often drives their instinctive attraction to a prospective partner. Many marriages are formalised following the birth of a child.

When their betrothal was announced, Molly and Taliesin were granted a beautiful grace and favour apartment in the south wing of the palace. A suite of light airy rooms facing the mighty river Danu, it had beautiful views of the harbour and upriver to the shimmering lake and beautiful mountains beyond. The rooms were furnished in the same elegant style as the rest of the palace, yet still cosy and comfortable. Taliesin's duties as Queen's Warrior and Justiciar meant he had to divide his time between the palace and Tigh Falloch. Tigh Falloch would be their main residence, and as the palace accommodation was pleasant and comfortable, the happy couple were quite content.

The betrothal came and went in a dazzling swirl of frost and snow. The Great Hall was splendidly decked out in lavish greenery, enveloping the palace in the exhilarating scent of pine, spruce, and fir, intertwined with great branches of holly, mistletoe, and ivy, crowding every spare inch of wall and windowsill, their red and white berries adding bright splashes of colour amongst the greenery. Slender crystal candles nestled in the foliage, creating a welcoming glow, while hundreds of beautiful silver and frosted glass snowflakes, fashioned by local artisans, hung from the high hammerbeam roof, gently swaying, glittering in the crystal candlelight. The massive Yule log would burn bright in the huge hearth, drawn there earlier upon a beautifully decorated sleigh amid a great ceremony by two of Taliesin's pure white aurochs, their magnificent horns garlanded in mistletoe.

Molly hugged Morfan in delight. It was the morning of the betrothal and she had been desperate to come and view the preparations. People bustled about laying plates, dishes, and long-stemmed crystal glasses on top of snow-white tablecloths. Tables were arranged along the walls to leave the centre of the beautiful, polished oak floor free for the Solstice Ball. Stunning displays of white hellebore winter roses were arranged in elegant vases on every table, and the sound of musicians practising floated down from the minstrel gallery above the top table.

'It's like being in the middle of a magical winter forest!'

Morfan laughed. 'My mother loves everything to do with Yule and the Winter Solstice, as you very well know,' he said, 'but this year is extra special because of your betrothal!' He leant towards Molly and said, sotto voce, 'Actually, she's been a nightmare, but don't tell her I said that.'

Molly giggled merrily. 'She has been extra bossy — I saw two elves running for their lives yesterday — she was throwing oranges at them! Apparently, they were the wrong shade of orange!'

Morfan raised an amused eyebrow. 'Incorrigible as ever.'

'But it's all so wonderful!' exclaimed Molly. 'Everything's just perfect!'

'That's the Queen for you.' Lleu's mellifluous tones joined the conversation. 'This year is a very special celebration indeed, and heads will roll if all does not go to plan!'

Molly laughed nervously, being fully aware of Ceriddwen's mercurial temper. 'I'm sure you don't mean that literally, Lleu!'

'Why do you think I am patrolling the preparations?' He grinned wickedly. 'I'm making sure all sharp instruments are kept well out of the Queen's reach! Yes, Kip, I'm just coming.' He smiled down at a little page boy, tugging on his tunic. 'Please excuse me, my dears, I have been summoned.' He swept them a little bow, and with Kip clutching his hand, allowed himself to be dragged towards the Queen, who appeared to be tussling with a huge bunch of rampant ivy.

~

There was an involuntary and audible intake of breath from the assembled guests when Molly made her appearance that evening. She was ravishing in a sleeveless russet gown of shot silk, chosen to match the rich tones of her glorious hair, coiled at the back of her head and secured by two golden pins. Her bare arms were adorned with heavy golden bracelets while a matching torc gleamed around her neck, her eyes seductively ringed in black kohl. The guests, including Ceriddwen, were already at their places, standing ready to applaud as she joined Taliesin, equally magnificent in his Queen's Warrior dress uniform. This was fairy protocol at its finest. They were the guests of honour, and as such, sat in the centre of the top table on the raised dais opposite the Yule log that crackled and sparkled in the hearth at the other end of the hall.

Molly and Taliesin bowed to everyone and, as they took their seats, the hall erupted in thunderous applause which gradually slowed to a rhythmic clap as Lady Erena, a bard from the Crystal Tower, began to sing a traditional betrothal song from high in the minstrel gallery, her beautiful voice soaring and swooping through the hall, reducing some of the guests to tears.

Ceriddwen and Lleu sat next to Molly, with Lord Brude and Lady Adwena next to Taliesin, neither hiding the fact that they were bursting with pride and joy for their son. When the song finished, Ceriddwen, resplendent, yet understated, in a beautiful gown of cream velvet, rose to her feet again to make a speech about her joy at finding Molly and the happiness she had brought the Royal Family following the sad loss of Prince Gwion.

Molly found it difficult to remember much of Ceriddwen's speech, or any of the other speeches for that matter — she was lost in a scintillating haze of pure happiness, the warm scented air of celebration, the happy smiling faces, the gorgeous, subdued background music, and her hand lovingly nestled in Taliesin's strong, familiar grip. She sat enthralled as the palace dancers began their Winter Solstice dance, traditionally performed before every Solstice Ball.

The dancers made their graceful appearance, six dressed in gorgeous filmy white garments, six in similar black outfits and the thirteenth dancer wore a shimmering golden dress to represent the sun. The dancers twirled and leapt, legs flashing, hair streaming as they enacted the eternal battle between light and dark, day and night, the dark night forces battling with the forces of daylight, pushing the golden sun away, pushing backwards and forwards with the most beautiful intricate dance steps, until gradually, the black dancers gave way, and the white dancers formed a semi-circle around the golden sun. She pirouetted around them before finally leaping into the arms of a white dancer who held her aloft in triumph, amid great cheers from the audience; light has prevailed, the sun has returned, winter shall flee, and the long dark nights are over. The dancers took their bows and ran lightly from the hall, ecstatic applause, and cheering ringing in their ears.

After the sumptuous feast, the tables were cleared, and everyone prepared for the much-anticipated ball. The musicians struck up a rousing tune to encourage everyone onto their feet. Dressed in their solstice finery, the happy crowd thronged the floor, jostling for the best positions to show off their outfits — water fairies wearing iridescent gowns designed to expose their beautiful, finned wings, which either hung down their backs in rippling rainbow colours, or were displayed open, resplendent in their shimmering glory. The forest fairies were dressed in various forms of greenery and forest finds, gorgeous gowns made from different coloured lichens and delicate spider webs, little fitted tops stitched with a myriad, tiny finch feathers teamed with skirts woven from delicate plant fibres, jewellery and head-dresses made from nuts and berries fashioned into the most intricate designs. Everyone else swished and swirled in a glorious cornucopia of colour as people took up position for the first dance, a fast-paced partner-changing reel. Cernunnos and Lady Flidais led the charge, twirling the length of the rows of other dancers at break-neck speed before separating and taking a new partner, both couples now rocketing down behind the rows of waiting dancers and back up the centre. When it was their turn, Molly and Taliesin were swept along by Morello and Oonagh, followed by a breathless Tabitha partnering a huge mountain fairy, his silver hair flying around his face as he whirled her around with dizzying enthusiasm. Molly loved dancing, but never had she danced with such joy, surrounded by her dear friends and family, and held close in the arms of her beloved Taliesin.

The night belonged to Molly and Taliesin, of course, Ceriddwen keeping an uncharacteristic low profile, no hogging the limelight in her usual flamboyant style, even foregoing leading the first dance as she normally did at every other ball. Their guests assumed she was merely respecting the happy couple and felt free to pay her scant attention as they danced and caroused their way through the evening.

Ceriddwen never let her guard down, and tonight's celebrations were carefully monitored for any malign influences. Matters of state don't rest because of a party. The palace and surrounding area were on high alert, with troops discreetly placed at every vantage point. Ceriddwen was taking no chances. It was only two short months since the dramatic events of Samhain. Very few people, apart from Ceriddwen and her closest advisors, gave a thought to the goblin queen keening her grief in a bleak castle on her desolate island prison, nor to the ghost of the unfortunate Prince Jasper and the ever-present, malevolent spectre of Lord Nudd. Ceriddwen remained alert and watchful throughout the entire evening.

'Always expect the unexpected and never underestimate your enemy!'

This was an idiom that would eventually come back to haunt her. She may have felt the goblin king's unwelcome spectral presence, but he didn't present himself in person, and for that, Ceriddwen was very relieved. Molly's chilling and unexpected execution of Prince Jasper had shaken her to the core, though not because she disapproved. As a warrior queen, she would have performed the gruesome deed herself with alacrity. The prince was a participant in Nudd's ongoing war crimes against all the kingdoms and nations of their world. In her opinion his demise was just. There was a strong possibility that the courts would have sentenced him to death anyway. That Molly had undergone her transformation from gentle girl into fully-fledged Anunnaki dragon queen disturbed Ceriddwen more than the ignominious death of a goblin; prince or no prince. Morfan was forbidden to play the Anunnaki tune he had so innocently played at Samhain. No one had any idea what effect hearing it again might have on Molly. Nor did they wish to risk finding out.

Wine, beer, and mead flowed freely as the revellers danced and sang their way through waltzes, jigs, and reels, Morfan and Varik, enjoying the fact that Varik had his first evening off in weeks, got roaring drunk, dancing on the tables and singing marching tunes at the top of their voices. Molly had never witnessed the serious and very proper Varik letting his hair down, and she loved every fun-filled minute of it, cheering them on, and allowing herself to be whirled around the dance floor by each of them until she collapsed, screaming with laugher into Taliesin's waiting arms. Her happiness carried her effortlessly on to the end of the ball in the early hours of the morning. She kissed Taliesin beneath twinkling stars and a dazzling solstice moon as they clung together for warmth, their breath hanging in frosty clouds as they called and waved goodbye to the last of their guests crunching their way home through the silent wintry landscape. When the last reveller disappeared, Taliesin swept Molly into his arms and carried her joyfully to their long-awaited betrothal bed.

THIRTY

The Isle of Clouds

It was the middle of May, two weeks after Beltane. Molly and Taliesin were strolling through one of Tigh Falloch's beautiful woods, admiring the magnificent carpets of bluebells and other spring flowers. The air was thick with the heady scent of wild garlic, and pretty wood anemones filled the deep shaded spaces avoided by bluebells. Birds sang in the trees and bushes, and a cuckoo could be heard echoing through the woods.

'I'm pregnant.' Taliesin, bending over to point out a little purple orchid, turned his head to look at her in disbelief.

'What did you just say?'

'I said I'm pregnant,' Molly replied innocently, brushing her hand over wood-sorrel blooming on a bed of vibrant green moss carpeting a fallen log. He straightened up — orchid forgotten.

'But…but…when…how?'

Molly raised an eyebrow, suppressing a smile. 'How? How do you think?' Taliesin stared at her, dumfounded, and Molly burst out laughing. 'You should see your face. I wish I had a mirror!'

'I thought you said…?'

Molly nodded. 'Yes, I did say. I...or rather...we are going to have a baby!' Taliesin's face broke into a wide grin as he pulled her into a bone-crushing hug.

'You're pleased, then?' Molly gasped, wriggling out of his vice-like grip. In reply, Taliesin grabbed hold of her again, this time lifting her high in the air, whirling around until they collapsed dizzily in a fit of joyful giggles, cushioned by the soft leaf mould on the forest floor.

'I am ecstatic, my darling,' he said, finally catching his breath. 'But are you absolutely sure?' He laid his hand on her slightly rounded stomach. 'Do you know when the baby will be born?'

'Samhain.'

'Samhain!' he declared. 'A wonderful time of year! Our child shall be welcomed into the world amid much celebration!'

'I thought you'd be pleased.' Molly snuggled closer to him. 'It's my favourite festival, you know. I fell in love with you at Samhain.'

'I know.' He chuckled happily. 'This child will be special in so many ways. Who else knows?' he asked, helping Molly to her feet.

'Master Lenus and Brighid. I had terrible morning sickness at the beginning and Brighid guessed right away.' Molly grimaced at the memory.

'So, that's why you couldn't come to Tigh Falloch for the Spring Equinox.'

'I couldn't face the journey; the smell of horses made me worse!' She laughed ruefully. 'I was so disappointed, but really thrilled at the same time, and I couldn't wait to tell you, especially as you've been away for so long.'

'Not that long, my love, three weeks at the most.'

'It seemed much longer than that.' Molly pouted. By now, they were strolling through an apple orchard. The trees were smothered in blossom, filling the air with their delicate perfume.

Molly stopped as one obligingly dipped a branch, allowing her to bury her face in the pretty pink flowers, inhaling a deep breath of their scent.

'Did the trip go well?' she asked from the depth of the flowers.

Taliesin had been escorting Ceriddwen to the Isle of Clouds to discuss Grainne's imprisonment with Scatha. Coira, the island of Grainne's banishment, was part of Scatha's domain, and she was, in effect, Grainne's jailer. It was unusual for Ceriddwen to make such a trip. Normally, Scatha would have been summoned to court for instructions, but Molly suspected Ceriddwen was indulging in a little schadenfreude. She shuddered inwardly at the memory of her part in the debacle. *I would do the same again,* she thought grimly, involuntarily placing her hand on her stomach, *to protect my family and all my loved ones.*

Taliesin noticed the gesture. 'Are you feeling alright?' he asked anxiously.

'Yes, yes...I was just remembering what happened when... when Grainne...' her voice trailed off.

'She'll never bother you again, Molly, you do understand that, don't you?'

'If it was only her, but Gwynn ap Nudd is still as powerful as ever, and I do think it's strange that he hasn't launched an attack in retaliation — I did kill his son, you know!' she cried, almost hysterically.

'Molly, stop! Please!' Taliesin caught her shoulder and pulled her around to face him. 'Grainne has been banished forever. She will never escape from that island. Scatha will make sure of that. I, of all people, know that. She was my teacher and mentor, remember?'

Molly looked unconvinced.

'Please stop fretting. Nudd is no match for the fairy kingdom and our allies, and he knows it. He wouldn't dare. Mean little skirmishes are more his style. Cunning and deceitful, but cowardly!' He held her gaze earnestly. 'You are a very powerful Anunnaki dragon queen. He knows that now, and he will fear you. You are more terrifying to Nudd than you realise.'

She shrugged. 'I suppose you're right. Becoming a mother-to-be is making me over-sensitive. Why do I worry when I have you to protect me!' She threw him a coquettish smile.

'I think you are more than capable of looking after yourself, my love, and very few people would disagree with me.'

Molly threw her arms around his neck and kissed him soundly. 'I love you so much,' she said, linking her arm through his. 'Now, let's get back to the grange and you can tell me all about your trip over a nice cup of tea.'

'Speaking of my trip, you do know you'll have to tell Ceriddwen before you tell anyone else?'

'I know, I know. Thank goodness I had three weeks to prepare myself while you were gone.'

Taliesin chuckled. 'Ah, so now you're glad I was away!'

She gave him a playful push. 'You know what I mean. But you're right and I'll come with you when you go back to the palace. We can tell her together.'

Taliesin rolled his eyes. 'I can hardly wait!'

Molly chuckled. 'You know she'll be thrilled, but come on, I want to hear all about Scatha and Grainne.'

Taliesin's jaw tightened. This was one trip he wasn't about to forget in a hurry.

~

Taliesin was summoned to court because Ceriddwen had announced that the maiden voyage of Lord Dubh's sleek galleon, *The Lady Froya*, would be a sail to the Isle of Clouds. The main purpose of the visit, she explained to her slightly surprised officials, was the rather unpleasant task of delivering Prince Jasper's embalmed body to his mother for burial. As Grainne was a political prisoner, this was a matter of state security, and Ceriddwen had decided to deal with it herself accompanied by Taliesin and a contingent of warriors. Although she had no reason to believe the formidable Scatha would behave dishonourably, Grainne was still a sister queen, and protocol decreed that Ceriddwen put aside her personal loathing of the goblin queen to ensure Grainne was treated well. Taliesin, however, felt uneasy at Ceriddwen's offhand explanation for the journey. It didn't feel right somehow. Seafaring was most definitely not Ceriddwen's favoured mode of travel, and normally she would have sent Taliesin or Lord Varik to ensure correct protocols were being observed. But it wasn't his place to question the Queen, and he kept his misgivings to himself.

Admiral Sulis seconded Fleet Captain Midir to be ship's master, with Lord Ravenna's frigates as extra muscle should they come across any goblin pirates. According to Admiral Sulis' intelligence, pirates were active in the Western Sea and had so far evaded the best efforts of the fleet to intercept them, much to the Queen's disapproval.

On the morning of the maiden voyage, as Taliesin made his way along the harbour to *The Lady Froya*, he was surprised to see Ceriddwen had already made her way up the gang plank and was heading across the deck towards a nervous-looking Captain Midir.

'I expected the pirate problem to have been dealt with by now.'

Ceriddwen launched a furious attack on an alarmed Captain Midir, jabbing him viciously in the chest with the point of her crystal-tipped staff. Caught off-guard, he fell backwards against the bulwark. Ceriddwen scowled ferociously at him as he struggled to keep his footing. 'Lost your sea legs, Captain?' she snapped before flouncing off to the royal cabin with Ladies Tanith and Rowan scuttling behind her.

'Captain Midir, I presume?' Taliesin had come aboard, and seeing the captain's discomfiture, waited patiently until he composed himself before bowing politely.

'My Lord Justiciar! It is an honour to have you aboard.' Captain Midir was a stocky, well-built man with a weather-beaten face, veteran of many a sea battle, but now visibly shocked by the Queen's outburst.

'Do not mind the Queen, Captain.' Taliesin smiled, taking in the captain's ashen face. 'She is always like this at the beginning of a voyage.'

'Really?' Captain Midir replied weakly.

Taliesin leant towards him and whispered, 'She suffers terribly from seasickness, and must drink a special preventative potion brewed in her cauldron.'

'But we haven't yet left the harbour!'

'According to Her Majesty, she becomes ill as soon as her feet touch the gangplank. Psychosomatic, I fear.'

Captain Midir groaned audibly. 'And when can we expect Her Majesty's good humour to be restored?'

'As soon as she can be persuaded to take the medicine. It tastes absolutely foul!' Seeing the captain's look of scepticism, Taliesin made a face, admitting, 'I suffer from the same affliction myself and must partake of the same potion. Believe me, Captain Midir, consider yourself very fortunate you do not have to imbibe such an evil-tasting cure.'

'Have you had yours yet, my Lord?'

'Unfortunately, no. I am on my way to the royal cabin now. Her Majesty always prefers to witness the sufferings of others before inflicting the same punishment on herself!' He laughed ruefully, giving the captain a comforting pat on the shoulder as he left. 'Don't be downhearted Captain Midir, peace and harmony shall soon be restored.'

Ceriddwen glared furiously at Taliesin as he entered the cabin. 'I was about to send a search party to look for you, Lord Taliesin,' she complained. 'How good of you to finally join us!'

Taliesin bowed low. 'Forgive me, Your Majesty. I paused to greet Captain Midir.'

'Captain? He'll be reduced to the rank of rating if I so much as glimpse a pirate vessel on the horizon!' she spat. 'And Admiral Sulis needn't think her position is secure either. Pirates indeed! As if I didn't have enough to deal with.' She then rounded on Lady Rowan, hovering nervously, clutching a phial of greenish-looking liquid tightly in her hand. 'Well, don't just stand there like a fool!' she cried impatiently, waving her hand at Taliesin. 'Give him the draught before our breakfasts are disgorged all over the cabin floor!'

'Of course, at once, Your Majesty!' Taliesin reached out and took the phial from Rowan's shaking hand, and grimly swallowed the contents in a single gulp, his gorge rising as the foul concoction hit the back of his throat. He gritted his teeth until, thankfully, his stomach began to settle.

Ceriddwen eyed him suspiciously. 'It has worked?'

'As always, Your Majesty.'

Ceriddwen nodded. Her face was a definite greenish colour, and Taliesin knew she must already be feeling quite nauseated, hence her evil temper. She snapped her fingers impatiently at poor Lady Rowan, who jumped to attention, almost dropping the second phial she had just retrieved from its box. Ceriddwen snatched it out of her hand, and screwing her eyes tightly shut, swallowed the potion in one gulp before hurling the empty phial at the cabin wall where it shattered into myriads of tiny shards, narrowly missing Taliesin. Ignoring the broken glass glittering around his feet, he waited a few moments until the Queen's equanimity was restored.

'Your Majesty, shall I tell Captain Midir to weigh anchor?'

'Everyone on board? Troops with Lords Lleu and Morfan on the quay?'

'Yes, Your Majesty, all are assembled and waiting to wave you off.'

'Then let us be on our way, we have tarried too long!' Taliesin hid a little smile as she turned away, bowing deeply, before making his way back to the poop deck where Captain Midir waited impatiently for his orders.

Captain Midir and Taliesin stood on the deck as Ceriddwen smiled and waved elegantly to her husband and son, her bodyguards standing to attention at her back. Everyone on the quay cheered and waved as the little galleon set sail out of the harbour to a loud fanfare, heading down the broad blue waters of the river Danu towards the open sea where they would meet up with Lord Ravenna and their frigate escort.

'Is this your first visit to the Isle of Clouds, Captain?' asked Taliesin once they had safely navigated the mouth of the river.

'No, my Lord, I have made the journey several times.'

'Ah, good.' Taliesin nodded his approval. 'You will be familiar with the Beir, then.'

'Unfortunately, yes.' The captain gave a wry smile. 'Nearly sucked me under when I was young and inexperienced. I'll never forget it!'

Taliesin nodded sympathetically. 'The final test for those training at the warrior school is navigating the Beir alone in a tiny skiff. If you fail, you are either drowned or considered unfit to be a warrior should you have to be rescued.'

'Then it's a good job we have Lord Llyr's dolphins to guide us,' Captain Midir said drily.

Taliesin raised an eyebrow. 'Bearing in mind we have the Queen on board, Captain. It is no reflection on your navigational skills,' he said mildly.

'Indeed,' replied the captain hastily.

The Beir was a huge whirlpool, situated just short of Scatha's Isle of Clouds and the island of Coira where Grainne was being held, notoriously dangerous and difficult to navigate. It was typical of Ceriddwen to undertake such a risky journey with no thoughts of her own safety but causing everyone else great anxiety.

In the end, the voyage was pleasant and uneventful. The skies remained blue and the sea calm. The dolphin pod escorted them safely round the Beir, much to everyone's relief, and soon they were docking at Scatha's harbour with the island's huge mountain, Onomaris, rearing in front of them. Scatha's eyrie was high on the mountain, affording her spectacular views of the island and across the sound to Coira and Grainne's castle prison perched atop its granite cliffs.

Scatha and Ceriddwen rode side by side with Taliesin and his warrior band, with Captain Midir, Lord Ravenna, plus several of Scatha's trainee warriors bringing up the rear. Taliesin's initial unease about their visit was exacerbated by the fact that, although out of earshot, he could see that Ceriddwen and Scatha were engaged in what appeared to be a grim and tense conversation. His warrior instincts were on full alert — something was seriously amiss.

The sailors from the galleon and frigate escort were lodged for the night in the trainees' barracks. Their first task the following morning was to transfer Prince Jasper's remains from the galleon onto one of the frigates, then await the order to set sail for Coira to deliver the prince's remains to his mother.

Scatha's fortress was built into the side of the mountain with high thick walls topped by merlons and punctuated by dozens of arrow-slits. The walls clung to vertiginous sheer drops on three sides, and the only way into the fortress was over a massive drawbridge laid across a terrifyingly deep, dark gorge. The entrance was protected by huge iron studded gates and a portcullis. Ceriddwen and Taliesin were familiar with the fortress, as were the warriors, but the sheer, forbidding presence of the place still gave them all a frisson of fear as the great wooden gates slammed shut, followed by the metallic clanking of the enormous chains creaking and groaning as they were rewound around their windlasses to raise the drawbridge.

The interior of the fortress was just as Taliesin remembered. The bailey was surrounded by a gatehouse, guardrooms, storerooms, the granary, stables, and a forge. The keep was partially built into the side of the mountain with Scatha's solar, bedchamber, library, and bedchambers for guests on the upper floors, whilst the ground floor comprised of the Great Hall, kitchens, buttery, pantry, and a warren of corridors leading to the armoury, offices, a sick bay and various other rooms and chambers. Next to the armoury door, a long dark tunnel hewn out of the bedrock of the mountain led down to an ominous-looking iron gate guarded by two well-armed warriors. Taliesin was all too familiar with this passageway. It was the only way in or out of Scatha's dungeon.

Scatha wasn't a great believer in personal comfort. The fortress was sparsely furnished and functional. She wasn't overly impressed by the Queen's presence either, and laid on no special comforts and facilities for Ceriddwen, who knew Scatha of old, and wisely said nothing. She knew they must simply get on with the business at hand.

'Those of you who know me,' Scatha announced peremptorily, 'will be aware that I don't stand on ceremony. For anyone,' she added emphatically, obviously referring to the Queen. Ceriddwen's face wore an expression of studied nonchalance as Scatha continued: 'We shall eat once I have explained why you are here.'

The captains exchanged glances, thinking they were delivering the goblin prince's corpse to his mother, nothing more. Taliesin clenched his jaw in irritation. He had no time for petty subterfuge, and to think the Queen had brought him to his old school under false pretences was unthinkable. What on earth was going on? He could feel his notorious short fuse begin to smoulder and fought to keep his temper under control.

'Forgive me, Your Majesty, Lady Scatha, but are we to understand that we are not delivering the goblin prince to his mother as planned?'

Ceriddwen nodded to Scatha, who quickly replied, 'Yes, of course — the goblin shall have her son, but we have bigger fish to fry, Lord Taliesin, much bigger fish indeed.'

'May I be so bold as to ask what that would be, exactly?'

Attendants had placed food and drink on the large scrubbed wooden table in the centre of the room. Scatha waved everyone over to the plain, uncomfortable looking benches set around it. 'Please be seated, and, with Her Majesty's permission, I shall explain.' Everyone made their way to the table and once they were settled, Scatha called for attention.

'First of all, please excuse the obvious subterfuge. I sent word to Her Majesty explaining the gravity of the situation, requesting that she come as quickly as possible, telling no one the real purpose of the journey.'

Seeing the bemused faces, Ceriddwen took up the tale. 'I did my best to maintain an attitude of normality because there was no point in alarming everyone while we were at sea.'

Captain Midir, the brave sea farer with a chest full of medals, shuddered inwardly. Just being in the capricious Queen's presence alarmed him. She was their Queen. She should be ensconced in splendour, surrounded by attentive courtiers, not sitting in a draughty castle kitchen about to eat plain fare. He studied her surreptitiously. She was dressed in twill breeches and a leather jerkin, her hair pulled back into the warrior's braid, and her face bare of her usual cosmetics. She looked for all the world like any other warrior and not the most powerful fairy in the land.

He had heard the tales of her unpredictability and her fearsome temper tantrums, and he inwardly cursed Admiral Sulis for sending him on this mission. He wished fervently to be at the helm of his beloved battleship, *Orion*. Anywhere but here.

'Are we boring you, Captain Midir?' He almost leapt out of his skin as the Queen's sarcastic comment cut into his thoughts.

'N...n...no, Your Majesty, not at all.' He stuttered in terror, shrinking into his seat.

'Then we are extremely relieved to hear it!' she glowered at him before continuing. 'What Lady Scatha is about to reveal will explain the need for extreme secrecy. The venality of this matter almost renders me speechless.'

To Captain Midir's increasing horror, Scatha now focused her attention on him. 'Captain Midir, tell us about these pirate raids the fleet has been trying to intercept.'

Taliesin was frowning by now. His initial unease at the Queen volunteering to make the trip when she loathed sea journeys was proving to be correct. Captain Midir choked down a mouthful of bread he had absently popped into his mouth and patted his lips with a napkin as he quickly tried to arrange his thoughts.

'We have been called out several times in the last two months to try and run down two particularly persistent goblin ships, but so far they have managed to elude us.'

Ceriddwen was mightily unimpressed. 'The entire fleet has been unable to apprehend two pirate ships. How can this be? Haven't you been using dolphin trackers? King Ossian of the Fianna seems able to deal with goblin pirates more effectively than the Royal Fleet! This is becoming embarrassing!'

Lord Ravenna cut in smoothly before the flustered Captain Midir could answer. 'The pirate ships in question have trained orcas, Your Majesty, and they have killed eight of our best dolphins. Lord Llyr is most reluctant to send more.'

'He had no problem sending the pod to guide us here!' Ceriddwen snapped.

'Um… that was only because Your Majesty was on board the galleon, otherwise, they would not have been sent.'

This was too much for Taliesin. 'Permission to speak, Your Majesty,' he snapped, immediately gaining everyone's attention. 'This has been going on for two months, and I, Queen's Warrior and Justiciar, have not been informed. Why?'

Ignoring the uncomfortable silence, but noticing the furtive glances between Ceriddwen and Scatha, he ploughed on. 'Orcas aside, in what way are they more dangerous than the ships raiding King Ossian's waters? Are you sure they are goblins? The fact that you have been unable to intercept and apprehend them is most disconcerting. It's almost as if you were pursuing someone familiar with fairy seamanship and defence!'

As soon as he uttered the words, he had a deep sense of foreboding as once again he caught the furtive glance that passed between Ceriddwen and Scatha. 'As always, Lord Taliesin, you get straight to the nub of the matter,' Scatha said grimly. 'They are goblin ships, but it is not goblins at their helms.'

'How do you know this, Lady Scatha?' Captain Midir ventured, bravely casting a fearful look in Ceriddwen's direction.

'Because we have captured one of them,' Scatha replied. The captain swallowed nervously as Ceriddwen frowned at him, and to make matters worse, his stomach rumbled rather loudly, a sure sign his nerves were getting the better of him.

This was bad, very bad. Ceriddwen's enchantment rendered the island of Coira invisible to everyone apart from specifically chosen Tuatha de Danaan fairies. He dared to think the unthinkable, but terror rendered him dumb, so he said nothing.

'Fortunate for you, and you also, Lord Ravenna,' Ceriddwen growled at the equally nervous frigate captain, 'but especially fortunate for Admiral Sulis. Had we not captured this ship and made our startling discovery, all of you would have been reduced in rank to midshipmen, if not dismissed altogether. We are most displeased.' She eyed them beadily and Taliesin was simmering with impatience.

'Where is this ship? I didn't see a goblin ship in the harbour.'

'Ah,' said Scatha, 'they thought to avoid the Beir by sailing their ship around the back of the island, but unfortunately a sudden storm blew them onto the Skean Reef.'

Taliesin scoffed. 'Only someone familiar with these islands would take such a calculated risk, not only to avoid the Beir, but to avoid being seen. Someone who knew the western side of the island wasn't guarded because of the reef.'

'Exactly!' said Scatha.

'And who might this captive be?' Taliesin was beginning to feel extremely uneasy. 'Forgive me, Your Majesty, but this would appear to be some sort of cat and mouse game, and I'm finding it difficult to work out who is the cat and who is the mouse!' He closed his mouth abruptly, hoping he hadn't been too assertive, but Ceriddwen ignored him, staring impassively ahead.

'All in good time, my Lord Justiciar,' Scatha said in a placatory tone. 'Eat your meal, and then we shall pay our guest a visit.'

Eating was now the last thing Taliesin and the good captains felt like doing, but they dutifully ploughed their way through the generous portions placed in front of them for fear of offending the prickly Scatha. Ceriddwen ate with her usual gusto, clearing her plate and calling for more fruit pie while the others waited impatiently.

Before they left the table, Scatha advised them to be prepared for a shock. 'Especially you, Lord Taliesin, this will be particularly onerous for you, I am afraid. Her Majesty has had time to digest the implications, but alas, we had to maintain the utmost secrecy until you arrived.'

Taliesin nodded. 'Understood.'

'Good,' said Scatha. 'Now, if everyone will follow me, we shall proceed to the prisoner.'

She led them through the castle corridors to the dungeon tunnel. It would have been a dark, oppressive space but for the crystal sconces flooding the narrow passageway with light. They made their way in silence to the dungeon gates, smartly flung open by the burly guards who saluted and bowed as Ceriddwen and the others swept past them into a large square lobby. It contained three heavily bolted cells on each side and four rooms in front of them housing an interrogation room, a sitting room for the guards, a storeroom, lavatories, and showers. The lobby was lit by a phalanx of very bright overhead lights. Scatha approached the middle cell door on the left-hand wall and slid the cover from the spyhole.

'Your Majesty,' she said, 'please satisfy yourself that the prisoner is exactly who I have identified them to be.'

Ceriddwen leant forward and peered into the cell, then straightening up, turned to the others, grim-faced. 'You are correct in your assertion, Lady Scatha, although I can scarcely believe my eyes.' She was quivering with barely suppressed fury as she turned to Taliesin. 'Lord Justiciar, allow me to present our prisoner.' Taliesin stepped forward and put an eye to the spyhole. Almost immediately, he reeled back in shock, his face a mask of disbelief. He looked again and turned to Ceriddwen.

'Your Majesty, I now understand the need for secrecy! This is beyond treachery!' Ceriddwen's eyes flicked towards the cell door and back to Taliesin, her lips pursed in distaste.

'I would have spared you this, Lord Taliesin,' she said brusquely, 'but protocol insists that as Justiciar, only you can deal with this. The interrogation, arranging the trial, and the outcome. This is unprecedented and we shall have to tread very carefully and swiftly.'

A quick bow was all Taliesin could muster. His professional training enabled him to quickly adopt an inscrutable appearance after his initial shock, but inside he was having difficulty processing what he had just witnessed. This was a very bad business indeed.

'Captains, please look at the prisoner and tell us if you have ever seen this person on any pirate ships you have pursued'

His lips were moving automatically, speaking as a Justiciar should, but his emotions were in turmoil. With Herculean effort, he pulled himself together and watched as the men took it in turns to observe the prisoner.

'Your Majesty, Lord Taliesin, I have seen this person before, several times.' Captain Midir mopped his brow nervously. His life was ruled by protocol, and he found the Queen's informal presence extremely disquieting.

Admiral Sulis conducted all business with great pomp, and the Queen's apparent insistence on making this journey low-key with no advisors apart from Lord Taliesin and a handful of warrior guards seemed alien to his disciplined mindset. He was also very curious as to the identity of the prisoner'What about you, Lord Ravenna?' Taliesin queried tersely.

'Looks very familiar — I've seen that face before, just can't remember where.' Lord Ravenna scratched his head as he tried to place the prisoner. 'Never mind, I'm sure it'll come back to me.'

'For your sake, I sincerely hope so.' Ceriddwen gave him an icy stare as Scatha slammed the spyhole shut.

'We shall retire to my solar to discuss this further and arrange the transfer of the prisoner from here to the palace where the interrogation can take place in front of the council. If that suits Your Majesty?' Scatha added, hastily deferring to Ceriddwen, who nodded abruptly.

'Yes this will be a very long night.'

Ceriddwen gestured imperiously to the guards who opened the gates with alacrity, bowing again as she stalked past them into the tunnel, the others trailing in her wake. The prisoner sat in her cell, wrists and ankles restrained by shimmering elfin rope, body bruised and aching from being dashed against the reef during the fateful storm, but her spirit remained unbowed. She couldn't wait to laugh in their faces. Morgaine smiled to herself. Revenge was a dish best served cold.

THIRTY-ONE

The Tongue That Cannot Lie

Taliesin watched morosely as Molly poured him a cup of steaming tea. 'I really don't want to tell you this, especially after your wonderful news.'

Molly's brow wrinkled slightly. 'It can't be that bad, surely? You're here, after all.'

'I'm sorry, my love.' He spread his hands in a gesture of regret. 'Had I known, I would have…'

'You would have come sooner and asked Ceriddwen if you could stay longer.' She passed him the milk jug. 'So, what's so terrible you don't want to tell me?' She gave a half-hearted laugh. 'Don't tell me Grainne has managed to escape?'

'I wish that's all it was.' The bleak expression on his face chilled her to the marrow.

'You'd better tell me then,' she said, laughter forgotten.

'Ceriddwen hasn't given me forty-eight hours to come and visit you. I've come to fetch you.'

'Fetch me? What do you mean?'

'You've been summoned to sit on the council while Morgaine is being questioned.'

'Morgaine?'

Taliesin let out a long sigh. 'Yes, Morgaine. I thought I would never see her or speak that name again.'

~

The meeting in Scatha's solar lasted into the wee small hours. The repercussions were potentially catastrophic, therefore Ceriddwen demanded utmost secrecy from everyone involved, until Morgaine was delivered safely to the palace.

Ancient long held tradition ruled that any fairy deliberately breaking protocol to the serious endangerment of other fairies rendered their entire family culpable. Families were responsible for ensuring everyone lived by the rule of law, which had kept the Tuatha de Danaan safe and in charge for thousands of years. Indeed, all the other nations and tribes of their world were grateful too, for the Tuatha de Danaan had protected them all, usually from the goblins, but generally from the ever-present threat of humans discovering Sidhthean really existed.

The following morning, Taliesin accompanied Ceriddwen and Scatha on the sail across the sound to deliver Prince Jasper's remains to his mother. Captain Midir was relieved to note his Queen was now suitably attired in a golden circlet decorated with rubies and the kingdom's four gate points studded with glittering diamonds. Her face was fully made up to accentuate her feline eyes and sensuous red lips, and she had flung a stunning cream-coloured fleece wrap around her shoulders over an extravagantly embroidered bronze-coloured velvet gown with a split riding skirt. She looked every inch the conquering queen.

As soon as they docked at Coira's tiny harbour, Ceriddwen, Scatha and Taliesin rode ahead on waiting horses, followed by their retinue, leaving Lord Ravenna to supervise the delicate task of safely manoeuvring the casket from the ship's hold and loading it onto a waiting wagon for the steep uphill climb to the castle.

Grainne's prison was a small, ruggedly built castle perched on a towering cliff overlooking the Isle of Clouds. It boasted a high forbidding curtain wall flanked by four towers and the entrance was protected by heavy wooden gates and a fierce-looking portcullis. Gulls and terns wheeled and screamed, adding to the noisy roar of the waves crashing onto the rocks below. Rather than try and compete with the noisy cacophony, the company approached the castle in grim silence, their mounts snorting and stamping impatiently, as Grainne's guards hurriedly opened the gates.

They entered a bailey much the same as Scatha's, only considerably smaller. A broad flight of curved steps swept down from an arched Gothic doorway leading into the keep. Grainne stood at the head of the stairs, staring impassively at her visitors. She was dressed in a severe, high-necked, black woollen gown, her blonde hair plaited and coiled around her head. She slowly made her way down the stairs, followed by two guards who emerged from the depths of the shadowy doorway, until she came face to face with the waiting Ceriddwen, haughtily clutching her crystal staff, its tip and the diamond points on her crown, glittering in the harsh sunlight.

Grainne reluctantly dipped a curtsey to Ceriddwen who nodded curtly as she regarded the goblin queen with contempt.

'If not for the fact that you are a sister queen, I would have had your head for what you attempted to do to us.' Grainne glared at her in undisguised hatred as Ceriddwen waved her hand in a dismissive gesture. 'However, we are magnanimous, are we not? Plus, you didn't bargain for a dragon queen either, did you? You didn't see that coming!'

Grainne's mouth twisted in fury. 'The bitch murdered my son!'

Ceriddwen gave her a cold look. 'She executed the prince because he was a war criminal and because you murdered her ancestors and were about to murder her family and MY subjects, so I think it was justified. The court agreed, as I recall.' She raised her hand again, palm upright, before Grainne could respond. 'Enough! I will hear no more of your complaints. You look well enough — you are obviously adequately catered for.' Head held high, she swept past Grainne and up the stairs. 'We shall inspect your quarters first. Make sure refreshments are provided while we await the arrival of your son's remains.'

This was too much for Grainne. She sank to the ground in a crumpled heap, sobbing bitterly, all attempts at queenly dignity forgotten. Taliesin and Scatha, both standing silent and watchful, began to follow Ceriddwen into the keep. Scatha turned and gestured to the guards to assist the lachrymose goblin to her feet, whispering to Taliesin beneath her breath, 'I must be going soft. I almost feel sorry for her!' Taliesin grunted in agreement, anxious to distance himself from the sound of Grainne's gulping sobs as she was half-dragged, half-carried up the stairs by two stone-faced guards.

~

The interior of the castle was far more comfortably appointed than Scatha's spartan dwelling. The entrance hall was hung with banners woven by the loving relatives of Scatha's students. A plethora of these colourful banners, all depicting family crests, meant that many of them had found their way to Castle Coira to decorate its many walls. The ground floor had a normal kitchen area with all the usual kitchen accoutrements, pantries, storage facilities, and staff quarters. A highly polished dining table dominated the seldom used Great Hall, with another beautifully carved table sitting in splendid isolation on a raised dais at the far end of the room. Again, the walls were hung with pennants and banners. Taliesin remembered a time when Castle Coira was in constant use. Feasts were held here in honour of visitors, also to celebrate the eight annual festivals, the walls steeped in centuries of song and laughter. He felt saddened that the castle was now a prison and would host no joyous celebrations for the foreseeable future.

Grainne's solar and bed chamber were on the upper floor. Ceriddwen roamed from room to room, running gloved fingers over every surface, inspecting for dirt and dust. Meanwhile, four of Grainne's attendants scurried nervously after her. Grainne was being kept at great expense, and Ceriddwen was making sure everything was exactly as it should be. She opened the solar's huge windows and stepped onto a pretty balcony overflowing with pots of spring flowers. Scatha's castle, sitting high upon Onomaris, was clearly visible across the sound, and far down to the right, several fishing boats were moored alongside Captain Ravenna's frigate. People were busy bustling about the harbour, stacking lobster pots and mending fishing nets. A little boatyard was situated at the far end and the sound of hammering carried on the brisk wind blowing incessantly around the island. The left of the balcony afforded a sheer granite cliff face rising from jagged rocks rearing out of the crashing waves. Ceriddwen stepped back inside, leaving the window's heavy brocade curtains billowing in the stiff breeze.

Grainne was imprisoned in restrained splendour befitting her queenly rank. She had been granted a generous wardrobe of warm clothing and footwear, a maid to attend to her personal needs and dress her hair every day, a cook, and staff to look after the household and stables. She had a comfortable bed, and comfortable furniture in her solar, books to read, plenty of wool and equipment should she choose to knit or weave, two little dogs for company, and she could ride out every day with some of her guards if she wished. The island wasn't very big, but large enough for a long exhilarating gallop. She was watched constantly, and Scatha reported that she seemed to bear it stoically enough, although it was quite hard to tell.

The dungeon and an ancient crypt lay beneath the castle, accessed like Scatha's, by a long tunnel. The crypt contained the sarcophagi of twelve revered warriors, Scatha's predecessors, and Ceriddwen had to convene an extraordinary council meeting to seek approval for Prince Jasper's internment in an antechamber well away from the remains of the Isle of Clouds' past warrior teachers. The suggestion was seriously unpopular and challenged by furious objections and cries of *Shame*, but as usual, Ceriddwen's will prevailed and the motion was passed, despite the anger and misgivings of most of the council.

After what seemed like an interminable length of time, the wagon bearing the goblin prince's casket arrived. Everyone breathed a quiet sigh of relief. There had been no question of small talk over tea and cakes. Everyone just wished to have the business over with as swiftly as possible.

The bier was carried on the shoulders of six burly guards, with Grainne walking stoically behind them, her eyes puffy and swollen, the others following at a respectful distance down the tunnel to the crypt and finally into the little room that was to be the prince's final resting place. Grainne had had the room cleaned and whitewashed. There were several small niches carved into the walls and she had filled these with vases of daffodils and beautifully perfumed hyacinths. Four crystal lamps glowed from wall sconces, bathing the room in soft light. The bier was lowered to the ground and the carved oak casket was gently lifted and placed in a purpose-built niche opposite the door. Once the casket was in place, the bearers filed out of the room.

'We shall leave you to mourn your son,' said Ceriddwen, 'which is more than you deserve, as is the comfort you enjoy on this island. But Tuatha de Danaan justice is always fair. More than can be said for your rule of law, goblin.'

'My son and I are unforgotten, and I shall be avenged!' Grainne spat back.

'I may forget you,' Ceriddwen replied mildly, 'but be assured neither my Justiciar nor Lady Scatha shall forget you. You shall be incarcerated here until the end of your miserable days.' With that, she nodded curtly at Grainne and swept from the room, followed by the others.

'Beware the wrath of the goblin kingdom!' Grainne screamed defiantly to their retreating backs.

Taliesin stayed well out of the way when Morgaine was being transferred from her cell to the frigate. Although Ceriddwen had brought Taliesin along with her in his role as Justiciar, Morgaine was ostensibly Lord Ravenna's prisoner until they returned to the Southern Gate, where she would then fall under Taliesin's jurisdiction. Scatha rode with the conroi of warriors escorting Morgaine down the mountain. She was seething with suppressed fury and her contempt for her erstwhile student was palpable. Morgaine sat astride her mount, head held high, with an infuriating smirk playing about her lips. It took all Scatha's self-control not to knock her off her horse with a vicious blow.

The return voyage was not a comfortable one. The wet and windy weather caused the little galleon to lurch and roll drunkenly across the heaving waves, much to Ceriddwen's disgust. Taliesin thanked the gods no fairy believed in for the blessing of the cauldron's miraculous stomach-calming potion, then joined the Queen in throwing back dose after dose without complaint. They spent most of the journey privately closeted in the royal cabin discussing the implications of Morgaine's treachery.

Ceriddwen lifted her head from the documents containing Scatha's report on the pirate shipwreck and Morgaine's arrest. 'Scatha is adamant Morgaine was the only survivor, yet only three bodies were washed up.' She tapped her teeth with her pen. 'I am disturbed by this, Lord Taliesin. If we only have three bodies, we must assume the rest of the crew managed to survive. Do goblin ships have life rafts?'

'I believe they have small boats they keep on board for such emergencies, ma'am.'

'So, they must have rowed their boats out to sea to avoid capture around the Isle of Clouds or Coira?'

'The two pirate ships always work together. I would imagine the other ship avoided the reef and managed to sail to safety. Any survivors must have been picked up by the other ship.'

'A great pity, Lord Taliesin. Without one of the goblin pirates, we won't know if Morgaine revealed the fact that she could see Coira and they couldn't. I don't relish the thought of having to find somewhere else to incarcerate that infernal goblin. Coira is perfect, or at least it was!' She pushed the document away in exasperation.

'Forgive me, ma'am,' Taliesin chose his words carefully, 'but why do you think Morgaine would be able to see Coira? I thought only a chosen few were granted that privilege.'

'Yes, I know that, thank you!' Ceriddwen snapped irritably. 'But some families have the gift naturally without the aid of my enchantments, and I am afraid Morgaine's family is one such as those!'

'I was not aware of that,' Taliesin responded in a shocked voice.

'It's not something that is broadcast — the families who can see through glamour are bound by honour to reveal their gift to me and no one else, but we now know Morgaine is entirely devoid of honour,' she spat.

'Scatha is on high alert,' Taliesin replied. 'Both islands are being patrolled night and day, and she has doubled the guard on Coira.'

Ceriddwen harrumphed tetchily. 'It's the best we can do now until we question Morgaine and get some answers.'

'I fear she won't speak. Like all of us, she has been trained by the best to withstand torture and mind-bending.'

Ceriddwen glared at him. 'This is unprecedented, Lord Taliesin! I don't have to remind you how far-reaching the implications of this creature's treachery could be. It has the potential to bring down some of the most important families in the land.' She lifted one of the empty anti-seasickness phials, turning it between her fingers. 'I am afraid she will have to be tested by the cauldron, aristocratic warrior or not!'

Taliesin was aghast. 'I understand what you are saying, ma'am, but what about *The Tongue That Cannot Lie*? Will the council or Mother Arianrhod allow such a step?'

'Have you forgotten she is Morgaine's grandmother? This is not the time for pandering to aristocratic sensitivities! We cannot be seen to bestow special favour. Mother Arianrhod must step down until this matter is resolved. The law is clear — ALL family members shall be placed under arrest for the duration of the investigation.'

Taliesin looked at the Queen in horror. He was aware of the law — he just hadn't imagined any fairy breaking it. Fairy nobility consisted of many ancient and powerful families; they were embedded into every aspect of government. There was also an unspoken understanding that no trained warrior should ever expect to be tested by the cauldron. Their loyalty was regarded as unimpeachable. When warriors took their oath, they drank a potion from the cauldron, a gift from the Queen called *The Tongue That Cannot Lie*, and thereafter a warrior's word was considered sacrosanct. Ceriddwen regarded Taliesin's stricken look with growing impatience.

'You are Justiciar whether you like it or not, Lord Taliesin, and this is just as unpleasant for me as it is for you. Correct me if I am wrong, by the way, but as far as I am aware, Morgaine did not complete her warrior training after Lord Nuada's accident?' Taliesin nodded grimly. He had no desire whatsoever to be reminded of this chapter in his life, and now here it was, being forced upon him whether he liked it or not. 'Have you also forgotten that Lord Varik is Morgaine's cousin? Not only shall you be, temporarily I hope, deprived of your deputy, but my son shall be deprived of his partner. I have the unpleasant task of telling him.'

Taliesin's mind raced as he tried to formulate an effective plan. The task was monumental, and he knew he would have to act swiftly. They were due to dock in two days. 'I think it would be prudent to send word to Lord Lleu and the most trusted members of the council to forewarn them,' he said.' We shall have to issue warrants for the confiscation of every pigeon flock belonging to Morgaine's family, and they must be issued swiftly. I don't for one moment believe Morgaine's family knows anything about her treachery, but we must be prepared for all eventualities. Word of this must not be allowed to spread.'

'It is already done, Lord Taliesin. I have also issued an order to my husband that Lord Nuada's family also be included in the warrants. I hope you do not think I am stepping on your toes?' Ceriddwen arched an eyebrow.

Taliesin quickly nodded his head in agreement. 'Of course not, ma'am.'

'Good. Now, leave me please. I have much to do, as have you, I imagine.'

THIRTY-TWO

An Unexpected Arrival

The horses stamped and snorted in the cool dawn air. Taliesin, mounted on Luath, waited on the quay with the Morrigan and two conrois of her best horse warriors. Lord Ravenna was supervising Morgaine's removal from the frigate into Taliesin's keeping. The rising sun threw a spear of golden light across the eastern hills and down through the valley, glinting on warriors' shields and helmets and gilding the choppy river wavelets. Ceriddwen wished Morgaine to be transferred to the prison tower as quickly as possible before too many people were up and about.

Lord Ravenna appeared on deck and, at the Morrigan's signal, a conroi took up position at the bottom of the gangplank. Morgaine, hands securely bound, was ushered off the ship and helped onto a horse by two guards. She was immediately surrounded by the mounted warriors, spirited along the harbour and through the huge gates into the palace precinct followed by Taliesin and the Morrigan.

The Lady Froya, being smaller and swifter, docked a full half-day before Lord Ravenna's frigate, giving Ceriddwen and

Taliesin a few hours to bring Lleu and the remaining council members, not related to Morgaine or Nuada, up to speed. The Arianrhod had been informed, and although deeply shocked, willingly placed herself under house arrest. Her deputy, Lady Nimue, would become the Arianrhod until the matter was resolved. As soon as Lleu received Ceriddwen's message, he immediately issued warrants placing all members of Morgaine and Nuada's families under house arrest until further notice. Messages were swiftly sent to officials in every corner of the realm to ensure not a single member of the proscribed families was roaming free.

Once Morgaine had been officially processed and handed over to Lord Erien, the prison governor, Taliesin steeled himself for his first confrontation. Morgaine was housed in the only cell on the top floor of the tower, a semi-circular room with bare white walls, furnished with only the basic requirements. Accompanied by Lord Erien, with two prison guards standing by the door, Taliesin had his first good look at Morgaine in years. She was dressed in the usual prison garments of loose, blue cotton trousers and a long-sleeved top, her feet encased in slip-on canvas shoes. She stared defiantly at Taliesin, her beautiful brown eyes narrowed in contempt, and her hair, once worn long in anticipation of a warrior's braid, was now cropped short, framing her face in soft curls.

'How ironic it is that you should be my jailer,' she sneered before Taliesin had the chance to open his mouth.

'Lord Erien is your jailer, but I take your point. How ironic that YOU should betray your people when you were once prepared to take the Warrior's Oath,' he countered.

'You betrayed me!' she spat back. 'Your jealousy destroyed my life and the life of an innocent man, yet here you stand, Justiciar of The Four Gates. You have risen high despite your own treachery.'

Taliesin could hardly believe his ears. 'After all these years you're still peddling this fantasy?'

'What? You're actually going to deny it?'

'I refuse to discuss this nonsense any further.'

Taliesin's short fuse was begging to be lit and he fought to keep his temper under control. He held up his hand to silence her before she could say anything else. 'I am here to inform you that you will be questioned by the council next week, the day after your parents. You shall be tested by the cauldron, and once we have the truth of the matter, you shall be arraigned for trial.'

'You're bluffing,' she said warily, paling slightly, Taliesin noticed. 'You can't use the cauldron on warriors. It's forbidden.'

'But you are not a warrior, Morgaine. You left the Isle of Clouds before completing your training. Have you forgotten?'

'I am still a warrior!' she cried. 'I have centuries of warrior blood running through my veins!'

'You are a traitor, and the cauldron will soon reveal the depths of your treachery. Good day, Morgaine. We shall meet again at the hearing.' He gave her a curt nod and strode from the cell followed by Lord Erien, the guards slamming the door shut behind them.

'Come back! I am still a warrior! I am a warrior!'

He could hear her screaming all the way down the stairs and out of the tower, and he was shaking with fury as he made his way to the stables to fetch Luath for the journey back to Tigh Falloch and Molly.

~

By the time Molly and Taliesin returned to the palace, the Southern Gate towns and villages were in a state of heightened apprehension. As soon as Morgaine and Nuada's families were arrested, word spread like wildfire, and every shop, market stall, tavern and meeting place was alive with gossip and speculation. It was such a rare occurrence that no one could remember anything like this ever happening before. Feelings were running high, and people were besieging the courthouse to try and book seats for the expected trial. This was unprecedented, and the court officials were tearing their hair out until eventually, Taliesin had to send in guards to secure the court premises and order everyone back to their homes.

The first council meeting before Morgaine's questioning was conducted, unsurprisingly, in a very intense and charged atmosphere. The remaining council members were furious that several of their wise and trusted colleagues were under house arrest for the crime of simply being related to Morgaine and Nuada. When some asked if it was possible for those remaining to be impartial under the circumstances, they were silenced by Ceriddwen's announcement that Morgaine would be subject to questioning by the cauldron, their protests about warrior exclusion vanishing when Taliesin produced a document from Scatha's records confirming that Morgaine and Nuada did not complete their training after Nuada's accident, thus removing any impediment to this line of questioning. After a few more heated exchanges, it was decided that Morgaine and Nuada's parents would be questioned the following day, and Morgaine the day after. There was still no sign of Nuada, but Ceriddwen was confident Morgaine would reveal his whereabouts whilst under the influence of the cauldron.

~

Ceriddwen invited Molly and Taliesin to dine in her private apartments that evening as she hadn't seen Molly for several weeks and hoped that she would cheer Morfan up — he was deeply upset by Varik's house arrest and the fact that he wasn't allowed to visit him, either. Molly decided that this might be the best time to tell the family about the baby.

Brighid bustled around, fussing and chiding Molly for riding Flambeaux up from Tigh Falloch instead of travelling in a well-sprung carriage. 'You must take care of yourself and the little one now, not go charging about the countryside on a huge, flighty unicorn. Anything could have happened!'

'Flambeaux couldn't be flighty if he tried, Brighid — you know he's a big pussy cat and safe as houses.'

Brighid pursed her lips in disapproval as she laid out Molly's dress, looking her up and down with a critical eye. 'Perhaps you should have a word with Mistress Holda while you're here and have the seamstresses make clothes for your pregnancy — thank goodness she's not a member of either proscribed family!'

'I know, Brighid, all these poor people having their lives disrupted and possibly ruined in an instant.' Molly had been shocked to discover that Oonagh from the hospital stud was under house arrest — apparently, she too, was Nuada's cousin. The tentacles of Morgaine's treachery were far-reaching and very damaging indeed. Tabitha considered herself fortunate that no one at the royal stables was related to either of them. 'I'll have a word with Mistress Holda soon.'

She glanced ruefully at her still trim figure in the beautiful ornate cheval mirror.

'Hard to believe in a couple of months I'll be the size of a house. Enya offered to run me up some maternity clothes, you know.'

Brighid let out a snort. 'Run you up some clothes? You are a princess — no one just "runs you up" clothes! I never heard the like!'

Molly laughed. 'You are such a snob, Brighid! Do you think I run about the estate in beautiful gowns, wading through streams and across muddy fields in velvets and silks?'

'A princess shouldn't be doing anything like that, either,' Brighid said, hugely unimpressed by Molly's tales of life on a country estate. She hadn't taken kindly to being left behind in the palace rather than look after Molly at Tigh Falloch. Molly had very wisely foreseen the possibility of fireworks had Brighid permanently invaded the inestimable Enya's domain.

Taliesin tapped on the door. 'Ready?'

Molly gave the protesting Brighid a bear hug. 'Wish me luck, Brighid! I'm telling the Queen about the baby tonight.'

Taliesin was in a sombre mood as they strolled through the palace. 'You're very quiet, my love, I do know what a strain this must be for you,' Molly said.

Taliesin squeezed her arm. 'I'm just upset all this had to happen now of all times. I can't help feeling that what should be a joyous announcement will be forever tainted by this treachery.'

'They'll be thrilled, I'm sure of it, and it will help take everyone's mind off tomorrow.'

'Yes, perhaps, but it should have been under happier circumstances.' Molly sighed and patted his hand as Ceriddwen's major domo announced their arrival.

To begin with, dinner was quite tense, and, for most of the main course, the discussion concentrated on the following day's questioning and whether it was feasible or not that any of the two families knew what was going on. Eventually, Ceriddwen decreed that they would discuss the matter no further and turning to Molly asked how things were faring at Tigh Falloch. Molly decided this was the moment to tell all.

'Everything's running smoothly, Grandmother, the orchards are in full bloom, and we have plenty of healthy calves and lambs. Melusine has increased the fish stocks admirably, too.'

'Wonderful, my dear, and I must say you are positively blooming! Is there something you would like to tell us?' Molly gaped at Ceriddwen in amazement. How did she know? Then she remembered. Upon their arrival, the Queen had greeted her with a kiss on both cheeks. Of course, her fairy senses! She had sensed the baby when they embraced.

Molly coloured prettily. 'Actually, I was just about to announce that Taliesin and I are expecting a baby at Samhain!'

Ceriddwen clapped her hands, beaming from ear to ear. 'This is wonderful news! I am so happy for both of you!'

Lleu jumped from his seat and rushed to hug Molly and shake Taliesin's hand. 'Well done, well done! Just what we need. Good news to cheer us up.'

The announcement even roused Morfan from his misery, and he too enveloped Molly in a great hug, before giving Taliesin a congratulatory thump on the back.

'A little niece or nephew! I can't wait to have a baby in the family again. And if you're desperate to know if it's a boy or a girl, my lady mother will be only too happy to tell you!'

They all laughed. Another of Ceriddwen's talents. 'We'll let you know,' Molly said, smiling happily. 'We're still adjusting to the news.'

~

'Please be upstanding for Her Majesty the Queen and the Royal Family!' announced the council clerk as Ceriddwen swept in and settled into her ebony chair followed by Lleu, Morfan and Molly.

Seated in her usual chair next to Morfan, Molly took in the all-pervading sense of unease and confusion, mixed with a real sense of fury and discombobulation amongst the council members. Outside, May was blooming in all her glory — the air was filled with the scent of lilacs, clematis scrambling over garden walls and birds singing joyfully in the sunshine but, inside the council chamber, the atmosphere was one of stygian gloom. The business with Melusine had been disturbing and treacherous, but she had been blackmailed horribly, and everyone knew that water fairies were notoriously fickle anyway, although never to that extent, but Tuatha de Danaan warriors? Although Morgaine and Nuada weren't ordained warriors, they both came from long lines of warrior tradition and had undergone years of arduous training. It was an unprecedented situation.

Molly recalled a conversation when Mistress Holda likened the fairy people to bees who lived in harmony, working to protect themselves and their Queen. She reflected on the fact that most of the peoples throughout this beautiful, magical world embraced the same goal. They might squabble and fall out with each other occasionally, but their loyalty was to Ceriddwen and the preservation and protection of their world. The biggest threat was the goblins with their incessant desire to possess control of the portals and gain access to the human world. They envied humans their wealth and technology and wished to be part of it. Molly suppressed a shudder; she remembered very little of her previous life, but knew enough to understand if that ever happened, this beautiful, although imperfect, world would be changed forever, and not for the better.

Ceriddwen banged her staff for quiet. Lord Ruka stood up, and after clearing his throat apologetically, he announced Morgaine's parents, Lord Adarn and Lady Etain. As protocol decreed, they were shown into the council chamber by Taliesin in his role as Justiciar. Lord Ruka greeted them on behalf of the Queen and council, inviting them to sit facing Ceriddwen in the same chairs Prince Jasper and his cousins had occupied a few months earlier. No one enjoyed this humiliation of two good families and most council members had difficulty looking these respected members of fairy society in the eye.

Adarn and Lady Etain were both retired warriors. They lived on the other side of Lord Cernunnos' vast forest domain on their estate, Tarant Hoo, where their main business was carriage building and saddlery. Although wearing civilian clothing, their hair was dressed in warrior braids to emphasise their warrior status. They sat, straight-backed and proud, bewildered faces haggard through worry and lack of sleep,

It quickly became apparent that Morgaine's parents had no idea what their daughter had been up to. They were horrified and deeply embarrassed. As far as they knew, she was living deep in Western Gate territory with Nuada and his family who owned a famous winery. They were mortified to admit they had lost contact with their daughter due to a terrible argument about breaking her betrothal vows to Lord Taliesin. They shot apologetic looks at Molly, who felt achingly sorry for them. Unsurprisingly, Morgaine refused to see them when they arrived, despite Ceriddwen's magnanimous offer. Ceriddwen just shrugged. It made no difference to her.

Nuada's parents, Lord Igor and Lady Loti, were interviewed after lunch. Strained-looking and furious, they had a similar tale to tell. They believed that Morgaine and Nuada had gone to train troops for King Ossian beyond the Northern Gate. When questioned about their apparent lack of concern regarding their son's whereabouts, Lord Igor told them they had quarrelled over Nuada's accident on the Isle of Clouds. Nuada had always been a reckless, wayward child, thoroughly spoilt by his mother, a comment eliciting a venomous look from Lady Loti, as he went on to explain it became very clear Nuada was beside himself with jealousy when Morgaine became betrothed to Taliesin. He had assumed that Morgaine would be his and proceeded to go out of his way to win her back, fully aware he risked dishonour in doing so. Far from being sympathetic when Nuada had to leave the Isle of Clouds after the accident, Igor was furious and told his son he would never forgive him for so wilfully ruining his chances of becoming a fully-fledged warrior and dishonouring the family name. He refused to acknowledge Morgaine as Nuada's partner, blaming her for encouraging him, and for betraying Taliesin. They were both dishonourable and he wanted nothing more to do with them. Taliesin winced inwardly, recalling with appalling clarity, the day Lord Igor came to the Isle of Clouds to make a grovelling apology to Taliesin and his parents for his son's behaviour.

Both parties were beyond reproach. All were warriors sworn to lay their lives down for the Tuatha de Danaan and every other nation under their protection. Honoured by *The Tongue That Cannot Lie*, no one doubted for a second the veracity of their testimonies. The two couples were dismissed but would remain under house arrest pending the outcome of Morgaine's trial, and unpleasant though it was, Lord Igor and Lady Loti's entire family would remain under house arrest for as long as it took to track down Nuada.

The next morning, they were once again sitting in the council chamber. Ceriddwen had said very little during the previous day's proceedings. The parental interviews were a mere warm-up for the main event — Morgaine's interrogation, but today, the Queen would take charge of the questioning. The atmosphere was hushed and expectant. The morning sun streamed through the high, stained-glass windows, catching dancing dust motes in its beams, and spilling colourful rainbows of light across the walls and onto the huge, polished council table. All eyes were on the big double doors and a few people jumped at the sound of three loud knocks. Guards threw the doors open and Taliesin strode into the room, bowing to the Queen and council before announcing Morgaine.

'Good morning, Your Majesty and Honoured Members of the Council. It is my grave duty to bring before you Lady Morgaine, daughter of Lord Ardarn and Lady Etain of House Tarant.'

Morgaine, looking pale and drawn, was ushered in by two guards, her head held defiantly high, quickly hiding a flicker of dismay as she glanced nervously at Lady Tanith and the Ladies of Astarte gathered around the cauldron. She stood silently between the two guards, dressed in her prison garb, hands bound in shimmering elfin rope. This was the first time Molly had laid eyes on Morgaine, and she felt a quick stab of jealousy. Morgaine was beautiful and she understood why Taliesin had fallen for her.

Lord Ruka stood up. 'Thank you, Lord Taliesin. Please show the prisoner to her seat.'

Morgaine was placed in the chair her mother had occupied the previous day. Ceriddwen glanced at her contemptuously. The Queen was in the foulest of moods, snapping at her attendants and finding fault in everything. She, who normally slept like a baby, had lain awake for most of the night worrying about the implications of Morgaine's behaviour. There was no doubt about the trial, and even depending on the outcome of today's questioning, the outlook for Morgaine was grim. As usual, Ceriddwen would have the final say on the court's judgment. Morgaine was no Melusine trying to protect her child, and there could be no magnanimous gestures allowing her to while away imprisonment on some comfortable aristocratic fairy estate. There would be no Taliesin speaking up for her. The only people speaking up would be those who demanded the ultimate penalty.

Ceriddwen frowned at the papers scattered in front of her. She was at her most regal, dressed in a black and silver brocade sheath gown with a heavy tooled silver torque around her neck and wearing a jet-studded silver coronet on her head, her hair pulled back in a severe chignon. Her eyes were heavily outlined in her trademark kohl and her lips a slash of red in her pale, furious face. If Morgaine was intimidated, she hid it well. Ceriddwen looked up again and fixed her with an icy look.

'Lady Morgaine, I will come straight to the point. Please tell us why you are apparently a crew member of the goblin pirate ship that foundered on the Isle of Clouds?'

Morgaine stared directly back at Ceriddwen. 'I do not recognise the authority of you or this council. You are no longer my Queen, and I will answer to no one in this room.'

A terrible stillness came over the chamber. Outside the birds still sang merrily in the gardens and the sun continued to flood the room with colour and light. Everyone held their breath, and no one looked at the Queen.

A pulse began to throb in Ceriddwen's temple, and her face became even whiter, her knuckles whitening too, as she gripped the arms of her ebony chair in fury. Everyone knew what was coming.

Thrusting herself out of the chair, she grabbed a sheaf of papers from the table and flung them at Morgaine.

'When these documents contain proof of your treacherous behaviour,' she snarled, 'you dare insult me in my own council chamber?' Ceriddwen's eyes were bulging with rage. 'I am not your Queen? You forget, Lady Morgaine, I am High Queen of every realm in this world and I, and I alone, will decide your final fate! Be very mindful of what you say!'

'Lord Nudd does not recognise you as High Queen! He challenged you for the High Crown, but you dishonoured yourself by lying about a non-existent crown prince.'

Molly listened in horrified silence. Morgaine was either completely ignorant of the facts or she was deliberately goading Ceriddwen.

Ceriddwen digested Morgaine's words for a few moments. 'I was going to give you a chance to explain yourself,' she hissed. 'I even considered that perhaps you are ill, and could be cured by the cauldron, but how foolish of me to think that. You care not a jot for the harm you may have done this kingdom or indeed your own family.' She drew herself up to her full height and threw her arm out dramatically, bejewelled fingers glittering as she pointed to Lady Nimue, sitting in the Arianrhod's chair.

'Do you see your grandmother seated at this table?' she screamed, two spots of crimson glowing furiously along her cheekbones as her rage took hold. Lady Nimue, a sturdy, well-built woman with startling green eyes, sat placidly as Ceriddwen continued her verbal attack on Morgaine. 'Your grandmother, the most esteemed and venerable Mother Arianrhod, is under house arrest because of your actions! Are we to believe that you did not consider what harm and chaos your treachery would bring down on your own family?'

No one moved a muscle, not one piece of paper rustled, not even the scratch of a pen, the scribes sat motionless, pens poised in mid-air as the drama unfolded.

'Well?' Ceriddwen thundered, banging her staff so hard that everyone jumped, and the papers that were scattered on the table flew into the air.

Morgaine maintained a serene expression as she replied, 'I have no family. I have renounced the House of Tarant.'

Ceriddwen made an impressive effort to control herself. 'Well, Lady Morgaine, you will remain a member of the House of Tarant long enough to be questioned by the cauldron, then, when we have the truth, until your trial, your only family will be the other prisoners in the tower!'

'You cannot subject me to the cauldron. I am a warrior.'

'Why, whatever gave you that idea, Lady Morgaine?' Ceriddwen gave her an acid smile.

'I trained on the Isle of Clouds with Lady Scatha. My parents are warriors as am I.'

Apart from raising a quizzical eyebrow at Morgaine's mention of parents she had just so forcefully denied, Ceriddwen ignored her. 'Ladies of Astarte, is the cauldron ready?'

Morgaine was now looking a lot less serene. 'I refuse. You cannot make me! Warriors are exempt!' she babbled. 'I am a warrior. I do not recognise this council!'

'The cauldron is ready, Your Majesty,' Lady Tanith replied.

'Very well, bring the potion.' Tanith placed a goblet in front of Morgaine just as she had placed goblets in front of Prince Jasper and his cousins. 'Drink!' Ceriddwen commanded.

'I refuse! This is illegal! I demand legal representation!'

Ceriddwen was in no mood for nonsense. 'Lord Taliesin, have the prisoner restrained and force the potion down her throat.'

Taliesin, standing impassively behind Morgaine, ordered two guards to hold her arms as he took hold of her jaw in one hand, forcing it open, and with the other, lifted the goblet and poured the liquid down her throat before clamping her jaw shut, forcing her to swallow, all the time ignoring her eyes blazing hatred into his face.

Molly watched the proceedings dispassionately. It looked more violent than it was, with only Morgaine's pride being injured. Molly felt no sympathy for her. She was accused of betraying her people and may possibly have been involved in Grainne's ill-fated attempt to rescue Prince Jasper. Many people had died then. Molly shuddered inwardly, placing a protective hand over her belly. She was a gentle person, but a ruthless, primal element of her nature had been unleashed by Morfan's mysterious, magical Samhain music, changing her forever. She would stop at nothing if her loved ones were threatened and this woman, along with the goblin kingdom, threatened everyone and everything she held dear.

As with Prince Jasper and his cousins, Morgaine quickly fell into a relaxed, acquiescent mood. Ceriddwen began by asking mundane questions about her childhood, gradually introducing more relevant topics. Morgaine chattered on as though she was enjoying an afternoon tea party, the council scribes assiduously writing down every word.

Gradually it all came tumbling out. After leaving their furious families, Morgaine and Nuada were recruited by Lord Ossian to train troops as the goblin raids on his kingdom and territorial waters were becoming too frequent for comfort. During a training exercise at sea, they happened upon a goblin pirate ship. After surrounding and boarding the ship, they came face-to-face with its captain, none other than Prince Idris himself. Idris possessed a charming, charismatic personality, and lost no time in offering them a better deal than Lord Ossian's. A deal with the goblin prince was treasonous of course, but Morgaine and Nuada harboured deep resentments, taking no responsibility for their own actions, and thus required very little persuasion to join the prince's pirate fleet. Idris knew their warrior training would be a tremendous asset to the goblins.

'Tell us why you were in the waters surrounding the Isle of Clouds when your ship struck the reef?' Ceriddwen asked conversationally. She was keen to find out if Grainne would have to be moved.

'We were heading for the Anunnaki lands, but we were blown off course by the storm.'

Molly stiffened; ears pricked. This was becoming much more interesting.

'Why did you not try and drop anchor around Coira? You sailed past safe anchorage and on to the Isle of Clouds, obviously running the risk of foundering on the reef?' Ceriddwen asked. 'A somewhat strange decision for an experienced captain to make, is it not?'

'Yes,' Morgaine replied readily, 'I couldn't understand that either. He acted as though Coira wasn't there. I asked him why both ships were avoiding shelter at Coira. He looked at me as though I was mad. I suppose, for some reason, he just thought it was too dangerous. No one questions a goblin captain. I just obeyed orders.'

Everyone noticed Ceriddwen visibly relaxing. The goblins hadn't been able to see Coira, the glamour enchantment worked, and Morgaine obviously had no idea Grainne was imprisoned there. Ceriddwen breathed a sigh of relief.

She nodded. 'Of course, very wise. Now, perhaps you could tell us why you were going to the Anunnaki lands?'

Morgaine settled herself more comfortably into the chair. 'Well, we're trying to set up a dragon breeding programme, but they're becoming harder to track down; they go into hiding now when they realise we're around'.

'Why would you want to breed dragons?' Ceriddwen asked innocently. At that moment, Morfan glanced at Molly and was shocked to notice that, just for a second, a nictitating membrane flicked across her eyes.

His heart sank. *Please Molly, not in here, not now*, he thought, grabbing hold of her hand and squeezing it tightly.

Morgaine prattled on. 'It's because they don't live very long, of course. The fire-breathing minerals kill them eventually, so we need to breed more. Nuada's ship must have managed to ride out the storm, and I imagine they'll have arrived by now. He's probably rounding up the horrible creatures as we speak.'

Molly's heart began to pound, and she could feel the tell-tale prickle down her spine as dragon scales began to emerge over each vertebra. She struggled to pull free from Morfan's grip as he noticed with horror that the pupils of her eyes were now vertical slits. She was watching Morgaine with an intense, predatory look on her face.

Ceriddwen was blithely unaware of this as she continued to draw information from Morgaine.

'And who is based in the Anunnaki lands? Surely the crew of a single ship would not be capable of capturing and transporting several dragons? They are very large creatures, are they not?'

'Why, Nuada, of course!' Morgaine was now in full flow, revealing everything. 'That's why we were returning. We'd just delivered four dragons, and we were on our way back. He also trains goblin troops there and maintains the dragon pits. That's where they keep the captured dragons until they have enough to ship. It's always better to have baby ones, though, they're more tractable, you see, so quite often we have to kill their mothers.' This was too much for Molly, and she wrenched free from Morfan's grip, violently throwing her chair back as she leapt to her feet.

'We?' she shouted at Morgaine. 'We kill their mothers! You dare to sit there and tell me you kill my children?'

Ceriddwen turned to gaze at Molly in shock. Again, Molly appeared clothed in the same otherworldly glamour she had worn when confronting Grainne. She seemed taller, more robust this time, and her eyes! Ceriddwen couldn't stop staring at her eyes. Morgaine, on the other hand, simply blinked in surprise at the interruption.

'How rude!' she began and then it dawned on her who Molly was, and, to everyone's consternation, she began to giggle merrily. 'Oh, this is too funny for words. You're the dragon queen everyone's talking about, aren't you? Oh my! I wouldn't like to be in your shoes, oh no, absolutely not, because Idris is going to kill you for murdering his brother and imprisoning his mother! Dragon queen or not, you're a dead woman!'

Before Molly could open her mouth again, the council erupted in fury at Morgaine's insolence. Taliesin ordered the two guards to restrain her as he rushed to Molly's side. She was white with rage, and he was horrified to see green scales beginning to spread from behind her ears. Just as he reached out to put his arms around her, she suddenly doubled over, groaning in pain while clutching her stomach.

'Molly, what is it?' he asked urgently. 'Is it the baby? Shall I fetch Master Lenus?'

Molly cried out again in distress. Ceriddwen barked at Lord Ruka to close the meeting, ordering the guards to return Morgaine to the tower, as Lord Ruka shooed the startled and bemused members from the chamber. Molly was moaning in pain, beads of sweat standing on her brow and upper lip.

'I feel as though I have a dragon in my belly clawing to get out!' she gasped; her waters broke in a gush as Lady Nimue appeared by her side with a speed and agility that belied her bulk. She frowned in concern at Molly's grotesquely swelling belly, her fine cotton gown tearing at the seams as the others looked on in horror.

'I have midwifery skills, but I have never seen anything like this! Princess, may I examine you?'

Molly gave a brief nod, but Taliesin swept her into his arms. 'You can't examine her here!' he grunted, heading for the anteroom, Morfan throwing open the door as he rushed through to place Molly on one of the room's large couches.

Lady Nimue ran practised hands over Molly's abdomen, telling her to breathe deeply and slowly. 'I've done this before, you know!' snapped Molly, remembering in an instant of clarity, her previous long hours of labour, then it was gone. Lady Nimue said nothing, just making soothing noises as she finished her examination. Patting Molly's hand, she stood up and turned to Taliesin.

'When is the baby expected to be born, my Lord?'

'Not until Samhain!' cried a distraught Taliesin. 'What is happening, Lady Nimue?'

'This is unprecedented and not within my level of expertise,' she replied. 'The baby's head is engaged, and I am afraid birth is imminent — the princess is fully dilated.'

'But...but how can this be?' Taliesin flew to Molly's side as she shrieked in pain, gripped by another fierce contraction.

Lady Nimue knitted her brows in consternation. 'I am no expert, but this obviously has something to do with the princess's Anunnaki blood.' she lowered her voice so that Molly couldn't hear what she was saying, and turning to include Ceriddwen, said, 'I think it's stress related. Lady Morgaine's revelations about the dragons may have triggered this reaction. I haven't practiced midwifery for a long time, so I can't be sure. We need the Taweret and Master Lenus.'

Ceriddwen sent one of her attendants flying to summon Master Lenus and Mistress Mesket, the incumbent Taweret or chief midwife just as Molly gasped, 'The baby's coming, the baby's coming!'

Twenty minutes later as Master Lenus and the stocky, robust little figure of Mistress Mesket came hurrying breathlessly into the room, followed by a red-faced and worried Brighid, an exhausted Molly was resting in Taliesin's arms, both gazing in joy and wonder at their bouncing eight-pound baby girl with her shock of red hair and tiny green scales peeping from behind her ears, sleeping peacefully at her mother's breast.

THIRTY-THREE

The Anunnaki Lands

While Harry and Xander were taking care of business in Glastonbury, Laura was discovering that Molly's profusion of paintings were the perfect aids for her recovering memories. She persuaded Molly they should be catalogued chronologically, and they busied themselves with the task of sorting and collating every single painting — dozens of beautifully crafted, meticulously detailed canvases. They were paintings Molly had thought were simply figments of her imagination but were really a pictorial diary of her fairy life, including delightful paintings of her children, Alaria and Ares, with Taliesin's parents and the Royal Family.

'Did you go full term with Ares, or did he come as quickly as Alaria?' asked Laura, admiring a painting of the children playing with a roly-poly amarok puppy.

'I was practically wrapped in cotton wool!' Molly sighed, screwing up her face at the memory. 'To be honest, Brighid, Enya and Mistress Mesket almost drove me round the bend! They meant well, but I felt suffocated for the whole nine months.'

Laura nodded sympathetically. 'I suppose they were just trying to keep you and the baby safe.'

'Of course, but with Brighid and Enya fussing around like mother hens, not to mention Mistress Mesket watching my every movement, constantly poking and prodding me, it was exhausting.'

'What about Taliesin? What did he have to say about it?'

'Well, that was the thing, you see. Believe it or not, I hardly saw him at all during the entire pregnancy and do you know, he was even sent away for a while immediately after Alaria was born.'

~

Ceriddwen wasn't sentimental when it came to matters of state, baby, or no baby. The information obtained so far from Morgaine's interrogation had established that Nuada had been heading for the Anunnaki lands. The news he was training goblin troops and hunting dragons alarmed her, and she immediately summoned Admiral Sulis along with Captains Midir and Ravenna to an urgent meeting meeting. Taliesin had a couple of days respite until the admiral and her captains arrived from the Western Gate and strategy plans were drawn up, and he spent as much time as possible with Molly and their baby daughter, who they decided to name Alaria.

'It's an ancient water fairy name meaning *One Who Brings Beauty*,' Taliesin said, gently lifting the sleeping baby from her cradle. 'What do you think, my love?'

'I think it's a beautiful name, it suits her perfectly!'

'We really should be having her Naming Day quite soon,' Taliesin murmured as he stroked Alaria's downy cheek, 'but I fear it shall have to wait — I've just been ordered to accompany the fleet to the Anunnaki lands to find and arrest Nuada.' Seeing

Molly's stricken face, he gently placed Alaria back in her cradle. 'I'm sorry, Molly, I must go. The Queen cannot let this threat go unchallenged. Please don't be upset.'

Molly bit her bottom lip as she fought to hold back tears of disappointment. 'I'm not upset, not really,' she said unconvincingly. 'It's just a touch of the baby blues.'

'Baby blues?'

'It takes a few days for hormones to settle down after giving birth, and it can make new mums a bit weepy, that's all. I'm fine, really, please don't fuss,' she added, seeing concern spread over his face. 'I just don't understand why you have to go when Admiral Sulis has the entire fleet at her disposal!'

'I've been assigned command of one of the troop ships. Varik's been assigned to another now he's been released. Morfan's as unhappy as you are — he'll probably console himself by spending time with you and Alaria.'

Molly sighed; arguing was pointless. Taliesin was at the Queen's command, day and night. She knew she would be sharing him with Ceriddwen when she agreed to marry him. Duty came first — unquestioningly. But it didn't mean she had to like it.

~

Laura pulled out a painting of a smiling Alaria sitting in what looked like an old-fashioned high coach-built baby pram.

'That's looks like a Churchill pram!' she cried. 'Did you really have a Churchill pram in Sidhthean?'

Molly laughed. 'Honestly, Laura! Just because they don't have motor cars, high-speed trains and aeroplanes doesn't make them backward, you know! They're highly sophisticated, and yes, I had a coach-built baby carriage. It was a gift from Morgaine's parents, believe it or not!'

A few days after Alaria's birth, the beautiful cream-coloured pram and matching pushchair were delivered to their palace apartments courtesy of Lord Adarn and Lady Etain. They were keen to make amends for their daughter's misdemeanours and restore themselves to good favour in the eyes of Taliesin and his parents, not to mention the Queen's.

They were perfect gifts as far as Molly was concerned. She loved nothing more than wheeling Alaria along the dappled, leafy lanes of Tigh Falloch into the little estate village, the beautifully sprung pram hardly bumping at all on the narrow, cobbled streets. She soon became a familiar figure, getting to know the villagers, swapping baby stories with other new mums, having tea in the quirky tea shop, and just generally shopping and wandering around the market stalls. The villagers weren't in the least fazed by the fact she was a princess. She was Lord Taliesin's lady and that was enough for them. If they ever noticed the two bodyguards who discreetly followed her everywhere, they said nothing. She was royalty and commanded royal protection, but Molly had no airs and graces, and they loved her for that.

She did the same when staying at the palace, wheeling Alaria all over the vast grounds and into town, shopping in the artisan quarter and visiting all her friends, with Brighid and the ever-watchful guards in tow. One day, she even pushed Alaria all the way along the broad white road to the Crystal Tower, intending to visit Lady Nimue but, as soon as she entered the huge, glittering foyer, she bumped into Lorien, who fell into paroxysms of delight at the sight of Alaria, instantly, to Molly's consternation, engulfing the baby in a miasma of alcoholic fumes as he leant over the pram for a better look, ignoring Brighid tutting her disapproval at his back.

'Oh, how precious! I have already started a poem for her Naming Day, but now I have seen our little princess in the flesh, I fear I haven't done her justice!'

'I'm sure your poem will be just fine.'

Lorien jumped back, an affronted look on his face. 'Oh no, Your Highness, I would never settle for a poem that was "just fine", as you put it, my poems must be excellent and incomparable in every way or there would be no point!'

'Yes, yes, of course, Lorien.' Molly hastened to reassure the overly sensitive bard. 'I simply meant that your poem will already be incomparably excellent.'

'Well, yes, quite so,' he agreed, slightly mollified, rummaging about in his pocket for his ever-present flask of hazelnut mead, 'but it could probably do with just the teeniest tweak and that's why we must keep the creative juices topped up.' He saluted Molly with the flask before downing a good swig. 'Good afternoon, Your Highness, we shall meet again at the Naming Day, no doubt.' And with a cheery wave, he wove his slightly inebriated way out into the sunshine.

Molly was practical. She knew there was no point in fretting over Taliesin's absence and resolved to carry on regardless. She loved Tigh Falloch and continued to immerse herself in its day-to-day running, pushing the pram through the estate, taking long walks around the beautiful lake and through the muddy yards of various farms and stables. Visiting Melusine in her tiny fish tannery was a particular pleasure. She and Melusine were now firm friends, and it delighted Molly to see how well she had settled into her enforced way of life, and to watch little Luss thrive and grow into a robust, happy toddler under the watchful eye of Mistress Tansy. Happily, he seemed unaffected by his ordeal at the hands of the goblin queen. Alaria's lovely nanny, Nuala, was a great help, too. Recommended by Enya, she soon became an indispensable member of the household, and both Alaria and Molly grew to love her dearly.

The first few months of Alaria's life passed uneventfully, and although Molly missed Taliesin dreadfully, she busied herself with her baby daughter and her chores.

She divided her time between the estate and the palace — Ceriddwen demanded her presence for various council meetings and insisted upon seeing her great-granddaughter at every available opportunity. Alaria's palace nursery was bursting at the seams with gifts from her doting great-grandparents, much to Brighid's intense irritation, as she was running out of cupboard space for the endless stream of toys and baby clothes. Molly quietly dealt with the problem by every so often having some of the items discreetly shared amongst the babies and children of the palace and surrounding town, sending equal amounts back to the estate to be divided between the estate workers and villagers. She was careful not to offend by appearing to play Lady Bountiful. There was no need in fairy society. No one went without, and all Molly had to do was ask Brighid and Enya to barter the toys and clothes for a little token something in return.

~

'What I don't really understand,' said Laura as she buttered a slice of bread, 'is why you weren't desperate to go and rescue the dragons yourself. I mean, wasn't it the shock of learning what Nuada was doing that caused you to go into premature labour?' They had decided to have a break, and were lunching in their local Wetherspoon's, enjoying a meal of fish and chips.

'Well, I can assure you if I hadn't gone into labour and thinking I wasn't due to give birth until Samhain, I jolly well would have gone, and no one would have stopped me!'

Laura rolled her eyes. 'I can imagine.'

'Obviously, there was no question of me making a dangerous sea journey like that with a newborn baby, so I had no choice but to stay behind when Taliesin left. Alaria was my priority — *is* my priority!' Molly threw down her knife and fork and reached into her handbag for a tissue. 'Oh Laura, my children must wonder why I've left them. I can't bear it! I wish I hadn't remembered them.' She burst into floods of tears, blowing her nose, and ignoring the curious stares of other diners.

Laura adopted a soothing tone and reaching over, gently took hold of her friend's hand. 'Molly, we've talked about this. The time thing — I'm prepared to bet that they haven't even noticed you've gone. And anyway, we haven't reached that part of your story, have we? You haven't remembered it yet.'

Molly dabbed her eyes and blew her nose again. 'Oh, I know, I'm just being silly, but it hurts, it really hurts. I do think you're right, though. Just ignore me.'

'Okay, then! Hurry up and finish your fish,' Laura said briskly, 'I want to order sticky toffee pudding for afters.'

~

Ceriddwen received regular bulletins from Taliesin via homing pigeons, though not the pigeons familiar to Molly's human world. Fairy pigeons were preternaturally swift, using their ability to sense magnetic field energy to guide them through tiny wormholes, enabling them to return to their home lofts almost in the blink of an eye. This ability to disappear into wormholes, protecting them from predators, resulted in an almost fool proof communication system, and news was coming thick and fast.

Taliesin advised Ceriddwen that Lord Llyr had secured the help of Selkies, a strange race of water fairies who could shapeshift into seals at will — the usual water fairy shapeshifting laws didn't apply to Selkies because of their lifestyle. They were a nomadic people who lived in and around the many islands surrounding the Anunnaki mainland. They hated and feared the aggressive goblins and managed to escape the Anunnaki and flower fairy genocides by shapeshifting and successfully hiding. They were also infuriated by the kidnap of the Sirens and sea dragon. As soon as Grainne's huge man-of-war appeared over the horizon, they took refuge in their usual hiding place, a series of underwater lava tunnels, unaware of the goblin plans. The goblins had no idea these tunnels existed, and Taliesin and Varik planned to use them to launch an attack on their unsuspecting quarry.

Two Selkie leaders, Lady Arnemetia and Lord Rodon, were discussing manoeuvres with Taliesin and Varik. 'You are positive that the goblins don't post guards?' Taliesin sounded deeply sceptical.

Lady Arnemetia, a small dark woman dressed in sealskin, shrugged and replied, 'Why would they? They are unaware of our existence, if we think they may have observed us we simply shift into our seal bodies. They believe they are entirely alone on the islands.'

Lord Rodon, a burly, bullnecked man, cut in gruffly, 'We are familiar with the goblin camp. We can lead you there, but it will not be an easy journey.'

Taliesin and Varik nodded. 'No matter. We do what we must.'

The goblins' main camp was situated in a deep glen on the eastern side of the great Lake Dovann at the bottom of a heavily forested hillside. This lake occupied the centre of the peninsula and was an effective division between Taliesin's troops and the goblin camp. The troops would be led through a tunnel that opened on to a wooded area overlooking the glen. It would be a perilous journey. The entrance to the lava tunnel was underwater, and each soldier would not only have to dive into the water, fully equipped and in battledress, but also swim quite a distance into the tunnel before they could surface. The rest of the tunnel ran just above the water level of the lake, and timing was of the essence, as during wet weather, the tunnel often flooded. It was also low and narrow, and the men would have to crawl for much of the way. Another two Selkies, Lady Ceto and Lord Varun, would guide more troops, led by Harek, a tough elfin lieutenant, through another tunnel, emerging on the far side of the glen, effectively creating a pincer movement.

The Anunnaki main island was some five hundred miles long, no more than seventy miles wide, and surrounded by many small islands. Surmising that as Nuada had headed there from The Isle of Clouds, probably landing on the east coast, Admiral Sulis decided to take the fleet the long way round hoping to arrive, completely unobserved, on the west coast. She set her course up past the Northern Gate, hugging King Ossian's coastline, staying well away from the goblin territories bordering the Fianna lands. The course would then eventually cross the Northern Sea to sail the length of the Anunnaki west coast to the peninsula at the southern tip of the island where they anchored, out of sight, in a deep bay surrounded by high cliffs.

Three goblin ships were anchored in a small bay near their camp. Blissfully unaware of the imminent attack, the only guards seemed to be a pod of their trained orcas leisurely swimming around the bay. On the other side of the peninsula, Admiral Sulis moved the fleet out of the bay to sit behind a promontory further along the coast. From this vantage point she could readily blockade any exit from the goblin bay should the goblins decide to make a tactical retreat to the sea. A platoon of marines was preparing to go to the northern end of the glen to engage any goblins fleeing towards Mount Dovann, the extinct volcano at the head of the lake. The marines could make this journey unobserved through another tunnel below the rim of the volcano.

The Selkies were prepared to risk their lives to be rid of the goblins. Their spies displayed outstanding bravery, reconnoitring the goblin camp and shapeshifting into seals to spy on their ships, despite the ever-present danger of the killer whales. Their spies were everywhere, and they communicated by using a series of coded calls mimicking various birds. In this way, they were never out of contact with each other and relayed continuous information about the goblins' movements.

'The three ships are unattended, guarded only by orcas,' reported Lady Arnemetia.

'That means there must be about four hundred and fifty goblins in the camp, or out hunting for dragons,' mused Taliesin. 'Three groups of fifty on the northern side of Mount Dovann hunting a dragon and her two whelps.'

'A hundred and fifty men to catch three dragons?' queried Varik, who had sauntered up to join them. 'Surely it can't be that difficult?'

'You have obviously never witnessed a mother dragon defending her young,' retorted Lady Arnemtia.

'But I have,' said Taliesin softly, 'believe me, I have.'

Varik was immediately apologetic. 'Sorry, my Lord, I didn't mean to speak out of turn.'

Taliesin made a dismissive gesture. 'It's nothing, don't worry.' But seeing the Selkie's look of incomprehension, added quietly, 'My wife is the only remaining Anunnaki dragon queen.'

'How can that be?' Lady Arnemetia was incredulous. 'The goblins wiped them out!'

'Unbeknown to the goblins they had descendants with human blood, such as my wife. And very fearsome she is, too!'

'If that is so, Lord Taliesin, why is she not with you? Our task would be so much easier with someone who can control dragons.'

'She has just given birth to our first child, otherwise, I assure you, my wife would be here.'

'Ah.' Lady Arnemetia nodded. 'Of course. I understand.'

Now he knew the goblins were already hunting on the mountain, Taliesin changed strategy. He sent word to Admiral Sulis advising that the marines be despatched immediately with their Selkie guides under strict orders that no dragons be harmed and making sure every single marine could identify Nuada if he was with the hunting party.

'I know the man you speak of.' Lord Rodon spat on the ground contemptuously. 'He kills the mother dragons to capture the whelps. He has a hook instead of a hand and he takes pleasure in his butchery.' The Selkie's voice trembled in fury.

Taliesin shook his head in despair. 'It saddens us greatly that a man raised to respect every sentient being in this world should abandon every principle he was taught and embrace goblin cruelty.'

'I should like to kill him myself!' growled Rodon. His hatred for Nuada and the goblins was palpable.

'Queen Ceriddwen would rather he was captured alive. He has much to answer for and must be tried for his crimes.'

Rodon snorted in derision. 'Maybe so, but I would throw him to a dragon or give him to their orcas to play with. They would enjoy ripping him apart.' Seeing Taliesin's frown, he shrugged and held up his hands in a placatory gesture. 'But I will, of course, do my best to help you capture him alive.' Taliesin didn't look convinced.

They decided to leave at first light the following morning. Admiral Sulis ordered the marines on Mount Dovann to scout out the hunting party on the other side of the mountain, and as soon as they were located, prepare to attack. Each man had a full description of Nuada burned into his memory with strict orders to capture him alive if possible.

With Lady Arnemetia in front, and Lord Rodon bringing up the rear, Taliesin and his men followed the Selkie into the dark, still waters of the lake as she dived down several feet before disappearing into an underwater cave. This was the opening to the lava tunnel and the men had to hold their breath and swim quite a distance before finally breaking water, gasping for air, into a narrow, dank tunnel. Dripping wet, they painstakingly crawled or walked half-upright, occasionally banging their heads on small stalactites, until they emerged at last, blinking into the light, breathing fresh air redolent with pine and honeysuckle, to peer across an enormous expanse of trees spangled in moisture from a recent shower, dotted with meadows where wild ponies and deer grazed on the lush green grass.

'Is our camp close by?' Taliesin shaded his eyes as he scanned the area.

Lady Arnemetia nodded. 'Everything's in place. As soon as all the men are through, we'll make our way down.'

As this would take about another hour, Taliesin spent the time discussing strategy with Arnemetia and Rodon. 'Our spies and scouts have reconnoitered the entire area. The goblins are using an old Anunnaki manor house overlooking the bay as their camp headquarters, with most of their men bivouacked in the surrounding grounds.'

Lord Rodon cleared his throat and spat into some shrubbery. 'They can keep an eye on their ships, and the nearer they are, the easier it is for them to transport the dragons, especially the bigger ones.'

'How many do they have?' Taliesin didn't relish the thought of dealing with dragons, even if it was just to set them free. He fervently wished Molly was with him.

'Too many!' Rodon growled in disgust. 'They have five pits, three of them containing two adults and a half-grown whelp. My spies tell me they intend to leave as soon as they catch the three on the mountain.'

'No sea dragons, I hope.' Taliesin's stomach churned at the very thought of going anywhere near a sea dragon. He could still picture the hideous creature wrapped around Molly's neck when she rescued it from Grainne.

'Not a chance,' asserted Arnemetia. 'They would never have caught the one Grainne had if your friend Nuada hadn't been in possession of a blowpipe and stun darts!'

'Nuada has stun darts?'

'Not anymore he hasn't. He blew every dart he had at that dragon before he managed to knock it out. They're lucky the darts are fast-acting because it was just launching itself out of the water, all six heads snapping at once, when it collapsed.'

'How do you know he doesn't have more blowpipes and darts?'

'I heard him tell the goblin queen. They were so intent on catching the dragon they took no notice of us basking on the rocks in our seal bodies,' continued Arnemetia. 'He boasted he stole them from Scatha when he left the Isle of Clouds.'

Taliesin clenched his fists in anger. 'To think someone who was hoping to take the Warrior Oath could sink so low.'

'Hopefully, he'll be in for a nasty surprise when the marines catch up with him,' Varik said, leaning against a large rock, his wet clothes steaming in the warm sunshine.

'If he's actually on the mountain!' Taliesin took his fury out on a grassy tussock, kicking it with such force he uprooted it, sending it flying. 'He could still be in the camp.'

At last, the stragglers finally stumbled out of the tunnel, shielding their eyes from the bright sunlight. Once Taliesin had made sure everyone was accounted for, they headed to the Selkie camp located in a secluded clearing deep in the forest. They would rest until dawn before engaging the goblins in what they hoped would be a surprise attack. The forest was home to wild animals and Taliesin had made sure there were several forest fairies amongst the troops as their skills would be essential for guiding so many men safely and quietly through this dangerous, unfamiliar environment.

The men whiled away the hours snatching some sleep, drying their clothes, and checking their weapons. Others threw dice or talked quietly amongst themselves. It was going to be a long night.

Just before dawn, they began to advance on the goblin camp. Using their coded bird calls, Lady Ceto advised that Harek's troops were in position to the north-east of the goblin camp, and ready to engage as soon as they received orders. Taliesin and his men made their way through the awakening forest, the hooting of owls and shrill cries of foxes giving way to a glorious dawn chorus of birdsong. Fingers of sunlight began to penetrate the trees, illuminating the Anunnaki manor house in the distance. All was still and quiet, no goblins appeared to be up and about their duties. They moved silently through the last of the trees and undergrowth, coming out behind a line of large tents. They could hear the plaintive cries of the captured dragons, and much as they wished them to be free, most of the men desperately hoped they were securely caged.

Taliesin had the Selkies signal Harek to advance and after checking all were in position, ordered the attack. Too late. Just as they were inching forward, a forest fairy tried to wave them away from a large patch of undergrowth just as a startled wild boar and her piglets charged out and rushed, squealing loudly, the full length of the tent line.

Trying not to lose momentum, Taliesin urged his men on as the goblins tumbled out of their tents, raising the alarm, crying, 'To arms! To arms!' as soon as they realised they were under attack. Taliesin's troops, weapons drawn, launched themselves at the goblins and were soon engaged in ferocious, bloody, hand-to-hand combat with a seemingly never-ending force of fearless goblin warriors. In the heart of the melee, Taliesin spotted a huge bear of a man rush from the manor house wielding a vicious-looking halberd. He ran headlong into the fight slashing ferociously left and right, decapitating one man and disembowelling another as he charged straight towards Taliesin. By his size and the set of his shoulders, Taliesin thought it was Prince Idris, but as the man drew closer, he realised it was another of Nudd's sons, Prince Hywel. Taliesin ducked and parried as Hwyel lunged and stabbed at him. Taliesin was nimbler and faster than the huge goblin and landed a few good blows, but Hywel seemed impervious to pain until finally, Taliesin managed to duck under the halberd and stab the goblin in the groin. He fell to his knees, still slashing at Taliesin who kicked him to the ground, grabbed the halberd, and rushed back into the fight. The noise was deafening — men screaming and shouting and dragons roaring, excited by the scent of blood. Taliesin's men were struggling, with many of their number dead or seriously wounded, but thankfully, shouting 'Danaan! Danaan!' the fairy war cry, Harek's troops finally charged into the fray, and very quickly overpowered the remaining goblins. Varik issued orders that no prisoners were to be taken and those goblins still alive or wounded were despatched swiftly and mercilessly. Ceriddwen was sending Lord Nudd an unmistakeable message: Make war on the Tuatha de Danaan and suffer the consequences.

Some of the goblins fled to the bay, and in their panic plunged into the water, intending to swim to their ships, forgetting all about the orca pod. The orcas launched themselves into a feeding frenzy, herding, attacking, maiming, and ultimately having fun with their prey, throwing the hapless goblins high into the air before catching and eating them. No one taught the orcas how to differentiate between goblins and fairies.

Leaving Harek to supervise the collection of the goblin bodies for later cremation, Taliesin and Varik decided to check out the manor house for its suitability as a temporary field hospital for wounded men too ill to be transported back to the fleet. So far there was no trace of Idris or Nuada — both must be on the dragon hunt.

The Selkies, who had remained hidden in the forest during the fighting, surveyed the bloodied corpses and body parts scattered all around, stepping over entrails and pools of congealing blood, trying to ignore the groans and screams of the wounded. Harek's men were tending to the wounded fairies and separating the bodies into groups of fairies and goblins. The Selkies kicked and spat on the dead goblins.

'Bastards!' hissed Lady Arnemetia. 'Burning's too good for them!' She looked around and snapped her fingers at two Selkie guides helping Harek move the bodies.

'Come, we have a good deed to do!' She pointed at the ignominious jumble of dead goblins. 'Find three good-sized bodies, strip them and haul them over to the dragon pits.'

Harek heard her and came striding over. 'Excuse me, madam, but you can't go near the dragon pits!'

'Don't tell me what to do, young man!' Arnemetia snapped. 'I've forgotten more about dragons than you'll ever learn!'

'But...but what are you planning to do?' Harek was bemused.

'Why, feed them, of course! Dragons aren't the monsters here, you know. You think the goblins bothered to feed them?'

'But...but won't you be encouraging them to kill and eat us?' spluttered Harek, who knew he was completely out of his depth. Arnemetia was correct, he knew nothing about dragons. Apart from being terrified of them.

She gave him a pitying look. 'Dragons are carrion eaters. They don't eat live creatures. Once they've eaten these goblins, they won't need to feed for months. We can let them go and they'll go back to their lairs. They won't be interested in us at all. The only dragons you need worry about are sea dragons, they *do* hunt live prey, but they live in the ocean and are kept under control by the Sirens.'

'Well, if you're sure you know what you're doing. Our orders are to free them unharmed, anyway.' Harek was still a bit dubious.

'We Selkies have lived with dragons for thousands of years. They harm no one. We leave our dead out for them when we die. It is the way of things in this land. The goblins invaded and murdered the Anunnaki and the flowered ones and are now doing everything in their power to destroy this beautiful kingdom. Your Queen is right to kill them!'

She turned on her heel and made her way towards the dragon pits, huge holes in the ground with metal grids over them, secured by heavy bolts. Dragons like to shelter in caves, they dislike rain and love to bask in the sun when it's not too hot, but these pits offered no shelter from the rain, nor from the burning heat of the sun in high summer, so they suffered exposure from rain, sunburn or freezing cold. The goblins often kept them confined in these pits for months, starving them into submission for easy transport onto their ships.

When the dead goblins were brought over, Arnemetia slid back the bolts on the first pit and opened the grid wide enough for the body to be pushed in. The dragon cowered in fear, roaring at them half-heartedly, until Arnemetia closed the grid and left him to his meal. They did the same with the other two dragons before walking back to Harek.

'We should be able to release them in a few hours once they've eaten, poor things. They're terrified as well as starving.'

Harek grimaced. 'I'll take your word for it, madam.' He gave her a little bow. 'Now, if you'll excuse me, I have much to do.'

'Of course. Thank you. My kinsmen shall be happy to continue helping you.' Arnemetia nodded as the two Selkies followed Harek across the bloody, gore-spattered ground. She turned to see Lady Ceto and Lord Varun hurrying towards her.

'Lady Arnemetia,' Ceto panted, obviously out of breath, 'where is Lord Taliesin? We have grave news from the mountain!'

Arnemetia pointed to the manor house, and with a quick nod, the pair ran towards the crumbling, multi-turreted house, trotting along its avenue of weird, sculptured, stone beasts peering at them from beneath their tangled cover of vines and brambles. They pushed open the heavy wooden door, slowly rotting beneath an arched lintel decorated by a disconcerting relief sculpture of a sea dragon, three of its six heads twined together on each side with its body squatting on the apex of the arch.

Their voices echoed through the empty building as they called out Taliesien's name. It was obvious this had once been a great house, but was now in a state of serious disrepair, with signs of goblin vandalism everywhere. Taliesin and Varik were in the stable yard behind the house making sure no goblins were hiding there. They hurried indoors when they heard Lady Ceto calling.

'Lady Ceto, Lord Varun, you bring news from the mountain?' Taliesin didn't like the look on their faces. Lord Varun cleared his throat to speak, but Lady Ceto was quicker.

'Forgive me, Lord Taliesin, but it was a bloodbath, not as bad as this,' she indicated towards the heap of bodies piled beyond the avenue, 'but bad enough.'

Taliesin and Varik were aghast. 'How so? Did the goblins escape? Do the marines have Nuada?'

'Yes, my Lord, but I'm afraid he is dead.'

Taliesin let out a furious curse before demanding, 'Well, what happened?'

Lord Varun cut in. 'The goblins had the mother dragon and her young trapped in a cave at the bottom of a ravine. They obviously realised they would have to try and kill her to capture the whelps, but she's a mature, experienced female with thick scales, so their spears and arrows just bounced off her. They were trying to shoot her in the mouth or eyes but weren't having much success. The marines' orders, as you know, my Lord, were to make sure the dragons, as well as Nuada, weren't harmed, so they decided the best plan would be to ambush the goblins from behind while they were concentrating on the dragons.' Varun paused as Ceto took up the tale.

'The ravine is long and narrow. The dragons were at one end, the goblins in the middle, and so focused on the dragons that the marines caught them completely off guard. They just swooped down on them. The goblins didn't stand a chance, although they did retaliate ferociously. We were with the troops watching from above. It's difficult to see clearly into the ravine because of the trees and bushes, so it was almost impossible for them to use their blowpipes accurately for fear of shooting their own men in the confusion, but in the end, they didn't have to. The goblins were caught in their own trap. Nuada and the goblin prince, Idris, were at the front fighting the dragon when the marines attacked. They must have realised they were never going to escape capture.'

This all came out in a rush, so intent was Ceto on not missing anything out.

'So, what happened to Nuada?' Taliesin demanded roughly when she paused for breath.

'He committed suicide along with Idris, rather than be taken alive,' Varun said quietly.

'Suicide?' Taliesin and Varik were astounded. 'What do you mean?'

'When the marines cut down the last of the goblins and it was just Nuada and Idris left standing in front of the dragons, they looked at the marines, then turned and ran straight at the mother dragon!' Ceto and Varun chuckled malevolently at the memory. 'It was a sight to behold! Have you seen the size of a full-grown dragon's jaws and the size of their teeth?'

Taliesin suppressed a shudder. 'I hardly think this is the time for levity,' he said stiffly.

'Well, no offence intended, Lord Taliesin, but we rejoice wholeheartedly every time a goblin dies, and this was poetic justice, pure and simple.' Ceto was unrepentant.

Taliesin rubbed his forehead in despair. 'You're not the one who has to tell Queen Ceriddwen!'

'Forgive me if I don't sympathise, Lord Taliesin,' Ceto was almost cackling with pleasure, 'but it goes with the job, does it not?'

Taliesin sighed wearily, looking at his blood-stained hands and clothes. 'Indeed it does, Lady Ceto, indeed it does.'

A few hours later, the marines trudged into camp, battle-worn and weary, but triumphant despite the fact they had failed to capture Nuada alive. They brought with them three large, wheeled cages intended for the dragons, drawn by sturdy native ponies. The bodies of the goblins were thrown unceremoniously into one cage and the bodies of the marines in another, with the wounded marines in the third. They also had the bodies of Nuada and Idris, retrieved once the dragons had made their escape, hideously mutilated by the mother dragon, tied across the backs of another two ponies.

Taliesin had already ordered Hywel's body be separated from the others as it was to be embalmed, along with what was left of Nuada and Idris, for transport back to the Southern Gate. Ceriddwen would require proof that Nuada was dead, and that the two dead goblins were indeed Nudd's sons. Taliesin knew that once they were formally identified, she would make a point of returning them to their father as a warning and to drive home her victory. The bodies were removed to the stables behind the manor house for embalming by Admiral Sulis's medical team while the wounded troops were hurriedly installed in several of the house's empty rooms, and a makeshift operating theatre set up in another. It would be several weeks, if not months before some of the injured would be fit to travel. Taliesin set up a temporary office in one of the ground floor reception rooms. He needed somewhere private where he could discuss ongoing plans with Varik, Admiral Sulis, the rest of the officers, and the Selkie leaders. He sent immediate word to Ceriddwen and a few hours later, after they had eaten, everyone was summoned to discuss Ceriddwen's response.

Soon, all were seated, some on battered chairs found lying around the old house, others on makeshift benches rustled up from logs and planks of wood, while Taliesin and Varik sat on a wide window seat overlooking the grounds. Taliesin thanked them for their hard work, their bravery in carrying out their duty, and made sure the men received extra rations to keep their strength up as there was still much to be done the following day.

'We are all exhausted,' he began, 'it's been a long, harrowing day, and it grieves me that we have lost so many men and that so many more are grievously wounded. Our grateful thanks to Admiral Sulis for her rapid deployment of the fleet's medical team.'

Admiral Sulis inclined her head graciously. At least the Queen wasn't baying for her blood following the marines' failure to capture Nuada alive. The admiral was grateful for small mercies. Feet stamped and voices rose in agreement as Taliesin continued.

'However, although we have achieved much of what we intended, it is unfortunate we failed to take Nuada alive. The Queen is disappointed, of course, but as a warrior herself, she understands the vagaries of battle, and I am glad to say, is not pursuing the matter.'

He paused to drink from his mug of ale, noticing the intent, expectant looks on the faces of the four Selkie leaders. Shrugging off a nagging sense of unease, he continued delivering the plans for the rest of the evening and the following day.

'As previously discussed, our Selkie allies will remove the grids from the pits and set the dragons free tonight. Please ensure all men remain in their quarters until the dragons have left the pits. No trips to the latrines, or anywhere else, until the all-clear is sounded.'

'I was told the dragons wouldn't be interested in us now they've been fed,' Harek interjected indignantly. 'Are you now suggesting, my Lord, that these creatures are a danger to us after all?'

'Of course not!' Lady Arnemetia cut in hotly before Taliesin could respond. 'Once they've climbed out of those infernal pits, they'll have to exercise their wings before they can take off.'

'So why all the fuss about staying out of sight?' Harek was like a dog with a bone. Arnemetia gave him a withering look.

'Because they're wild animals, extremely traumatised wild animals. They can't tell the difference between us and goblins. There's no telling what they might do if they see even one man and think they're going back into those pits. Believe me, you do not want three terrified dragons rampaging through this camp!'

Other voices were now raised in concern, and the Selkies were becoming more and more irate.

'I'm beginning to think you lot are just as bad as the goblins,' roared Lord Varun. 'You know nothing about dragons, yet you question everything we tell you. It's insufferable!'

'Enough!' thundered Taliesin, thumping his fist on the windowsill. 'You will obey my orders without question or suffer the consequences! Do I make myself clear?'

He glowered around the room, defying anyone to contradict him. When order was restored, he turned to Arnemetia.

'Lady Arnemetia, if you would be so kind as to advise us what to expect when the dragons come out of the pits.'

Arnemetia stood up and turned to face the assembled officers, her face still flushed in anger. 'The dragons have been held in these pits for many weeks, they have been unable to exercise and haven't been fed, so they will be stiff and weak. I imagine they will have to stretch and flap their wings for a few hours before they feel strong enough to fly off. I cannot stress strongly enough that these creatures are not interested in any of us at all unless we are dead bodies. I have already explained this to Lord Harek. They are carrion eaters. They are also very shy and avoid confrontation, but if threatened, they are extremely dangerous. I cannot be any clearer than that.'

'Thank you, Lady Arnemetia. You have been most helpful.' Taliesin cleared his throat. 'Now, to the rest of our business. The men will construct pyres tomorrow for the cremation of the goblin bodies. Lord Harek, you have that in hand?'

'Yes, my Lord, the men have their orders, they start at first light, providing the dragons have gone!' Harek couldn't resist another dig.

'Thank you,' Taliesin said curtly, moving on before Harek warmed once more to his theme.

'What we thought was a walled garden in the grounds is an Anunnaki cemetery, and I propose we bury our fallen there. Unfortunately, there are too many to be embalmed and shipped home for interment in the Cave of Crystals or family burial grounds. Does anyone have any objections to that?' He glanced around the room. 'Good. Lord Varik will take charge of the burials, and liaise with the bard, Fili, for the service.' Turning to Admiral Sulis, he asked, 'Do you wish your bard to join with us in our service, Admiral, or shall you bury your marines at sea?'

The admiral replied without hesitation. 'Thank you, but they will be buried at sea.'

'Good, good. You will all be aware that many of the wounded are too severely injured to be moved, therefore the Queen has decreed that a garrison be set up here until they are well enough to travel. According to the doctors, we are talking about three months at the most before we can leave.'

Taliesin discovered very quickly why the Selkies had been so intensely interested in the proceedings. Lady Arnemetia leapt to her feet — her face once more suffused with rage.

'A garrison? One garrison for three months and then you leave? Have you no shame?'

Taliesin stared at the furious Selkie in dismay. 'The Queen commands it...I am at a loss to understand why you are so angry, my Lady.'

He was genuinely perplexed, but Arnemetia was in full flow, a seemingly unstoppable force.

'We waited and waited for you to come and avenge the Anunnaki and the flowered ones. We waited for you to come and rid us of the accursed goblins. We waited while they raped and plundered our lands, stole our dragons, cut down our forests, slaughtered our wildlife, and laid waste to our precious lands. You never came. Not even one ship to check for survivors or check the damage. Why, Lord Taliesin? Why did the Tuatha de Danaan abandon us?'

Taliesin was shocked to the core. Not only was he deeply uncomfortable at the Selkie's onslaught, but he also felt deeply ashamed. He had often asked himself this question in private, but no one dared question the Queen on the matter. He knew she was furious, the goblins had deliberately tried to blame the Tuatha de Danaan for the genocide and Gwyn ap Nudd had been spreading rumours for years that Ceriddwen knew her family was responsible and didn't care. Knowing Ceriddwen as he did, Taliesin knew she had probably decided to file it away until she had exacted retribution from the goblin king. Retribution of the sort she was delivering now. His queen imprisoned and three of his sons dead along with the traitor Nuada.

Arnemetia's strident accusations were piercing him like stinging arrows. 'We offered to help you overcome the goblins because we thought, at last, you had come to right the great wrong the Tuatha de Danaan have done the Anunnaki and the flowered ones, but instead we discover that you were only interested in capturing one of your own traitors before sailing home to your safe lands and leaving us once more to the mercies of the goblins!' She sat down heavily, taking great gulps of air as Lord Rodon attempted to calm her down by patting her arm, sighing stoically as she shrugged him off. Ceto and Varun just glared at Taliesin in silence.

'I am so sorry, Lady Arnemetia,' he said quietly. 'I have no alternative but to obey my Queen. I am Queen's Warrior and Justiciar of the Four Gates. I cannot gainsay my vows.'

Arnemetia snorted in derision. 'You are married to a queen! An Anunnaki dragon queen no less, and your daughter is an Anunnaki princess.' She now had the room's full attention. This was news to everyone apart from Varik.

'This has nothing to do with my wife! How dare you bring her into this conversation!' Taliesin's voice shook in fury.

'Ah, but it has everything to do with your wife, Lord Taliesin. Why is the Queen of the Anunnaki languishing in the Land of the Four Gates and not restoring her kingdom to its former glory?' Everyone now looked expectantly at Taliesin, who was, for once, lost for words. 'Yes!' Arnemetia crowed triumphantly. 'You know I speak the truth. Do you and your queen deny your wife and daughter their birthright? Is Queen Ceriddwen a jealous queen?' She swept aside Taliesin's attempt to reply, jumping to her feet and crying, 'Our dragon queen has been restored to us and she must come home. It is her sacred duty.'

THIRTY-FOUR

Benign Deceit

'So,' asked Xander as he raked fallen leaves into a heap, 'did you ever get to the Anunnaki lands?' Harry and Xander had finally returned, and they were all pottering around in the garden. What difference they thought raking up a few fallen leaves would make to the imminent goblin arrival was anyone's guess, but it helped to keep busy.

'No,' replied Molly, as she piled leaves into the garden refuse bin, 'I didn't. I was too busy being a wife and mother, and how could I go, anyway? I would never ask Taliesin to forsake his oath of honour to the Queen.'

Xander nodded, remembering their encounters with the fearsome warrior. 'Yes, I can understand that. IS Ceriddwen jealous of you, by the way?' he asked curiously.

Molly laughed. 'No, of course not. She's thrilled that the Anunnaki bloodline lives on in me and my children, including you, I might add. I think she has dynastic plans, but we haven't discussed it very much. A marriage between the Tuatha de Danaan royals and my Anunnaki children would strengthen Ceriddwen's position enormously, and backfoot Lord Nudd.' She gazed at Xander speculatively. 'I'd bet my bottom dollar she has big plans for you!' Molly, of course, had no idea Xander planned to go and live in Sidhthean if they succeeded in stopping Lord Nudd. He leant on the rake and gazed across the garden to the sinkhole. Molly had told Harry and Xander as soon as they arrived about the tapping coming from it, and sure enough, the sound was becoming louder each day.

'No one will be starting any dynasties if we don't stop Nudd.' He reached out and took hold of her hand, still encased in its gardening glove. 'We can't think about anything else until this ordeal is over,' adding grimly, 'one way or the other.'

Molly looked at her gloved hand encased in his and her eyes filled with tears. Apart from the time she hugged him, the last time she had had any physical contact with him was on the day she left the hospital forty years ago. She gave him a watery smile as he warmed to his theme.

'So much depends on you at this end. Ceriddwen is mustering all her allies and planning an attack on Nudd before he starts sending his troops through and...' He stopped in mid-sentence as he realised Molly was looking at him very strangely.

Molly's smile froze on her lips. If she kept herself busy, she could keep her terror at bay. Laura had been wonderful over the last week or so, insisting they catalogue the paintings, go out for lunch, take long walks along the river and on the moors, anything to stop Molly dwelling on what was coming. Dead of night was the worst. She would lie in bed, ears straining at the slightest sound. Although the rational part of her brain knew very little would happen before Samhain, even though it wasn't guaranteed that the goblins would succeed anyway, she was filled with an overwhelming sense of dread. Part of her hoped it was something else entirely and nothing to do with Lord Nudd and dragons. She knew it was a vain hope.

Who am I kidding? she'd thought one night, tossing and turning, sleepless as usual. She'd climbed out of bed, shoved her feet into slippers, and grabbing her dressing gown, then padded downstairs and out into the garden. The late October night air was chilly, and her feet had grown cold as the wet grass soaked her slippers. She made her way around the pond, nearly jumping out of her skin as the pale ghostly form of a barn owl swooped silently in front of her. Peering into the darkness of the sinkhole, her heart had missed a beat as she heard a distant sound, and she'd leant further in, listening intently. There it was again; a distant, eerie, tap, tap, tap. Molly knew the sinkhole carried on indefinitely beyond the narrow opening at its far end. Was this reverberating sound definite proof that the goblins had almost perfected the co-ordinates and were on track to break through at Samhain? She shivered, not with cold, but in sheer terror.

Xander realised he had made a major blunder. He had forgotten they intended to break the news of their visit to Ceriddwen over dinner that evening.

'You...you've been to see Ceriddwen? You went behind my back?' Molly was dumbfounded and outraged at the same time. She really didn't know whether to be angry or pleased, whether to laugh or cry. She just felt terribly bewildered. 'Why would you do that?' she accused. 'Apart from the fact it could have been very dangerous, don't you think you should have asked me first?'

'You were in no fit state to make rational decisions, Molly,' Xander answered gently.

'How did you manage to contact Ceriddwen?' she cried, ignoring him. Then, pursing her lips, she nodded to herself. 'Yes, yes, I get it now. You went down to Aunt Gwynnie and Mum. How could you? They're old ladies — anything could have happened to them!' She was now shaking with rage, leaning on the refuse bin for support.

Harry and Laura, making tea in the kitchen, hurried out as soon as they heard Molly's raised voice.

'What's going on, folks? Molly, you look as though you've seen a ghost!'

'Don't act the innocent with me! I bet you knew all about this too,' she barked at Laura.

'Knew what? What are you talking about, Molly?'

'That Harry and Xander went to visit Ceriddwen,' she cried. 'They made Mum and Aunt Gwynie take them. You all went behind my back!'

Laura stared open-mouthed at Molly before turning to Harry and Xander. 'Well?' she demanded.

'Look, let's all calm down,' Harry said quietly. 'We'll go inside and talk about this sensibly over a nice cup of tea.'

'Sensibly?' Molly retorted, 'I haven't felt sensible since all this started. I don't even know who I am anymore!'

Xander ignored Molly's attempts to shake off his arm as he gently guided her back into the house. He sat her on a chair in the living room, settling himself down beside Harry on the sofa as Laura poured the tea. As soon as their cups had been filled, Harry began to explain.

'You were distraught, and a bit confused by the fact there's a portal in your garden. We had no way of knowing whether Ceriddwen was aware of this or not, so Xander and I decided to take the bull by the horns and try to contact Ceriddwen ourselves. We didn't force your mum and Aunt Gwynnie, Molly. They weren't keen, I'll grant you that, but they did understand the seriousness of the situation and they agreed to help — well, it was your Aunt Gwynnie who summoned Morfan, but that was all.'

Molly sat white-faced, biting her lower lip to stop herself sobbing, but unable to stop the tears now coursing down her face. She couldn't help herself from blurting out, 'Did...did you see Taliesin?'

Harry suppressed a grimace of distaste. He didn't wish Molly to know he found her husband insufferable. Xander, aware of his father's jealousy and antipathy towards Taliesin, quickly said, 'Yes, we did, and I have to say that your husband and Queen Ceriddwen are about the scariest people I've ever met in my life!'

Molly, despite her tears, gave a little hiccupping chuckle. 'Sounds about right! But is Taliesin well? And what about Alaria and Ares?'

'Yes, he's fine, but very worried about you, obviously — that's what made him scary! I'm sorry, but who are Alaria and Ares?' Harry asked, raising a questioning eyebrow.

'My children — my babies — didn't you see them?' Molly's face crumpled as Harry stared at her in astonishment.

'Your children? You had children while you were there?'

'Well, what's so surprising about that? Do you think you're the only man I should have children with?' Molly sobbed convulsively, then quickly apologised at the sight of Harry's stricken face. 'I'm sorry, Harry, that was unforgivable, I don't know what I'm saying — please don't be angry with me.'

'No, of course I'm not angry with you — you have a right to be upset and to be angry with us!' Harry shook his head. 'It's actually just sinking in how long you actually lived there, it never occurred to me that you'd been there long enough to have babies. It's mind blowing!'

Seeing how upset Molly was, Xander tried to smooth things over. 'We didn't see or discuss your children I'm afraid, Molly. The visit was all about the goblins and the portal into your garden.'

'So, tell me,' Molly blurted through her tears, 'what are Taliesin and Ceriddwen going to do? Are they going to stop Nudd from coming through the portal? Are they going to attack them?'

'Yes,' replied Harry, 'but the goblins have mined deep into someone else's territory, someone called the Cailleach.

Apparently, her father is King of the Trolls. Do you know anything about these people?'

Molly wiped her eyes and blew her nose loudly as she searched her memory. 'I've never heard of anyone called the Cailleach, but I do know Ceriddwen doesn't think much of King Jontar. As far as I can make out, he dislikes her authority, but I do know the trolls hate the goblins.'

'Well, that's got to be a good thing,' said Xander. 'The goblins have technically invaded his land via the mine, so he has the perfect excuse to go after them.'

'But only if he is prepared to help his daughter,' mused Harry thoughtfully. 'The Cailleach appealed to Ceriddwen for help because her father did nothing. Taliesin and Varik were sent to investigate. They were appalled by what they found. This lady and her people were living at subsistence level thanks to constant pillaging and harassment by the goblins and the sheer cruel neglect of King Jontar. Ceriddwen sent troops and relief supplies immediately.'

'But what is Ceriddwen doing about the portal?' Molly's fear was palpable now. 'The goblins are coming closer to accessing it with every hour that passes! She is aware of that, isn't she?' she cried desperately.

Harry turned to Laura with an odd look on his face. 'Laura, I don't know why I haven't asked you this before,' Laura looked at him expectantly, 'but would you describe to us in detail what happened when you went through the portal and found yourself in Australia?'

Xander and Molly exchanged puzzled looks as Laura quickly replied to his question. 'I'll never forget it! I crawled towards the back of the sinkhole where it narrows to that tiny opening, but before I got there, the air began to shimmer, and when I inched forward a bit I was sort of whooshed through a lot of coloured lights and there I was, sitting in Jimmy Thomson's back yard...'

'Are you absolutely sure you didn't touch the wall at the back of the sinkhole, you didn't put your hand on it?'

'No, I didn't touch the back wall, I didn't get down that far — what are you getting at, Harry?'

Harry looked perplexed. 'I'm not really sure, I don't know much about the theories behind portals and wormholes, but I'm sure they operate to different "laws", if that's the correct terminology.'

'What are you talking about?' asked a puzzled Laura. 'What's the difference between a portal and a wormhole?'

'A wormhole enables you to travel through great distances in an instant, but a portal is a doorway into another dimension. Ceriddwen's world has both. I'm trying to work out whether this is important or not.'

'So how would that affect us?' Xander asked before Laura could ask any more questions.

'Do you remember when we came back through the portal?' asked Harry.

Xander nodded. 'Yes, of course.'

'Now think. What did Morfan do to open the portal?'

'He placed his hand on the wall to open it, at least that's what he did when he brought us back. I don't know what he did when we came through the first time, I was too frightened to notice.'

'I don't think it's the same when you go back through, because it's already open — it's the initial opening methodology I'm interested in. If Laura didn't touch anything and was just *whooshed though*,' Harry gave Laura an apologetic grin, 'then I think she entered a wormhole. When we went through the portal, it was just like walking through a curtain of light; totally different.'

'So, what does all this mean, then?' asked Molly nervously.

'I wish I knew,' Harry said with a shrug. 'I guess we'll just have to soldier on regardless and hope for the best. Wait a minute...' He turned to Xander. 'Is there nothing about portals and wormholes in the musical spells Ceriddwen gave you?'

'What spells? Ceriddwen gave you musical spells?' Molly asked, shocked.

'She gave me a bundle of Anunnaki sheet music...' Xander began tentatively, but Molly cut him off.

'That's the music a goblin sold to a stallholder in the market—it was Gwion who taught Morfan one of the melodies and when he played it at Samhain, I became very ill; it affected my system and triggered a genetic memory affecting my DNA. Why has Ceriddwen given you this music?' Molly's voice rose hysterically as the words tumbled out.

'I was just about to explain when you interrupted me!' Xander remonstrated mildly.

'Sorry...sorry, it's just a bit of a shock, that's all!'

'You think this whole business hasn't been a shock for all of us?' Laura said irritably. 'Could we just get on with the explanations, please?'

Molly held up her hands in apology. 'Okay, okay, let's hear it, Xander.'

'Thanks.' Xander tried to keep the exasperation out of his voice. 'Apparently, this music is crucial because it will encase us in a protective bubble, which is very important now that Ceriddwen's enchantment has come to an end. These sheets of music are sonic spells.' He paused, noticing Laura's look of incomprehension. 'Let me try and explain what that means. Sonic spells are sound spells. The musical notes create a magical spell—a manipulation of certain elements either in the air or in surrounding organic materials, like the way the music affected Molly when Morfan played it, if that makes any sense?'

'Yes, I think I understand,' said Laura. 'It makes sense.'

'Good.' Xander warmed to his theme. 'I can read Annunaki script, and each of these music sheets concerns different things.

Some of them are about protecting and enhancing the Anunnaki power over dragons, and what that means for you, Molly, because, as you have remembered, you are an Anunnaki dragon queen.'

Molly nodded miserably. 'And I don't have particularly happy memories of my last outing as a dragon queen, either.'

'Well, if my understanding of the spells is correct, as long as each spell is played through at least once, whatever happens to you as regards your…er…dragon queen alter-ego, for want of a better expression, you will be protected for at least twenty-four hours.'

'Protected from what, I wonder?' Molly sucked in a deep breath and let it out slowly, trying to stay calm. 'And what exactly am I expected to do?'

'Let's just say at this stage of the game we'll play it by ear.' Before Molly could respond, he added grimly, 'If these sonic spells are correct, Lord Nudd has a very nasty shock in store!'

'All very enigmatic,' said Laura sarcastically. 'I'm sure Molly and I are hugely reassured by that explanation. Maybe we'll be the ones having a nasty shock if we all find ourselves being sucked into a wormhole instead of saving the world from goblins!'

'Well, that's all the explanation you're getting!' Harry snapped. 'Look, this is not the time to be sniping at each other. Xander and I have discussed the contents of these spells and it really is best if we stop speculating about them until Wednesday when we'll find out one way or the other — okay?' He glared at the others, defying them to disagree with him. 'Good. Now, maybe we can speculate about what Ceriddwen and Taliesin are doing at their end?'

THIRTY-FIVE
The Wormhole

To the casual observer, the scene at the Eastern Gate was one of utter chaos. Four huge canal barges were disgorging their cargoes down massive gangplanks — herds of shaggy longhorn aurochs, flocks of bleating sheep, huge snorting warhorses, unicorns with their lethal horns encased in padded sleeves, and dog handlers with snarling, barking amaroks on tight leashes. All the livestock, apart from the amaroks, were quickly driven into large holding pens while the canal barges continued unloading supplies onto dozens of waiting wagons. Officers barked orders at the thousands of troops now converged on the gate waiting for the signal to pass through, with more joining the line every few minutes carrying backpacks, holstered weapons and shields slung over their shoulders, laughing, joking, and exchanging banter, others quiet and watchful, fearful of what lay ahead of them on the other side of the wormhole.

Lord Brude surveyed the frenetic activity with a grim look on his usually jovial face. He ran a very tight ship and was determined that this operation should run like clockwork as

Taliesin was due to arrive at any moment with the Queen and Lord Lleu. He patted his mount's neck soothingly as it nervously sidled away from the Morrigan's huge black stallion, baring its teeth as she drew up alongside. He gave her a polite nod. She was arrayed in an armoury of lethal weapons and wearing her magnificent trademark raven's feather cloak and matching winged helmet. A fainter heart than Lord Brude's would have quailed at the sight of her.

'Lady Morrigan?'

'When will the wharf be cleared, my Lord?' she snapped imperiously. 'I was under the impression that civilian merchants and traders were instructed to stay out of the way.' She glowered furiously at the pens of livestock and people still milling about.

'The animals are securely penned, and all other merchandising has been stored in the warehouses until the armed forces have gone through,' Brude replied patiently. The Morrigan was every bit as difficult and mercurial as the Queen, but the Morrigan was equal to him in status, so he would brook no nonsense from her. 'What exactly has irritated you?'

'The Queen will be here any minute, and I don't want civilians rushing up to her with their usual requests and demands for boons and blessings. We are engaged in preparation for war, not a royal procession, and that should take precedence.'

'Do not presume to tell me my job, Lady Morrigan,' Brude replied. 'I am as seasoned a warrior as you and, in case you have forgotten, Legion Commander of this garrison. I have passed thousands of people — warriors and civilians alike, through this gate for more years than I care to remember.' He held up his hand to silence her as she opened her mouth to protest. 'You do your job, my Lady, and I'll do mine.'

A loud fanfare announced the arrival of the Queen, and Brude smiled to himself as his faithful old warhorse made a vicious lunge at the Morrigan's stallion as they turned to greet the royal party, nearly unseating her as it reared up in a futile attempt at retaliation.

'Greetings, Your Majesty.' Brude bowed from the saddle, giving the Queen a welcoming smile. Ceriddwen was resplendent in a beautifully tooled leather breastplate, which accentuated her magnificent breasts. She wore matching vambraces and greaves with a diamond studded Four Gates coronet gracing her head. No way was she being upstaged by the Morrigan and her feathered outfit. Brude also bowed to Lleu and Taliesin, trying and failing to keep his delight at seeing his son from his face. 'If you would come this way, Lady Adwena is waiting with refreshments.'

'My Lord.' Ceriddwen nodded graciously, before turning her attention to the Morrigan who was in the process of using her horse to shoulder two merchants out of the way as they attempted to catch the Queen's attention.

'Lady Morrigan,' she called sharply, 'why are you abusing my subjects in such an unseemly manner? Let them approach!'

The Morrigan's face darkened in fury at the public humiliation, reining her stallion back to allow the men passage. Brude gave her a pitying look, which only enraged her further as she sat silently fuming. The Queen spoke kindly to the merchants, thanking them for their patience, explaining that the gate would soon be clear. Once the men had stuttered their thanks and backed away, Ceriddwen turned a furious face on the Morrigan.

'Lady Morrigan, if I ever see you abusing your position again, you shall be stripped of your office and reduced to the ranks. Do I make myself clear?'

The Morrigan, thoroughly humiliated in front of everyone, could only manage a terse, 'Of course, Your Majesty. I do apologise. It won't happen again.' Ceriddwen glared at her.

'Good! Our subjects depend on us for their peace of mind and safety. This disruption to their daily lives should be treated with compassion and respect. Take your temper out on the goblins, not your own people!'

With that, she wheeled Arien about and headed into the courtyard of the garrison manor house where Lady Adwena waited to greet them.

Shortly afterwards, while Ceriddwen and Lady Morrigan, their altercation forgotten, were chatting with Lady Adwena, Brude took Taliesin aside, concerned by the strained, worried look on his son's face. 'Any word from Varik?'

Taliesin nodded grimly. 'The cryptanalysists are having problems deciding whether it's actually a wormhole like this gate, or a normal portal.'

'How so?' Brude asked.

'Apparently, there are large quantities of shocked quartz, and the rest of the deposits are normal quartz — extremely unusual to find two different kinds of quartz in the same place, because, as you know, shocked quartz is formed at far higher pressure than normal quartz. Shocked quartz facilitates wormholes and normal quartz, portals.'

'Yes…yes, I can see that is unusual, but why is this a problem?' Brude sounded puzzled.

Taliesin heaved a great sigh. 'Because the analysts think that the combination of both types of quartz means that sometimes it's a portal and sometimes it's a wormhole.'

Brude scratched his beard as he processed this information. 'So, a wormhole could open up in a completely different location to a portal?'

'Yes. Molly's son and his father said that a man from an entirely different part of Earth came through the portal.'

'But how does that prove the portal or wormhole theory?' Brude was a warrior, science wasn't his thing. He controlled access to and from the Eastern Gate wormhole, he didn't question why it was a wormhole or how it worked.

'That's not what's worrying us. It's the fact that Nudd could potentially have two means of access to the Earth dimension. One into Molly's part of the world and another thousands of miles away on the other side of the planet. He would be able to move vast numbers of troops just as we are now.' Taliesin turned a stricken face to his father. 'All the signs were there, you know. Scatha reported unusual shipping activity. They were moving huge numbers of troops and loads of timber for months, and we just let them pass by the Isle of Clouds without question.'

'We had no reason to question them.' Brude placed a soothing hand on his son's arm.

'Protocol getting in the way as usual,' Taliesin spat. 'We always have reason to question the goblins. We should have learned that by now! Lord Ravenna told me on the way back from the Anunnaki lands, and I just dismissed it. How could I have been so stupid?'

Brude could see the worry etched on his son's face. 'Are the analysts sure about the dual function theory?' he asked, changing the subject as he could see Taliesin was becoming overwrought.

'No, Varik said it's a possibility, but one we must be aware of.'

'Well, I reckon the sooner you get through our wormhole and engage with the blighters the better! I'd be first in line myself if I wasn't tied to this blasted gate, as you very well know.'

Taliesin smiled, despite his worry, and clapped his father on the back. 'You'll never cease to be a warrior, my Lord Father, and the Queen would trust the Eastern Gate to no one else but you — you are indispensable!' With his arm around his father's shoulders, they strolled back to Ceriddwen and the others.

'Ah, Lord Taliesin, perfect timing,' Ceriddwen said briskly, putting her cup down and rising to her feet. 'Thank you for your hospitality, Lady Adwena, Lord Brude, most enjoyable, but now we must be on our way. Your son has a wife to rescue, and I have no wish to lose a granddaughter and another crown prince, either.' Ceriddwen was putting on a very brave face but fooled no one. She was beside herself with worry.

Lord Brude escorted them back to their waiting mounts, then past the lines of troops and through the gate towards the shimmering energy of the wormhole, watching sombrely as they disappeared through the coruscating brilliance.

THIRTY-SIX

Castles in the Air

Apart from a few short weeks after her birth, Taliesin didn't see Alaria again until she was nine months old.

When he returned from the expedition to find Nuada, Lady Arnemetia and Lord Rodon had insisted they return with him as they wished to petition the Queen for a permanent Tuatha de Danaan presence in the Anunnaki lands until their rightful dragon rulers resumed their reign. Ceriddwen refused to see them at first, making all sorts of excuses, the truth being she was embarrassed by her failure to deal with the issue sooner and was somewhat unwilling to face their opprobrium. Eventually, the council, headed by Lord Ruka, convinced her it was in everyone's interests to protect the islands from the goblins, and appoint a temporary governor until something more permanent could be arranged. Taliesin was inevitably ordered back with a large contingent of troops to oversee the defence fortifications, along with the organisation of staff and workers. Naturally, he would much rather be with his wife and daughter, but matters of state came first, and he reluctantly resigned himself to another lengthy absence.

Molly was devastated to learn he would be leaving again so soon. He sent a message asking her to join him at the palace as quickly as possible, hoping they might have a few snatched hours together before he left. She dropped everything, bundling Alaria and Nuala into their swiftest carriage and hurtled the thirty miles to the palace at breakneck speed, stopping only once to rest the horses.

'I'm sorry, my love,' Taliesin murmured to her as he held her in a tight embrace, his face buried in her burnished copper curls. 'I wish I didn't have to go.'

As he kissed her lips, her eyes, her face, Molly's fingers trembled as she pulled at the buttons on his jacket in her haste to undress him. 'Let's not waste what few hours we have,' she whispered, voice husky with desire. 'Take me to bed — I've missed you so much!'

They tumbled onto the bed in their beautiful palace bedroom, Alaria now sleeping soundly in her crib, and gave themselves up to passionate lovemaking until, spent and sated, they lay in a tangle of arms and legs, gazing into each other's eyes.

'I never imagined I would find a woman like you,' Taliesin said, lifting Molly's arm to shower her with kisses, starting at her wrist and up to the soft skin inside the crook of her elbow, before stroking the curve of her hip and along her sleek thighs. 'You are the most beautiful woman I've ever seen. How shall I bear not seeing you again for months?'

Molly put her finger against his lips. 'Hush, my love, we've already had this conversation. You belong to the Queen, you must do her bidding, and no matter how much I hate it, we must bear it together.' As Taliesin leant forward for another kiss, Alaria gave a gurgling little cry to let them know she was awake. He savoured his kiss before reluctantly letting Molly go.

'Our daughter demands attention!' he pointed out, laughing ruefully, trying to ignore the renewed stirrings of desire as

Molly rolled off the bed and strolled languorously to the crib, lifting their precious daughter and putting the squirming infant straight to her breast. Alaria nuzzled hungrily at her mother's skin, searching for the nipple before latching on and sucking greedily, her chubby hand pulling on Molly's hair as it cascaded over her other breast in a shimmering red gold veil. As Molly slid back into bed, Taliesin piled pillows at her back, then gave himself up to the sheer joy of watching his wife and baby, fixing the scene in his memory, knowing he wouldn't see them again for many months.

~

Molly stood disconsolately on the quay with Alaria in her arms, both warmly bundled up against the unforgiving March wind knifing through the assembled crowd, blowing salty air upriver from the sea, scattering their clothes with sparkling droplets of spray from dancing foam-capped waves. Draught horses clopped along the quay, their harnesses jingling as the carts rumbled over cobblestones, while dockers scurried to and fro, supervising the huge nets of supplies being loaded and unloaded from other ships. Curious onlookers lined the harbour walls to gape at the Queen and the huge battleship now tied up beside the merchant ships and fishing boats they were familiar with.

Admiral Sulis had decided to put Captain Midir in charge of the fleet taking the latest contingent of troops and workers to the Anunnaki lands, and he was delighted with the weather, advising Ceriddwen they would make great headway unless the wind changed direction. Ceriddwen harrumphed and gave him a nod. If she wasn't on board, she couldn't care less what the weather was like. She was feeling a little twinge of conscience, having witnessed Taliesin's heart-wrenching goodbyes to Molly and baby Alaria. Ceriddwen was besotted with Alaria and could well imagine how she would feel if Taliesin was taking his wife and daughter with him. However, she reminded herself that the business of state would come first, and placed a comforting arm around Molly's shoulders as Taliesin made his way up the gangplank.

'Safe journey, my love!' Molly called to his retreating back, trying and failing to stop the tears of misery pouring down her frozen cheeks. As soon as he was onboard, Taliesin turned for a final goodbye wave, then he was gone, swallowed by the crowds of sailors, troops and civilians all working flat out loading horses, livestock, and other supplies into the ship's hold. The gangplank was raised, and Captain Midir's beloved ship, *Orion*, gradually eased itself out of the harbour, into the river, and downstream to the welcoming arms of the sea and the waiting fleet.

Ceriddwen breathed a secret sigh of relief. The Selkies' visit had been a trial of diplomacy, testing her patience to the limit. Lady Arnemetia was strident and uncompromising in her insistence that Molly should return with them to sit on the Anunnaki throne.

'Why is she languishing here in your realm when she should be striving to return and restore her own lands to their former glory?' she had demanded of Ceriddwen. 'Do you fear her power and therefore keep her here under your control?'

The palace courtiers and officials collectively held their breath, nervously avoiding Ceriddwen's eyes, afraid one of her legendary rages would erupt amid shocked mutterings at the Selkie's boldness.

Ceriddwen clutched the arms of her throne, knuckles whitening as she fought to contain her fury; she couldn't afford another diplomatic incident, relations with Lord Llyr were still somewhat strained following the Melusine incident, and although the Selkies were a law unto themselves, shapeshifting in and out of their seal bodies at will, they were still ostensibly Lord Llyr's responsibility.

'Lady Arnemetia,' she said coldly, fixing her with a glacial stare, 'Princess Molly is free to do as she pleases. She is fully aware of who and what she is, and the power that bestows, but as you are aware, she is married to Lord Taliesin, my Justiciar and Queen's Warrior, and she chooses to be a wife and mother. It is not for us to dictate how she should live her life.'

'If you are not keeping her here against her will, you must insist she takes the Anunnaki throne!' The Selkie was not going to be easily dissuaded. Lord Rodon was sweating profusely; he had heard many tales of Ceriddwen's ferocious temper, and feared his wife was treading dangerous waters.

Ceriddwen made a supreme effort to control her temper. 'I will do no such thing.' Her voice was icy with contempt. 'It is not for me to order the princess to do anything. I may order YOU to carry out anything of my choosing, and you would obey me, Lady Arnemetia; believe that, if you believe nothing else.'

Arnemetia bristled with indignation, apparently impervious to imminent danger, shaking off Lord Rodon's warning touch on her arm.

'The Rain Bird has returned to the Anunnaki forests!' she flashed defiantly at Ceriddwen. 'Bringer of Life! A portent that cannot be ignored!'

A murmuring rippled around the room. The legendary Rain Bird had mysteriously vanished after the genocides, and the assembled fairies in the room were unsettled by this revelation. The Rain Bird was much beloved by the flowered ones and flourished in their care, only to completely vanish after the genocides. Its return, if true, was a matter of great import. Pushing her luck, Arnemetia continued.

'It hasn't been heard for years, but shortly after Lord Taliesin arrived, it began to be heard throughout the forests again. It is surely announcing that the Anunnaki and the flowered ones have risen again to reclaim their lands! How can you deny this, Your Majesty?' she challenged Ceriddwen, unable to keep the triumphant note out of her voice.

Ceriddwen glared at her. 'Why, if the Rain Bird has decided to return to the Anunnaki lands, that is indeed a wondrous thing, it has obviously heard the good news that the bloodlines of the flowered ones and the Anunnaki live on in my grandchildren,' she answered, rolling over Arnemetia's triumphalism with a heavy layer of sarcasm. 'But I am sure that nowhere is it written that I must banish my family against their will, Rain Bird or no Rain Bird! My grandchildren will visit the Anunnaki lands when they see fit to do so.' She rose abruptly to her feet, two of her cats sinuously slinking to her side from beneath the throne. 'The audience is over. You may leave,' she snapped, striding from the chamber without a backward glance, Lord Ruka and several council officials scurrying after her.

~

'I know you're sad now, my child,' whispered Ceriddwen, giving Molly a comforting squeeze as they watched *Orion* sail round the curve in the river and out of sight, 'but very soon your world will be filled with joy again!'

Molly gave a watery smile in response, kissing Alaria before handing her to Nuala. 'Don't worry, poppet,' she whispered, 'Daddy will be home soon.'

Alaria waved her arms happily as they climbed into the royal carriage beside Ceriddwen. Molly settled herself into the comfortably upholstered seat, glad, despite her misery, for the welcome warmth of the crystal heater beneath. The carriage made its way out of the harbour, clip-clopping along the cobbled main street of the little town, followed by half a dozen mounted palace guards. People cheered and clapped the royal party from shop fronts and half-timbered upper storeys, until the carriage finally swung onto the broad tree-lined drive leading to the palace gates. Molly stared miserably out of the window, blind to the glorious swathes of daffodils spilling around the trees and beyond into the deer park, their golden yellow trumpets bravely defying the blustering east wind.

She spent the next few months travelling between the palace and Tigh Falloch, much of this necessitated by the fact that when Ceriddwen told Molly at the quayside she would once more be filled with joy, she had unerringly detected that she was once again pregnant. Ceriddwen was taking no chances risking a repeat performance of Alaria's swift entry into the world, and a reluctant Molly was placed under the auspices of the formidable Taweret, Mistress Mesket, aided and abetted by her ever-watchful partners-in-crime, Brighid at the palace and Enya at Tigh Falloch. She resisted their efforts to control her life, regularly galloping out on Flambeaux with Tabitha and Morfan, or riding tough little moorland ponies, rounding up the huge aurochs on the estate.

In response to their continued attempts to rein her in, a frustrated Molly eventually threw a tantrum, yelling at them, 'I have yet to see a goblin or a dragon at Tigh Falloch or the palace! To my knowledge there are no sea dragons lurking in the Danu trying to lure me away, nor in any of the lakes and rivers around Tigh Falloch, either.' She paused for breath, eyes flashing with spots of high colour burning furiously on her cheeks, a bemused Brighid and Mistress Mesket staring at her open-mouthed as she resumed her tirade. 'Furthermore, be advised your unwanted ministrations and interference in my life are more likely to bring about a premature labour than the appearance of goblins and mistreated dragons simply because you all infuriate me so much! I wish you would just leave me alone!' Molly glared down at them from Flambeaux, Brighid having run to fetch the Taweret as soon as Molly had indicated she was riding out. To emphasise her point, she dug her heels into a startled Flambeaux and cantered swiftly down the lane towards the Watermeadows road.

'We're going to the hospital stud,' explained an unapologetic Tabitha to the outraged matrons as she quickly urged Merrily after Flambeaux.

'Well, really!' spluttered an affronted Mistress Mesket. 'This will not do at all. We must inform the Queen at once!' She pursed her lips and bustled off towards the palace, calling over her shoulder to a discomfited Brighid, 'Well, are you coming? The princess is your mistress after all, you can explain her intransigence to Her Majesty!' Brighid stalked indignantly after her. Mistress Mesket had ideas way above her station and would have to be put in her place very soon.

~

As Molly's pregnancy blossomed, Alaria was growing fast, delighting Molly by taking her first steps on a visit to Melusine. They were sitting amongst the flowers in Melusine's pretty garden having tea with Mistress Tansy, when Alaria grasped hold of Molly's favourite amarok hound, Jassie. She hauled herself to her feet before letting go to launch herself on a wobbly but determined toddle after sturdy two-year-old Luss, before plopping down with a loud infectious giggle, as the ever-protective Jassie anxiously licked her ear.

It saddened Molly that Taliesin was missing out on these important milestones in their daughter's life, but they wrote regularly, and Molly kept him up to date with anecdotes about Alaria's development and all her endearing little foibles.

In turn, Taliesin kept Molly (and the Queen) appraised of the ongoing work in the distant Anunnaki lands. For all the Anunnaki tribe along with the flower fairies had only numbered around two million souls, Taliesin reckoned it would take months to make a proper assessment of the damage. The abandoned farms and manor houses, the derelict villages and towns, the ravaged forests and countryside all had to be identified and accounted for, and the job of surveying the country was immense. The small peaceful population had made it easy for the goblins to take them by surprise, and the destruction wrought by the goblins was incomprehensible to most of the people tasked with trying to restore some sense of order; they worked with a single-minded tenacity to heal the damaged environment.

As well as sending thousands of troops to protect the land from further goblin attack, Ceriddwen called for skilled volunteers to accompany them and help with the enormous task. She could have ordered any number of people to go, but preferred volunteers as she believed in the premise that one volunteer was worth more than twenty pressed men. Her call was taken up with alacrity and many of the volunteers brought their families and loved ones, which meant the farms, towns and villages would once more have a growing population as Ceriddwen believed many of them would choose to stay.

They might not have Anunnaki blood, but as Taliesin told Lady Arnemetia, 'You will have to be content in the knowledge that this work is being done to right a great wrong, not by the perpetrators, but by those who will ensure this land is ruled by Anunnaki blood in the future. You must learn patience, Lady Arnemetia.'

In her heart, Arnemetia knew he was right. The Selkies could hopefully resume the peaceful lives they lived before the genocides. They could follow the seasons again, moving freely from island to island, changing into their seal bodies to hunt the sea for fish, play with the sea otters and cavort with their friends, the bottlenose dolphins. They no longer had to stay close to the lava tunnels to hide from the goblins. The Sirens would once more sing their symbiotic songs, weaving the magical strands that kept the sea dragons small and the rest of their world safe. They were free again, and she knew they should be grateful to Ceriddwen. Lord Rodon had berated Arnemetia for her rudeness to the Queen, but she wasn't sorry, she may not have persuaded Ceriddwen to insist Molly assume the Anunnaki throne, but what she had achieved instead was a prize indeed.

Taliesin worked tirelessly, travelling up and down the country to familiarise himself with what had to be done. It was a beautiful land, wild and rugged in the north where many of its jagged mountains had mysterious, strange-looking castles built into their sides with fortified towers clinging precariously around their peaks. Many of these castles could only be accessed by wondrous bridges that seemed to hang in the air, unsupported, high above the vast gorges they were spanning. When Taliesin wondered how these structures were built, or indeed, how the castles could be built on top of the mountains, his Selkie guide, Tepi, told him most of these castles were built over ancient dragon lairs, and had housed Anunnaki aristocracy whose sole purpose, handed down through generations, was to protect the dragons beneath the castles. 'Yes, but how did they build these castles and bridges?' Taliesin was puzzled.

'Don't you know why the goblins killed the Anunnaki?'

'Well, I thought that was obvious. To capture the dragons!' Taliesin tried to keep the irritation out of his voice.

'I'm afraid you misunderstand the goblins' reasons for wishing to control the dragons, my Lord.'

'Do I?' Taliesin was tired and growing impatient with the Selkie's pedantic manner.

Sensing Taliesin's darkening mood, Tepi quickly explained. 'The goblins want the power of flight. They heard how the Anunnaki flew on the backs of the dragons as they carried materials up the mountains for the rope bridges across the ravines and gorges, to enable the Anunnaki to build these beautiful bridges and castles.'

Taliesin shielded his eyes from the morning sun as he squinted at the magnificent hanging structure shimmering in the distance. It looked far too delicate to be a functional bridge.

'They thought all they had to do was kill the Anunnaki and they would have control of the dragons, but little did they know that dragons only willingly do the bidding of Anunnaki royalty. They found the only power they had over the dragons they captured was to force feed them a combustible mineral they found in one of their infernal mines. It makes them breathe fire, and ultimately kills them.' Tepi turned to face Taliesin. 'You understand why the Selkie people hate the goblins?'

'Indeed, I do,' replied Taliesin grimly, his jaw set in utter loathing.

Rivers cut through deep gorges, rushing and tumbling over their rocky beds, others fell down the mountainsides in startingly beautiful waterfalls of glittering silver ribbons. Magnificent eagles soared from their eyries on high mountain ledges, riding the thermals, ospreys fished the deep dark lakes, snatching salmon and trout from beneath the water's surface with deceptive ease. Taliesin and Tepi were awed one afternoon by the sight of a huge dragon searching for carrion, its glossy green scales glinting in the sunshine. They held their breath as it flapped its strong leathery wings in a wide lazy circle, its long, sinuous neck moving from side to side, nostrils flaring as it detected the carcass of a dead stag. Swooping down, gracefully for such a large creature, it grasped the body in its powerful forelegs before heading back to its lair.

'Well, there's one beauty that escaped the accursed goblins!' Tepi punched the air in triumph.

'Beauty isn't a word I would use to describe dragons.' Taliesin suppressed a shudder, he would never admit to the Selkie that he was terrified of dragons. 'Although my wife would disagree with me.' Tepi threw him a sidelong glance. He knew who Lord Taliesin's wife was, but wisely kept his thoughts to himself.

The south of the country was blessed with rolling green hills, limpid lakes and fertile fields with gentle rivers meandering through water meadows alive with wildfowl and game. The ancient Anunnaki forest stretched the length of the country, and, like the rest of the forests throughout Ceriddwen's world, was home to many wild animals including bears, wolves, wild boar, and lynx. Unfortunately, much of the southern forest had been damaged over the years by the goblins, and urgently needed proper forest management, one of the first projects Taliesin set in motion.

What he didn't reveal to Molly in his regular letters were the grave pits full of slaughtered Anunnaki, hundreds of them scattered from one end of the country to the other, and around the perimeters of towns and villages. They found wells choked with skeletons in the grounds of eerie crumbling castles and mansion houses left forlorn and empty, many of them almost completely covered in shrouds of vegetation, witnesses to unspeakable horror and cruelty. Other victims had been herded into barns and burned alive — everywhere they went the fairies were sickened by goblin atrocities. Many dappled forest groves where the flower fairies lived had also been ravaged by fire, fragments of teeth and bone found among the charred and blackened remnants of magnificent oak and beech trees that bore testimony to the number of flowered ones who had perished. Dense thickets of blackthorn, hawthorn and holly had sprung up in defensive circles around these groves, protecting the pathetic remains. Fragrant honeysuckle twined through the thickets, perfuming the air with a sad sweetness, whilst the centres of the groves were carpeted in memorials of delicate woodland flowers.

He didn't tell her about the bleached bones of mother dragons and their mates killed protecting their young or the pathetic bundles of bones that had once been juveniles, dead from mistreatment and left to rot in the fetid goblin dragon pits. Day on day, his horror and disgust grew to such an extent that he doubted he would ever meet another goblin without wanting to kill them on the spot, but he swallowed his hatred and applied himself to the task in hand, reasoning the sooner the Anunnaki lands were restored and protected from further goblin attacks, the sooner he would be home with his beloved family.

It took almost nine months for a temporary government to be arranged, with Lord Conal of the Sidhe, a branch of the mountain fairy clan, highly trusted and respected by King Ossian and Ceriddwen alike, being installed as governor. He and Taliesin were firm friends from their warrior training days, and comrades in many a battle with the goblins. He was an experienced commander and administrator, the perfect choice for protecting, restoring, and running the Anunnaki lands justly and efficiently. Taliesin breathed a huge sigh of relief.

A few weeks later, on a bitter winter's day, he stood on the stern of Lord Ravenna's frigate, buffeted by a freezing north wind as he watched the rugged granite cliffs of the Anunnaki lands grow smaller beneath a sullen snow-filled sky, the beautiful farewell song of the Sirens fading into the distance. Lady Arnemetia, Lord Rodon and several other Selkie friends escorted the frigate with a pod of bottlenose dolphins, shape-shifting in and out of their seal bodies at will to wave and call their goodbyes until they, too, gradually disappeared over the horizon.

Lord Ravenna, a tall slim man with hooded black eyes and a hawk-like nose, noticed Taliesin's hands clenched firmly around the guard rail, and the slightly greenish tinge to his face. 'Are you feeling seasick, my Lord?' Taliesin reacted by hanging over the rail and retching violently. Lord Ravenna gave him a sympathetic pat on the shoulder. 'A most unfortunate affliction, especially on a long voyage like this.'

'You think so?' Taliesin growled, spitting into the sea. 'If you have nothing constructive to say, please don't say anything at all!'

'I do apologise, my Lord. I just wanted to say that unfortunately I am not in possession of Her Majesty's special sea sickness potion, but I do have a very good ginger root tea.' Seeing Taliesin's sceptical expression, he quickly added, 'It is extremely efficacious. I do urge you to try it.' He extended an arm towards the stairs leading to his cabin immediately below them. Groaning and clutching his stomach, Taliesin stumbled down the twisting stairs and collapsed onto one of Lord Ravenna's comfortably upholstered benches.

An hour or so later, having consumed three or four mugs of steaming ginger root tea, Taliesin was pleasantly surprised to find that he was feeling very much better, and quite amenable when Lord Ravenna suggested they have a chat.

'As you are aware, Lord Taliesin,' he began, 'Admiral Sulis sent me to patrol the Anunnaki waters as she wasn't convinced the goblins would just surrender the land without a fight.'

Taliesin lifted an eyebrow. 'Apparently, they have, although to be fair to Admiral Sulis, I do agree with her. It is uncharacteristic to say the least.'

Lord Ravenna gave an eloquent shrug. 'Well, they may be thinking discretion is the better part of valour, but Lord Nudd is a wily foe, and Captain Midir thinks he may be planning something else.'

'With all due respect, how would Midir know Nudd's plans?' Taliesin couldn't help himself scoffing.

A pained look crossed Lord Ravenna's face. 'May I remind you he is not the captain of a warship for nothing, my Lord! He is an extremely experienced marine warrior, and like yourself, seasoned in many a battle with the goblins and his sources are usually impeccable.'

Taliesin shifted uncomfortably in his seat, scratching his nose. 'I apologise Lord Ravenna, that was uncalled for and unprofessional. I spoke without thinking, something I am not usually in the habit of doing.'

'Indeed,' his companion replied neutrally, 'do you wish me to continue?'

'Please do,' answered a glum Taliesin.

'Lady Scatha has advised the Queen and Admiral Sulis that goblin ships loaded with troops, accompanied by a man of war battleship, are regularly cruising by the island of Coira and the Isle of Clouds along the sea lane that borders on troll territory.'

'Does Scatha think they have worked out where Queen Grainne is?'

'No, not at all, that's not the problem, it's just the fact that these sightings are very regular. The ships pass by obviously heavily loaded with cargo and return apparently empty.'

'And what is the significance of this, I wonder?' Taliesin mused thoughtfully; glumness forgotten. 'I have no love of goblins, especially after the atrocities I witnessed on the Anunnaki mainland, but as long as they are not pirate ships, they are entitled to sail wherever they please, unless they are being overtly aggressive.'

'Yes,' Lord Ravenna conceded, 'but this seems to be a new phenomenon. They have never been seen in these waters before, apart from the pirate ships Morgaine and Nuada sailed with. As I said, they are making regular trips, always with lots of troops on board, and often with cargos of timber. If large numbers of troops are involved, they must be up to something.'

'Have they been challenged?'

'Well, no, not yet. They haven't done anything that merits a challenge, and really, as they are sailing mainly in troll waters, it is rather outwith our jurisdiction.'

'As I thought, Lord Ravenna.' Taliesin looked thoughtful. 'But yes, you are correct to draw my attention to this. No doubt Admiral Sulis has notified the Queen and I expect she will wish to discuss the matter with me upon my return.'

'Forewarned is forearmed, my Lord — more ginger tea?'

THIRTY-SEVEN

The Waters of Forgetfulness

One bright morning, Taliesin was chatting to Tabitha as he tightened Luath's girth, the spring sunlight gleaming on the stallion's glossy flanks as he tossed his head, dancing impatiently on the spot, eager to be off. Taliesin was heading to Tigh Falloch for a welcome week's leave, Molly, Alaria, and their son, Ares, having left a few days earlier after the fun and excitement of the Beltane celebrations and bonfires. He had just placed his foot in the stirrup when one of the Queen's equerries hurried breathlessly into the stable yard.

'Lord Taliesin!' he gasped, red-faced and sweating from the exertion of running at top speed through the palace. 'Thank goodness I managed to catch you! The Queen wishes to see you immediately in the private audience chamber.'

Taliesin gave a resigned sigh, took his foot out of the stirrup, and handed Luath's reins to Tabitha. 'Unsaddle him, please, Epona, I have no idea how long I will be.'

He strode into the carriage and wagon yard where his wagon master and the rest of his men were waiting patiently for the order to move out. After telling them to stand down until further notice, he reluctantly followed the equerry back through the palace, the bright expectations of the lovely morning vanishing as his stomach clenched in apprehension. Ceriddwen knew he was looking forward to his break, and capricious as she was, spite was not one of her failings. It must be something important for her to summon him at such short notice.

Her private audience chamber was at the far end of the Throne Room, and as usual the room was thronged with people going about palace business. Courtiers, officials, and petitioners milled about chattering, shouting, and vying for the attention of beleaguered staff behind rows of desks down one side of the room. Cleaners were trying to mop the floor around dozens of feet, they were up ladders cleaning windows, beating dust out of tapestries, flags and banners, and polishing crystal light fittings. The noise and constant activity made Taliesin long even more for the peace and tranquillity of Tigh Falloch.

When he was shown into the audience chamber, he knew at once something serious was afoot when he spied the Arianrhod sitting with Ceriddwen. A grim-faced Lleu and Morfan were also present. The private audience chamber was a beautifully furnished, welcoming room with tall windows opening onto a balcony overlooking the palace harbour. Under normal circumstances it was a lovely place to sit and chat. Taliesin knew instinctively he hadn't been summoned for pleasant conversation.

Ceriddwen waved him towards a comfortable green leather armchair. 'Please take a seat, Lord Taliesin, and thank you for coming so quickly.' Her voice was taut with suppressed emotion. Taliesin lowered himself apprehensively into the chair.

'I'm very sorry, but Mother Arianrhod has just advised me of something I had persuaded myself not to think about, but oaths must not be broken, and so here we are. The moment has arrived. You do know what I am talking about?'

Taliesin swallowed hard. Like Ceriddwen, this was something he had pushed to the back of his mind. 'Yes, Your Majesty, I'm afraid I do.'

When Taliesin asked for Ceriddwen's permission to marry Molly, she briefly explained how Molly would eventually have to go back to her own world, but only for a short while, and then she would return. Ceriddwen hadn't said when this would happen, in fact, she had been extremely vague about it, and Taliesin, being so besotted with Molly and desperate to marry her, hadn't treated the matter with the gravity it required. He looked at their concerned faces. Ceriddwen was obviously trying her best not to burst into tears. He knew how she felt.

Swallowing hard, he blurted out, 'But why now, Your Majesty? What about our children? They are barely more than babies — how will I explain their mother's absence?'

He deliberately didn't mention his greatest fear of all — a fear he shared with Ceriddwen — that once returned to her own world, Molly might wish to remain there and never come back. The Arianrhod deftly took over the conversation before Ceriddwen could reply.

'Because we promised to return Molly after a certain length of human time — a few hours of their time, years of ours. That time is up, and we must honour that promise.'

Taliesin could feel a rush of blood to his head coming on and fought to control it. But what about our children?' he repeated angrily.

'They are still very young, they will hardly notice she is gone, Lord Taliesin. They are used to being left at Tigh Falloch or the palace when you and the princess leave on diplomatic trips. They love their nurse, they love Enya and Brighid, and they will still have all their playmates. Children are very adaptable. Before they know it, their mother will have returned as if she'd never been gone.'

'I don't mean to be rude, Mother Arianrhod,' Taliesin replied stiffly, 'but I know my children better than you, and they most certainly *will* miss their mother.'

'As I said,' replied the Arianrhod smoothly, 'children are adaptable, and in this instance, they will have to be, because Molly must leave, and that is the end of it, Lord Taliesin whether you like it or not!'

Taliesin bit back a furious retort. He wasn't the Queen; he couldn't verbally abuse the venerable Arianrhod and get away with it. He knew he was defeated, nodding his head in acquiescence as he tried to think of a suitable reply. One of Ceriddwen's many cats sprang lightly onto his lap, purring loudly as he absently stroked its sleek fur. It began kneading his thighs with its soft paws and the gentle rhythm coupled with the soothing sound of the purring helped focus his mind, as the Arianrhod spoke on in quiet, measured tones.

Taliesin continued to stroke the cat mechanically, listening with mounting dismay as the Arianrhod began to issue him with instructions. He was to drug Molly.

'Drug my wife?'

His mind was in turmoil, and it was only his superb warrior training and discipline that prevented him tossing the cat from his lap and storming out of the room. Ceriddwen had thought carefully about where he was sitting, facing the window with the sunlight streaming into his eyes. Ceriddwen, Morfan and Lleu were facing him, and he couldn't read the expressions on their faces; all he could hear was the calm voice of the Arianrhod potentially destroying his life.

The drug, provided in a little crystal phial, was to be administered around supper time that evening. By morning, Molly would be completely pliable and amenable to whatever Taliesin asked her to do. They were to return to the palace the following day, when Molly would be met by the Ladies of Astarte, and escorted deep into the bowels of the citadel to the Cavern of the Mysteries. This cavern was the source of the cauldron's power, coming from a spring of mysteriously charged water that welled up and flowed, before being channelled along a crystalline conduit, into the torpid waters of the River Lethe. The Cavern's ancient worn steps led down to a sandy beach where the river was diverted through a pool contained within walls of sapphire crystal. Taliesin bristled immediately at the mention of the pool. The Waters of Forgetfulness were used in extreme cases for criminals deemed too controversial for execution, and Morgaine, with her powerful family connections, had fallen into this category. She had been submerged in the pool and banished for life to an obscure farm many miles from her home.

Noticing Taliesin's darkening expression, Ceriddwen cut through the Arianrhod's speech. 'Molly must remember nothing,' she explained quickly with an apologetic look to the Arianrhod for rudely interrupting her. 'This is the only way, Lord Taliesin, and it is the kindest.'

Molly would be submerged in the pool where the River Lethe's magical waters of forgetfulness would wash away all memory of her life with the Tuatha de Danaan.

'How can forcing my wife underwater like a criminal be kind?' he retorted furiously. 'And how will she know when it is time to return? Are we to invade the human world and kidnap her like thieves in the night?' He was shaking with temper and fear.

'The Queen and the Ladies of Astarte will be with the princess at the pool, she will be told it is a game and as she will still be under the influence of the drug you shall administer tonight, she will think nothing of it.'

The Arianrhod spoke placatingly to Taliesin, but he remained unconvinced.

'You still haven't told me how my wife will know when it is time to return.'

'She will still be under my enchantment,' Ceriddwen replied hesitantly, 'and the enchantment will begin to wear off after forty years of human time, which, as you know, translates into only a few weeks of our time. When her memory is restored, she will know to return to the rock in the forest where she entered our realm.'

'And if she chooses not to return?' There, he had said it, the outcome that he and Ceriddwen feared most.

'That is her choice, and if she makes that decision, there is nothing we can do. You know, Lord Taliesin, we do not hold humans here against their will, despite the stories they frighten each other with.' Ceriddwen's voice shook with emotion. 'Let us hope her love for you and her children transcends all else.' She stood up and crossed to Taliesin's chair, lifting the purring cat from his knees. 'Now go to your loved ones, go with our blessings and love, spend tonight in the arms of your family and return with the princess tomorrow.' She smiled sadly at him, hugging the cat to her bosom, eyes glittering with unshed tears as Taliesin bowed formally, turned on his heel and left the room.

~

Once more, the fleet-footed Luath lived up to his name, his powerful legs and stout heart eating up the thirty-mile gallop to Tigh Falloch. Talisesin was again reminded of his headlong flight to the Western Gate in his bid to head off Grainne. He was madly in love with Molly then, and even more so now. The thought of losing her was almost more than he could bear. The rhythmic sound of Luath's hooves seemed to mock him as though they were beating out *Molly's going away! Molly's going away!* During Luath's rest breaks, Taliesin tried to mentally prepare himself for what lay ahead, doing exercises from his training on the Isle of Clouds, training that was used to prepare warriors emotionally for battle. This was going to be worse than any battle he had ever known. At each stop, he went through the exercises, losing himself in the flow of the movements and deep breathing, until eventually, as they neared the gates of Tigh Falloch, he felt calm enough to behave as normally as possible.

The amaroks set up a loud barking as Luath trotted around the lake, over the little bridge and along the curtain wall of the grange. The gates were quickly thrown open, and Jassie rushed out, leaping around him, yowling her delight, dodging the vicious kicks Luath aimed at her. As he dismounted, Alaria flew from the house, followed by Ares as fast as his chubby little legs would carry him. 'Daddy! Daddy! Sassy's had puppies!'

'Thathy had babieth,' lisped Ares. Despite his misery, Taliesin laughed as he swept them both into his arms.

'Puppies, is it? And how many do we have?'

'Thix, Daddy,' Ares confirmed, gravely holding up six fat, miniature fingers just as Molly came to the door and leant against the frame, arms folded across her chest, smiling happily at her family.

'On your own?' she queried, noticing the absence of the wagons and lack of noisy men and horses clattering and shouting around the yard. 'Where's everyone else?'

'Oh, Luath was very fresh,' he explained as nonchalantly as possible, carefully putting the children down and taking them both by the hand. 'I just gave him his head. The others will be here soon. Now, you two, let's go and see these puppies!'

They spent a pleasant half hour before dinner watching the children romp with the roly-poly amarok puppies. Taliesin's heart felt like a lump of lead as he put on a brave face, laughing at the antics of the children and the puppies, trying not to squeeze Molly's hand too hard, holding it as tightly as he dared, lest she should suspect something was amiss. He showered and changed for dinner, making sure the little phial was safely concealed in his pocket, fretting over when and how he was going to slip its contents into Molly's wine.

He needn't have worried. Finlas served dinner as usual, and Molly chattered happily about Beltane, meeting up with her friends and telling him Lord Cernunnos and Lady Flidais had stopped for a brief visit the previous day with their son, Lord Pan. They were on their way to the Western Gate to finalise a deal on timber with Admiral Sulis and had decided to make a point of visiting friends on the way.

'I like Lady Flidais a lot,' Molly confided. 'She was very kind to me when Ceriddwen took me to Fell Oak.'

'Yes, I remember...'

Taliesin had just started to reply when Nuala interrupted them, bobbing a curtsey as she entered the room. 'I'm sorry to interrupt,' she gave them an apologetic smile, 'but do you think you could come and decide which pudding the children should have? We've a bit of foot stamping going on, and I think a tantrum might be imminent!' The children normally ate with their parents during the day, but, until they were older, the evening meal was reserved for adults only. They had their dinner either in the kitchen or in the nursery. Molly smiled ruefully and put down her fork.

'Is it a toss-up between ice cream and chocolate sauce or Enya's wonderful trifle, I wonder?'

As soon as she left the room Taliesin swiftly took the phial out of his pocket and emptied the contents into Molly's wine glass, giving it a quick stir before quickly sitting down again. Molly returned a few moments later.

'Ice cream for Ares and trifle for Alaria!' She laughed. 'What about you, my love? Will you have room for pudding after these lovely cheese dumplings?' Taliesin's heart lurched as she raised her wine glass. 'A toast to us and Enya's lovely puddings!'

Just about managing to raise his glass and fix a smile to his face, he watched Molly drink the doctored wine and he felt sick with guilt and shame.

'To Enya's lovely puddings!' he repeated, downing a large gulp, covertly watching Molly for any immediate reaction to Ceriddwen's tincture, but to his relief it obviously wasn't a fast-acting potion.

Later, he felt guilty making love to her, but he couldn't help himself, he couldn't bear the thought that this could be the last time he ever held her in his arms. He held her and kissed her with such ferocious passion, tasting her and breathing in her scent, taking her again and again until he feared she might question his sudden insatiability, but Molly, still showing no effects of the drug, responded with equal intensity.

'You weren't as passionate as this when we'd been separated for months!' she teased when they were lying exhausted in the afterglow. 'Has someone fed you an aphrodisiac?'

'You're the only aphrodisiac I need,' he murmured, curling a thick tress of her hair around his hand. 'Every time I look at you, I want to make passionate love to you.'

'I thought you just did!' Again, the throaty, teasing laugh that drove him wild, making him feel crushed by misery and grief.

What if she doesn't come back? he thought frantically, hoping she wouldn't notice his heart starting to thump rapidly. *I couldn't bear it, and what about the children?*

'I'm sleepy, my love, night night...' Molly's voice trailed off as she drifted into sleep, distracting him momentarily from his thoughts.

'Goodnight, beloved,' he whispered, tucking the blanket around her shoulders, knowing he stared a sleepless night in the face.

Finally, as little golden streaks of light filtered through the curtains, he awoke from a fitful doze to a glorious dawn chorus competing with the rousing crowing of the yard cockerel. He climbed reluctantly out of bed; Molly was still fast asleep, pink and rosy, breathing steadily with her mouth slightly open.

Feeling tired and groggy, Taliesin rubbed the stubble on his chin as he headed into the bathroom for a cold, invigorating shower. He stood under the icy water as the grange gradually came to life, beginning the usual business of the day — horses whinnying for their breakfast, buckets banging, dogs barking, cattle lowing in the distance waiting to be milked. As he stepped from the shower, the smell of baking bread wafted up from the bakehouse. Everything was perfectly normal and as it should be, except that it wasn't.

He towelled himself dry and shaved before heading into his dressing room, trying to work out what he was going to say to Nuala and Enya about Molly's imminent absence. They would have to be told, of course, along with the rest of the household and estate staff. The most important thing was not to upset the children in any way. Nuala and Enya were experienced enough, and he knew they would allay any fears the children might have about their mother's absence.

He managed to catch them in the kitchen as breakfast was being prepared and once over the initial shock, they agreed to secrecy, going along with everything he said, to prevent alarming Molly or the children.

Shortly afterwards, Molly appeared, bright-eyed and bushy tailed, hugging the children as they tumbled through the door, helping them up onto their chairs around the big, scrubbed kitchen table, the morning sunlight streaming through the window, spreading a warm golden glow around the room.

'Good morning, everyone, it's going to be another beautiful day, by the look it!' she said cheerfully. Then, addressing the children, asked, 'Do you remember where we're going today?'

'To visit Tuke, Mummy, to see Toffy's piglets!' Since retiring as undefeated Truffle-Hunting Champion, Tuke had settled down to raise prize pigs on his farm at the other side of the Falloch estate. He loved children, having children and grandchildren of his own whom he doted on, and was a great favourite of Alaria and Ares. They turned their excited faces to Taliesin, eyes shining, babbling in excitement. 'Are you coming, Daddy? Please, please, please!'

'Luth ith coming too, Mithtwess Tanthy thaid he wath!'

Ares' lisping enthusiasm was almost too much for Taliesin, and he looked at them sadly, his heart almost breaking at the sight of Alaria's happy, expectant smile.

'I'm very sorry, my darlings, but Mummy and Daddy can't come with you today. Your great-grandmother, the Queen, wishes to speak to us about a very important matter and we must leave straight after breakfast.'

He gave Molly a quick glance to see if she was going to argue, but Ceriddwen's potion seemed to be working — she was smiling cheerfully at Alaria and Ares.

'Don't worry, children, Tuke won't mind if Mummy and Daddy aren't there this time. He loves to spoil you and you know he won't spoil you so much if we're there, don't you?'

The two little faces, about to pucker up into howls of disappointment and outrage, paused for a moment's reflection, then lit up again at the thought of the forbidden treats Tuke always managed to produce. Mummy was quite right; they would get more treats if she wasn't there. Then a moment of hesitation.

'So, who will come with us, then?' asked Alaria. 'Because Nuala and Mistress Tansy won't let us have treats, either!' Both faces took on a mutinous look.

Nuala, who was helping Enya dish up breakfast, quickly said, 'Oh, Mistress Tansy and I shall be VERY busy shopping in Tuke's store. He will have to look after you, we shan't have time.' Nuala crossed her fingers behind her back, hoping they wouldn't ask her what they were buying. Somehow, the thought of cuddling little piglets and then buying bacon and sausages wouldn't go down well. Fortunately, they seemed satisfied by her answer and Taliesin heaved a silent sigh of relief. So far, so good.

'If we're leaving immediately after breakfast, I'll have to go and change, I can't ride in this,' Molly said through a mouthful of scrambled egg, pointing her fork towards her flower-sprigged cotton dress.

Taliesin marvelled at the efficacy of the drug she had ingested. No questions asked, no queries about the Queen's summons, just complete acceptance that this is what she was doing today. 'Will you ride Flambeaux, or Abraxas?' he asked. 'I'll have them saddled up while you change.'

'I'll ride Flambeaux, he could do with a good ride out.'

Taliesin nodded. 'I'll see to it. We'll leave in half an hour, that should give you time to change and say goodbye to the children.'

He swallowed hard; he felt like a traitor watching Alaria and Ares chatter excitedly to Molly about their trip to Tuke's farm. She wiped egg yolk from Ares' chin with a napkin and then set about buttering bread soldiers for both children to dip into their eggs. Just another happy morning. Molly finished her own breakfast then ran lightly upstairs to change into a riding outfit for the journey as Enya produced a packed lunch, drinks and snacks to put in their saddlebags for the journey. Taliesin smiled ruefully as she handed him the packages.

'Don't worry, Taliesin,' she said quietly, patting him gently on the arm, 'she'll be back before you know it.' Seeing his mask slip momentarily, revealing his real, desperately worried self, she added, 'The children will be fine — they've plenty to keep them occupied, Nuala and I will make sure of it, and they won't doubt for a moment their mother will be back soon.'

'I hope you're right, Enya.' He managed to give her a lop-sided grin, aware that the children were watching and listening. 'And thank you — what would I do without you?' Alaria and Ares crowed in delight as their big warrior father wrapped little Enya in a huge bear hug.

'Me nextht, Daddy!' shouted Ares, scrambling down from his chair. 'Hug me too!' Unable to stop himself laughing, Taliesin released the spluttering Enya, her face pink with pleasure, and lifted Ares into his arms, squeezing the breath out of him. 'Thtop, Daddy, too hard!' Ares screamed in delight as Alaria tugged on Taliesin's sleeve.

'Me too, Daddy, me too!' she pleaded, jumping up and down. Taliesin bent down and grabbed her just as Molly came back into the kitchen.

'What a noise! What on earth is going on in here?' she demanded, laughing at the sight of her husband wrestling with both children in his arms.

'Daddy hugged Enya, so we get hugs, too!' Alaria explained.

'Of course you do, my darlings,' agreed Molly. 'Can I have hugs too, before Daddy and I leave to visit great-grandmother?'

Ares wriggled out of Taliesin's arms. 'Hugth for Mummy, too!' and as Molly enveloped him in her arms he asked, 'Will great-grandmother alwayth be a queen, Mummy?'

'Yes, she will,' replied Molly. 'Why do you ask, poppet?'

'Becauthe then you wouldn't alwayth have to go when she askth,' he said, very matter-of-factly.

'She is the Queen, and we must do as she asks. That's just the way it is, my darling.'

He thought for a moment, his little brow creased in concentration, then said gravely, 'Well, she doeth give uth lotth of presentth, tho I thuppothe it'th all right!'

Molly and Taliesin exchanged glances, then smiled fondly at their son. Ares' lisp was very endearing, but they both hoped he'd lose it when his second teeth came through. Speaking with a faux heartiness he didn't feel, Taliesin ruffled Ares' hair and patted Alaria's russet curls, so like her mother's.

'Right then, everyone, into the yard to wave goodbye, we must be off!'

He strode from the kitchen, through the hall and along the passageway that led into the courtyard with Molly following, ushering the children in front of her. Rudi and Draco, their escorts, were already mounted and waiting. Taliesin had decided to ride Storm back to the palace, and he stood patiently beside Flambeaux with their groom, Dru.

Taliesin gave Molly a leg-up onto Flambeaux, then swiftly mounted Storm with a lithe agility that always set Molly's pulse racing. The unicorns side-stepped and rolled their eyes, fresh and keen to be off as Molly and Taliesin waved their goodbyes and blew kisses to the children before trotting through the big wooden gates, across the little bridge and along the lake shore, its water sparkling in the bright morning sunshine, the children's goodbyes ringing in their ears.

As far as Molly was concerned, she was having a pleasant outing in warm spring weather and chattered normally along the way, admiring the miles of frothy cow parsley, pretty bluebells, and the pungent aroma of wild garlic. They cantered through shady tunnels of beech and oak, Molly loquaciously admiring the beauty of the chestnut trees resplendent in their glorious tall candle-like flowers, the hawthorn bushes and trees with beautiful May blossom tumbling across their branches like foaming waterfalls, filling the air with their distinctive musty perfume. Taliesin was blind to all of it, focusing entirely on what was about to happen. It took all his discipline and strength of character not to grab Flambeaux's reins and gallop off with Molly into the wide blue yonder. Anywhere rather than lose her. Molly was oblivious to his silence, in thrall to Ceriddwen's potion and relishing, as always, time alone with her husband, with Rudi and Draco maintaining a discreet distance as always.

They stopped for lunch at their favourite spot beside the river where Molly insisted they go for a swim. This had become a ritual during fine weather after Taliesin had promised to take Molly swimming here when they stopped on her first trip to Tigh Falloch. They swam in a bend of the river out of sight of the others, Molly stripping off and racing Taliesin into the water. Reluctant at first, he soon forgot his worries, caught up in her enthusiasm and the ache of desire in his groin as she dived gracefully into the lazy current, startling a family of grebes feeding in the shallows. They dived and splashed in the clear cool water until Taliesin could contain himself no longer and pulled the laughing Molly out of the river onto the grassy riverbank, her wet skin gleaming in the sunshine, dripping hair spread amongst the pink ragged robin and cuckoo flowers. She wrapped her legs around him as he pushed into her, thrusting against him, making little mewing sounds of pleasure until he came in a groaning rush, collapsing on top of her, panting, hands wrapped in her hair, nuzzling her neck.

'Our first swim of the season,' she murmured languidly into his ear. 'The first of many I hope.' Taliesin rolled off and lay on his back, staring into the cloudless sky. Molly propped herself up on one elbow.

'Are you sure you haven't taken an aphrodisiac?' she said with that same throaty chuckle, an amused smile playing about her lips. 'I mean, how many times last night and again just now?'

'Are you complaining?' he asked, trying to keep his voice light, as though he was enjoying their post-coital banter.

Molly gurgled with laughter. 'Not at all!' She took his hand and held it against her belly. 'I was thinking we've probably made another baby — wouldn't that be wonderful?'

Taliesin's blood froze in his veins. Molly might be pregnant? He hadn't factored that possibility into any of this. His mind raced frantically as he attempted to process this new thought. *Ceriddwen must have considered the possibility*, he reasoned, resolving to find out as soon as they arrived at the palace.

'Well,' Molly's voice intruded into his thoughts, 'that would be lovely, wouldn't it?'

'Yes, of course it would, my love.' He sat up and pulled her into his arms, planting a kiss on her lips. 'Absolutely wonderful.'

All too soon the dark forbidding walls of the citadel loomed in front of them, with the rest of the vast palace buildings and gardens gradually coming into view as they started their descent into the Danu valley. Taliesin had been instructed to enter by the North Barbican where the entrance to the Cavern of the Mysteries was situated. As soon as they reached the perimeters of the palace, he sent Draco ahead to announce their arrival.

They trotted through the huge, fortified gateway into the cobbled courtyard to find Morfan and Lleu waiting with heavy hearts and forced smiles of welcome. Taliesin dismounted, handing Storm's reins to a waiting groom and clasped Lleu's arm, as Morfan helped Molly down from Flambeaux.

'Good to see you both,' Lleu said with a heartiness he didn't feel. 'I hope you had a pleasant journey.'

Morfan, playing along, hugged Molly and clapped Taliesin on the back.

'At least the weather stayed fine. How are the children?' He turned back to Molly. 'No doubt running Nuala ragged!'

Molly laughed. 'Correct!' she agreed, twisting her hair, still loose and tousled after her post-swim lovemaking, into a passable braid. 'They're going to Tuke's farm to see his prize sow's piglets and their excitement is at fever pitch. Nuala and Tansy will have their hands full!'

Lleu and Morfan nodded and laughed dutifully, trying to keep things as normal as possible just as Lady Tanith slipped silently from the arched entrance of a passageway beneath the flight of stairs leading up to the massive, iron-studded doors of the north entrance.

She curtsied to everyone, then addressing Molly said, 'Greetings, Your Highness. The Queen has sent me to fetch you.'

'Oh, how kind. Thank you, Lady Tanith!' Molly exclaimed happily. 'But where are we going? I don't think I've ever been to this part of the palace.'

'Well, this is the oldest part of the citadel, and most of the palace business takes place, as you know, at the southern end.'

'Of course, but where are we going?' Molly asked again, linking arms with Tanith as she was led through the archway and down the dark passageway without a backward glance.

Taliesin made to follow them, but Lleu grasped his arm.

'No, Taliesin, you cannot follow. The Queen and her ladies are in charge now. You may accompany Morfan when he takes Molly back through the portal, but that is all.'

After an agonisingly long three-hour wait, Taliesin, accompanied by Lleu and Morfan, was summoned to the Queen's private apartments. When they arrived, Molly was sitting beside Brighid, whose eyes were red and puffy from crying, staring vacantly into space, obviously unaware of her surroundings. She was wearing the same cheesecloth shirt and bell-bottom jeans she had arrived in. Her glorious hair was scraped back into an unkempt ponytail, and she didn't look at all like her usual vibrant self.

Ceriddwen turned as the men entered the room. She was dressed in an indigo velvet sheath gown, its high neckline encircled by a heavy tooled silver torc, and long sleeves that tapered to points on the back of her hands. Her head was adorned with a diamond and silver diadem with her trademark white curls framing one side of her face. She had dressed appropriately to mark this upsetting and important occasion.

'Ah, Lord Taliesin.' She smiled sadly at him. 'The deed has been done, and Molly is ready to return to her own world. Do you wish to go with Morfan when he takes her through the portal?'

Taliesin gazed in horror at his beloved wife.

'Is this what living in the human world does to people?' His voice shook with emotion. 'She looks so different!'

'Lord Taliesin, you must remember, she was very ill when she came to us.'

Ceriddwen's voice washed over him like a soothing balm; she was weaving an enchantment to console him, to keep him from damaging the new enchantment she had placed Molly under. If Taliesin unleashed his ferocious temper, he might also unleash his own inherent fairy powers and negate at least some of her work. All fairies had power and the ability to shapeshift, but over thousands of years, they had learned to control it. Extreme stress or duress could break that control. If he broke Ceriddwen's enchantment, it could potentially do untold damage.

'I have healed her and, when she returns to her world, she will no longer be ill.' Taliesin sat down, hypnotised by Ceriddwen' voice. 'I have already explained this to you, if you remember, but I shall tell you again, just to be sure. Molly will be under my enchantment, and my powers shall keep her safe for forty human years. She will live a human life, but under my auspices. She will have no more children in the human world, for she is once more pregnant with your child and this pregnancy shall lie dormant until she returns to us in a few short weeks.'

Taliesin nodded. 'She thought she might be pregnant; I did wonder if you had thought about that.'

A Dynasty of Dragons

Ceriddwen laughed mirthlessly. 'Lord Taliesin, I am not Queen of the Tuatha de Danaan for nothing! I knew as soon as she joined us this afternoon.' She held her hands up in a placatory gesture. 'I know you are worried that Molly may not wish to return to us, as am I. When my enchantment wears off, she is free do to as she pleases. If she chooses to remain in the human world, we must respect her wishes. It is the price we pay for always honouring our word. You know that as well as I do.'

He stared at his feet and replied gruffly, 'Of course, Your Majesty.'

'Good!' Ceriddwen nodded curtly. 'I'm glad that's settled.' Turning to Brighid, who was tightly clutching Molly's hand, her face still wet with tears, she said gently, 'Mistress Brighid, it is time. Let the princess's hand go. She must leave now.'

Stifling a sob, Brighid helped Molly to her feet. Molly was obviously completely unaware of anything and moved like an automaton. Taliesin swiftly moved to her side and put a protective arm around her shoulders.

'Thank you, Brighid,' he whispered, 'I'll take her from here.'

Brighid nodded and stood wringing her hands helplessly as Taliesin, accompanied by Morfan, led Molly through the door, along the sumptuous long gallery that led to the Queen's apartments, through all the lovely halls, corridors, and courtyards of this part of the palace, until finally they made their way along the wall walk to the flight of stairs leading down to the portal passageway.

Anwyn was waiting for them and lumbered down the ancient steps to unlock the gates. He bowed respectfully as the two men carefully guided Molly down, then stood back to patiently await their return. At the end of the passageway Morfan stood in front of a wall of gleaming quartz and, turning to Taliesin, asked, 'Ready?'

'As I'll ever be,' Taliesin grunted, kissing the top of Molly's head, feeling as though his heart would break. He felt like a broken reed instead of the mighty Queen's warrior he was supposed to be. Morfan nodded and touched the wall with the palm of his hand. The wall began to shimmer and sparkle, taking on the appearance of liquid light. Morfan stepped through, and with his heart in his mouth, Taliesin followed, clutching Molly.

He looked around cautiously. They were in a forest clearing beside a tumbling stream, and they were standing in front of an immense rocky outcrop covered in moss, ferns, and trailing ivy. All was quiet apart from a flock of jackdaws chattering to each other in the trees high above them. 'Have you been through this portal before?' Morfan's question broke into Taliesin's fevered thoughts.

'No, I've had no call to enter the human world before, believe it or not.' He pulled the unresponsive Molly closer. 'I've had no reason to travel through any portals, only the Eastern Gate wormhole.'

'Of course, I realise that — the other portals are well guarded and anytime my Lady Mother is summoned, the humans are always thoroughly checked out.'

Morfan knew he was just babbling, Taliesin wasn't remotely interested in portals and other humans, he was only interested in Molly's wellbeing.

'Okay then, we don't have much time until Molly's family returns.'

He peered along the rough track leading into the clearing to make sure no one was about then asked Taliesin to bring Molly over to the fallen log she was seated on before. Molly obediently sat, propping her feet on a protruding root, wrapping her hands around her knees. She sat, staring into space without uttering a word or acknowledging their presence.

Taliesin would have lingered, reluctant to just leave her sitting there so helplessly, but Morfan was insistent, speaking sharply. 'Taliesin, move, now!'

Taliesin cupped Molly's face in his hands, ignoring her blank expression, to kiss her one last time before following Morfan through the coruscating light.

THIRTY-EIGHT
Let Battle Commence

The camp was a hive of frenetic activity; soldiers polishing armour, sharpening weapons, people erecting tents, digging latrines, raised voices shouting orders, horses whinnying and the snarling and barking of the amarok fighting dogs straining on their leashes, sensing the tension in the air. Messengers and pigeon handlers dashed to and fro with correspondence from commanders waiting on orders. The sense of urgency was palpable, and every single soldier and warrior knew that their futures depended on preventing the goblins from breaching the new portal. Not only was Princess Molly's life in danger, but their precious world and way of life would be lost forever if humans discovered any of the portals. This was not just a personal fight to the death for each man and woman, but a fight to prevent the death of their world.

Ceriddwen ground her teeth in anger and frustration as she surveyed the massed goblin troops arrayed in the valley plain below. This valley was contained within a sloping, crescent shaped, sandstone ridge, the open end blocked by piles of spoil from the mine at the bottom of the north side, piles of lumber and long wooden sheds obviously used for accommodation and storage purposes. The south side of the ridge was dominated by a large wood and the north side covered in acres of prickly yellow gorse. Ceriddwen's camp was situated along the centre, affording her a clear bird's eye view of all goblin activity.

Thousands of goblin troops crowded the plain as the sun shone opaquely though the smoky pall of their campfires. They presented a seething mass of bodies constantly on the move — mounted warriors patrolling the perimeters and occasionally galloping along the bottom of Ceriddwen's camp, hurling insults, challenging Ceriddwen to come and fight them, wisely staying just out of range of retaliatory fairy arrows. The ground troops constantly changed position as men took their turn to eat and warm themselves at their fires. They were obviously alert and disciplined — ready for whatever the fairies might have in store for them. Ceriddwen had quickly spotted the goblin king astride a huge blue roan warhorse, instantly recognisable by his mane of red hair and huge powerful shoulders. He wore no armour, and confidently rode through the crowded ranks of men, fully aware that he was highly visible and apparently unconcerned, stopping to chat and encourage men as they practised archery at the butts, his stentorian voice joining in rousing battle songs with others.

'He obviously hopes this show of strength will demoralise us,' Ceriddwen murmured to Lleu as Lady Tanith handed them mugs of steaming tea — the winds across the exposed top ridge were bone-chillingly cold. 'He's only fooling himself — he'll be having a hard job maintaining his men's morale. No doubt they know how large our armies are.' Ceriddwen took a sip of hot tea as Lleu nodded in agreement.

'Not that Nudd cares,' he growled. 'He knows his troops are dangerously exposed. He's using them as a barrier to slow down our attempt to get to the mine — he knows the game's up.'

'He's got to try and hold us off as long as possible before he gets the portal open — see how the bulk of his army and his best warriors are concentrated around the mine. Once we clear the plain, we'll have to get through the goblin stormtroopers...wait a minute...what's going on now?' Ceriddwen shaded her eyes with her free hand as she squinted into the distance through the haze of smoky sunlight. Something was moving through the long morning shadows cast by the sheds and stacks of timber.

'They're moving the dragons! They must think they're about to breach the portal!'

Ceriddwen and Lleu watched intently as three wheeled cages were drawn towards the mine entrance, each containing the unmistakeable shape of a large, winged dragon.

Ceriddwen turned to a hovering attendant. 'Fetch Lord Taliesin, now!' she barked at the shivering youth who had been stamping his feet and blowing into his hands to warm them. He turned on his heel and fled in the direction of the main body of the camp.

It hadn't been an auspicious start to their campaign as Nudd was obviously well-informed by his network of spies. When Ceriddwen passed through the wormhole, she found herself in an enormous forested area of goblin territory where they were immediately pounced upon by waiting bands of guerrillas who harried them mercilessly, killing and wounding many of Ceriddwen's troops before melting back into the seemingly impenetrable forest. This onslaught continued until Cernunnos' fearsome forest fairies came through the wormhole, swiftly pursuing and despatching many goblins in a massive rout. No one managed forest warfare better than forest fairies and Nudd lost many of his finest guerrilla warriors. Despite the loss of so many of her own men, Ceriddwen still felt a grim frisson of satisfaction.

The entire campaign was fraught with worry and stress. Although Nudd had been very clever about hiding his mining activities, he knew very little about humans, and certainly misunderstood their nature and willingness to use their vastly superior weapons technology on any invader perceived as a serious threat. He hadn't considered that the territorial and aggressive humans would probably view him as an extra-terrestrial alien, that they would panic and throw everything they had at him. Apart from risking his own life and the lives of his men, he was blind to the fact that once the humans understood another world lay beyond the portal, they would invade and take over *his* world. This, of course, apart from their concern for Molly, was the fairies' greatest fear — that their thousands of years of vigilance and protection were about to be thrown away by a foolish, power-hungry goblin. Nudd would no doubt have succeeded in entering the human world, oblivious of the consequences, had he not fatally underestimated the Cailleach's survival instincts. That was his biggest mistake.

As soon as he was found out, Nudd lost no time in flooding the entire area with thousands of troops. He reasoned that the more troops he packed into the narrow valley plain, the more time he would have to breach the portal. He knew Varik had Ceriddwen's cryptanalysists and engineers working on the Cailleach's side, and as their technology was better than his, time was of the essence. He pushed his workers mercilessly, trying desperately to reach the quartz crystal deposits of the portal before Varik. He was also unaware that Varik's mining engineers had successfully removed the enormous area of shocked quartz deposits on their side, seriously damaging the wormhole aspect of this portal.

Lady Tanith was collecting the empty tea mugs after wrapping a thick fleecy cloak around Ceriddwen's shoulders, when Taliesin galloped towards them, Storm snorting puffs of steamy breath into the icy air as he skidded to a halt. Taliesin quickly dismounted and bowed low. His anxiety for Molly was making him short-tempered and bellicose; he wanted to be down in the plain, fighting his way through to the mine. He had to be at the portal entrance before the goblins broke through, and Samhain was drawing closer with every passing hour.

'Your Majesty?'

'Yes, yes, get up!' Ceriddwen snapped impatiently. 'Look over there!' She pointed peremptorily across the plain. 'They're moving the dragons towards the mine.' Taliesin's sharp eyes immediately took in the distant activity as he resolutely suppressed his terror of dragons.

'Have you heard from Lady Morrigan?' he demanded, as Cernunnos and Lady Keres, the Morrigan's second in command joined them.

Ceriddwen was waiting for the Morrigan to indicate her troops were in position hidden amongst the woods on the south side. King Jontar's troops were lying in wait, out of sight, a distance behind the sheds and lumber piles blocking the open end of the little valley. Cernunnos' son, Lord Pan, was leading a squadron of bark-skinned forest fairies, impervious to sharp gorse thorns and hiding out of sight amongst the bright yellow bushes on the north side, both armies waiting for the Morrigan's signal. Ceriddwen anxiously scanned the sky for peregrine falcons, a sure sign that pigeons had been sighted, and peregrines released to intercept them. Fairy pigeons were preternaturally swift, using unseen wormholes to dodge falcons, but nonetheless, peregrines were a deadly danger.

Taliesin had no sooner uttered the words when a young soldier came puffing up, bowing and asking permission to speak.

'Out with it, then!' barked Ceriddwen.

'W...word from the...the Morrigan, Your Majesty,' he stuttered. 'She is in position and is waiting for permission to attack.'

Ceriddwen punched her fist into her other hand. 'Excellent!' she exclaimed. 'There's your answer, my Lord. I assume your men are ready and waiting for the order to attack?'

Taliesin smiled thinly. 'They are, Your Majesty.'

Lady Keres and Cernunnos nodded in unison. 'As are ours.'

'Very well, let us be about our business. Tell the grooms to bring our mounts,' she ordered the young soldier, who obeyed with alacrity, adrenaline pumping at the thought of cutting his teeth on his first battle.

Taliesin rubbed his face before donning his helmet and fastening the chinstrap. He pulled the noseguard down as he wheeled Storm about, saluting Ceriddwen as he reined in the restive unicorn who was arching his neck and fighting the bit, eager to be off.

'I will sound the signal to attack, Your Majesty.'

Ceriddwen nodded, her face pale in the frosty morning light. 'At once, if you please, my Lord.'

As soon as the attack was trumpeted across the valley, the goblin troops reacted immediately, their mounted warriors forming themselves into defensive rows in front of the foot soldiers, now clattering spears on their shields and defiantly howling battle cries as they quickly got into formation behind the cavalry, covering their heads with their shields to protect them from fairy arrows. At the same time, Taliesin, Lady Keres, Cernunnos and the Morrigan led a terrifying cavalry charge down the western and northern slopes of the ridge, followed by hundreds of foot soldiers screaming their battle cry, 'Danaan! Danaan!' The amarok dog handlers ran alongside, unleashing their ferocious charges as they went. The forest fairies stayed put — they would bide their time until needed, once the cavalry charge had broken through.

All Taliesin could think about as Storm plunged down the frosted slope and across the plain to the waiting goblins, was

Molly and his children. They were his sole focus; the thought of their trusting little faces waving goodbye to him, and Enya and Nuala trying to stifle their sobs as he rode off to war, was almost too much to bear. No goblin was going to deprive him of his beloved wife, nor his children their mother. He wore his hatred of goblins like a warm protective armoured jacket.

The goblin cavalry, although heavily outnumbered, fought with ferocious determination. Storm, along with all fairy warhorses and unicorns, was superbly trained in warfare, lashing out with hooves and teeth as Taliesin slashed left and right with his battle-axe and sword, dodging attempts to unhorse him, pushing Storm through the roiling mass of goblins, horses and unicorns, his fellow warriors fighting just as fiercely in vicious, bloody, hand-to-hand combat. He watched several of his men go down, their horses cut from under them, the screams and agonised shouts adding to the din of weapons clashing, men shouting, trumpets blaring and the thud of hooves smashing shields and skulls.

He urged Storm on, cutting, thrusting, parrying blows, cursing in pain as a goblin mace landed a heavy blow on his armoured thigh, swiftly twisting to dodge the next aim as he hit the goblin a killer blow on the side of his head with his battle-axe. Storm plunged on, lowering his head to stab and slash with his lethal horn, lashing out with his iron-shod hooves, and leaping into the air to back-kick any goblins unfortunate enough to be behind him.

As he despatched the goblin, Taliesin saw the forest fairies rush in, swarming over the goblin troops, stabbing with their razor-sharp knives and blowing poison darts from short, lethal blowpipes, the goblins finding it difficult to cut through their incredibly tough, bark-like skin and armour. He could see the Morrigan in her winged helmet in the distance and Andraste's elven crystal ropes flying across the melee as the elves incredibly lassoed goblin cavalry, pulling them off their horses and overpowering them. Ceriddwen's men drew inexorably closer to the goblins surrounding the entrance to the mine and it had been agreed that as soon as they were halfway across the valley, a signal would be sent to Jontar's troops, still hidden out of sight in woods behind the mine slag heaps.

Through the sweat running into his eyes, Taliesin was relieved to see Jontar's troops pouring between the slag heaps, timber stacks and sheds. Waves of foot soldiers and mounted warriors charged into the fray and Taliesin felt a grim thrill as he watched the previously disciplined goblin troops break ranks as the full force of the troll army smashed its way towards them before splitting in two, one half headed for the mine troops and the other charging into the general melee. Fresh troops made all the difference as both sides were rapidly tiring, and Ceriddwen's troops fought with renewed vigour as it became obvious that the goblins were faltering.

Nudd had been galloping in and out of the battle, encouraging his men, but spent most of his time standing beside a wheeled cage containing the largest dragon. High on the central ridge, Ceriddwen sat astride Arien, accompanied by Lleu mounted on his magnificent bay stallion, Roja. They watched the battle scene intently, messengers constantly running backwards and forwards with information and casualty numbers. They had been watching Nudd's movements carefully, too, and were now focused on his behaviour at the mine entrance. Several goblins now surrounded the cage of one of the smaller dragons; they held long chains, and as the door was pulled open, they pulled hard, dragging the unfortunate creature out by its neck, almost choking it. As its body was gradually eased out, more chains were thrown around it and viciously tightened until the dragon couldn't move.

'I don't like the look of this.' Ceriddwen lowered her crystal spyglasses and handed them to Lleu. 'I hope I'm wrong, but it looks as though they are about to set a fire-breathing dragon on Jontar's troops.'

Lleu peered through the glasses and cursed loudly. 'That's exactly what they're going to do!'

The goblins produced a long funnel and loosened the chains around the dragon's neck just enough to allow access; they thrust the funnel down its throat then poured a sand-like mixture into it. The dragon struggled pitifully, and when they had finished, after securing its muzzle again, dragged it away from the cage to face the trolls. Apart from chains securing it to heavy stakes in the ground, they released it after swiftly removing the chain around its muzzle. The dragon immediately roared in fear and pain as it tried to pull itself free, throwing huge bursts of flames at the trolls, burning dozens of men to a crisp before they had time to scramble out of the way. Again and again the pain-maddened creature vomited flames at the trolls, forcing them into a short, terrorised, temporary retreat before they hurled themselves once more at the goblins. When the unfortunate creature collapsed and reassured that the exhausted dragon was going to stay down, the battle paused for a few seconds as everyone, including goblins, stared in appalled horror at the agonised dragon and the blackened remains of dead trolls. Those at the back of the battlefield who couldn't see what was happening were assailed by the smell of burning flesh as the wind blew plumes of greasy black smoke over the battlefield.

Taliesin, fearing a loss in momentum, stood up in his stirrups, holding his sword aloft, yelling, 'Danaan! Danaan!' before plunging back into the thick of the fray, surrounded by his valiant warriors, cutting their way steadily forwards through the crush of goblins fighting furiously to keep them from reaching the mine.

They slowly cut a bloody but deadly swathe towards their goal, gradually gaining more and more ground. Through the crush of fighting bodies, Taliesin cursed as he saw the dragon cages being dragged towards the mine — the goblins had somehow managed to manhandle the unfortunate fire-breathing dragon back into its cage where it was lying comatose, barely breathing, with its long neck lolling through one of the bars. The mine entrance was heavily guarded, and the only reason Taliesin could see what was going on was due to Storm's great height. It was clear the goblins were not going to give up the mine without a tremendous struggle. Once the last cage disappeared into the depths, huge numbers of goblins blocked the entrance, obviously prepared to fight to the death.

The trolls had made excellent progress despite the dragon attack — they were tough, aggressive soldiers who detested goblins, relentlessly mowing them down, settling long held scores. Inch by inch they fought their way closer to the mine, the goblins pushing back ferociously. Taliesin realised he had no idea how many goblin troops were already in position deep inside the mine, ready to rush into Molly's garden as soon as the portal was breached. He turned and barked at the warrior beside him, 'Ride to the Queen as fast as you can and tell her we need more troops down here, now!'

The exhausted, blood-spattered man saluted Taliesin, turned his mount around and urged it into a swift gallop, plunging through gaps in the fighting, dodging attempts to unhorse him as he sped across the plain. Taliesin watched grimly for a few moments before throwing himself back into the bloody task of fighting his way through the waves of screaming, defiant goblins.

THIRTY-NINE

The Day of the Dead

It was the morning of 31st October — Samhain — Hallowe'en — Day of the Dead — whatever you wish to call it, and Laura was knocking gently on Molly's bedroom door.

'Molly...Molly? Are you awake? It's half-past-eight already. I've made tea...'

No answer.

Laura frowned. This was unlike Molly, who normally rose with the lark every morning no matter what. She rapped the door a bit harder and raised her voice. 'Molly?'

'Go away,' came the muffled reply, 'leave me alone!'

'Are you ill? Shall I bring you some paracetamol?'

'I said just leave me alone. Go away!'

'But Molly, you must get up! Today's Hallowe'en — you haven't forgotten, surely?'

'Go away, I said!' Molly's voice was hysterically high. 'I'm not getting up. I don't care what day it is.'

Laura retreated downstairs and into the back garden. They were staying with Molly until whatever was going to happen was over, and Harry and Xander had been up for what seemed like hours, mooching around the garden and sinkhole, studying the sonic spell sheets, and trying to decide where to position themselves to play the music and keep an eye on whatever might happen. They were also worried that Guisers or Trick or Treaters might descend on them because it was Hallowe'en, but Molly reassured them that Heathervale Avenue was not known as a welcoming haven for Hallowe'en revellers, and in all the years she had lived there, no one had ever come to their door. In fact, Mr Morrison who lived next door, had got into the habit of letting his dogs, his current one being a huge Labradoodle called Buster, out into the garden every evening, and he had encouraged them to bark very loudly at anyone who passed by. They only wanted to play, but few people knew that and avoided the avenue like the plague after dark.

'It's because you're all too posh and stiff-necked to entertain plebs!' Xander said good-naturedly.

Molly had laughed along, but he had hit the nail on the head. No way would Fred, Mr Morrison and the likes of Dolores allow Hallowe'en revellers to darken their doors unless it was a specially arranged fancy dress charity ball someone was throwing in one of the bigger houses.

Breakfast forgotten, Laura rushed into the garden to tell the others Molly was refusing to get up.

Harry frowned. 'I was afraid of this. It's all getting too much for her. She's terrified.'

'But...but she has to get up!' Laura stammered. 'What are we going to do?'

'Leave it to me.' Harry strode across the lawn into the kitchen, poured fresh tea and milk into a mug, then padded upstairs to Molly's bedroom. He knocked on the door, calling softly, 'Molly, it's Harry. May I come in?'

'No! Go away! I don't want to talk to anyone.'

'I'm sorry, Molly — I'm going to be rude and come in anyway, ready or not.' He turned the handle and pushed the door open, surveying the bump that was Molly huddling beneath the duvet. He crossed the floor, placing the mug of tea on the bedside table before settling himself on the edge of the bed. 'You might as well come out. I've brought tea.' A silence ensued. 'I'm going to sit here until you do, so stop being silly and sit up.'

'I'm not being silly.' said a voice coming from the duvet. 'Why is wanting to have a day in bed being silly?'

Gritting his teeth and suppressing his jealousy, Harry replied, 'That's not silly at all, it's just wanting to stay under a duvet on the very day you will probably be reunited with Taliesin that sounds silly.'

The duvet moved around a bit.

'I need to pee.'

'I'm not stopping you, off you go.'

A tousle-haired Molly emerged, pale and looking exhausted, with huge dark shadows bruising the skin beneath her eyes.

'You look awful,' Harry said unsympathetically.

'Piss off!' Molly spat as she pushed back the duvet and dashed to the bathroom.

'Better now?' he enquired innocently as she emerged from the bathroom and hopped back into bed. She glowered at him for a moment, then let out a great tremulous sigh.

'I can't believe today's finally arrived. I thought if I just stayed in bed I might wake up and discover it's all been a dream.'

Then, to Harry's consternation, she burst into floods of tears, great wracking sobs, her shoulders heaving and her body shaking uncontrollably. He wrapped his arms around her and rocked her back and forth, stroking her hair and making soothing sounds as though he was calming a small child, his denim shirt becoming soaked in tears in the process. He reached over to the bedside table and grabbed a box of tissues, offering them to Molly as she spluttered and snorted, trying to wipe the snot pouring from her nose with her hands. She pulled some tissues out of the box, gratefully blowing her nose and dabbing at her eyes.

'I bet I look even more awful now,' she gulped tearfully. 'You know, Harry, I don't think I can do this.'

'Yes, you can.' Harry was gentle but firm. 'You can and you must. There's no one else, only you.'

'What if I can't stop it? What if Lord Nudd tells his dragons to burn us all to a crisp and I can't stop him?'

'Well, as I recall, Ceriddwen told us you can communicate with dragons, and they will do whatever you tell them. You're supposed to be a dragon queen and you're the one who calmed a sea dragon, the most fearsome dragon there is!'

Harry tried to sound confident — he didn't want Molly to guess he was absolutely terrified at the thought of being anywhere near a real live, fire-breathing dragon.

'But what if I've lost that power? What if being here for forty years has cancelled out my Anunnaki blood?'

'Do you really think Ceriddwen would be risking your life, her people's lives and the whole of her world if she thought for one minute that you weren't up to this? Plus, we have the Anunnaki sonic spells, and we know they're spells of protection, so if we play the music as we're supposed to, everything should be fine.'

Harry mentally crossed his fingers behind his back as he smiled reassuringly at her, and she stared back for a few seconds, then dropped her eyes.

'I...I hadn't thought of it like that — no, you're right.' She looked up at him again, this time more resolutely. 'Ceriddwen wouldn't throw me to the wolves. She must know what I am capable of.'

'You are capable of anything, Molly, if it means being reunited with your husband and your children.' Harry smoothed her hair back from her face. 'And you have no idea how much I envy them.' He pressed his forehead against hers, then kissed her lightly on the lips. 'Now, get showered and dressed. We'll be ready for this when it comes!'

FORTY

The Mine

Taliesin and his men fought on, gradually gaining ground, pushing the goblins into the path of Jontar's troops, who were still cutting a deadly but efficient path towards the mine. The trolls seemed unperturbed by the goblin numbers, as Jontar had kept his word, sending thousands of troops who just kept streaming through the slag heaps.

Taliesin rushed to defend a warrior frantically trying to disentangle herself from her stirrups as her flailing horse, mortally wounded by a goblin pike, collapsed on its side. The goblin was about to swing the pike at her when he was momentarily distracted by the ringing cries of 'Fianna! Fianna!' accompanied by the thunder of hundreds of hooves galloping across the plain. Taliesin's messenger had made it through the battlefield to Ceriddwen — King Ossian's troops had arrived in the nick of time, followed by Lord Dubh's men mounted on their shaggy, feisty little ponies, sweeping through the enemy soldiers, spearing them without mercy before the goblins realised what was happening. Ossian's troops swiftly aligned themselves with the Morrigan, and Lord Dubh's men joined Lord Pan and Queen Andraste on the western flank.

The horse-killing goblin's hesitation was his undoing as Taliesin detached his head from his shoulders in one mighty blow. The fairy warrior patted her faithful mount's neck for one last time before swinging up onto a riderless horse, saluting Taliesin in gratitude. Taliesin spat contemptuously on the goblin's body, gathering his warm jacket of hatred closer around himself, and urged Storm back into the fray. Across the battlefield he could see the fiercely disciplined trolls were now throwing goblin bodies out of the way as they fought through them; well-schooled in battle tactics, they understood that if they were to gain the upper hand in the mine, their way couldn't be blocked by dead bodies. Heaps of both dead and injured trolls and goblins began to pile up — those on the battlefield were left where they fell, but the entrance to the mine and access to the portal had to be kept clear at all costs.

Taliesin had been trying to keep a tally of how many of his mounted troops were lost, a difficult task in the heat of battle, when everyone was fighting and concentrating on staying alive, but he had a good idea that most of them were still fighting on, although many had fallen. Surprisingly for such a skilled warrior, Taliesin hated war — he was a supreme fighting machine, the best in the land and at the height of his powers, but it sickened him. He knew it was a necessary evil to prevent Lord Nudd and his goblin ancestors before him causing the destruction of their world and, as such, believed every fairy, man or woman who had the ability to be a warrior should dedicate their lives to the protection and survival of their world without exception. It was the way of the Tuatha de Danaan, and it had served them well for thousands of years. They would prevail, they would defeat Nudd. There was no alternative, and this is what kept these warriors fighting. Nothing else mattered to Taliesin, apart from Molly and his children.

A great swelling cheer went up as the trolls finally broke through the goblin defences. Taliesin was heading Storm towards the mine just as another messenger pulled his lathered horse up beside him.

'M...my L...Lord,' he panted, bowing to Taliesin, his horse's heaving flanks steaming in the bitingly cold air. Taliesin nodded in return.

'Out with it man!' he said gruffly. He was bone weary and in no mood for stuttering, incoherent messengers.

'The...the Queen says to tell you Lord Varik has broken through from the Cailleach's side of the mine.'

Taliesin's eyes gleamed, weariness forgotten. 'Excellent! Tell Her Majesty the mine entrance has been breached and we are about to enter.' The messenger saluted and headed back across the battlefield to the waiting Queen and Taliesin galloped across to the troll commander, a huge man with a scarred face and a flattened nose, seemingly unconcerned by blood oozing from a cut above his left eye. He bowed respectfully to Taliesin.

'Commander Vix at your service. How are we going to work this, my Lord?'

Taliesin gave Commander Vix a quick nod of acknowledgement, warrior to warrior.

'Do we have any idea how many goblins are in the mine?'

The commander jutted his chin towards several emaciated figures shivering in the shelter of one of the huge sheds. At Taliesin's raised eyebrow, he quickly explained.

'Slave miners. They were dragged out to help the goblins load that accursed dragon back into its cage. They don't look strong enough to lift a spoon, never mind anything else!'

'And?'

Commander Vix chewed his lip, sensing Taliesin's impatience. 'The goblins were in such a hurry to get those cages into the mine, that once the dragon was loaded and this lot collapsed on the ground exhausted, they just left them where they lay, really stupid, if you ask me.'

'I'm asking you how many goblins are in the mine!' growled Taliesin, patience hanging by a thread.

'Yes, I'm sorry, my Lord. We questioned them, of course — the goblins sent most of the troops in the mine back to defend the entrance. The only people down there are the rest of the slaves, Nudd himself and about eight hundred troops, including those who pulled the cages.'

Taliesin lifted his helmet off his head, rubbing his eyes and forehead. 'Queen Ceriddwen has just sent word that Lord Varik has broken through from the Lady Velecia's side of the mine.'

The troll commander's mouth tightened at the mention of the Cailleach. 'A very great lady and badly done by,' he murmured. 'But I'll deny I ever said that if you repeat it.'

'You'll get no arguments from me,' Taliesin replied tersely. 'A brave woman indeed, but we don't have time to engage in polite conversation about the Cailleach, do we, Commander?'

'No, indeed!' The troll inclined his head in agreement.

'The veil is thinning, Commander, I am sure you can feel it, too.' Taliesin gave Vix a searching look. 'I take it you understand what that means?'

The troll commander looked affronted. 'What inhabitant of this world doesn't, my Lord?'

'Exactly!' Taliesin gave him a look of approval. 'Every portal becomes vulnerable for the next twenty-four hours, and this new portal is the most vulnerable of all. The future of our world depends on what we do next, Commander — we must not fail!'

'We await your orders, my Lord.'

'Lord Varik has plenty of troops, so all going well, we should be able to trap Nudd and his men between our troops and his.'

'And the dragons?' Vix demurred. 'We have already seen what one is capable of — I lost many men, if you remember.'

'How could I forget!' snapped Taliesin. 'Commander, you know as well as I that this is a fight to the death. If we lose this struggle, we lose our world. We shall have to face the dragons head on whether we wish to or not. Do I make myself clear?' Vix nodded unhappily. 'Good!' Taliesin massaged the bridge of his nose before replacing his helmet. 'Prepare to enter the mine.'

The commander saluted, pulled down his visor and swung back to his waiting men. Taliesin surveyed the battlefield, littered with dead and wounded; agonised screams and cries for help were almost drowned out by the thud of weapons on shields, the clashing of swords and the whinnying and snorting of horses. The Morrigan's troops had routed the goblins on the southern flank; they were retreating in their droves, hotly pursued by Ossian's men, while Lord Pan and Lord Dubh's troops were engaged in mopping up the centre.

Taliesin ordered the warrior nearest him to round up his men — Taliesin had his own band of elite warriors, and they lost no time in making their way to his side. They were exhausted, having suffered quite a few losses, although not as many as Taliesin feared. The men and women gathered around him, sweating and panting, many bleeding from superficial wounds, awaiting their orders.

'Lord Varik has broken through from the Cailleach's side, and the trolls have cleared the entrance to the mine. Our job is to get into that mine and stop Nudd from accessing the portal.' Taliesin paused for breath, noticing a large gash on Storm's shoulder. Quickly refocusing, he continued: 'Together with the trolls, we outnumber Nudd's forces, but he has three dragons in there. I'm not forcing any of you to come — I will understand if you do not wish to face fire-breathing dragons, so if you're not coming, please return to the battle because we cannot delay any longer.'

Not a single warrior moved a muscle to leave; instead, they raised their swords in the air, defiantly shouting, 'Danaan! Danaan!' at the top of their voices. Taliesin could feel tears pricking his eyes. Dipping his head brusquely in acknowledgment, he wheeled Storm around and led them swiftly across the churned-up ground to the trolls kicking their heels impatiently by the mine. The huge entrance to the mine was chiselled out of the living rock, and the cavernous interior yawned in front of them, lit by torches, the floor littered with detritus and piles of spoil yet to be taken to the slag heaps outside. It was shored up at regular intervals by huge wooden mine props and cross bars, and the air was rank with the unmistakable and peculiar, sweet rancid smell of dragons. Taliesin knew it was pointless trying to persuade their mounts into the mine once they caught the dragon scent, so they reluctantly left them in an enclosure next to one already containing several goblin mounts, including Nudd's huge blue roan stallion, who pawed the ground and snorted aggressively at the newcomers. He looked guiltily at the wound on Storm's shoulder, but as time was of the essence, it would have to wait.

After a short while, everyone was beginning to feel slightly deprived of oxygen as the atmosphere began to thin, a sure sign that the newly discovered portal would soon open spontaneously — the other portals were guarded by shields only accessible by the palm prints of a trusted few — but until this portal was secured, it was open to anyone. The fairies and trolls would gradually get used to the oxygen deficiency and after twenty-four hours, the atmosphere would return to normal. It would be twenty-four hours of terrible danger if they didn't reach Nudd in time.

A Dynasty of Dragons

Despite weariness and a shortage of oxygen, the army of warriors started to jog down the seemingly endless tunnel, eyes everywhere, checking out ventilation shafts and escape routes, ignoring the emaciated and terrified slaves who shrank against the walls as the fairy and troll forces streamed past them. Astonishingly, several of the braver slaves thrust pitchers of water at them as they passed by and the thirsty troops drank gratefully, passing the pitchers along the lines as they went.

They jogged on, following the pungent dragon odour. Taliesin was having difficulty second-guessing Nudd. He had the dragons, and eight hundred men, but in the confined space of the tunnel, his troops were just as much at risk from the dragons as Taliesin's. What was he planning to do? These thoughts tormented him until he was alerted by the return of his scouts — Nudd was about half a mile away fighting Lord Varik's troops, and the end of the tunnel, which opened into a huge natural cavern, had been blocked by rubble. Taliesin took a long drink from one of the slave pitchers and offered it to the scout who drank gratefully.

'Did you see anything that could facilitate a portal?' he asked. The scout nodded and took another gulp of water.

'There's an area of quartz on the right-hand wall, just a few feet beyond the section breached by Lord Varik. The goblins seem to be doing everything in their power to keep Lord Varik away from that wall — they've got the dragons facing it, too. Looks like that quartz wall is our portal.'

'You got that close without being seen?' Taliesin clapped the man on the shoulder. 'Scatha trained you well!'

'Sounds like the portal all right.' Commander Vix wiped sweat and blood from his face with a little water from one of the pitchers. 'Let's get moving and help Lord Varik out.'

Taliesin called the company to attention. 'Our sole purpose is to prevent Nudd getting through that portal, no matter the cost. Now, let's finish this, dragons or no dragons!'

Raising his sword in the air, he roared 'Danaan! Danaan!' and charged down the tunnel, the battle cries of the others ringing in his ears.

FORTY-ONE

Metamorphosis

Molly switched off the hairdryer and stared at her reflection in the dressing table mirror, Harry's talk of being reunited with Taliesin replaying constantly in her head. Would Taliesin even recognise her? Would her age repel him? Molly's sixty-year-old face stared wearily back at her. The glorious russet hair of her youth had faded to strawberry blonde, and with Fred insisting long hair looked ridiculous on anyone over thirty (to Laura's utter disgust), she had worn a no-nonsense, shoulder-length bob for years, just long enough for an elegant chignon when required. Lately, she had taken to wearing her hair up in a sort of messy topknot. As her brow became increasingly lined, she had decided to opt for a more flattering fringe. The skin around her eyes was quite wrinkled, and her jawline beginning to sag — Taliesin's young and vibrant Molly long gone. If only she'd listened to Fred! Every time they were in Debenhams or House of Fraser, he always tried to steer her towards the beauty counters, trying to persuade her to buy expensive Lancome or Estee Lauder face creams. But she pretended she preferred cheap-as-chips Nivea.

Truth be told, she found the immaculately made-up beauty consultants patronising and intimidating. Fred's dire warnings were right, though — she had turned into a prune.

Sighing, she unplugged the hairdryer and began to get dressed, pulling on a pair of joggers and a thick, hooded sweatshirt. Resisting the urge to dive beneath the duvet again, she resolutely made her way downstairs, thrust her feet into a pair of trainers, shrugged on a padded jacket, and wandered outside to join the others. She was beginning to feel guilty about her earlier tantrum. These three people — Laura, her best friend, Harry, the man she had ruthlessly cut out of her life forty years ago, and Xander, the baby boy she had abandoned with equally ruthless yet heart-breaking determination, were prepared to place themselves in great danger for the greater good of protecting a world they didn't know existed until a few weeks ago. She should be humble and grateful for their support instead of behaving like a spoiled brat.

Molly wondered when Xander would start playing his harp. She hated to admit it, but she found the beautiful music rather disturbing — it triggered unpleasant memories, but she certainly didn't want to say that to Harry and Xander who had made it clear that the musical spells were the only thing protecting them. Molly wasn't entirely convinced. She had a horrible feeling the sonic spells were being put in place to keep the outside world unaware of any goblin invasion for as long as possible, and nothing to do with protecting her. She suppressed a shiver of anxiety, her mind in turmoil. *I mean*, she thought irritably, *what on earth are the three of us supposed to do against the goblins if they arrive before Ceriddwen? Am I supposed to turn into a dragon and eat them?*

She quickly disabused herself of that notion and decided to give the garden a quick morning check. All was quiet and peaceful — it was a dull day, promising rain, and the air was saturated with moisture, prompting Harry and Xander to rescue her portable gazebo from the garage where it had languished since Fred's death. He had loved throwing garden parties every summer, especially for the gardening club, where they all laughed and brayed loudly about their dahlias and tomato plants whilst eating and drinking Molly out of house and home. Fred was a natural bon viveur and show off, completely in his element, holding court, master of all he surveyed. Molly was relieved neither Dolores nor any of the others had suggested she maintain the tradition.

Most of the plants had finished flowering with only a few providing a last valiant show of defiance as they waited for the first frosts to finally see them off. Molly squelched across the sodden grass to have a look at the gazebo. Laura discovered four portable garden seats in the shed, setting them around an old card table she found at the back of the garage. At least if it decided to rain, they would be nice and dry.

Xander was sitting tuning his harp. He had spent a lot of time studying the Anunnaki parchments, going over every word and musical note, line by line, finally understanding their purpose — spells of protection designed to cast a protective shield around Anunnaki royalty, with particular emphasis on shapeshifting events. He had voiced his suspicions about this to Harry on the way back from visiting Gwynnie and Morven; Molly and Laura were kept in the dark, the implications simply too shocking, and thus Xander very wisely decided to follow the parchment instructions and let the day unfold at its own pace.

It would take about an hour for the musical interlude to weave its magic around the house and garden, after which they would all have to stay calm and keep a sharp eye out for anything untoward that might happen throughout the day. Molly couldn't help feeling even more guilty at the prospect of Harry and Xander sitting outside all that time, but they had insisted; the vicinity of the sinkhole must be constantly guarded. Laura was already on top of it, providing them with hot water bottles and determined to do her bit by keeping them fortified with hot drinks and food. No one really knew when the portal would open, they simply had to stay alert, hope the sonic spells worked, and be ready to deal with whatever might happen. The whole scenario had a surreal, almost ridiculous quality about it, and Molly kept thinking she was going to burst into hysterical laughter. What on earth would Fred have made of all this?

Despite her misgivings about the sonic spells, they sat entranced while Xander plucked the haunting music from his harp, and minute by minute, a wonderful sense of peace began to wrap itself around the house and garden, the notes dancing amongst the branches of trees like delicate little hummingbirds and flitting across the still-flowering plants like beautiful butterflies, filling the rain-threatening sky with a sense of warm sunlight, even though it was such a dull, grey day, creating a haven of peace and tranquillity. It was all an illusion, of course, fairy magic at its best and a wondrous thing to behold, but as the day wore on, Molly began to detect a liminal feeling to the atmosphere. The others appeared not to notice, but she knew the air had a thinner quality to it — the branches of trees and plant stems, some of them festooned in beautiful, moisture spangled spider webs, shimmered in the fading late afternoon light. Crows began calling raucously from their plum tree roost in Mr Morrison's ancient orchard as though they, too, sensed the change. Molly glanced through the trees to the hazy hills beyond, the view rippling like a gently disturbed pond.

In all other respects, despite being inside their magical bubble, it had been a day like any other. Alan, the postman, sauntering along the avenue, whistling tunelessly as usual, people walking their dogs, Sainsbury and Tesco Home Delivery vans stopping outside houses, and later in the afternoon, excited school children dressed as mini witches and vampires skipped home from the village school Hallowe'en party. Molly had tried to keep busy, pottering around the garden, and was now about to check the bird feeders. As she made her way around the pond to the rowan tree, she paused as though something had caught the corner of her eye.

Harry, who had been watching as she approached the tree, saw her hesitate and make a half-turn, as though to look at something, before abruptly vanishing. Just as he was about to call the others, Molly re-materialised just as abruptly. As she turned to look at them, Harry noticed something odd about her eyes.

'We must help them,' she muttered vaguely, casting her strange eyes around the garden.

'Help who, Molly?' Harry probed gently, trying not to stare at her now decidedly reptilian eyes.

'My dragons — they're so sick and weak. We must help them.' She was becoming more and more agitated. 'They're all fighting — it's awful!'

'Who's fighting?' Harry was becoming increasingly worried. 'The dragons?'

'No...No! Varik's in there and...and I saw Lord Nudd!' Her voice was shrill now, and to Harry's horror, nictitating membranes kept flicking across her eyes. 'My dragons...I must help my dragons...so much screaming and fighting! Hurry...help me!' She was becoming more and more incoherent, clutching at Harry in her distress.

He turned and called urgently to Xander, still sitting doggedly, plucking his harp. 'The portal's open, Molly's been through!'

Before Xander could answer, Molly gabbled hysterically, 'Water...water...they need water...We need buckets, like that one...' pointing frantically to an enamel pail holding a bedraggled mop by the kitchen door, 'and I think there's another two in the garden shed.'

Laura, who was standing open-mouthed by the door, quickly dumped the mop then ran across the grass and handed the bucket to Molly, who promptly dashed to the pond and filled it with water, shouting at Harry to hurry up with the other two. Harry, heart thumping, quickly retrieved them and joined her.

'What are you going to do?' he asked fearfully, still trying not to stare at Molly's disconcerting reptilian eyes.

'You mean what are *we* going to do?' she cried, indicating he should fill the other two buckets. Then she called over to Laura, who had retreated to Xander's side, 'You two as well! Grab those buckets, we must go through, now!'

Xander, Harry and Laura, apprehensively clutching their water-filled buckets, followed Molly into the unknown and found themselves witnessing a scene of utter chaos. Having only ever witnessed pretend hand-to-hand combat in films, the horror of the real-life screaming and fighting was almost too much for them; unfortunately, they had no alternative but to trust Molly's instincts and do as she asked.

The time difference between dimensions meant Molly was in the portal cavern for much longer than a few seconds, giving her time to absorb what was going on. When she first came through, it took a few moments for her senses to process the enormity of the scene before her. The noise, the smell, and the suffocating heat were almost overwhelming. She was in a huge, natural cavern, lit by flaming torches, with tunnels leading off in several directions. The torches were also the source of the overpowering heat, and Molly could see terrified people creeping along the walls, frantically replenishing torches about to burn out, trying to avoid being injured by the crowds of fighting soldiers, or coming too close to the dragons. As she looked in dismay at the three dragons trapped inside the cramped cages in front of her, something caught her eye on the other side of the cavern. Although she hadn't seen him for years, she recognised

Gwynn Ap Nudd immediately; she would know that flowing mane of red hair and those broad shoulders anywhere. He was screaming encouragement at his men and lunging towards another warrior. As Molly glanced beyond him, she saw, in a single heart-stopping moment, the equally unmistakable figure of Lord Varik, roaring and swinging his battle-axe like a huge Viking warrior. If Varik was here, surely Taliesin must be too, battling it out somewhere amid this frenzy.

The three dragons had set up an incessant roaring and crying. These normally shy and retiring animals were traumatised to the point of madness, the smallest of them groaning in agony from its burns, desperate for water. The goblins were determined to keep the fairies away from the portal wall, focusing all their attention on what was in front of them, ignoring the dragons behind. Only the dragons noticed Molly materialising through the glittering quartz wall, watching her carefully, as her shocked eyes took in the carnage before her. Breathing hard, she looked again at the dragons, and unbidden, her long-forgotten Anunnaki power began surging through her body with such ferocity that she stumbled backwards and found herself once more standing in her garden.

Back with precious water, Molly, now thinking and speaking in Anunnaki, crooned soothingly to the dragons as she approached. Ceriddwen was right, the dragons were instantly reassured by Molly's presence. Their emaciated condition both horrified and further infuriated her — their eyes were sunken and dull, their wide, flaring nostrils, usually bright red, were pale and shrivelled through dehydration and ill-treatment. She took in the condition of their scales, normally the colour of oak leaves with their leathery wings a shade lighter and rimmed in red, matching their nostrils and the rings around their eyes. Not so these unfortunate creatures. Their skin and scales were pale and diseased-looking, with weeping sores where heavy chains had bitten cruelly into their flesh. Biting down her fury, she offered water to the dragon with the burned throat — it thrust its head into the bucket, sucking it up in deep, shuddering draughts.

The others, almost paralysed by fear at the sight of the dragons on top of everything else, stood rooted to the spot, close to dropping the buckets of water in sheer terror.

'Give them the water!' Molly hissed. 'They won't harm you — they know you're with me and we're helping them. Xander, unbolt the cages!'

She quickly scanned the ferociously fighting warriors; she couldn't see Lord Nudd or Varik among the seething mass of bodies and no sign of Taliesin, either. She didn't want to think about seeing Taliesin or what could happen to him and Varik — she had to concentrate on the task at hand and thankfully no one appeared to notice their furtive presence behind the dragon cages. The other dragons, already calmed by Molly's presence, wove their necks to and fro, bobbing their heads submissively, desperate for water, ignoring Xander's terrified fumbling with the huge bolts as he struggled to open them. As Molly's rage intensified at the appalling cruelty, she tried to fight what was happening to her body, taking deep breaths to try and calm herself and stop her heart racing as intense pain seared through her muscles and joints, her skin beginning to feel unnaturally tight and stretched. Staggering in pain and shock, she grabbed hold of Laura, who was backing away from the dragons with a now empty bucket.

'Help me!' she cried, as Laura stared in horrified fascination at Molly's eyes and the profusion of green scales spreading from behind her ears and down her neck. 'I need to take my clothes off, hurry, please!'

'Wha....at?' Laura felt as though she was about to lose it — the horror of people fighting and killing each other a few yards from them, her terror at being in such proximity to real live dragons, and now Molly wanted to take her clothes off? She had an overwhelming urge to scream with laughter.

Fortunately, Harry, realising something was seriously wrong with Molly, dropped his bucket and started to pull her sweatshirt over her head, snapping at Laura. 'Get a grip, Laura! Help her take off her trousers!'

'Don't you think we should take her back through the portal?' Laura shot back, Harry's rebuke jolting her back to reality.

'Yes...yes...good idea.' Harry nodded as he ceased trying to wrestle the sweatshirt over Molly's strangely enlarged head.

'Molly, we're going back through, it's too dangerous to do this here. Someone could see us at any minute. Are you finished, Xander?' he called anxiously.

'Yes, that's it done,' panted Xander breathlessly, having just wrenched open the final bolt. 'Let's go!'

'Hurry, I need to take them off...' Molly clamoured, obviously in great distress.

'Quickly Laura, grab her legs,' Harry urged as he grasped Molly under both arms and stepped smartly backwards, and instantly they were back in the peace and quiet of the garden. Harry pulled the sweatshirt over Molly's head as Laura removed her jogging trousers. Molly grasped hold of Harry's hand.

'I have to be naked, no underwear.'

'Okay, Molly, okay,' he murmured. 'We'll go and let Laura help you now.' He patted her hand, trying not to stare at the strange, alien changes to her body, and nodded to Laura. 'We'll leave you to it.'

'Go away, all of you!' whimpered Molly as soon as Laura had relieved her of her bra and pants. 'Go into the house, I don't want you here, I have to be on my own.'

'But, Molly, we're worried about you, you're obviously in a lot of pain, and...'

'Go away!' This came out in a guttural scream, causing an ashen faced Laura to flee into the house, wisely followed by Harry and Xander.

If Molly's metamorphosis was difficult for her, it could be argued it was even more difficult for the others, especially Laura. At least Harry and Xander had been through a portal before, although had never witnessed the horror of real warfare or real live dragons. For Laura, though, what had been merely an abstract concept, was now a horrifying reality. Yes, she'd gone through what she thought was a portal where she met Jimmy Thomson and solved the mystery of the Australian wildlife; she had somehow managed to rationalise this in her head, convincing herself it was all part of her *New Age* beliefs and nothing to do with fairies and goblins. Why did she think like that? Because she had physically met Jimmy Thomson, had really travelled to Australia, and part of her believed that when the Australian episode was over, that was it — a temporary aberration in the natural laws of physics repaired by Jimmy's Ngangkari skills. Job done.

If she was honest with herself, she thought the rest of it was an elaborate game, a figment of Molly's vivid imagination, illustrated in stunning detail by the wonderful paintings in the attic. Laura was blinded by her obsessive desire to reunite Harry and Molly, the star-crossed lovers of her own imagination. She had never met any of Molly's Sidhthean family, and even although Harry and Xander said they had gone through another portal and met Ceriddwen, part of her was still in denial — pretending this was still just a game they were all playing. Who can fathom the human brain's capacity for self-deception? Now, having been dragged through the portal and witnessed the horrors therein, the normally confident and assertive Laura sat on Molly's sofa in deep shock.

Meanwhile, in the garden, shielded by the branches of two protective lilac trees, Molly writhed in agony as her body went through its first ever complete shapeshift. Her pain during Alaria's birth was nothing compared to this. She felt as though she was being tortured on some hideous invisible medieval rack — her joints being wrenched out of their sockets and her limbs being pulled into impossible shapes by horrible red-hot pincers. The agony seemed to go on and on until finally, she lay panting and exhausted on the grass beneath a pearlescent moon, its beams shining softly between the scudding clouds in the now dark October skies.

Xander and Harry stood by the kitchen window, peering into the pale moonlit garden. 'I wonder,' mused Harry tentatively after about ten minutes, 'if we should go outside and check on Molly?'

'I don't know if that's a good idea under the circumstances,' Xander replied rather grimly, so grimly, in fact, that it roused Laura out of her stupor.

'Wha...what do you mean by under the circumstances?' she asked.

Harry tried to control his irritation. 'Laura, why do you think she wanted her clothes removed? You saw her eyes? The shape of her head? The scales?'

'I...I don't really want to think about it.' Laura was now shivering in fear.

'Well, force yourself!' Harry shot back at her. 'She's shape-shifting into a dragon!'

'How come you're so sure about that?' Laura eyed the two men suspiciously.

'Because it says so in the parchments — that's why Xander had to play the sonic spells. They weren't just about keeping prying eyes away!'

The words were no sooner out of Harry's mouth when a deafening roar shook the house. Through the window, they watched an enormous shape rear up from behind the screen of lilac branches — a huge dragon, twice the size of the unfortunate dragons in the cavern. They could see a horned head on a long powerful neck, twisting this way and that, as though looking for something, as it flapped massive leathery wings. The moonlight silvered a ruff of spikes across the massive shoulders.

'Oh, Molly, what has happened to you?' Harry murmured, more to himself than anyone else.

'Wh…what do you think it…I mean she…means to do?' quavered Laura, clutching at Harry's arm.

'Go through the portal, of course!'

'To fight the goblins?'

'I really don't know, Laura,' Harry said flatly, shaking his head. 'I don't know if she's retained any of her human personality, or if she is a completely different creature in all ways. I think her main purpose will be to rescue those dragons, and that could be the catalyst for attacking the goblins.'

'What about the fairies? Do you think she'll know the difference?' Laura wondered, trying to stop her teeth from chattering.

'Again, who knows? What we do know is as soon as she went through the portal, she changed, and all she wanted to do was help those dragons. She never mentioned Taliesin at all.'

'Yes, I did notice that,' Laura agreed. 'I thought she would have been desperate to know if Taliesin was there.'

'Well,' said Harry, with a determined thrust of his chin, 'we'll just have to follow her through and see what happens. Are we all agreed?'

'I'm not going back through!' Laura screeched, her voice shrill with fear. 'We could be killed or trapped there — what if the portal closes again?'

'Well, I have to go back!' Harry retorted harshly. 'We promised Ceriddwen that we would keep Molly safe — you stay here if you wish.'

'That dragon doesn't look as though it needs keeping safe from anyone!' Laura snapped.

Xander lifted his hand in a soothing, placatory manner. 'No, it's okay, Laura, Dad didn't mean you.' He shot a warning look at Harry. 'We need someone to stay here and look after things this end just in case something happens and we're held up a bit.'

'You mean in case you both get killed!' By now, Laura was on the verge of hysterics. 'You're going to blindly follow that... that thing Molly has become without knowing anything about it...her...whatever?'

'She's become a dragon, Laura, not a thing!' Harry snapped irritably. Their collective nerves were becoming visibly shredded.

Ignoring Harry and hugging herself for comfort, Laura peered nervously through the window at the huge creature in the garden, now hunkered down behind the lilac branches, head up, as though scenting the air.

'I don't think I've ever felt this afraid or helpless in my life,' she muttered, half to herself.

'We don't know what will happen, or what's happening just now, but no matter what, we'll be there for Molly.' Xander sounded more confident than he felt. He wasn't at all sure if Dragon Molly would regard them in a friendly manner, or even be able to tell them apart from the goblins and fairies. They were just going to have to trust everything to fate.

'How long will the musical spells last?' Laura had retreated once more to the safety of the sofa and sat nervously hugging a cushion for comfort.

'I'm hoping a full twenty-four hours, but to be honest, I don't really know,' admitted Xander.

'All the more reason why we should go and see what Molly's up to.' Harry, having decided on a course of action, shrugged on his parka and headed for the kitchen door. Xander grabbed his Aran sweater and followed him.

'You won't need warm clothes once you're back in that cavern...' Laura called after them.

Laura's voice carried into the garden, disturbing the stillness and alerting Molly. The horned head, still up scenting the air, turned towards the sound, snaking its long neck across the screen of branches to stop directly in front of Harry and Xander, nostrils flaring, huge reptilian eyes fixing them in unblinking, terrifying scrutiny. Both men stood rooted to the spot, illuminated by the kitchen door security light, hardly daring to breathe, until Harry plucked up the courage to say as gently as possible, 'It's only us, Molly, we mean you no harm.'

The great horned head tilted one way and then the other, as though deciding what to do, then a deep, soft rumble came from somewhere at the base of the very long neck until finally, the huge eyes blinked at them, perhaps in recognition; they had no way of knowing. The great head lifted, and as the long neck turned, the screen of branches sprang back to their normal position, the light from the door casting an eerie tree shadow towards the portal entrance.

Now revealed in all her terrible magnificence, silhouetted against the moonlit sky, Molly flapped her huge wings once more, giving voice to another terrifying roar before springing forward and disappearing through the portal. Jolted out of their horrified stupor, Harry and Xander hurried across to the sinkhole, stopping just short of the portal entrance.

'Are you absolutely sure about this?' Harry placed his hand on Xander's arm. 'It could all end very badly.'

'You've changed your tune.' Xander regarded his father thoughtfully. 'When I suggested that to you before, you almost ridiculed me, if you remember.'

'I hadn't really thought it through at that stage. It was all very dreamlike and surreal — still feels that way, to be honest.'

'Look, Dad, I've already told you if we survive this, I want to live there, my future isn't here, it's with Ceriddwen and...' he stumbled over his next words as though he was afraid to say them out loud, 'and with Molly...my...my mother.'

'I know...I know...look, ignore me. I'm really, bloody terrified! I suppose I'm looking for an excuse not to do this.'

'Dad, if anyone else could hear us talking, they'd be sending for the men in white coats! It IS terrifying and I'm as scared as you, but I guess we've wasted enough time prevaricating, so let's just do it, okay?'

Harry took a deep breath and giving Xander a quick nod, both men stepped forward into the unknown.

FORTY-TWO
The Dragon Queen

Taliesin's troops jogged resolutely down the tunnel, their first task being to unblock the passage opening into the large cavern. The goblins had forced their slaves to fill it with huge rocks, causing Taliesin and his men to waste precious time and energy clearing this barricade. Already exhausted from fighting all day, the troops were almost overwhelmed by the shortage of oxygen and the fetid, overpowering stench of dragon, but when they finally broke through, the sight of Varik and his men powering into the goblins gave them the encouragement they needed, and they threw themselves once more into battle.

Taliesin paused for a moment to catch his breath, panting as he blinked the sweat from his eyes, trying to get a sense of the goblin's latest plan of action. Sandwiched between Taliesin and Varik's men, they seemed to be deliberately compressing their shield wall on both sides, leaving the centre clear.

'What are they doing?' Taliesin muttered to himself. He wondered for a moment if this was a futile effort to protect the dragons, but why? Nudd must surely know he was beaten — there was no way he was going to fight his way out of this, especially with Varik's superior numbers and fresher men.

The thought had barely crossed his mind when a movement on a slight incline to the left-hand side of the cavern caught his eye. To his utter dismay, goblin troops were pouring down an escape shaft into the space created by the compressed shield walls. He cursed loudly at his stupidity in not sending someone to check the escape routes earlier. Too late now. As the goblins streamed into the cavern, Lord Nudd was ushering men towards the dragon cages, several of them carrying bins containing what Taliesin supposed were the fire minerals they intended force-feeding the dragons.

He turned, barking at an exhausted warrior by his side, 'Go! Run as fast as you can, find a horse and tell the Queen we must have fresh troops, now!' The man saluted and stumbled back through the tunnel as fast as his weary legs would carry him, the defiant war cries of the goblins ringing in his ears.

The goblins began to advance once more on Taliesin and Varik, emboldened by their influx of fresh men as the fairy forces quickly reformed their own shield walls making ready for yet another round of gruesome hacking, stabbing, and slashing as each side tried to overpower the other. Taliesin's men had been fighting all day and were nearing exhaustion, but still fought fiercely, the future of their world driving them on. After another bout of bloody and exhausting combat, Commander Vix turned to look at Taliesin in surprise as the goblin shield wall began to falter, despite their initial ferocious push back.

'Something's happening, my Lord,' he panted, nodding in the direction of the dragon cages. Sure enough, the men carrying the fire minerals were backing away from the cages, ignoring Nudd's apoplectic fury, and the reason soon became obvious. 'The line's breaking!' Vix yelled, as the goblins began to mill about in confusion.

'Stand your ground! Stand your ground!' roared Taliesin as his men moved to take advantage of the gaps in the shield wall. He had to make sure this wasn't a goblin trick — pretending to run away, then regrouping for attack. He peered through a gap in the fighting, his blood freezing in his veins.

When Molly told Xander to unbolt the dragon cages, she knew what she was doing. The sight of the goblins advancing on them with their chains and fire minerals terrified the dragons so much that they began to thrash about their cages in panic, causing the unlocked doors to swing open, allowing them to scramble out. They were now roaring in fear, frantically exercising their cramped wings to try and fly out of danger. Even in their weakened state, three unfettered dragons were a terrifying sight and many of the goblins were caught in panicked indecision — risk being killed by the fairy forces or die in a dragon's jaws.

The thought of his carefully laid plans going awry, further enraged the goblin king who was screaming, red-faced with fury, at his men, cracking a massive bullwhip as he tried to drive the dragons towards the portal. The dragon handlers fled into the midst of the fighting and were promptly set upon by several of Varik's men swarming through the broken shield wall. The fresh goblin warriors, initially fighting fiercely, began to falter as it became apparent that Nudd had completely lost control of the three dragons, who were now lunging, huge jaws snapping at anyone foolish enough to come too close. Without the massive chains and powerful goblin warriors to restrain them, they were set to rampage into the midst of the battle.

As Taliesin fought to control his fear of these huge beasts, he gasped in horror as the largest and strongest of them managed to launch itself into the air, swooping across the men, its honey-coloured underbelly brushing the tops of their helmets as it flew in a circle fruitlessly seeking an escape route before clumsily flapping back to the others, exhausted by the effort.

Nudd's commanders were trying in vain to rally their troops back into a defensive position as Varik pushed forward mercilessly. Nudd had lost many men, but showed no signs of admitting defeat, kicking, whilst screaming orders at the men nearest him, exhorting them to try and overpower the dragons. Again and again, they approached the beasts, but were forced back by snapping jaws and powerful claws.

'We need the nets, Lord,' gasped one of the men. 'We should have brought the nets!'

This oversight only further enraged Nudd, who was about to hurl a battle-axe at the unfortunate man, when the largest and most terrifying dragon he had ever seen in his life suddenly materialised through the quartz wall. Twice the size of the other dragons, it stood surveying the chaos in front of it, lashing its huge tail in fury, an enormous ruff of vicious spikes standing proud across its massive shoulders as its long neck snaked this way and that, reptilian eyes glittering in the torchlight.

The soldiers in the centre of the melee fought on, too intent on trying not to be killed to notice anything but the men they were fighting. Taliesin and Vix, however, had deliberately positioned themselves near the area where they expected the portal to open, and Varik, coming from the Cailleach's side, had employed the same strategy.

'I saw a dragon queen,' Vix said, and spat out a tooth with a mouthful of blood, looking hard at Taliesin's visibly paling face. 'when we fought with the Anunnaki against the goblins many years ago before the great genocide. I recognise that as a dragon queen!' He looked pointedly at Taliesin. 'You seem unnerved, my Lord.'

Despite the clash of weapons, the cries and groans of the wounded, and the bellowing of Nudd's commanders bullying their troops back into action, a strange stillness came over Taliesin as he remembered Molly hovering between life and death as her human and Anunnaki DNAs fought to overpower each other, the scales behind her ears and Alaria's dramatic entry into the world. He stared at the mighty leviathan glaring malevolently into their midst and suppressed a shudder as he allowed himself to acknowledge the unthinkable.

'Forgive my frankness, Lord,' Vix was like a dog with a bone, 'but am I correct in assuming that the bravest warrior in all the lands is afraid of dragons?'

Taliesin began to mutter, 'I wish it was that simple…' when an urgent cry went up: 'Shield walls up! Shield walls up!' The goblins had decided to make a determined two-pronged attack on Varik & Taliesin's shield walls, taking advantage of the distraction caused by the huge dragon. Cursing himself for allowing his attention to wander, Taliesin immediately threw himself into the attack, roaring 'Danaan! Danaan!' to rally the men, all thoughts of dragons momentarily banished from his mind, until he became aware of a terrified screaming, not just agonised battle screaming, but screams of pure terror. He steeled himself to lower his shield and gasped in sheer horror — there, in the centre of the battleground, stood his worst nightmare: six enormous hideous heads filled with ferociously sharp teeth, on six long necks all darting in and out, plucking goblins, only goblins, from the fighting, shaking them as a dog shakes a rat, before throwing them against the cavern walls. The great dragon queen had shapeshifted into a mighty sea dragon and was despatching every goblin she could catch. Taliesin's head began to swim, and he could hear Vix shouting in the distance, 'Stay beneath your shields, don't look at her! Stay beneath your shields.'

Vix's previous dealings with dragon queens were standing them in good stead as he ran up and down the shield wall, telling the men what to do, signalling to Varik on the other side to do the same. Varik waved grimly in acknowledgment as all his men quickly covered themselves with their shields. Taliesin became aware of someone touching his arm.

'Lord Taliesin, hide beneath your shield!' Taliesin didn't move, the voice was louder this time, Vix now pulling on his arm. 'My Lord, do not antagonise her, come beneath the shield wall!'

Frozen in appalled fascination, Taliesin allowed himself to be unceremoniously hauled beneath the shields, and crouched, heart pounding, as the screams of the unfortunate goblins, accompanied by the roaring of the dragons, morphed into an appalling macabre and hypnotising sound reverberating in a blood-curdling cadence around the cathedral heights of the cavern.

Harry and Xander unfortunately chose this moment to come through the portal and stood rooted to the spot in shock, survival instincts screaming at them to leave immediately. But it was too late, one of the dragons, sensing their arrival, snaked its great horned head around to confront them, hissing threateningly.

'There's gratitude for you,' Harry whispered nervously. 'Obviously doesn't remember we gave it water!'

At the sound of Harry's voice, the dragon hissed even louder, opening its jaws so wide that they could see every massive tooth and fang in its mouth. Instinctively, Xander began to jabber softly in Anunnaki, and to their immense relief, this seemed to calm the beast, and with a final foul-smelling hiss, it turned away to resume roaring at the goblins.

Neither man had ever seen anything so hideous as the six-headed monster in front of them, not in real life, anyway, and fighting their fear and revulsion, now that the dragon seemed to have forgotten about them, they stealthily crawled beneath one of the cages for safety. They lay on their stomachs, watching in mounting horror as goblins tried desperately to escape from the six bloody fanged jaws intent on killing them. Unable to flee through the mine, they rushed towards the escape shaft their reinforcements had recently used, trampling over each other in their panic.

'I...I feel sick — I can't believe what I'm seeing.' Harry's face had taken on an almost grey pallor. 'Is...is that thing Molly?'

He couldn't stop trembling and was beginning to fear he might soil himself in sheer terror. The heat, the smell, the roaring and screaming, and the sickening thud of goblin bodies hitting the cavern walls was almost too much to bear. Perhaps Laura was right — they should have stayed where they were. Hindsight is a wonderful thing. He turned his head at a sudden sharp crack behind them to see Xander being pulled from beneath the cage.

'Dad! Dad!' he yelled, frantically clutching at the undercarriage as he was relentlessly dragged out. Harry managed to manoeuvre himself around to see who or what had grabbed him and saw a huge, red-haired man grimly pulling Xander towards him. He was wielding an enormous bullwhip which was tightly wrapped around Xander's leg. Two burly warriors stood beside him.

Where were the dragons? Why weren't they attacking these goblins, because the man's stature and red hair told Harry that this was none other than the goblin king, Gywnn ap Nudd himself. He steeled himself to look across the cavern and watched, dumbstruck, as Molly, if the six-headed monster was indeed Molly, followed by the three dragons, headed across the cavern to the escape shaft to pick off the remaining goblins.

Scrambling out from under the cage, Harry made to rush at Nudd, but one of the bodyguards stepped forward, pushing him in the chest and growling threateningly.

'Stay where you are! Do not attempt to approach a king without permission!'

If Harry had felt fear before, it was nothing to the icy cold fingers of terror now clutching his heart as the goblin king held a wicked looking seax to his son's throat. Despite his mouth being dry with horror, he managed to shout, 'What do you want with my son? Release him immediately!'

'Leave him!' Nudd waved away the guard who prodded Harry again with a menacing look on his face. 'He is nothing.'

The guard stepped back, and Nudd looked Harry up and down, a contemptuous sneer on his face.

'Go back to your own world, old man, what can you do here? Your father gave up his birth right and left you powerless!'

He laughed at Xander's furious and futile struggles as the other guard expertly tied his hands behind his back.

'Why am I powerless?' Harry found a reserve of courage he didn't know he possessed. 'My son and I are under the protection of Queen Ceriddwen and I'm pretty sure Lord Taliesin is out there under one of those shields.'

Nudd's face darkened in fury at the mention of Ceriddwen and Taliesin. 'A pair of cowards!' he spat. 'The proud warrior Queen skulking on her hillside and the great Lord Taliesin cowering from his own wife beneath a shield!'

'Lord Taliesin's wife will kill you when she sees you have her son!'

'Ah, you think?' A malicious smile played about Nudd's mouth. 'I disagree. Watch and learn, human, watch and learn!'

To Harry's disbelief, Nudd confidently frog-marched Xander across the cavern, hesitantly followed by his reluctant guards. He stood a little way behind the enormous dragon, ignoring the other three who turned in unison, roaring a warning to Molly.

Nudd called out, 'Dragon queen, if you value your pup's life, let me pass!'

'Nudd has Molly's son,' gasped a shocked Taliesin jumping to his feet, thrusting his shield aside.

'Molly's son?' queried Vix joining him. 'The dragon queen has a son?'

By now, many fairies had bravely emerged from beneath their shields to view this latest turn of events.

'We have a son and a daughter, but Xander is my son by marriage. He is Ceriddwen's crown prince, and Nudd knows how valuable he is, he means to use him as a bargaining tool!'

Vix stroked his chin, digesting this information. 'Hmm, he is taking a huge risk — who knows what goes on inside the mind of a dragon queen?'

'You more than most, apparently!' Taliesin snapped irritably.

In the few seconds it had taken for this conversation, apart from the groans and cries of the wounded, all else fell silent, even the three dragons ceased their roaring as six monstrous heads, fangs dripping goblin blood, turned towards Nudd and the hapless Xander.

'I am waiting, dragon, I grow impatient!' Nudd pricked Xander's throat with the seax, drawing a trickle of blood. Varik, standing a few feet behind them, growled in fury.

All six dragon heads swooped directly in front of Nudd's face, one of them placing itself directly between Xander and Nudd's ears. Xander gasped as Nudd forced the point of his knife a little deeper into his throat. The head immediately withdrew and joined the other five, hissing in fury.

'You think I won't kill him?' Nudd snarled. 'You thought nothing of killing *my* son — you think I wouldn't return the compliment?'

Vix watched the proceedings with an increasingly worried frown on his face.

'Is there something I should know, Commander Vix?' demanded Taliesin, sensing the troll was deeply troubled.

'I fear she cannot keep this up much longer. Dragon queens can only maintain a shape shift for a short time, and your wife, Lord Taliesin, has also shape shifted twice — a tremendous strain on her, I am afraid. She could revert at any moment; she has expended much energy, and now this!'

The great dragon queen seemed to hesitate, as though unsure of her next step, drawing back slightly, enabling Nudd to start inching towards the escape shaft. The largest of the three dragons made a sudden lunge at one of Nudd's bodyguards as they attempted to follow, distracting Molly, who turned her heads to look, allowing Nudd to dive into the shaft, swiftly followed by his other guard.

Harry, who had been watching in disbelief, now lost all self-control as he was engulfed in a searing surge of white-hot molten fury. He grabbed the battle-axe Nudd had discarded earlier and charged towards him. 'Old man, is it? Let my son go or I'll show you who's an old man or not!' he screamed.

'Harry, no!' roared Taliesin. 'Go back, go back!'

Molly turned at the sound of both Harry and her beloved Taliesin's voices just as one of Nudd's guards hefted his spear, and flung it straight as an arrow, hitting Harry with such force he was flung backwards and lay screaming in a pool of blood with the spear protruding at a hideous angle from his shattered left shoulder.

The effect on Molly was instantaneous. With a piteous cry, she sank to the ground, the six great necks falling around her as her body began to convulse and heave, drawing the necks back into her shoulders behind the great spiked ruff around her neck as she returned to her original dragon queen form. She stood up, massive tail lashing from side to side, roaring defiance at anyone who attempted to approach Harry. She stood over him as he lay, now mercifully unconscious, whilst chaos erupted around them as men rushed to try and apprehend Nudd and rescue Xander.

Unfortunately, his guard's quick thinking had provided Nudd with the perfect opportunity to make his escape. Those of Varik's men nearest to the escape shaft were unable to pursue them because the other three dragons were blocking the way, and the fairies fumed in impotent rage. They weren't foolish enough to take on three dragons.

Ceriddwen chose this moment to arrive, preceded by her bodyguard, clearing a path for her through the melee. Commander Vix dug Taliesin in the ribs to alert him to the Queen's arrival, and he whirled around, bowing low as she hurried towards them.

'Your Majesty,' he said. 'My messenger made it, then?'

'Yes, a brave man, Lord Taliesin, we came as quickly as we could, but a little too late I fear, you seem to have drawn the battle to a close without us. Some of the poor slaves told us Lord Nudd has run away. I have sent men after him, but I fear he will have made good his escape by the time they return to the entrance.'

Ceriddwen and Lleu stood with a small retinue of men-at-arms, the rest hunting for Nudd. Ceriddwen looked across at Molly, Harry's body hidden behind her great bulk, and then to the other three dragons.

'I see there are many casualties, have we lost many men?' she asked, her eyes never leaving Molly.

'No, not many, my Queen, the goblins bore the brunt.'

'And the portal is secure?'

'Yes, Lord Nudd didn't manage to breach it all.'

'Good — we shall have the cryptanalalysists work out the co-ordinates and secure it for our use only. Goblins will never be allowed near it again.' Still staring at Molly, she finally said, 'I saw three dragon cages being taken into this mine, but a dragon the size of that one,' she nodded to Molly, 'can only mean one thing, and if I am correct, that is Molly in her dragon queen form.'

She had just placed her hand on Taliesin's arm, waiting for his reply, when the cavern was suddenly filled with hauntingly beautiful singing. It echoed around them, becoming louder with every passing second until a luminous sphere appeared above Molly's great horned head, and hovered there for a few moments before transforming itself into three smaller globes. Inside each glowing sphere stood the hologram of a tiny being.

Ceriddwen clutched Taliesin's arm tightly as the rest of the company stood mesmerised by the ethereal singing and shimmering balls of light. 'The Sirens! What brings them here? Who or what has damaged the web, Lord Taliesin?'

'Your Majesty, I am afraid the princess shapeshifted into a sea dragon to kill the goblins, she could no longer abide their cruelty to the three captured dragons.'

Ceriddwen gave a mirthless chuckle. 'Worked well for us then, my Lord, did it not?' Then, more seriously added, 'But they would not go to such lengths for a temporary shape shift, the princess is not a danger to the order of things, quite the opposite. No, they have come for another reason, have they not?' She looked quizzically at Taliesin, who shifted his feet nervously.

'I...I...well, yes, Your Majesty, there has been a most unfortunate incident, well, actually, two unfortunate incidents.'

'Very important incidents if the Sirens are summoned.' Taliesin watched as Ceriddwen's face grew paler by the second. 'Summoned to comfort Molly in her hour of need.' Her voice rose hysterically. 'And obviously not because anything has happened to you, Lord Taliesin, so, tell me, what has happened?'

Lleu put his arms around her. 'Ceri, stay calm, everyone is watching, remember you are their Queen, you must bear this in a queenly manner, whatever it is.' He gave Taliesin a curt nod. 'Tell us, Lord Taliesin, what has summoned the Sirens to Molly's side?'

Taliesin, his former rancour towards Harry forgotten, braced himself to tell Ceriddwen that Harry was gravely injured.

Swallowing hard, he bowed and said in a low voice, 'My Queen, your grandson, Harry, has been grievously wounded by Lord Nudd's guard.'

Ceriddwen closed her eyes in horror, swaying slightly, supported by Lleu's loving arms.

'How grievously, Lord Taliesin? Is he near death?'

Taliesin shrugged helplessly. 'We know not, my Queen, no one dares approach while the dragon queen guards him.'

Ceriddwen turned to Lleu and whispered, 'We've just found him, please let us not lose him as we lost his father.'

'We must bear it in public, Ceri, you are the Queen, we still have much to deal with.' He patted her hand. 'Now, my dear, let us to work!'

Ceriddwen gripped Lleu's hand and turned tearful eyes to Taliesin. 'What else should I be aware of?'

Taliesin turned to Vix and indicated he come forward.

'Your Majesty, allow me to introduce Lord Vix, commander of King Jontar's troops. He has knowledge of dragon queens from times gone by, and he fears the strain and shock maybe too much for her. This may be another reason why the Sirens have come to her aid.' Ceriddwen acknowledged Vix's bow.

'We thank you for your concern, Commander Vix. Anything you can tell us will be most welcome.'

She turned back to Taliesin, voice trembling with emotion. 'Why was Harry here? Did he come through the portal with Molly? And where is Xander, I do not see him anywhere.'

Taliesin's heart sank to his boots. He looked at Ceriddwen's white, shocked face.

'Didn't the slaves tell you?'

'Tell me what, Lord Taliesin? What else should they have told me?'

'Lord Nudd has taken Prince Xander hostage — Harry was wounded trying to save him.'

This was too much for Ceriddwen and she staggered as her legs gave way in shock, only held up by Lleu's powerful grip.

'He will kill him in revenge for Prince Jasper,' she whispered, her voice hoarse with fear.

'He is much more valuable as a hostage,' Taliesin replied tersely. 'Nudd could not have a better bargaining tool!'

'Lord Taliesin is correct, Ceri,' Lleu affirmed. 'Nudd won't harm Xander, and hard as it is, we must accept that for now and focus on what is happening here.' He turned and beckoned to Lady Tanith standing with the men-at-arms. 'Lady Tanith, the flask!'

'Yes, my Lord.' Tanith scurried forward and thrust a cup into Lleu's outstretched hand before unscrewing the lid of the flask she carried in a leather bag across her body. She poured the liquid into the cup and waited as Lleu wrapped Ceriddwen's hands around the vessel and ordered her to drink. He waited a few moments, and then held out the cup for a refill. After the second drink, Ceriddwen became more composed and began to look and sound like herself again. Satisfied the cauldron had once more worked its magic, Tanith rejoined the retinue.

Ceriddwen surveyed the scene before her; the three dragons, were now crouched sleepily by the side of the escape hatch, soothed by the Siren's singing. The Sirens had now hidden Molly and Harry behind a shimmering veil of light emanating from the three globes.

'Do you know what they are doing now, Commander Vix?' demanded Ceriddwen, now fully restored and back to her normal self.

'I believe they are protecting the princess as she shifts back to her normal body — it…it's not always an easy process.'

Taliesin frowned. 'How so?' he asked, desperately worried about his wife.

'If it happens too fast, it can kill them, their hearts can't take the strain,' Vix replied.

Taliesin, sick with apprehension, watched and waited; nobody moved, the stillness was palpable as the magical music placed the conscious wounded into a pain-free sleep and hypnotised the exhausted surviving warriors into an almost soporific stupor, at the same time providing a heart-rending elegy for the scores of dead goblins and fairies, lives needlessly lost through Nudd's obsession and greed. Ceriddwen stood patiently, vowing silently that she would not rest until he was hunted down and Xander safely returned.

Initially, after what was an agonising wait for Taliesin, the shimmering veil began to dissipate, revealing a naked Molly curled in the foetal position with one arm across Harry's chest, the ground around his head stained red by the blood seeping from his shoulder. The three globes hovered above them, the Sirens within still singing softly.

'Lady Tanith, give Lord Taliesin my cloak!' Ceriddwen had entered the mine still wearing the cloak Tanith had placed around her shoulders that morning, removing it when the suffocating heat of the mine became too much to bear.

'Go and tend to your wife, Lord Taliesin, and protect her modesty!'

Taliesin took the cloak and carefully approached Molly.

'Molly, my love, are you alright?' he asked hesitantly. 'Let me put this cloak around you.'

To his shock and consternation, Molly screamed at him, 'Go away, go away! Don't look at me! I'm old, I'm an old woman now!' before breaking into convulsive sobs.

Taliesin drew back in shock at this outburst, looking in confusion at Molly's slim body, her glorious russet hair streaming down her back. 'What do you mean, Molly? You're not old? Why would you think you are old?'

'I am!' she cried, still not looking up. 'I'm old like Harry. Oh, poor Harry! Nudd has murdered him and it's all my fault.'

She began to sob again, her shoulders heaving in grief. Taliesin hovered, uncertain what to do next.

'Harry's not dead, Molly.' Ceriddwen was now standing beside them. 'You must get up and let the medics attend to him before he does die from shock and lack of blood.'

Molly lifted her head and blinked at Ceriddwen. 'How can you bear to look at me, I'm so old and decrepit!'

'Enough of this nonsense, Molly!' Ceriddwen snapped impatiently, beckoning to one of Varik's men who happened to have a particularly worn and shiny shield. 'Look at your reflection in this shield — do you see an old woman? What makes you think I would allow you to grow old? You have been protected by my enchantment.'

Molly looked in wonder at her reflection. Her skin was smooth and unlined, her hair cascading over her pert, naked breasts. Gasping, she snatched up Ceriddwen's fleecy cloak and wrapped it around herself, then held out her hand to Taliesin and flung herself into his arms, burying her face in his unyielding armoured chest.

Field medics quickly placed Harry on a stretcher and bore him away for treatment and transfer into the care of Masters Lenus and Heka as soon as he was stable enough to travel back to the palace hospital.

A short while before Taliesin's messenger staggered out of the mine, Ceriddwen and Lleu had ridden down to the battlefield to take stock, meeting up with the Morrigan, Andraste and Lord Pan for confirmation of their victory, a tally of the dead and wounded, and to follow Taliesin into the mine to make sure Nudd had been prevented from breaching the portal. Ceriddwen wouldn't be satisfied until she was sure this final part of the operation was secured in their favour. The messenger's news wasn't encouraging, and with a large troop of men-at-arms, Ceriddwen and Lleu hurried to the mine only to find their horses also refused to enter, the smell of dragons still strong and powerful. Reluctantly, they dismounted and started trekking through the tunnel on foot instead.

Ceriddwen looked around in wonder as they passed through vast and valuable crystal deposits. Nudd was a fool, mostly ignorant about speleography, simply ignoring the vast crystal wealth uncovered by his crude mining methods in his all-consuming obsession with the portal. She made a mental note to send a team in to assess everything as soon as possible. She was also deeply concerned and angered by the presence of so many cowed and emaciated slaves trotting along beside them, discovering many were the Cailleach's people. She promised them if all went well, they would soon be returned to their lady. Her fury drove her on, until finally they made their way through the narrow passage that opened into the huge portal cavern.

Ceriddwen was used to wars, she had fought many of them in her time, but the horrors witnessed on the battleground above, followed by the sight of so many bloodied, battered bodies inside this cavern were nothing compared to the news that Harry was seriously injured, and Xander had been captured by the crazed goblin king. This outrage would require a whole new strategy, but the immediate aftermath of today's conflict would have to be dealt with first.

Leaving Taliesin and Molly to some privacy, Ceriddwen discussed the problem of the three dragons with Commander Vix.

'We can't just leave them to make their own way out of the mine, they will create terror wherever they appear.'

'I don't think that will happen, ma'am.' Vix chose his words carefully — he didn't want to appear more knowledgeable than the Queen, he had heard all the stories about her terrible rages should anyone offend her.

'Why not?' Ceriddwen snapped back.

Vix spread his hands in a placatory gesture. 'The Sirens won't allow it. The dragons must be fed and rested, and then the Sirens will guide them home to the Anunnaki lands.'

'Yes, of course. Forgive my sharpness, Commander Vix.' Ceriddwen appeared surprisingly apologetic. 'I may be a Queen, but I know very little of dragons. Let us feed them then, the sooner they are on their way, the better.'

Vix cleared his throat, scratching his nose before saying, 'Um, you know they are carrion eaters, ma'am? They only eat dead meat.'

'Well, give them meat then, there must some around here…' the words were no sooner out of Ceriddwen's mouth when she realised what he meant. 'Ah, I see,' she said doubtfully.

'If I may be so bold, ma'am, I know you don't wish to disturb Lord Taliesin, but if you will take my word for it, he told me when he was sent to find Lord Nuada in the Anunnaki lands, the Selkies fed dead goblins to the captured dragons to help them regain their strength and fly off to freedom. In the wild, dragons are shy and retiring creatures; they only attack if they are threatened or protecting their young.' This all came out in a great rush, and Vix prepared himself for a torrent of abuse for his impertinence. To his surprise, Ceriddwen nodded in agreement.

'Hmm, the redoubtable Lady Arnemetia,' she said, rolling her eyes. 'See to it, Commander. The Sirens appear to be waiting for us to get on with it.'

Sure enough, each dragon, still sitting calmly, had a Siren globe hovering above it. As soon as three stripped goblin corpses were placed in front of the dragons, the Sirens surrounded them with another shimmering veil, allowing the starving creatures to eat in privacy and peace.

Satisfied the dragons were no longer a problem, Ceriddwen turned her attention to Lord Varik and his team of cryptanalysts, not leaving until she was convinced the portal would be secured, allowing no unwanted incursions in or out. Suppressing a shudder at how close Nudd had come to destroying their world forever, she resolved never to let anything like this happen again.

As Lleu and Varik began issuing orders to clear the cavern of the dead and wounded, Ceriddwen joined Taliesin and Molly sitting on some rocks with Lady Tanith, who had insisted Molly drink a cup of cauldron liquid to calm and revive her. Despite her deep concern for Harry and the missing Xander, although she had no doubt he would soon be safely home, Ceriddwen smiled to herself at the sight of Taliesin holding onto his wife as though she might disappear in a puff of smoke, Molly's hand crushed in a firm grip.

All three stood up as she approached, and after Ceriddwen had enveloped Molly in an uncharacteristic hug, she waved them back down. Although the heat was stifling, Molly was still encased in Ceriddwen's fleecy wrap; Ceriddwen couldn't help chuckling,

'If only Brighid could see you now, my dear, she would be outraged at your most unroyal state of undress!'

To Ceriddwen's consternation, Molly burst into floods of tears.

'Oh, you have no idea how much I've missed you all, and I didn't even know I was missing you. I forgot all about you for forty years. I thought I had grown old!'

'Ha!' Ceriddwen flapped her hand dismissively. 'Old, what nonsense! Simply an illusion! We missed you too, but you played an important part in preventing, I am ashamed to say, an unforeseen disaster on our part.' Then added briskly, 'And remember, you were only away a few weeks of *our* time.'

Molly turned her tear-stained face to Taliesin. 'Yes, and now I want to go home. I want to see Alaria and Ares and then we can concentrate on Harry and Xander — take me home to Tigh Falloch, Taliesin!'

'Yes,' agreed Ceriddwen, gladly sharing Taliesin's obvious relief that Molly showed no signs whatsoever of wishing to return to the world of humans. 'We shall go home and plan our next move. This is not a victory to celebrate. Nudd's vision of an inter-world goblin empire may have been dealt a serious blow, but it has cost us dear. To paraphrase the words he spat at us the very evening you first joined us, we may have won this battle, but we have yet to win the war.'

~

Laura closed the curtains and locked the doors, then switched off the lights and climbed the stairs to her bedroom. 'The time thing,' she muttered to herself, 'means they'll probably be back in time for breakfast…'

Acknowledgements

I would like to thank the following people for helping to make this book possible...

My wonderful editor, Kathryn Hall, for her professionalism, expertise, suggestions, and wise input. I doubt this book would have ever seen the light of day without her very generous encouragement. She is an inspiration.

Many thanks to my lovely son, Kyle Hopwood, for drawing the map, his technical expertise, and for his infinite patience. I must have driven him nearly mad at times.

My dearest friend, Shireen Truitt, for patiently reading through every chapter, and encouraging me on my very long journey.

My friends at Leven Litts writing group in Alexandria for sitting through endless chapter readings, for their constructive criticism, unstinting encouragement and support, and just being there for me. Thanks to all.

Special thanks to Jill Smith for taking on the task of beta reading the finished manuscript. Thank you so much Jill.

Printed in Great Britain
by Amazon